UNFORGIVEN

UNFORGIVEN

The Forbidden Bond Series

Cat Miller

Published by Montlake Romance, Seattle

www.apub.com

Amazon, the Amazon logo, and Montlake Romance are trademarks of Amazon.com, Inc., or its affiliates.

ISBN-13: 9781477822852
ISBN-10: 1477822852

Cover photo and design by Regina Wamba

Library of Congress Control Number: 2013922268

Printed in the United States of America

To the readers who took my stories to heart and spread them farther then I ever could have on my own. Your enthusiasm and support have been a priceless gift. Thank you from the bottom of my heart. I share this dream come true with you.

To my family. Without your love, patience, and encouragement none of this would be possible. I love you beyond words. Thank you.

One

In order for there to be a rebirth, something in you must die. If part of you died, would you miss it? Would anyone else miss that part of you? Would they even notice it was gone? What if you were always the shadow in the corner of a room full of beautiful, bright beings, and one day you stepped out into the light? Would anyone see you, or would the shadows follow the less brilliant beings into the light? Brandi Vaughn was about to discover the answers to these questions.

She admired herself in the wall mirror in her huge walk-in closet. There were piles of clothes littering the floor around her, ready for the Salvation Army. All the clothes hanging from the racks still wore their tags, and her trendy new shoes were still in their boxes. She'd been planning this transformation for months and today would be the big reveal. She was a vampire with a whole new outlook on life. Of course, at first everyone would think that she had simply dolled up for her half sister's bonding to Chase Deidrick, Brandi's secret childhood crush. No one knew that Brandi had always had the hots for Chase. She'd watched him in the halls at school and drooled just like the rest of the girls, but Brandi had the added benefit of seeing him regularly at vampire functions and at the Council Hall.

It had broken her heart the day she caught her twin sister, Samantha, having sex with Chase in the pool house. Brandi couldn't possibly have looked any less like her twin, even if she had tried. Samantha was beautiful, tall, model thin, and blond. At the time, Brandi hadn't grown into a womanly form. She was a head shorter than Samantha and she had the same dark chocolate hair that seemed to run in the Vaughn family. Most days Brandi looked like a nerdy tomboy in a jersey and a pair of jeans or sweats. She enjoyed sports and was a natural athlete. She took great pride in getting straight *A*'s in her advanced gifted and talented classes. Fashion took a backseat to comfort and functionality in her mind—Samantha was just the opposite.

Oh, Samantha was just as smart as Brandi. They'd both graduated from high school at sixteen years old, but Samantha preferred to derive attention from her pretty face and flawless figure. The boys had always fawned over her and competed for her attention. She dated a lot, but Samantha only wanted the one guy who paid her no attention. Chase Deidrick.

Brandi figured it was the challenge that drew Samantha to Chase. She enjoyed the hunt more than the prize. Samantha wanted the prize to be hers and hers alone, at least until she became bored and tossed the guy aside like so much garbage. Who knew, if Brandi had developed early, as Samantha had, she could have been the same way. She wouldn't have needed to compete with Samantha for their mother's attention in the only way she knew, with her brain. Intelligence was the only attribute Brandi exuded that her sister didn't bother to flaunt.

Brandi had gotten home from a trigonometry study session on a particularly hot day at the end of her senior year of high school and decided to jump in the pool for the first time that season. She entered the pool house and was surprised to hear water running and voices coming from one of the shower stalls. She recognized her sister's hushed moans and went to investigate. Brandi thought it would be hysterical to catch her sister with the pool boy she'd been ogling, or a gardener. Who else would be around for her to dally with? Brandi would never let Samantha live it down.

He wasn't the pool boy. The shower curtain was open about an inch and Brandi could clearly see the side of Chase's beautiful face, his muscular, water-slicked body sliding against Samantha's Barbie perfection. They were getting it on and Brandi wanted to die. It was the end of her childish fantasies of a future with Chase Deidrick.

Brandi quietly backed out of the pool house, leaving behind a small piece of her heart, and much of the closeness she shared with her twin. Things had never been the same between them after that day. It served Samantha right to have Chase end up with their half sister after all of the plotting she'd done to trap him.

Looking at herself in the mirror now, years after that awkward day in the pool house, that shy tomboy was nowhere to be found. Brandi hardly recognized herself now that she wasn't hiding behind her frumpy yet comfy tracksuits and oversize jerseys. She could see the woman she'd grown into staring back at her.

Brandi was lush and curvy in a way that reminded her of her half sister, Danielle, instead of a tall, willowy creature like Samantha. She would never again envy Samantha's looks and popularity. Brandi would do whatever it took to find a sense of self-worth and stand out in a crowd, even if it meant part of her had to die. The quiet, bookish girl of her past had to step aside to make room for the woman she was now determined to be.

She checked her hair and makeup one last time, loving her new haircut. Her mother was going to have a shit fit when she saw the shorn locks that curled and wrapped around Brandi's jawbone. The stylist had given her the perfect haircut for a woman who wanted to look good but didn't have time for a lot of primping. The new cut used her natural waves to advantage in a style that reached midway down her neck, with long layers that tickled her face. She looked great straight from the shower with nothing more than a little product and a pick. It dried to a wavy and stylish perfection. Today she wore several sparkly pins in her hair that peeked out of the curls to accent the shiny beads on her lavender dress, which caught the light and made her appear to shimmer. The Brandi of old was gone. Looking to the future was exciting and terrifying at the same time.

Griffin, Brandi's father, was the first to see her transformation. When she reached the bottom of the stairs, she found him in his tuxedo, looking as much like a movie star as any she'd ever seen on a red carpet. His vampire genetics had slowed his aging to a crawl now, so he only looked to be in his late twenties and very much in his prime. He stared at Brandi and made a slow circle around her to take in the changes. He said nothing at first and her self-esteem began to plummet. Her father would tell her the truth no matter what, and if he disapproved, he wouldn't hold his tongue. He looked at her with the grave expression of a man about to break some very bad news. It was the serious face he used in the Council chamber when deliberating with the other Councilmen. Finally a smile split his face and softened his expression into that of her daddy.

"Now what am I going to do with you?" He folded her up in his arms and kissed the crown of her head. "I would assign armed warriors to guard you, but they would likely fall in love. Then I'd have to have good men executed." He shook his head. "The one precious child I never had to worry about had the nerve to become a beautiful woman and break her daddy's heart."

He held her there against his chest, swaying back and forth for several moments before pulling away with suspiciously shining eyes.

"I love you too, Daddy." She beamed up at him. The relief of his acceptance and pride in her was overwhelming to Brandi. "Shouldn't we be leaving now? Where are Sam and Mom?"

"It seems your mother is having trouble resigning herself to attend the bonding and Samantha feels she shouldn't have to attend, given her past with Chase. Not to mention her unreasonable distaste for Danielle. I gave them both fifteen minutes to get down here about thirty minutes ago."

Griffin looked around the room and ran his fingers through his perfectly groomed hair. The white highlights he was born with were believed, by their people, to be a sign of great power, and they stood out starkly against the dark coffee color of the rest of his hair.

"I'm going to go ahead without you in my car. I can't be late. Will you hurry them along and follow in the limousine?"

Her father looked so forlorn it made her heart ache for him. The past six months had been a balancing act and an exercise in patience for Griffin. After discovering his supposedly dead first mate and daughter had been alive and well for twenty-one years, he had to deal with Brandi's mother and sister, who wanted nothing to do with the girl, Danielle, or her human mother, Tessa. The fact that Danielle's mother was human was still a shock to their people. No one had believed it was possible for a human to carry a vampire child and survive. Almost everyone ignored Tessa at the bridal parties, and Brandi assumed they would shun Dani as well if it hadn't been for her transformation into a full-blooded vampire. Brandi believed her mother felt threatened by Tessa. Of course, Griffin hadn't admitted to Sarah that he still longed for Tessa, but it was impossible not to see it when they looked at each other.

This was all groundbreaking stuff. Up to this point, as far as she knew, once a couple was bonded they happily kept only to one another until one of them died. Then the surviving mate would either bond himself to another in order to end the suffering, as Griffin had done, or waste away in loneliness, longing for the lost mate. Griffin had been too young to live out his days alone so he quickly moved on to the mate of his parents' choosing.

"I'll do my best, Daddy. If I can't get them moving, I'll be along without them." She embraced her father again. "Everything is going to work out. Mom will come to terms with this addition to our family as soon as she realizes they aren't going away."

With a disbelieving smile that didn't reach his eyes, Griffin replied, "I hope so, baby. I really hope so." He kissed her on the cheek and headed out the door.

———•◆•———

Brandi had been waiting in the foyer for an hour. She had made several trips to her mother's and sister's rooms in an attempt to get them out the door. It seemed odd the way her mother kept checking her watch as if she was waiting for something. Maybe her intention was to miss the ceremony and show up fashionably late to the reception. "Mother, I'm leaving without you. I'll see you later tonight," Brandi informed Sarah's back, because she refused to turn around to acknowledge her. This brought Sarah's head whipping around to scowl at her.

"You will not leave this house without me, Brandi! Your sister and I will be down shortly, and you will stop making a nuisance of yourself. Go wait quietly in the foyer. It's bad enough you cut off all your lovely hair. Must you be a pest, too?" Sarah turned back to the mirror, dismissing Brandi entirely.

On the way down the stairs, familiar warmth started to spread in her core with the growing aggravation she felt with her mother and sister. What the hell did her hair have to do with anything? Taking calming breaths and forcing down the heat licking at her belly, she sat and practiced the calming meditative breathing techniques Doc Stevens had been teaching her during her recent secret weekly visits. Brandi's developing extra-elemental power was wreaking havoc on her life. She was pyrokinetic, the first fire starter in hundreds of years. It was a volatile and, as far as she could tell, useless ability. The research she and Doc had done suggested that elemental vampires had been more prevalent in the past and they tended to be feared by all due to the destructive nature of their talents.

Finally, Sarah swept down the stairs, her head held high, looking lovely in a black dress, the one she wore to funerals. Griffin was not going to think that was funny. Samantha looked dour in a matching shade meant to let the world know she was in mourning.

The ride to the vampire-owned country club, where many such ceremonies and events were held, was almost too quiet. Samantha continued to look as if she was going to vomit, and Sarah appeared smug and satisfied. They were surely going to be late and would have to wait in the hall so they didn't interrupt the bonding. Maybe Sarah's intention was to barge in and cause a disruption.

The limo pulled up to the building and Brandi realized the lights were out inside. She knew it was to be a candlelight reception with additional pale lighting used so as to not ruin the view of the stars in the clear night sky, but she hadn't heard any mention of the bonding being held in such darkness. Then she noticed a van parked up on the curb at an odd angle and a chill skittered down her spine. Something was wrong here. She could feel the tension in the air. Brandi leapt from the limo as soon as it came to a stop and ran for the stairs leading to the chapel.

"Brandi, get back here, now!" her mother exclaimed, but Brandi was almost to the doors by the time Sarah and Samantha had exited the vehicle. Sarah called her back again but she kept going. She wanted to rip open the doors and go storming in but the instinct that told her when to shut up and listen kicked in, so she slowly slid through the door and crept over to a coat closet off to the right. It would give her a place to observe her surroundings for a moment. She needed to be sure her creepy feeling wasn't just her imagination working overtime. Storming into Danielle's bonding ceremony like gangbusters only to find she was wrong would not be the ideal way to smooth things over between the Vaughns and the Deidricks. Not to mention, it would be embarrassing.

Brandi heard voices and a struggle in the hall. The owners of the voices came into view. One was very familiar and the other less so, but he reminded her of someone she couldn't quite place. The first was Darren, the vampire warrior who had disappeared from the warrior ranks after rumors of his connection to a rogue vampire surfaced. He was carrying a lifeless Danielle. The other guy was carrying a mean-looking gun and covering Darren's back. Darren had tricked Danielle into following him six months earlier, and had given her to the rogue who had been hunting Danielle and other vamp youth for months in order to rob them of their extrasensory powers.

Darren's motivation had been to force Dani to bond with him. It hadn't worked and he'd been trying to get back into Dani's good graces since his betrayal. Brandi's fears of foul play were confirmed. She'd just walked into a very dangerous situation. The warmth in Brandi's belly grew swiftly. She struggled to hold it back. Just then the front door flew open and Samantha walked directly into Darren. Danielle moaned with the impact. The other guy spun around, pointing the gun at Samantha's face.

"Back away and you won't get hurt, Sam," Darren said calmly, but the guy with the gun seemed less sure of Sam's safety. In the background Brandi could hear people pounding on the chapel doors, trying to get out.

"Take her." Samantha put her hands in the air and moved away from the door. "Make sure you get the job done this time. She's like a bad song stuck in my head. No matter how hard I try to forget her, the bitch just refuses to go away."

Brandi had to find a way to stall them until help came, and Samantha was providing a great distraction. Brandi rummaged around the closet, all the while fighting to contain the flames that were attempting to escape the confines of her body. She breathed deeply and imagined the fire in her gut was a tiny flicker of light, instead of the bonfire that was testing her limits. She had to keep it together. After practically ripping the closet apart, she finally came across a set of golf clubs. Lucky thing the country club had a golf course, because the clutch purse she carried wouldn't have done her any good in this situation. She exited the closet behind the armed man, with a club raised over her head, ready to swing.

Samantha looked her right in the eye and yelled, "No, Brandi, let them take her! We will all be better off this way!"

The armed guy spun around to face her. The club struck the shoulder of his gun arm instead of his head. It knocked the weapon loose, but he caught the gun, and his balance, as Brandi rushed him. She only had to keep them from leaving without getting shot. That's what she told herself, but she wasn't fast enough. The rage looking back at her from behind the dark eyes of her opponent froze her in place.

He twisted her roughly with one arm, trapping her against his chest and slamming the muzzle of the gun into her temple. Samantha yelped in protest behind her and the sound of people banging on the chapel doors from the opposite direction grew louder. The pain in her head from the impact of the gun made her stomach roil. Pain and rage spread through her like the flames she'd been fighting to contain. A little of her hard-earned control slipped, and the heat crept though her hands, scalding her captor. He released her quickly and pointed the gun at her head again. His incredulous look and the struggle went unnoticed by Darren, who had already shouldered his way through the doors and was heading down the front stairs. Samantha was cowering in the corner.

The guy lowered his voice and whispered to Brandi, "Look, I don't want to hurt you or anyone else. Just stay where you are. You can't win. Please, just back off."

His entire demeanor had changed and he suddenly seemed as young and as frightened as Brandi. She could do nothing but stare into the sable depths of his haunting eyes while he backed out the door. The spell was broken when the door shut and the sound of his retreating footsteps faded. Shaking herself, Brandi went to the door after retrieving her golf club from the floor. Her mother entered with a smile on her face.

"Well, that was entertaining, wasn't it, girls? I guess we won't have to suffer through the bonding after all."

Samantha jumped up from her hiding place and tried to stop Brandi's exit.

"Where do you think you're going? You can't fight them with a golf club!" The sound of squealing tires echoed from outside.

"I'm going to try to slow them down, or at least keep up with them until help comes. Either help me, or get the hell out of my way, Sam." Brandi glared at her twin. Samantha folded her arms across her chest, silently communicating her unwillingness to help Danielle. Brandi pushed past her and sidestepped her mom to streak through the doors into the night.

"Tell Daddy to call my cell," she shouted over her shoulder.

Running full tilt in heels was no easy task, so she discarded them and sprinted to the waiting limo. The driver stood stunned, gaping after the retreating van in the distance. Brandi hopped behind the wheel. She drove straight across the lawn all the way down the hill. Luckily the driveway leading to the country club was long, so they hadn't turned onto the main road yet. She would see which direction they turned. Her belly burned and the heat from her hands was causing the steering wheel to become sticky as it melted slightly. The breathing techniques and calming exercises were impossible to perform during a mission to save her half sister's life.

Brandi followed the van at a distance for a few miles but their sudden erratic driving made her think she'd been spotted. The van veered off into the city park, sped off the road, and onto the walking paths that led back into the trees and hiking trails. Thank God it was dark outside. She prayed no one would be walking in the park when she hopped the curb for the second time and sped through the trees. The instinct that told her when to stop and listen made her pull over and quickly cut the engine. Listening closely, she followed the sound of a running engine and male voices. Being careful not to be seen, she crept forward on her bare feet.

"Look, you sick bastard, this is not part of our mission! We are to retrieve the girl and take her in. You don't have permission to act out your sick fantasies on her!"

The younger man's voice was full of disgust for Darren. They were standing in the beams of the headlights and Brandi hoped that would make seeing her in the darkness more difficult. The van's side door was wide open and Danielle's white dress was visible in the shadows.

"This is not a sick fantasy, you ass! She is my mate and I have every right to do with her as I wish. I need to speak with her. I need to tell her I love her face-to-face. I need to apologize. I think if we exchange blood again, now that she has changed fully to a vampire, the bond will be complete." Darren paced, nervously raking his hands through his blond spikes.

"You didn't exchange blood the last time! You forced the bond you suffer from now. I can't believe you talked him into trusting you with the Hypnovam. Do you plan on giving her a choice this time, or will you steal her blood again?"

Darren didn't reply, only looked at the guy sheepishly. Shit. He was going to do it again. He planned to force his blood down her throat to solidify his bond with Dani.

"What do you think he is gonna do to you when he realizes you duped him?"

The guy looked in Brandi's direction, and she ducked, but his gaze continued around the clearing. Darren paced to the other side of the van and the guy followed. This was her chance. No way could she stand by and wait for backup while this freak forced Dani into a deeper bond. The blood bond was a sacred union to be given freely, not stolen by whomever wanted your obedience and affection.

She didn't have time to stand there planning a rescue. She had to just do it while they were arguing and out of sight. If Darren took off with Dani again, they might never find her. Brandi emerged from the trees and sprinted toward the van. Danielle looked to be uninjured. There was no visible blood or broken bones, and her eyes were open.

"Can you hear me?" Brandi whispered. Danielle blinked once.

"Can you move at all?" she asked, but Danielle only stared.

"Okay. I'll take that as a *no*. I'm getting you out of here."

Slowly, she dragged Danielle to the door of the van and listened to the heated discussion a moment longer before hauling Danielle over her shoulder in a fireman's carry. Brandi was strong, being a vampire, and she had no trouble lifting her petite half sister and running toward the woods. Just as she entered the trees, Darren and his gun-toting accomplice circled the van to find Danielle gone. A sound somewhere between a scream and a roar ripped through the trees from behind her and Brandi let her instinct take over. She couldn't outrun the older, stronger males. She needed to slow them down.

Turning, she sank to her knees. Still holding Danielle with one arm, Brandi pointed her palm toward the van. She let all the anger and fear swelling in her gut explode in a blast of energy that blew back her hair and caused Danielle's gown to ripple around her face. Thank goodness she hadn't chosen a big, puffy gown. The fireball that emerged from within Brandi raced toward the van. Both men leapt for safety to avoid the flames. The van exploded, making the night brighter than midday for a few long moments as Brandi lifted her half sister, got back to her feet, and ran for the limo.

"Holy shit! Holy shit! I can't believe I did that. I hope I didn't burn you," Brandi told Danielle.

She finally reached for the car door, depositing Danielle unceremoniously onto the floor of the backseat. She had no time to buckle her in. Brandi rushed around to the open driver-side door. She was startled by the report of a gun, and stopped when sharp pain bit into the left side of her back and slammed her against the vehicle. A second shot struck her higher and to the left. Stunned by the impact, Brandi righted herself and climbed behind the wheel.

"The bastards shot me! Twice!"

The shock of that realization didn't really sink in. She had no time to think, only time to drive. She slammed the door shut and was thankful for the use of her right arm. Her left arm wasn't cooperating. The pain in her chest and back throbbed with her heartbeat, and every beat caused a hot river to run down her front. The red heat bloomed across her new gown as she drove.

"Dani, I'm going to drive as fast and far as I can. I need you to hold on if you can, because if I kill you in a car wreck after saving your ass and getting shot, I'm gonna be so pissed off."

Her words at the end sounded sluggish to her own ears, but she needed to gain Dani's promise of silence. No one knew of her pyrokinesis except Doc Stevens and she wanted to keep it that way. If her parents found out, they would lock her away to protect her from the Rogue. She could only pray Darren and the other guy hadn't seen her and didn't know where the flames had come from.

The speeding limo careened onto the main road, nearly hitting a passing car.

"I'm driving toward home. I don't know if you know what happened back there, but if you do I expect your vow of silence in exchange for saving you. I'm not ready for anyone to know yet."

Dani made no response, but Brandi hoped she understood. She raced toward home, running red lights and nearly hitting two other vehicles. The world whizzed by and Brandi could feel herself slipping away. A puddle of her own blood spread across the seat and dripped to the floor of the limo. She began to cry, shaking with shock, and weak from blood loss. She pulled to the side of a street she believed to be very close to home, not wanting to pass out behind the wheel and harm anyone else. At least she was numb, now that the throbbing ache had passed. She didn't bother trying to brush away her tears. Her hands were covered in blood and it wouldn't do for her father to find her body with blood smeared across her face. She spoke and hoped Danielle could hear her. She was going to die there on the side of the road. She could feel her life slipping away and pooling on the seat next to her, but she had a few things to say before that happened.

"Tell Mom and Daddy I love them and I'm sorry. Tell them I believe sometimes loving someone means you have to let go in order to save each other. Tell Samantha her soul is a deeper, more beautiful place than she wants to admit, and it's time to grow up. Tell J. R. his big sister loves him more than chocolate chip cookies."

That had been a private joke between her and her brother, because nothing was better than chocolate chip cookies, except her little brother.

"I'm so sorry we didn't get a chance to know each other better, Danielle."

Brandi didn't know why, in her final moments, she was thinking of the guy who had held a gun to her head and had probably shot her in the back. When her eyes drifted shut, all she saw was the deep, dark sadness in his eyes looking back at her. With her final words she granted absolution to the captivating stranger.

"Tell him I forgive him. The guy didn't want to do it. Did you hear him fighting with Darren? He warned me not to follow. He didn't want to hurt anyone."

With that thought and the memory of the fresh, sun-dried-laundry-and-citrus scent she had taken deep into her lungs when he held her tightly against his chest, Brandi let oblivion swallow her whole.

Two

An hour earlier . . .

He was a vision in black. Chase was the most beautiful man Danielle would ever see, and he belonged to her. He'd insisted on the contrasting colors they wore on the day of their bonding ceremony. He told her that she was everything light and good in the world and he'd known no real light until the night her lips touched his for the first time. That's when the sun, his Lovely, his Soleil, found his heart and filled it with light. He was convinced that he would continue to have dark corners and shadowed places inside himself until she truly became a part of his soul at their bonding. He had a white suit to change into after the ceremony to signify his entrance into the pure light of her soul.

He was such a romantic, but the world would never know about the soft center lurking beneath the nonchalant exterior he carried like a shield. That part of him was only for her, and someday, their children.

Chase smiled at her from the other end of the chapel and the world narrowed down to just the two of them. She took in every detail, committing to memory the way his dark, nearly black, hair shone in the light of the chandelier, and his blue-green eyes that made her think of the ocean on a perfect summer day. The open adoration she felt for him was reflected back at Danielle in his gaze as he took her in as well. This moment would be burned into her memory and cherished always.

She began the slow march down the aisle to meet her mate while he fidgeted slightly in front of the altar. No one else would notice the telltale flexing of his fingers. She smiled even wider then; he was just as eager to seal their blood bond as she was. She'd only made it a quarter of the way when Chase left the altar and strode purposefully toward her. She laughed and wrapped her arms around his neck when he stopped and bent to kiss her. She let every bit of the passion and love she held in her heart pour from her mind into his while they held each other tight.

Dani blushed fiercely when people began to applaud and whistle in approval of the open show of love and affection. She'd almost forgotten where she was. Chase raised his head and smiled at the crowd, taking Dani's hand to lead her the rest of the way down the aisle. There were so many people here that she didn't know, but that was to be expected. Her new mate would one day be a member of the ruling council of vampires, just as every male in his line before him had been.

Dani beamed at everyone they passed. She noticed a grandmotherly vampire at the end of the row ahead. The lady was one of the very few vampires Dani had seen during her short acquaintance with the species who actually looked elderly, which meant the lady had to be very old. Then Dani smiled at the man behind the lady. The guy wore all black so he didn't stand out until you focused on what he was wearing. His attire, a pair of black cargo pants and long-sleeved black T-shirt, seemed out of place and informal while everyone else wore tuxedos and fine suits. He stared at Dani with purpose; an edgy twitch had him moving from foot to foot. Something inside of her screamed danger and Dani's steps faltered. Just as Chase turned to look at her, she saw the guy shove the older lady into the aisle. The lady yelped in surprise and Chase jumped to stop her fall.

The chapel went dark and a distressed cry arose from the crowd. In the same instant, a stinging bite to her hip took her to the ground. Unable to move, she couldn't fight when she was scooped up and over the shoulder of a man she knew wasn't Chase. He smelled all wrong. She heard the sound of the chapel doors slamming before she was passed to waiting arms that cradled her gently against a massive, hard chest. Her powers were completely out of her reach and her stomach did a nauseated flip when Darren began to whisper nonsensical love words and apologies into her ear.

No . . . not this again.

She wanted so badly to fight, but he had drugged her, and this time there was no fighting it. She was a full-blooded vampire and she knew from past experience that the drug was engineered for use on her kind. The darkness became thicker and dragged her down to a silent depth Danielle could not escape.

⚬

The bouncing and rocking was making her sick. She wished Chase would be still and stop rolling around in bed. He must be having another bad dream. He'd told her about his recurring dreams of the night Darren had carried her away to be his lifelong mate. Chase could do nothing to stop him. Usually if she snuggled up and held him tightly he would settle into a restful sleep, but she couldn't reach him tonight. Oddly, her arms wouldn't move, so she tested her legs—they, too, were useless. Then the voices drifted in from someplace far away and the memories came rushing back to her in a tidal wave. She wasn't in bed with Chase. She had been taken from the chapel by Darren. She believed herself to be in a moving vehicle. The movement of the car, compounded by the drug he had used, made her stomach roil, and acid burned the back of her throat. Two people argued vehemently as her head flopped around against the metal floor with the sharp turns of the vehicle. Still unable to move or really understand the words of her kidnappers, she slid forward into the front seats as they came to a sudden stop.

Shit. How was she going to get out of this one? She had to have used up her nine lives by now. Danielle's mind began to wander. She was counting the number of times she should have died in the past year to see if there were any spare lives left. Then a familiar face came into her line of vision. Brandi. How had she gotten there? Had they taken her too? Brandi took Danielle's chin in her hand and looked into her eyes. Danielle still couldn't hear but she could clearly read Brandi's lips when she asked, "Can you hear me?"

Not knowing how to let her know that she'd understood, Danielle blinked. She hadn't realized she could do that, but Brandi seemed to get her acknowledgment.

"Can you move at all?" Brandi asked.

Danielle remained unblinking, hoping to express her helplessness. If she could just get at her powers, she would mentally kick her captors' combined asses, but they were locked away from her. She had telepathic and telekinetic ability. Her unheard-of ability to telepathically control other vampires was what she longed for now. A moment later the world tilted on its axis when Danielle was dragged upside down from the open vehicle that she could now see was a van. Brandi quickly moved into the night. Her eyes still open, all the world's sounds came back in a rush as Brandi knelt down and let loose an amazing fireball from her hand that ripped the van apart. The explosion was hot and beautiful. Danielle wanted to applaud her half sister. She was awed by the extrasensory power Brandi possessed and wondered for a moment why she hadn't known Brandi was so powerful. Why hadn't Griffin ever told her during his many visits to the condo she shared with Chase?

Brandi turned and ran like the devil was on her heels. Maybe he was. If the Rogue was with Darren, then Brandi had just exposed herself to an incomprehensible evil and would now be a target too. Danielle could never pay back her half sister for the risk she was taking. Brandi dropped her in the back of a limo and slammed the door. A moment later the sound of gunshots echoed around the compartment of the limo and Brandi hissed from the driver-side door. "The bastards shot me! Twice!"

No, no, no . . . this couldn't be happening. Brandi had become a friend and had risked her mother's wrath to attend Danielle's bridal parties. She had risked her safety and exposed her pyrokinesis to save Danielle. Now she had been shot! Griffin would never forgive her for this.

Brandi broke into her thoughts. "Dani, I'm going to drive as fast and as far as I can. I need you to hold on if you can, because if I kill you in a car wreck after saving your ass and getting shot, I'm gonna be so pissed off."

It surprised Danielle when her normally shy and quiet half sister made a joke at such a stressful time. The coppery tang of Brandi's blood permeated the limo. After several moments of bumping around, Brandi spoke again.

"I'm driving toward home. I don't know if you know what happened back there, but if you do, I expect your vow of silence in exchange for saving your ass. I'm not ready for anyone to know yet."

Danielle would keep all the secrets Brandi had in order to protect her, and she tried to tell her that but nothing came out. They drove on in anxious silence for some time while Danielle prayed the gunshot wounds Brandi received weren't life threatening. Brandi finally pulled over. Danielle thought they'd made it to Griffin's home, but when Brandi began to speak she realized they had stopped for a reason. Brandi could no longer drive. Her speech was slow and Brandi struggled to get out every word. Danielle's heart screamed her pain when she realized Brandi was saying good-bye.

"Tell Mom and Daddy I love them and I'm sorry. Tell them I believe sometimes loving someone means you have to let go in order to save each other. Tell Samantha her soul is a deeper, more beautiful place than she wants to admit, and it's time to grow up. Tell J. R. his big sister loves him more than chocolate chip cookies."

Dani's eyes burned with tears. How could she tell their precious little brother that Brandi was gone from this world because she'd saved Dani's life? He wouldn't understand.

"I'm so sorry we didn't get a chance to know each other better, Dani." Sincerity and regret rang in her voice.

Dani was also very sorry to be running out of time with this brave younger sister of hers. Brandi was quiet for a bit before she continued.

"Tell him . . . I forgive him. The guy didn't want to do it. Did you hear him fighting with Darren? He warned me not to follow. He didn't want to hurt anyone."

After that cryptic remark there was silence, but the faint sound of Brandi's heartbeat was reassuring. Brandi must have been talking about the man she'd heard arguing with Darren. Dani hadn't been able to make out the words, but it was clear there was a disagreement. Time seemed to pass slowly, but Dani knew the influence of the drug had skewed her senses. The steady cadence of Brandi's heart began to stagger and pause too frequently. Frantic to help her, Dani began to try telepathically calling to her family and friends. She couldn't hear any answering replies and didn't know if it was working, but she continued giving all the information she could give concerning their condition and whereabouts.

After what felt like an eternity of trying to reach someone, anyone, and listening to Brandi slip further and further out of reach, the sound of squealing brakes and a slamming car door set Dani's heart pounding. The door nearest to Dani's head was ripped open to admit her beautiful and frantic mother. Tessa was rambling and cursing all vampire kind as she checked Dani for injuries.

"I should never have allowed you anywhere near these people! I should have run again when they found you! I won't let them hurt you again!"

Tessa was fretting over Dani and kissing her face. The only movement Dani had available was her eyes so she darted them repeatedly toward the front seat. Tessa had to get help for Brandi, *now.* When Tessa finally looked over the front seat to see the other girl slumped over, she cursed a blue streak and scrambled out to grab her phone. Calling for help, she climbed into the front passenger seat to assess the situation. Holding the cell between her ear and shoulder, she used her shawl to put pressure on the wound.

"Griffin, we are about two blocks south of your driveway, in a limo. Brandi is badly injured. I think it's a bullet wound, maybe two. Danielle is semiconscious. We need you now!" Tessa let the phone fall from her awkward grasp without hanging up to focus on Brandi. "Shit! I'm losing her!"

Dani was crying again. The fear and anguish in her mother's voice was tearing at her. With tears and makeup running down her cheeks, Tessa put her head over the seat to look down on Dani.

"Your dad is on the way, baby."

Tessa dug around in the glove box before giving up to lean all the way over the seat and grab a decanter full of liquor from the bar. She climbed out of the limo, and the sound of breaking glass startled Dani. She slowly began to take inventory of her body's ability to function. She had to get moving in order to help her mom with Brandi. The sudden sweet aroma of human blood flooded Dani's senses and caused her fangs to drop painfully from her gums. Her mother was bleeding. She'd cut herself to give Brandi the blood that would save her life.

Greyson's unit had been called in, along with several others, earlier in the evening when the daughter of a Councilman was kidnapped from her bonding by a crazed mate. Baffled as to how a mated vamp could be bonding again, he questioned the other guys. They'd looked at each other with grim expressions and promised to fill him in later.

Greyson had just recently transferred from California when he was promoted to the Wrath. The Wrath was the elite class of warriors who took on the more dangerous and sometimes sensitive assignments. They had to be able to function as a team in the outside world without drawing the attention of the human authorities. They were the special forces of the vampire nation and he was proud to have been selected to serve in their ranks.

Adjusting to the climate in upstate New York wasn't his only obstacle. Back home things were much more relaxed, and the stress of relocating to the Enclave that housed the leaders of his class of warriors was unnerving. The legendary Council worked closely with the Enclave. Guarding the Council members and their homes was part of the duty bestowed on his new Enclave, and given the small bits of recent history he'd heard so far, it was a very important duty. There was a traitor in their midst, Greyson knew, but in his short time on the Enclave, he hadn't yet been given the whole story.

The Wrath was spread out and covering ground in the area surrounding the country club looking for a trail to follow when the call came to move toward Griffin Vaughn's palatial home and search for a limo. Greyson's crew of six Wrath guards hit pay dirt two blocks away from the Vaughn estate. Mitch was driving, Greyson had shotgun, while Linc, Ray, Garrett, and Troy filled the back of the van, along with an arsenal of weapons for any situation. He was the first out before the wheels even stopped rolling. The scene that met him inside the limo was something straight out of a horror flick.

Blood.

So much blood it caused his fangs to drop, and he knew for sure his eyes had turned from his usual emerald green to obsidian black. Behind the wheel was a female with the look of a pixie. Her head of dark hair, dotted with shiny pins that sparkled in the low light, lolled to the side as if it would topple off her shoulders. Except the pixie with the delicate features had fangs and a nasty exit wound in her upper left chest. Everything from her mouth down was drenched in blood. Only small patches of the light purple color her gown had been were visible. Blood dripped off the seat onto the floor of the car.

The sweet smell of human blood had every vamp behind him pulling back to await instructions, except for Mitch, who moved to call in their location. The human in question was also in the front seat. She also wore a bloody gown, but it looked like most of the red saturating her was from crawling across the front seat. It was the pixie's blood. The only obvious injury to the human was a gash across her right wrist. Greyson knew then what had happened. The human had bled herself to save the vampire pixie. There was way more to this story than he had time to contemplate at the moment. Troy climbed into the rear of the limo.

"I've got another one back here." His voice carried through the open window that separated the chauffeur from the passenger. "It's Danielle. Damn, I've missed this girl. She kicked my ass too many times in sparring matches. She doesn't seem injured, but she's down for the count. Shit. I think she was drugged."

A litany of curses floated to him from outside of the vehicle. These guys obviously knew and cared for the girl in the rear of the limo. He peeked over the seat and got a jolt at the sight of her beautiful flowing dark hair streaked with white and red. Power. This girl must have some awesome power. She wore a white gown, so that would make her the bride-to-be. The pixie wore purple. He didn't know why it pleased him to know the pixie was not the one about to be bonded.

Greyson tuned out the chattering of the other men as he began to assess the condition of his patients. Greyson Drake was a doctor turned warrior. That was a life he tried not to think about, but the instinct to jump in and help the sick or injured still lived in his heart. There wasn't much he could do for the human who had lost too much blood, but he needed to wrap the gash on her wrist to stop the bleeding. He thought the vampire pixie might survive with some blood and time to heal the gaping hole in her upper chest.

"Get me the first aid kit from the truck. I'm gonna need some light, and we will need to move these ladies quickly," he barked.

He knew he'd need to find the pixie some blood sooner than was possible, or she might not make it to the Enclave. She only lived now because of the human woman's sacrifice. He turned to survey the area and zipped off to a nearby house, using his preternatural speed. When the human occupant answered his insistent pounding on the door, Greyson was glad to find a portly man glowering at him. Larger people could deal better with a little extra blood loss. Greyson easily grabbed hold of the man's mind. Within seconds he had carried his would-be donor back to the waiting pixie. He sank his teeth into the man's wrist and held it to her stained mouth. Instinctively, she latched on and sucked greedily at the life-giving offering. The sight of her lips and tongue lapping at the blood while her throat worked to take it in transfixed Greyson. She licked and sucked, and he imagined her full lips working at his neck while she rode him hard.

Damn.

———————

Griffin paced the lawn of the country club in his tux and watched Mason try to contain his distraught son. Chase was to be bonded to Griffin's daughter, Soleil-Danielle, earlier that evening. What her name was depended on whom you spoke to. Griffin drifted back and forth between the name she was given at birth, Soleil, and Danielle, the name her mother had given her in order to hide her from his family.

The bonding hadn't taken place. His little girl and Chase's future mate had been snatched right out from under them. Chase was in a full-blown rage, fangs flashing, onyx eyes full of pain, and he was attempting to join the search for Soleil. This was not the first time she had been cleverly extricated against her will. There was a Rogue out there on the hunt for talented young vamps. His goal was to drain them of their strengths. It was much easier to take the power of a youth, before they came into full strength, than to arrest it from an adult. Mason counseled patience to Chase. "If you run off, and we can't reach you or they bring her back here, you will regret leaving. Sit tight. Let the Wrath do their job."

"You know damn well the Wrath aren't looking for Soleil! They're looking for Brandi! If they gave a shit about my Lovely we would have had security tonight, but we didn't, did we? It's been six months since the warriors have so much as looked her way, by order of your damned Council!"

That wasn't entirely true. Kayden had been making regular rounds of Chase's building and covertly watching after Danielle the whole time. He reported back to Griffin daily. Kayden and Chase had been lifelong best friends until Danielle came between them last year. Kayden didn't want Dani, which was the name he preferred to call her, or Chase to know he was in the shadows protecting them. He'd been out there tonight patrolling the grounds in silent support of the bond Chase and Danielle were forging when he was struck down by a needle to the thigh. They'd found him unconscious. He was still completely unresponsive.

Griffin's phone rang in his breast pocket and the argument

around him stopped. Mason and Chase both froze and waited for the other shoe to drop. The caller ID showed him it was Tessa calling, his human mate . . . ex-mate. This made his heart pump harder with joy and fear, simultaneously. In the six months since he'd given her his number and told her to call him for any reason at any time, she had never used it. The fact that she did now could not be good news.

"Tessa?" he answered.

"Griffin, we are about two blocks south of your driveway, in a limo. Brandi is badly injured. I think it's a bullet wound, maybe two. Danielle is semiconscious. We need you now!" She was frantic.

Griffin didn't get a chance to reply. She had obviously dropped the phone, but left the connection open.

"Shit! I'm losing her!" he heard Tessa curse. There was a shuffling noise.

"Your dad is on the way, baby." She was talking to Danielle.

Griffin looked up to find two matching pairs of ocean-blue eyes burning a hole through him. The sound of shattering glass drew his attention back to the phone. "Tessa!" he shouted into the phone, but got no response. "We need a car. Tessa found the limo with both girls in it two blocks south of the gate at my house."

The double doors of the country club flew open and Samantha stepped out before anyone could move. "Mason, we need you in here. Now. Debbie has apparently been in labor for most of the day, but didn't want to disrupt the ceremony. For the last two hours she's been squeezing my mother's hand and panting. So unless you want your baby delivered by Dr. Sarah Vaughn, you'd better get moving."

Samantha said it so dryly it took a moment for the words to sink in. She shrugged her shoulders and went back inside, as if she didn't care either way if Mason attended the birth or let Debbie tough it out on her own. The three men looked at each other in stunned disbelief until reality rushed in and got them moving.

"I'm going to get a car." Chase rushed off to the parking lot.

Griffin continued to listen to the eerie silence on the other end of the phone. Mason looked torn between standing beside his wife for the birth of their second child or going with his son and his best friend to find Danielle and Brandi.

"Go to Debbie, Mason. She needs you now. Chase and I will bring the girls back, but I need you to have Doc Stevens come meet us." Tessa's words finally sank in along with the continued silence. "Brandi has been shot."

Griffin met Doc Stevens' disgusted glare. Tessa had cut herself to give Brandi the blood she knew the girl would die without. It was a sacrifice he could never repay. And Tessa was dying because of it. When Griffin arrived he had almost cut himself to feed Tessa from his vein, to try to turn her in order to save her life. Doc knew what he was about to do and tried to hurry him along. Tessa was already Griffin's mate so it made sense for him to do it. Griffin had no idea how it would affect his weak bond to Sarah, but at that moment he hadn't cared. He was Tessa's only chance, and he loved her so much his heart struggled to break free from his chest.

Griffin raised his wrist to his mouth. He bared his fangs and was ready to open his vein when Sarah grabbed him by the collar of his shirt and pulled him from the limo. She had just shown up and caught him hovering over Tessa while Brandi was being carried to a waiting vehicle.

"What are you doing touching that piece of filth?" She sniffed in disdain and turned Griffin to face her. "Let's get our baby home. These people have done enough harm to our family. Let the others clean up this . . ." she looked at Tessa's still form for emphasis. ". . . trash."

Griffin walked behind her halfway to the van and stopped. He had to maintain his relationship with Sarah. He was a Councilman and his relationship with Tessa had already brought undue attention to his family. His parents were pissed about the negative publicity. Fortunately, society didn't believe a true bond was possible between a vamp and a human, so his bond to Sarah hadn't been called into question. He was being looked upon as a man who'd had a wild youth and made a mistake. That was just how Sarah wanted it. She called it his "human phase."

Griffin stood between the open door of the van that held his injured daughter and the blood-soaked limo that held the love of his life. Doc Stevens was pulling Tessa's beautiful, blood-covered body from the limo. Sarah was in the van with Brandi and a Wrath warrior who used to be a doctor.

"Let's go, Griffin. We need to get her home. Now!" Sarah glared at him.

He looked back to the limo. Doc Stevens was doing chest compressions on Tessa. He was trying to restart her heart. All these years, all this time, he thought he couldn't feel her anymore because she was dead. His bond to Sarah had interfered and added to his belief that she'd lost her life after giving birth to their daughter. He had been wrong. There had always been profound warmth that had carried him through the darkest hours. There had been a soothing presence, like spring rain in his mind, to bathe away the heat of his longing and sorrow. It was gone now. That buzz of awareness in the back of his mind that always said he wasn't alone had ceased. There was no spark of consciousness flowing from her mind to his. He loved her so much and she was slipping away from him again. If she wasn't already dead, she soon would be if drastic action weren't taken right now.

Griffin stood with Sarah screeching at his back and watched Doc turn over the compressions to a warrior in order to hook up an IV. They had fluids on site, but no blood until they reached the Enclave.

His gaze moved to Chase in his black suit. He sat in the grass about ten feet from Tessa holding Danielle. They were a sight. Like yin and yang, he had wrapped himself so tightly around her. Chase was spouting love words and giving her the vows of the blood bond there on the street. The warriors around them stood vigilant and tried to pretend they weren't witnessing a future Councilman losing his mind over a female. Chase was chastising her for being so lovely that others couldn't help but want her. He begged her to wake up and talk to him. He demanded that she stop breaking his heart and find a telepathic connection to him. He pleaded, cajoled, kissed, and stroked her sleeping form.

Griffin had never been so torn in his life. All he wanted, all he had wanted for nearly twenty-two years, was to hold his mate, to kiss her, and whisper words of love and devotion. But he stood there afraid to move. If he went to Tessa, Sarah would make his life a new level of hell, deeper than the one he had been living in since finding his lost family again.

Tessa was dying; maybe she was already dead on the sidewalk only two blocks from his home. His heart revolted against the months of stern control he had exercised in staying far removed from her. She had been so close, but he stayed away for the sake of his family, for the children he'd brought into this world with Sarah, and for the pride and legacy of his family's House.

He stood there with his mate getting louder and nastier behind him, Doc Stevens passing judgment, and Tessa slipping away in front of him. Twice in his life he had failed the person he loved the most. Twice in his life he had let the woman he swore with a blood-bonded oath to protect and cherish, die with no action on his part to prevent it. Danielle wouldn't forgive him, any more than he could forgive himself. Griffin turned and climbed into the van, his heart a frozen block of despair, his face the picture of calm indifference expected of the leader of the mighty House of Vaughn.

Three

I need O negative hung and warm blankets now. We're almost there." Doc tried to speak in his usual calm tone to the nursing staff at the Enclave infirmary over the speaker of his cell phone. The phone was being held out to him by a Wrath warrior named Garrett because he was straddling his patient on the floor of the van performing chest compressions. He was known for being calm in the face of crisis, but the urgency pounding in his veins was seeping into his voice. The large crevasse opening in his composure was pissing Doc off. His hard-won reputation was one of stony unflappability, but he was going to lose this patient if they weren't prepared for his arrival, and she needed to live.

The van was overcrowded with warriors, weapons, and the enticing aroma of human blood. Air, thick with the tension of restraint and need, choked him. The blood was a near-irresistible temptation to the warriors now crashing from the adrenaline high of the previous hours. Doc's fangs were filling his aching mouth, his hands covered with the bright red essence of a human woman who deserved better than she'd received. Tessa smelled so sweet, like warm vanilla and female. *No.* He couldn't think of how delicious she smelled, or how it would feel to hold her to his chest, wrapped safely in his arms while the rich heat of her blood trickled down his throat, coating his tongue. Doc was also struggling with a rage that threatened to consume him after witnessing Griffin stand over his first mate—the woman he had pledged to protect with his own life—and watch her dying. Griffin could have started the change and it wouldn't have done him any harm. They were already bonded and it would have saved her life.

But no, the coward had walked away in fear of his second mate's anger. His family name and reputation were more important than the life of the woman who had spent the last twenty-two years loving him in spite of his betrayal. Who even knew it was possible to have multiple mates? Of course he had heard of parents giving blood to their children, or siblings sharing blood in an emergency to save their loved ones' lives. That would leave them with a permanent bond, but somehow their bodies knew the difference between a mate and a family member. There must be a marker of some sort in the blood that runs in families. He would have to research that in the future, but for now he had to deal with saving Tessa.

Continuing to perform compressions and breathing deeply as if he could breathe for her, Doc willed her to live, to fight and stay with him awhile longer. Doc's temper spiked at the memory of Griffin just standing there, looking lost while Sarah bellowed at his back and spat insults at the mother of his child. Doc was sickened by the weakness of the man whom everyone looked up to as a Council member and leader of their people. Griffin was no more than a puppet dangling from his parents' strings. He danced to whatever tune furthered his House's agenda and his position on the Council. This was exactly how he had lost Tessa all those years ago. His parents had tied him in a knot so tight that the love of his life and his daughter were strangled in the cords.

One of the warriors—he thought it was Troy—flung open the rear doors of the van as they turned onto the access road leading to the Enclave. Fresh air swept through the enclosed area, helping to clear his head. The gates stood open and the guards waved them through.

He checked her pulse again. It was so weak. They had managed to revive her with CPR and fluids on the scene, but he feared the end was near. Restarting chest compressions to keep Tessa's heart going, Doc prayed for the divine intervention he would need to bring her back around. When they came to a screeching halt on the curb of the Enclave, the warriors leapt from the vehicle, no longer able to tolerate the heavy blood scent permeating the van. A gurney was rolled over along with the blood and the IV pump he'd requested. Within moments Tessa was hooked up and he straddled her delicate body, continuing to assist her heart while the nurses wheeled them into the infirmary.

The damn beeping was getting on Brandi's nerves. Sam needed to turn off her alarm clock. Sam could sleep through anything, but the noise was coming right through the wall to wake Brandi. Sam had probably snuck out again. She likely wasn't even in her room to hear the annoying sound that would wake the whole house. It would serve her right if it woke Daddy and he came to check on her.

Brandi, being the sucker she was, contemplated going to turn it off so her twin sister wouldn't get into trouble, but decided not to. That was something the old Brandi would do. New Brandi wouldn't be such a pushover. But nobody had met *that* girl yet. Because . . . because she'd never made it to the bonding ceremony. She struggled with that knowledge. She knew something wasn't right but the memories were just beyond her grasp. Why hadn't she made her debut as the hip and fresh-faced Brandi Vaughn who was lurking beneath her baggy clothes and high IQ?

The beeping became more rapid and she tried to get up to go shut it off. She'd had enough of the noise. All she wanted was to go back to sleep. But when she moved, pain shot through her chest and had her gasping for air. Her stomach rolled and the pain made her want to toss her cookies. In the distance she heard a husky voice.

"Get Mr. and Mrs. Vaughn. I think she's awake."

Footsteps brought the voice to her bedside and a hand brushed her forehead.

"Hey there, Pixie. Are you ready to open those eyes for me? I'd love to see what pixie eyes look like. Can you hear me?"

The decidedly male voice was a deep rumble over her senses, soothing her back into sleep while simultaneously rousing her to find the source of the intriguing new voice. But was this voice really new? Had she heard it before? She struggled to recall the memory of a lifeline thrown to her from a distant shore. She had been floating away on a sea of pain when he came to haul her back in.

He'd held her and said, *"Drink now, Pixie. Drink and come back to me."*

She had done his bidding and drank the hot life pressed to her lips. A warm, calloused hand stroked her face, down her arm, and back up to brush her hair from her eyes.

"Come now. Open those eyes for me." He was checking her pulse; the large hand at her neck made her turn and snuggle her face into the warmth of it. Brandi was cold in spite of the feeling of being buried under a thick layer of blankets. A low growl emanated from above her and the voice came closer while a thumb stroked her cheek.

"I suppose this means sleepy pixies like to be petted? Are you ready to talk to me yet, Nymph?"

Brandi groaned and slowly opened her eyes while snuggling deeper into the comfort of his palm, and then she froze. Inches from her face, a pair of jewel-green eyes peered back at her. Beautiful, unearthly green beacons pulled her from the depths of sleep. He smiled at her sharply indrawn breath. Sandy hair lay over a tanned face with several days' growth adorning a square jaw. Was it right to call a man beautiful? It had to be, because *handsome* just wouldn't do it. Uncertain, she raised her hand to his whiskered cheek to see if he was real and not a dream as she told him what she thought in one word.

"Beautiful."

His eyes widened and New Brandi was proud. She had shamelessly, if weakly, given her approval of him instead of blushing and hiding from the man. And he was a man, not one of the boys she had dated in the past. Feeling a bit smug at having surprised him, she turned her head and pressed a kiss of thanks into his palm. She knew he had been there with her. He had saved her. Darkness drifted over her again and Brandi relaxed back into a deep sleep, feeling safe and protected by her unknown guardian.

The pixie had kissed Greyson's palm and nuzzled him like a lover. Such a gentle gesture had sent heat rocketing straight to his groin. Damn. She had called him beautiful and stunned him with the brush of her soft, rosy lips. Beautiful? Really? Some men may have taken offense at being called such a feminine thing, but Greyson wasn't at all offended. He was secure enough in his manhood to take the compliment as it was intended. He didn't necessarily agree, but far be it from him to dissuade the pixie. He found being called beautiful by this young lady made him feel oddly pleased.

It was so damn good to see some color in those lips and her cheeks. She had been so pale and lifeless just the night before. He'd sat by her bedside all night, pulling double duty as a Wrath guard and a doctor.

The ride in the limo to the Vaughn estate after his Wrath brethren and he had found her, along with her half sister and a human female, had tried his patience. He'd worked feverishly to stop the blood, which two humans on the scene had so kindly donated, from exiting her body through the holes in her chest and back. He'd continued his efforts with little light and the distraction of the pixie's mother screeching at her father, while the father stonily ignored her and held up his cell phone, utilizing the handy flashlight app to give Greyson more light for his work. There was a bullet still lodged in the pixie's upper chest near the clavicle. He hoped it hadn't nicked the artery resting very near the site. Without an operating room, the proper tools, and a couple of assistants, he wouldn't be able to fix that injury in time to save her life. The bullet was preventing her naturally speedy healing processes from taking over and clotting up the hole. It had to come out now, and he had to concentrate in order to make that happen.

Greyson finally snapped when the female simply refused to quiet down so he could work on her daughter. He leaned across the narrow space in the back of the van and grabbed her by the wrist, yanking her toward the doors behind him. He got right in her face and snarled.

"If you don't shut it I'm gonna toss you from this moving vehicle. Do you understand? I'm trying to save your daughter's life and you're worried about a human who is already dead."

The woman screeched even louder at his rough handling. Blood ran from his glove-covered hand down the woman's arm and she watched it drop from her elbow. Suddenly she looked at her daughter as if she had just noticed that the pixie in the van with them was bleeding out and dying.

"I thought you said she was stable?" she keened. Great, now she was crying and getting hysterical.

"I said she was stable enough to move. I need to remove the bullet from her chest," he barked in her face. He had to get it out before he moved her again. He needed her body's natural clotting and healing to help him along. The van came to a sudden and jarring halt. The side door slid open and two warriors, along with a host of other people in tuxedos and gowns, greeted him. Greyson turned back to Mr. Vaughn.

"I'm sorry, but we need this bullet out now." He forced the blubbering woman into the arms of the warriors standing by and slammed the van door shut, locking it. The warrior who had been driving turned around and added the light from his phone on the spot Greyson needed to see. Using the long tweezers, his fingers, and a Hail Mary, Greyson dislodged the bullet from her chest. Almost immediately the blood stopped flowing. He packed the site with gauze to protect it until he could get inside and stitch her up.

Griffin Vaughn stayed with him through the entire ordeal, acting as his assistant and nurse. In the immaculately clean and brightly lit kitchen of the Vaughn estate, on a steel table meant for food prep, Greyson cut the clothes off the pixie and thoroughly cleaned the area around the exit wound. Griffin stripped to his undershirt and scrubbed his hands and arms in the deep sink. He grabbed a pair of gloves from the med-kit and stood ready for direction.

The past crept up on Greyson for a moment and he fought to hold it back. The entire situation, the making do with what he had, the stress, the blood, and the near-death condition of his patient took him back to his days as a field surgeon in Vietnam. For a split second he was up to his elbows in blood, standing over the body of a twenty-year-old kid. The handsome kid hadn't known he'd seen his family for the last time, hadn't had a chance to say good-bye to his troop, or write one last letter to the sweetheart waiting for him at home in the States. He had died, in a foreign country on a metal table, with his chest blown apart.

Shit. Now was not the time to deal with his demons. Griffin stepped up and they set to work. Griffin never once complained about the strain of bending over the table, or winced at the blood and gore. He followed orders and, in the end, Greyson came away with a renewed respect for the Councilman.

During the surgery, a gurney, along with all the other equipment he needed, had been brought in from the Enclave. That made transporting the pixie to her room and monitoring her vitals much easier. The heart monitor had beeped reassuringly all night and into the next day before she had finally stirred for a moment. He continued to sit there with her face pressed into his hand after she slipped back into sleep.

The door pushed open behind him and Greyson reluctantly withdrew his hand. Her parents, along with her twin, who looked nothing like her, rushed into the room. The twin went directly to her sister's bed, knelt on the floor to hold her slack hand, and whispered encouragements for her to wake up so they could fight over the crazy stunt she'd pulled. He reassured them that she was doing well, and had awakened for just a moment, but that was a very good sign. She had seemed lucid and not in much pain until she moved to get up.

"Dr. Drake, why don't you let us make you up one of the guest rooms so you can get some rest? There are two guards at the door and a nurse on duty to monitor Brandi. You must be exhausted. Our family is indebted to you for the service you provided." Griffin shook Greyson's hand and pulled him in for an uncharacteristic man hug, pounding Greyson on the back the way men do when they're fond of each other.

"Please, call me Greyson. I haven't been Dr. Drake for a long time." He smiled a bit weakly. "If you don't mind, sir, I would prefer to continue monitoring Brandi myself." That was actually the first time anyone had bothered to mention her name in front of him. He liked it, but felt like *Pixie* or *Nymph* was going to stick. "I've been taking regular combat naps, and the blood and food you sent up hit the spot. It's been a while since I've had such a critical patient. Nowadays I usually don't do more than patch up my teammates on the fly out in the field." Okay, so he was making excuses to stay with the pixie. So what? He could admit that. To himself. Maybe.

"You still feel like she's critical, Dr. Drake? I thought you just said she was doing well." Mrs. Vaughn challenged him, but had the grace to look sheepish after her performance the night before.

"Brandi is not out of the woods just yet. She is doing well for someone who took two bullets to the back yesterday. Her body is healing nicely, but the amount of blood she lost combined with the extent of her injuries is going to take a toll on her immune system, and healing is going to be a taxing ordeal for her. We may heal quickly, but we are not impervious to all infection. She had a bullet removed in the back of a van and surgery on the kitchen counter. She will have a difficult time fighting off an infection right now, should one arise."

He looked to Griffin for help explaining when Mrs. Vaughn began tapping the toe of her stiletto and looking at him as if he were telling the teacher his dog ate his homework. Maybe she knew he was making excuses. Honestly, he had valid reasons for being concerned. Sure, the nurse could monitor Brandi just as well as he could, but who wouldn't want a trauma surgeon caring for their child instead of a rent-a-nurse? This bitch was . . . well, she was a bitch.

"Of course, we would love you to stay and provide the best care available for our child. Wouldn't we, Sarah?" Griffin eyed his mate until she nodded her agreement and went to the bed to take her daughter's hand. "I believe we have a rollaway bed that will be more comfortable than that chair. I'll have it sent in for you."

More pleasantries were exchanged before Greyson left the room to give the family privacy to visit with the resting pixie. He called to check in at the Enclave and got the green light to stay and care for the daughter of the Councilman. When he returned, the room was empty of visitors, and he quickly and professionally checked her wounds for infection and reviewed her vitals.

Looking down at her, he felt a bit ashamed for being attracted to such a young girl. Guessing a vamp's age could be tricky, but judging by her bedroom décor and her sister, she couldn't be more than twenty. After seeing her last night in a gown, dressed for a party, he had made some assumptions. She had been blood covered, so that hadn't helped, but her curvy body said "all woman" to his senses. She was beautiful even in her worst hour. With her face scrubbed clean of makeup and her curls hugging her cheeks, in sleep she was even more so. Maybe there would be a better reason than the Wrath teams for him to stay and adjust to life on the Enclave. Maybe a pixie could make him feel alive again.

⸻ ◆ ⸻

It was dark and the smell of old blood mixed with other bodily fluids and mildew assaulted Abel. Their failure to successfully complete their mission and return with the female had cost him dearly. He'd done his part and gotten her out of the chapel and away from all of her protectors. It was Darren who had botched the kidnapping, but that didn't matter. A failure was a failure, no matter who was to blame.

The sounds of a crying woman drifted to him from somewhere down the corridor. Was that his mother? Abel listened closely, but the sound was too faint to be distinct. He had really screwed up this time. The *Master*, as he liked to be called, was none too happy about the failure of Abel's latest mission. The goal was to abduct the girl from her bonding ceremony and bring her back to the Nest. Danielle Vaughn was important to the Master's plans for crushing the ruling Council of Vampires. Returning without her had brought a world of hurt down on Abel.

The Master had this insane, Hitler-like concept of the superiority of their species. He believed vampires, being at the top of the food chain, should rule the world, and humans should bow their heads respectfully and serve obediently or die. Naturally, he would be the leader, master of all, and all would worship at the altar of his genius for bringing about this new world order. No kingdom would survive the coming of his warped Shade army, the blitzkrieg of the vampire nation.

The Shade consisted of vampires from the darkest corners of the vampire nation organized into loose military units. They were thugs, thieves, and rejected members of society looking for a way to get out from under the Council's rule. The Master believed this roughneck band of misfits could defeat the warrior class of vampires who protected the Council and the vampire nation before they moved on to take over the human world.

Never mind the fact that vampires only made up about a fifth of the world's population, and who cared if the US military itself, without the help of the rest of the world, could crush his growing league of like-minded vampires. The ultimate goal of destroying the Council was all that mattered to the Master. First step, the Council falls, giving him control over the vampire nation. Then he planned to take over the world like some megalomaniac from a B movie.

The crying stopped when footsteps began to pound down the corridor of the underground network of cells where human cattle had been collected to keep the Master fed, alongside prisoners and vampires who had failed to please the Master. Chained to the floor, bloodied and defenseless, Abel waited for the end to come. Would this be the day to end his servitude to the evil he'd been forced into for longer than he could remember? Had the Master finally made good on his promise to murder Abel's mother if he wasn't completely obedient? It would be the killing blow to what was left of his fragile human psyche, if his failure had caused the death of his mom. His sweet human mother was the only thing holding Abel to this world anymore. He had murdered, kidnapped, stolen, and abused, all in the name of protecting the only family he had.

The footsteps passed his cell and stopped not far away. A shrill scream ripped through the darkness as the sounds of a weak struggle ensued. The woman was being taken to the Master. It was dinnertime at the Nest and she was the main course tonight. Panic and trepidation poured from the woman as she pleaded to be released, but the guard backhanded her. There was the too-familiar sound of skin striking skin before she fell silent. It was completely within their power to trance her into submission and make the experience comfortable, even pleasurable, for her, but they didn't. She was only cattle. Why worry about her feelings? Humans don't comfort livestock before they're slaughtered. The Master had no sympathy for his human delicacies.

Guilt battered Abel for being grateful the guard had come for the woman instead of him. His ravaged body might not survive another beating right now. Oh, he could fend off an attacker, but he submitted to the beatings, and being the half-human mongrel he was, healing from the last one would take some time. He was as strong and as fast as any full-blooded vampire, but when injured, it took twice as long for him to recover.

Abel had become a feared fighter in the Nest, because the best defense was a good offense. Preventing injury was the best offense against his bloodthirsty brethren. If his humanity were to come to light, he would be an instant target. It was the threat of exposure and the safety of his mother that kept him in line.

The Master could not be seen as weak or lenient. Abel took the beatings and smiled inwardly. He knew down deep the Master feared him. He was stronger, faster, and more deviant than any of the other soldiers. Abel had been raised on beatings as if they were mother's milk. The result was a vampire with a will to survive and take down anything in his path. No one could defeat him alone, and everyone, including the Master, knew it.

So the Master took great pleasure in making a show of beating the hell out of Abel at the slightest provocation, and in doing so, proving to the rest of the Nest that he was the greatest warrior. Only he could knock the pegs out from under Abel and then have him carried away and hidden to preserve the image of a perfect vampire. God forbid anyone find out the secret he and the Master kept by mutual agreement. If only they knew how he gladly accepted the beatings in exchange for his mother's safety. Now, when Abel was weak and vulnerable, the Master would come and remind him of his vows. He would remind him of his humanity and the fragility of being such a pathetic creature like his mother. How easily her life could end.

Again he felt shame for wishing the Master would just go ahead and kill him. It would be so much easier than being his whipping boy. It would be so much easier than going out and collecting cattle for the Master's pleasure. It would be better than wandering the streets, picking up human girls to bring back for the vamps in the Nest to abuse and drain. Human girls, who would have grown to be mothers just like his, followed him gladly until he entranced them into his web. He also captured vampire youth to be tested for power and killed whether they had any or not. He was a traitor to both races.

He was the perfect vampire. That's what the Master had told him. The humans couldn't resist vampire charms, and the vampires couldn't resist the faint, elusive scent of human blood. Yet nobody knew Abel was a demi-vamp mongrel. He wanted to die for his crimes against man and vampires because living with the guilt only made him meaner and colder by the day. But what would happen to his mom? If she wasn't needed to keep Abel in line, would she be the next woman dragged down the corridor, screaming and begging for her life? He didn't know the answer to that question and he never would.

A memory flickered in the back of his mind and Abel savored it for a moment. She had been such a surprise. In the chapel entryway, a little brunette fireball had tried to take his head off with a golf club. At first anger had swelled in his chest and he'd gripped her tightly, pressing the gun to her head. He would have killed her. He should have killed her, but the warm, honeyed scent of her had hit him, and the heat of her body against his chest made him hesitate. Until the heat of her hand literally burned him. She was pyrokinetic. The knowledge still shocked him.

The Master would kill for a prize like that and he knew he should have taken her. If he could've figured out how to do that without ending up well done. It would require waiting for another shipment of Hypnovam. But he didn't want to see her die at the Master's fangs. She had a spark, a fire in her that was about more than just her elemental ability. The fight he saw in her eyes needed to live on. The courageous fire starter needed to live and breed more vamps like her, if vampires were to have a chance of surviving people like him and his master.

Abel's head fell to the blood-blackened stone beneath him. Despair he didn't often allow himself to feel washed over him. Darren had pulled his weapon when he saw the little fire starter getting away with his mate. They'd struggled for the gun and just as Abel lifted his head, a fireball came roaring through the night to ignite the van fifty yards behind them. It had been magnificent. She was breathtaking, until Darren stood, braced his feet, and put two bullets in her back. He didn't know if she had survived, but when he got out of that pit—and he would eventually get out—he would find her. He had to know if the fire in her eyes survived. A foreign sensation twisted in his gut and he didn't like it. He couldn't allow himself to care. She wouldn't thank him for it. She wouldn't care for the bastard mongrel son of human woman.

Four

The ceiling above the bed Dani woke up in was, unfortunately, very familiar. She was really sick of coming to consciousness in the damn infirmary at the Enclave. How many times could one person end up there before the wing got renamed in his or her honor? Seriously, it should be called *The Danielle Vaughn Center for the Constantly Unconscious and Terminally Stupid.*

How the hell had she gotten into this situation again? She hadn't even really thought of Darren as a continued threat, but she was wrong. He'd betrayed her again, in spite of his supposedly undying love for her. She should have gone with her instincts and incapacitated him one of the few times he'd approached her wanting to talk since the Rogue's attack. He would be in jail now and she would be on her honeymoon. The problem was that something in her felt sorry for him. Knowing how her mother had suffered after the loss of her mate made Dani feel for him just a bit. Darren was paying dearly for his crime and she knew it, but she could no longer feel any pity for the man.

Dani realized that her mind was wandering and wondered how long she'd been out. Movement caught her attention and shifted her gaze from the familiar cracks in the plaster above her to the bottom of her bed. The sight that greeted her had her heart thudding instantly. Chase and Kayden stood facing off as if a battle would break out at any moment. *Shit!*

They had been best friends until Dani came between them, a fact that still weighed heavily on her heart. When she couldn't have the man she wanted, Dani had turned to another guy for comfort. Kayden gladly stepped into the role of her main distraction with full knowledge of her feelings for Chase. She'd prayed fervently that they'd come to an understanding, once all the smoke had cleared. It hadn't happened, and Kayden avoided her and Chase at all cost.

Now the two men stared at each other intently. The thick tension in the room had her holding her breath. Dani had had enough of their male posturing. If either one of them threw a punch she was going to give them both the mental smackdown of their lives. Then, she would lock them in a room together until they came out acting like grown men instead of stubborn little boys.

Kayden stepped closer to Chase, a challenge in his eyes and a smirk on his lips. Chase, never one to back down, stepped up and cocked an unimpressed eyebrow at his oldest friend, and then he smiled. Kayden shook his head and looked away. Then, by some miracle of fate, the two men embraced each other tightly. Chase was pounding Kayden on the back and smiling widely.

"I have missed you, brother," Kayden choked. "I'm sorry for . . . everything."

Chase pulled back slightly from the tight embrace to look Kayden in the eye.

"It's enough now, Kayden. You have punished yourself enough. I love you, man. Dani loves you so much. I know she's afraid to tell me how much, but I know. You were her best friend when I couldn't be. You protected her and supported her. You did the right thing when I was making all the wrong moves."

"I did not do the right thing. I hurt her more than any of the people who were out to harm her. She should hate me. I made promises. I told her she was perfect and I'd love her no matter what, but the first time I was tested I failed. I've stayed away because I don't want to see the disgust I know she must feel for me. But, I'll tell you this. She *was* perfect just the way she was and I *will* love her always. You are one lucky bastard and a better man than I could ever be."

"Are you done yet? Can you let it go? Because we already have. I made more mistakes and hurt her just as much as you did, Kayden. We were a couple of kids playing at being men. It seems like a lifetime ago. We have both learned from our mistakes and grown up. I want you in my corner. I need my best friend back in my life," Chase tried to reassure him.

"I think you should talk to Dani before we make any decisions about the future. The last thing I want is to make her unhappy." Kayden hung his head with a renewed bout of shame.

Finally, after months of silence and separation, they had both said their piece and come to an understanding. The past was in the past, and the future felt more secure with the two men she loved the most standing there like brothers instead of enemies. They had been an unstoppable force in the past and Dani believed they would continue to be overwhelming in the future. Only now, as men, they would conquer the enemies of their people and lead the future generations side by side. Kayden would be the backbone of the warriors and Chase would step into his post on the Council. Together they would create and enforce a new era of tolerance and acceptance in the vampire nation. It wouldn't be easy, but, together with the help of a few select Council members and youth of the nation, it would someday be done. This was the greatest wish in Dani's heart, and she finally released the pent-up air in her lungs, drawing the attention of both Chase and Kayden. Chase rushed to her side and pulled her into his arms, burrowing his face in her neck for a moment.

"Damn it, Lovely! I swear I'll be gray before I'm thirty. You scared the hell out of me." He began to place kisses on her neck and stroke her hair. Dani met Kayden's eyes over Chase's shoulder and smiled. In that moment it seemed as if a heavy burden was lifted from Kayden's shoulders. He took a deep breath and smiled back at her. He looked quickly away, embarrassed at watching her and Chase embracing each other.

"I'm sorry, Chase. I didn't mean to leave you at the altar. I hope you can forgive me." She nuzzled the side of his face and inhaled the essence of sunshine and home. Chase reached up and hit the button to call a nurse to her room.

"How do you feel? Does anything hurt?" Chase began to systematically check her limbs, testing for pain.

"I feel weak, but fine overall. Where is Brandi? How is she?"

Dani had to know what happened to her little sister, her rescuer. The last thing she remembered was the smell of her mother's blood and silence. *Oh God! Mom!*

"What about my mom?" Dani tried to push past Chase and get to her feet. She had to find her mom. Now!

"Hold on there, Angel." Kayden hurried to the side of the bed to comfort her. "That is actually the reason I stopped by to see you and Chase. Please, relax. I have news on both your mom and Brandi. Ms. Tessa is right down the hall. Doc Stevens is keeping a close eye on her. He hasn't left her side and he assured me that she's stable. She lost a lot of blood, and, to be honest, it was close, but she's expected to completely recover." He shyly took her hand after looking to Chase for approval. Dani pulled on his arm until he bent over and hugged her gently.

"Thank you, Kay. I've missed you so much. Please forgive me for pulling you into the mess my life has become. And please don't hold it against Chase if you can't forgive me. I asked too much of you and we both paid for it."

Kayden squeezed her tighter and didn't acknowledge her request for forgiveness. Instead, he sat back in a chair by the bed and continued to update them on everything they had missed.

"Brandi had two gunshots to her upper back. I went to check on her this morning. One of the bullets had become lodged in her chest and was preventing her blood from clotting and beginning the healing process. The other bullet exited her chest and only added to the blood loss. We had one doctor and two critical patients."

Kayden filled them in on the former trauma doctor who'd joined the ranks of the Wrath and his part in saving Brandi's life in the kitchen of the Vaughn estate. Chase and Dani both stared at him with open-mouthed amazement by the time he finished his story. A nurse bustled into the room accompanied by Doc Stevens. Chase and Kayden moved away to let them check Dani over. She tried to answer Doc's questions, while keeping an eye on the men whispering in the corner. After her exam was finished, and Doc explained Tessa's condition to Dani, he went to consult the guys while the nurse busied herself with removing her IV and getting her a set of scrubs.

No one else was aware that Dani had woken from her drug-induced sleep and that was the way they wanted to keep it. She still wasn't welcome on the Enclave and they only got away with taking her there because Doc insisted he have both of his patients in the same building. Now that they were both stable, even though Tessa had yet to awaken, they were being moved stealthily. Whether the Council or the Enclave was ready to admit it or not, there were traitors in their ranks. Moving the women before they drew any more attention was vital.

Dani had barely gotten dressed and was still barefoot when Chase scooped her up and headed for the door. Kayden had a car at the side entrance ready to go. Just ahead of them Doc had Tessa in an ambulance and was taking her to his clinic for observation. Within an hour of her waking, Dani was on the way to the condo she shared with Chase, and her mom was off to a state-of-the-art vampire clinic with Doc Stevens.

———— • ————

Chase had argued with his Lovely at the Enclave. After all the drama and mishaps of the past nine months, she hadn't wanted to wait another minute to become his mate. She wanted to exchange blood there in her hospital room before they went anywhere else. Soleil didn't want to take any more chances with their future; she sorely regretted waiting the six months it had taken to plan the bonding ceremony. It warmed him to his soul that she would be willing to hastily exchange blood and forgo any type of ceremony to ensure their bond happened immediately. He'd had one too many scares himself, but her suggestion was out of the question. They needed to move quickly before anyone realized they were gearing up for a swift evacuation.

From what he had seen in the past, Chase knew that once a couple was bonded it took them a while to get their heads on straight. He feared an attack on the way home, and if they were wrapped up in the growing blood bond, he might not see it coming until it was too late. The more than twenty-four hours they had spent on the Enclave was long enough for every warrior there to know that Danielle Vaughn was in the house and unprotected. Chase hadn't slept for fear someone would slip in and snatch her away from him again. The risk was too great to stay any longer.

Once at home, he had talked her into a meal and a nap. The drugs must have still lingered in her system, because in spite of her protest, she slept eight hours without stirring. Chase was glad he had waited until they were home and rested before they performed the bonding ceremony. They both needed clear heads and open hearts to begin the mating the right way. It needed to be special even if they had no family or friends there to witness the joining of their souls.

He stared sightlessly out the glass doors that overlooked his penthouse terrace and the city beyond it. He knew only the sound of his heart pounding in anticipation of his Lovely's entrance to their bedroom. She had gone to the guest room, wanting to prepare for the bonding alone while Chase prepared in their room.

Thinking back on the time before his Lovely belonged to him felt like reliving a nightmare. She had strolled into his life one night and changed him forever.

In the early days, when her vampire genetics had just kicked in and she had not yet learned to shield her thoughts when telepathically communicating, Chase had been able to read her like a book, and what he found there was shocking. His perfect little vampire goddess was actually a half-human demi-vamp who was terrified and still unsure of exactly what she was, or what he was, for that matter. He'd made huge mistakes and because of that she had actually lived out her greatest fears. She had been rejected by the vampires she cared for most. He loved her so much, and by some miracle, even after his past missteps, she loved him too.

He needed to make up for his blunders by making her life from now until forever the cocoon of love and acceptance she'd deserved from him and his people from the very beginning. A noise from the hall pulled Chase out of his reverie, and he turned to examine the room one last time, but his eyes caught on the beauty standing in the doorway. Slowly he made his way to the bed, never taking his eyes off of his bride as he crawled to the center of the bed to await her.

She was stunning, with dark chocolate hair twisting in waves to curl lovingly around her waist. The streaks of white hair she was born with gleamed in the candlelight, accentuated by dark red highlights that had appeared suddenly after her first taste of blood and had never faded away. The ice blue of her eyes seemed almost faceted and put the diamonds sparkling on her left hand and in her earlobes to shame. Chase held his breath, praying his Lovely wouldn't rethink her decision to be his mate. She was obviously getting the short end of this deal.

He sat still while she watched him, searching his eyes, for what he did not know. But he would wait as long as it took for her to be ready. He had already waited for nine months. Nine months . . . that didn't sound like a long time, but the beginning of the path that led them to this place felt like a lifetime ago. She was the sun that rose in his heart. Soleil was the center of his life already. Chase couldn't imagine how they could get closer. But they would.

She must have found what she was searching for in his eyes. Finally, she stepped into the room and shed her robe on the way to the bed. Moving slowly she crept up onto the bed to meet him in the middle. They knelt in front of each other, both breathing hard and waiting for the moment to feel right.

Danielle reached out to loosen the belt of his robe and push it off his shoulders. Once he dispensed with the barrier they both rose to their knees, needing to touch and be touched. Palm to palm. Wrist to wrist. Chest to chest they breathed each other in and they both knew. No words were spoken. They stared into each other's eyes and the vows they had practiced faded away.

It was all there in her face for Chase to see. Love. Commitment. Trust. Passion. Forever. The ceremonial daggers lay forgotten by the bed. They knew each other so well. By silent agreement when Danielle had entered the room and dropped her robe, revealing the expanse of her creamy skin, her lush curves, and the dusky rose of her peaked nipples, all thoughts of cutting and sealing the bond with a kiss disappeared like smoke. No. That wasn't what either of them wanted. They would make love and they would bite. Chase would draw the essence of her life, the light of her soul, into himself with his mouth at her throat, and her body wrapped in his arms, his body buried in her heat.

Danielle burned to be closer. Chase sat on the bed waiting patiently for her to make the first move. Hadn't that been his way since the beginning of their relationship? He waited, boring a hole in her resistance with his eyes. The fear of rejection still rode her, but she forced it down. For a long moment she watched him, waiting for him to remember that he was so far above her and he could clearly find a more worthy mate. He could find a mate who would surely live as long as he would and give him perfect, full-blooded vampire children.

There were so many unknowns in their future, not the least of which was whether or not she could be bonded to Chase. It hadn't worked out so well for Darren. The change he had brought about in her could have made her fully able to bond with Chase, but it also could have changed her life span and her ability to have children. Still, Chase sat and watched her with those piercing ocean eyes from under his ridiculously long black lashes.

They both knew the risks. She would give Chase the same love and commitment she would give to him if they were both human and blood bonds didn't exist. He would be her husband, her mate, whether the bond took or not. She loved him with every cell in her body already. The results of this evening wouldn't change that fact. Her fear was for Chase, not herself. She didn't want him to be hurt or suffer for loving her. It all boiled down to one question. Was there another woman in this world, vampire or human, who could love him more, or protect Chase's heart better than she could? Hell no! And she'd kill any woman who tried!

Before she knew it Danielle had crossed the room and crawled naked over the bed to meet her soon-to-be mate. He was gorgeous with sleek muscles under smooth, tanned skin. The only sound in the room was their breathing. She knew they wouldn't need the blades used in a traditional bonding. Danielle wanted to taste him on her tongue and feel the heat of his soul run down her throat while they loved each other thoroughly.

Simultaneously they fell into each other, and, chest to chest, their gazes held. Chase's eyes had gone black with passion and Danielle knew hers had done the same. She had to taste him on her tongue and leaned in to drink deeply from his mouth. He was a master at making her melt with his strong lips, and he plundered the depths of her mouth like a man starving. The kiss went on and on, but it wasn't enough. Pulling back, he looked down into her upturned face and growled. "I have to taste you, Lovely. All of you. I want to sear the flavor of you onto my tongue and into my mind." He grabbed her hips and pulled her more tightly against his body for a moment, rubbing his length against the junction of her thighs. "Mmm . . . you're already wet for me."

Danielle couldn't breathe while he licked and nibbled his way down her neck and across her collarbone. His questing mouth continued down to her breast, where he suckled and teased her nipples into stiff, aching peaks. Dani fought to hold still while he drew out her need. She felt her wetness slicking her thighs and remembered a time when that would have embarrassed her. Now she thought of her body's heated reaction as testament to her lover's skill. He knew just how to drive her insane. She felt the scrape of fangs against the underside of her breast and Chase froze momentarily. He'd broken the skin slightly, something he had always been able to control in the past. That told her a lot about his state of mind, and she felt a rush at knowing that she had pushed him over the edge of reason. Chase was running on pure instinct. He wiped at his mouth to remove any blood from his fangs.

"Not yet, Lovely. I want your fangs in me when I taste your blood. We will do it together."

He panted with the exertion of controlling the need to lap up her essence. Lowering his head to her breast, Chase sucked one taut peak into his mouth while he massaged the other. Danielle let loose a sexy little whimper when he released her breast with a pop. He had a goal, and that was to make his Lovely insane with the need to have him deep in her body and soul. He was a little saddened that she had stopped to give him a chance to back out before she entered their bedroom. She had learned a lot about her power and how to control it over the last six months, but, under stress, she still tended to broadcast her thoughts, if only to him. Now he was going to make her beg for his fangs. It would be a suitable punishment for doubting him.

The skin of her flat belly made his mouth water. Gently, he guided her down to the bed. Her expression was a mixture of anxious anticipation and desire. He'd give her what she wanted and take his pleasure in return. She was his mate no matter what and Chase was about to prove that to her. He slowly, painstakingly, made his way down her body, nipping, licking, and kissing every inch of her skin from her mouth all the way to her ankles, with the exception of her wet heat. She writhed and wriggled, trying to get his mouth where she wanted it. But he was in charge now and Chase would make her beg. He stopped on his way back up the inside of her thigh when she made a frustrated sound.

"What's wrong, Lovely?" He licked the damp crease between her hip and thigh. "Don't you like my mouth on your body?"

Oh God. He was going to make her say it. Chase wanted her to beg for the pleasure she knew he was withholding. She squirmed and grabbed his hair, trying to pull him up to her mouth. If her mouth was full, she couldn't talk. But he held steady and placed one long lick right where she wanted him.

"Chase, baby. Please. I need . . ." Damn it! They had been intimate for six months but it was still hard to say what she wanted.

"Tell me what you need, my Lovely. I want to give it to you." He purred and gave her another stroke of his tongue. Dani almost bucked him off of her. The force of her need was so great. She realized then that she had hurt him. The look on his face was intense, almost playful, but on closer inspection her senses were picking up sadness. He had felt her doubt before she entered the room and was hurt by it. She answered him the only way she knew how. With the truth.

"I need you, Chase Deidrick, to love me always. I need you to cherish my body, as I will cherish yours. I need you to understand my need to protect you from anything that could bring you harm. Even if that means protecting you from me. And I need you to be my one true mate in this life and all the lives that follow." She released a sigh of regret for hurting him tonight of all nights. "I need you to love me."

She had taken his breath away. Fighting tears of joy, Chase rested his forehead on her belly while gripping her rounded hips. She hadn't really doubted him. It was her worthiness to be his mate she had doubted. All thoughts of making her beg fled. He lowered his head again and gave her what she needed. He lapped at her ruthlessly until her cries of pleasure echoed off the ceiling and filled the room. Once assured that he had satisfied his mate's needs, he climbed over her and looked deeply into her obsidian, passion-filled eyes. When he rested himself against her, Danielle moaned a restless sound of needy longing.

"I will always love and cherish your body and soul. I have loved you since we first met. It just took me a while to realize how singularly unique a love so precious could be, and I will spend eternity proving the depth of my love to you. I will be your one true mate in this life and all the lives that follow."

With those vows of love, which were not the traditional bonding vows, Chase pushed forward to enter her slick body. It seemed to him that Danielle had been very careful to keep her distance telepathically during their love play, but her restraint snapped when his length filled and stretched her tight depths. He moved slowly in an effort to maintain control. His Lovely's mind had entered his own and the glory of their joined bodies and minds threatened to unravel him completely.

With every long stroke into her body he felt her pleasure at being entered as well as his own at feeling her heat grasp him and try to hold him. As he inhaled the intoxicating vanilla-and-lavender scent that followed her every move, he instantly knew her joy in the scent of summer that radiated off of him. He possessed her body and knew what it felt like to be possessed in return. He was close, too close. Chase pulled back slowly and slid his hand between himself and his writhing mate-to-be. Careful to still his body, Chase caressed her little bud of nerves with his thumb, and allowed her to move against him. It was still intense, but he needed to hold out. The sun was about to rise and he wanted to take his mate into his soul with her namesake sunlight glistening on her sweat-dampened skin.

━━━◆━━━

"I need to . . . I have to . . ." Dani panted. She wanted to explode with him but he was holding back.

"Yes, Lovely. Melt for me. I'm not done with you yet. Will you accept my bond in the light of day? I want to watch the sunrise on the first day of our bond to each other."

He was gritting his teeth and straining for control. Dani tried frantically to pull back some from their telepathic connection. She was about to lose it and she would surely drag him with her. It seemed to help and he breathed more easily. Dani couldn't hold off any longer. She bucked against his body and pressed herself into his hand. The world tilted and she came apart in his arms. Slowly, she drifted back to herself. Chase's need for release slammed into her the moment her leash on their link slipped, and his heart pounded with the aching of his flesh.

"I'm taking you out onto the terrace, Lovely. The sun is peeking over the horizon."

Chase lifted her from the bed still fully engaged with her body. When he stopped to open the glass doors, he leaned her against the wall to plunder her mouth and her body for a time before continuing to a chaise longue. He sat slowly and Dani sat astride his lean hips. The position was perfect for what they wanted to do.

"Baby," he hissed, "I need to taste you, need to feel you."

Chase's frenzy washed over her, but she sent back a calm, soothing wave of passion to counteract his fevered lust. He breathed more deeply and she moved slowly up and down his length. Dani twisted her hips and rocked steadily against Chase. He kissed her neck, and she knew when the combined scent of their lovemaking and the scent of the blood on her from his earlier scrape overwhelmed his best intentions. Chase looked up into her face and smiled. The sunlight was bursting over the horizon and through the clouds, washing everything in a pink-and-amber glow.

"I love you, Soleil Deidrick," he whispered.

Chase lowered his head and struck her hard and fast. His fangs sank into the space between her neck and shoulder, but before she had a chance to feel any pain, the most incredible rush of her life pulled her under. Chase was lapping at her and absorbing her into his body. He growled and pumped into her body.

Dani was so overwhelmed she didn't remember sinking her fangs into his flesh, but the taste of Chase on her tongue for the first time was something she would never forget. His flavor was familiar, yet strange. His blood was saltier than his kisses, but sweeter than the liquid heat of the releases she had swallowed. The blood running down her throat and the strong thrust of his body combined to shatter Dani. Her entire being seemed to blow apart and scatter in the wind. Place and time meant nothing for her and Chase while they floated together in the light of the rising sun. When they drifted back to their bodies, everything had changed. They were no longer separate entities but two parts of a whole, two beings with one soul.

It wasn't until that moment, in the aftermath of their bonding while Dani lay securely in Chase's arms, that she made an odd correlation in her mind between the way Chase reminded her of the perfect summer day, with his ocean eyes and the sunshine happiness of his scent, and her birth name. He was the perfect summer day and she was the sun. Chase's chest rumbled beneath her when she giggled. She was obviously broadcasting again.

"Obviously." He smiled and kissed the top of her head.

"I'm sorry you didn't see the sunrise. You were facing the wrong way, baby." She pouted. She had wanted his experience to be perfect.

"I saw it perfectly. I saw the light glistening off your skin. I saw the rays playing in your hair. I saw the sun rise in the eyes of my mate."

———◆———

Not far away Darren knew his mate was giving her body to another man, and he seethed. He was sick with the knowledge that some spoiled little rich kid had his hands, and everything else, all over his mate. Darren had had her in his arms for a few short, precious moments just the night before last. Now he sat in the place known as the Nest and listened to some psycho spout off about a new order of vampires. The Rogue thought he was building a new nation and his Shade army needed guidance. The nut would lead, and he believed everyone would follow once he took out the Council.

The *Master*, as he wished to be called, wanted Darren to be his second-in-command. He wanted a general to train and lead his Shade. They were a small army of like-minded freaks. Darren was only sticking around to have access to the Hypnovam. He needed it to bring in his mate. Now that she was a full-blooded vamp, they could exchange blood and solidify their bond. The problem was that she had grown too strong for him to get near her if she saw him coming. He just needed one more shot.

The nutcase was raving on about his plans for moving on the warrior class when a sharp pain ripped through Darren's shoulder and neck. He slumped back, startled for a moment before he realized what had happened. That little bastard had bitten his mate. He had sunk his dirty fangs into her perfect body. The asshole would have to die. But that wasn't the worst that was to come. Not by a long shot. His mate, his woman, who'd refused to take his blood, was drinking from another man? Danielle was attempting to wash away his bond to her. Rage so dark and deep bubbled up in his chest. He launched the heavy chair he'd been resting on across the room. It shattered against the far wall, startling the other vamps lounging around the room.

"I will do whatever you want," he hissed, trying to breathe through the sting of betrayal. "I will kill them all."

The Rogue smiled widely. "Good. Very good."

Five

Six months later . . .

Brandi leaned against the wall at Thirst and surveyed the crowd. The thump of the heavy bass vibrated through her chest. She needed to feed tonight. It had been several days since her last drink. She'd forced herself to leave the house to search for the warmth of a human host. Normally, to her mother's dismay, Brandi opted for drinking from a blood bag, juice-box style. It was a habit she picked up from her half sister, but tonight she needed to feel the heat of life run down her throat. She wasn't feeling like herself these days. She chuckled. She hadn't felt like the girl she had once been since the birth of New Brandi. She looked down at her body and wondered who exactly the girl in the black-sequined minidress and stiletto boots was. She just needed to feed. That was her problem. She needed to start feeding more often.

The practice of *juicing*, she laughed at herself again, came to her after she started dating Greyson. They had been together for nearly six months and it just felt wrong to her to get that close to another man. It was an odd mind-set for a vampire, but it was how Brandi felt. He had been her man since about a week after she woke up in her bed, having nearly been killed by the bullets of a madman. Tessa Vaughn, with the help of Greyson's quick thinking and surgical skills, also survived. Brandi chose to believe that Darren had been the one to shoot her twice in the back. When she thought of the other possibility, it left her feeling hollow.

It actually annoyed her that she couldn't seem to make herself believe that the striking, dark-eyed stranger who helped abduct her half sister could have shot her. He'd had plenty of opportunity to kill her when he'd stood in the entryway of the chapel with a gun pointed at her head. She had even tried to take his head off with a golf club, and all he had done was restrain her until she let the flames bubble up and scorch his ass. He had deserved it after knocking her brain around with the muzzle of his pistol. That pistol could very well have been used to nearly take her life. The bullet they dug out of her body could have come from that gun. She just couldn't reconcile that with what she had seen in his eyes. He was no angel, that was for sure, but something in him had reached for her. Something lost had wanted to be found that night, but she couldn't help a man who was on the wrong side of the fight between her people and the Rogue.

Once Brandi was recovering after the shooting, Greyson Drake, her doctor at the time, had announced that it was time for him to be heading back to the Enclave to resume his duties as a newbie Wrath guard. Brandi was shocked. This man who had a medical degree, amazing surgical skills, and a suntan to boot, was a warrior?

Brandi had thought she knew all of the warriors from the Enclave. They were all on rotation at the homes of the Council members. Even the Wrath took their turn on guard duty, but she had never before seen Greyson. Brandi didn't want him to leave, which was silly, because if it had been Doc Stevens she wouldn't have cared if he came or went. But this was Greyson. Greyson, the sexy, funny, intelligent guy who didn't treat her like a kid. They spent hours talking about everything from politics to sports. He listened to her opinions on the current state of the vampire nation and debated with her on their varying viewpoints. He explained her medical situation to her and the surgery she had undergone. Doc would have spoken to her parents and given her the kindergarten version of events, before he patted her on the head with instructions to be a good girl until he returned. Greyson made her think, and when he wasn't around he made her dream.

Brandi knew he was older, but she didn't care. In a few years her age wouldn't matter. Vampires lived a long time, as long as they didn't run around getting shot and setting things on fire. Greyson was hot and smart and she wanted to get to know him better. They had chemistry and Brandi knew she wasn't the only one who felt it. He liked her, too. As long as he was across the room in the cozy chair her father had brought in for him, Greyson seemed completely unaffected, but if he had to get close, he did his best not to make eye contact and breathed slowly and deeply. Her ego wanted to think maybe he was struggling for control.

So, when he was checking her over for the last time before he returned to his home at the Enclave, she took a chance. Greyson leaned over her bed to check her pupils with his little flashlight. When he was close enough for her to touch, she reached up and stroked his jaw with shaking fingers. She needed to show her interest and hoped he wouldn't laugh at her like she was a kid with a crush. Greyson froze. His expression mirrored the same curiosity she was feeling. He didn't pull away, so she pressed her lips to his for a lingering kiss. Brandi's heart fluttered around in her chest like a trapped bird when he began to kiss her back after only the slightest hesitation. Greyson's lips were strong, and he tasted like cinnamon gum. She felt desire rolling off of him.

It was the hottest kiss of her life. Greyson stroked her tongue gently at first, taking his time, making her want more. Brandi moaned into his mouth and that seemed to set him off. He began to explore her mouth more completely, touching and tasting her thoroughly. After losing themselves in the kiss for several long moments, Greyson pulled back and apologized. He felt as if he were taking advantage of his much-younger and vulnerable patient. He told her she was a temptation he had to resist and it was a daily battle. He wanted her, but he explained that it was his job as a professional to protect her best interests, even if that meant protecting her from him and his lasciviousness. That just made New Brandi more determined. He wanted her, but felt like a dirty old man. She had laughed and smiled up into his jewel-green eyes before she explained that she wouldn't be young forever.

A few guys Brandi had gone to high school with pulled her from her reverie when they blocked her view of the dance floor. They'd been friends and Brandi had actually dated one of them throughout their senior year. These guys were some of her jock buddies, as opposed to her geek friends. Brandi had a genius IQ and a love for all sports. Her two groups of friends didn't always mix well. She hadn't made many friends in college due to her age and heavy course load. She'd graduated from high school before she turned sixteen and had a bachelor of science in sports medicine at eighteen.

Since the birth of New Brandi, she had totally separated herself from everyone who had been close to Old Brandi. Those people had expectations of her. They would want her to behave as she always had, and that wasn't conducive to her new, more stylish, sophisticated way of life. She didn't play sports or compete in math tournaments anymore. She went to clubs and fashion shows. She did martial arts to stay in shape now. Seeing these guys actually made her feel bad. She had abandoned everyone, leaving them in the shadows when she stepped out into the spotlight.

"Hey, there's my girl!"

Nick pulled her away from the wall and into a tight embrace, sniffing her hair and rubbing against her. It was kind of offensive. They'd been intimate during their relationship, but when he headed off to college they broke it off. The long-distance thing just wasn't going to work. Neither of them was very hurt by the separation. So why after so many years did he think it was okay to paw on her? She wiggled free and moved back to the wall. Jason and Doug chuckled and leered at her body.

"It's nice to see you, Nick. When did you get back into town?" she asked.

"I've been home for a few days. I was hoping to run into you. I have to tell you, I didn't expect to find a bombshell when I did catch up to you. Whatever you've done to yourself, keep on doing it. I knew you had a hot little body under all those jerseys, but I never expected you to show it off. You look great."

Nick ran a finger down her arm while he ogled her boobs.

"Thanks, I think. Well, I'll see you guys around."

She tried to push past Nick, but he grabbed her arm and backed her into the wall again. The other two guys stood at Nick's sides, effectively blocking any escape.

"Hold on a minute, babe. I haven't seen you in years. Why don't we hang out? I'd love to get on the floor." Nick leaned in close to whisper next to her ear. Nick was a vampire, but Doug and Jason were not, and she knew Nick had used them as blood donors in the past.

"I have a friend I could share with you. Would you like to play with your food tonight? We could have a lot of fun, the three of us."

Okay. That was just wrong and creepy.

"No thanks, Nick. I already have plans. My boyfriend is meeting me later."

That was a lie. Greyson had been deployed for two weeks and she had no idea when she would see him again.

"Don't bother, Nicky. Ms. Vaughn here is way too important to be seen with a lowlife like you," Doug scoffed. "I'm surprised she remembered your name. Notice she hasn't spoken to me or Jason.

She sees us from time to time, but hasn't spoken a word in months. Snobby bitch."

Jason made no comment. He just looked around nervously.

"Say it ain't so, sweetheart." Nick pouted. "Are you a stuck-up bitch these days? And I always thought you would be better than the rest of your elitist family. You never minded my lower-class standing when I had you under me, did you, babe?"

He rested a hand against the wall on either side of her shoulders and got right in her face. Nick's eyes flashed black and she knew he was either highly pissed or seriously aroused. Neither of those was good news for her at the moment. Just before she thought she'd have to make the decision to fight, a scuffle broke out behind Nick and he was suddenly lifted away from her. Vince, the club's head of security, had grabbed the assholes and passed them off to his bouncers. The people on the floor parted to let the bouncers carry off the belligerent trio.

"Are you alright, little girl? Vince doesn't like ladies being harassed in his club." He looked her over with a concerned eye. Vince's way of speaking in the third person had always entertained Brandi.

"Thanks for the assist, Vince. They were just a little too aggressive."

She tried to downplay the fear she felt at being cornered by the large male vamp. Vince just nodded and calmly strode back to his post overlooking the action in the club.

Shit. She needed a drink. Maybe she could find someone who was tipsy. She'd done it a few times in the past, but didn't like the way alcohol made her feel out of control. Tonight, a little out of control was called for, in her opinion.

"Hi. You okay? I was watching the show just now. I hate pushy men. Why do they always think they have the right to touch a girl? It's so arrogant."

This came from a human girl who was propped up at a table near Brandi's position on the wall. She had the look of a scantily dressed goth chick with her torn fishnets, black fingernails, and folded-over combat boots. The only flaw in her costume was the platinum-blond hair. Hair like that should not be dyed black and Brandi was glad the girl had abstained from completing the look. She was beautiful.

"I'm good. Asshole didn't want to back off. I'm glad security showed up when they did, though." Brandi sighed.

"Yeah. I thought I was gonna have to put my boot in his ass." She smiled and pointed her toes as if she were wearing ballet slippers. They both laughed. The blonde rose from her seat and extended a hand in greeting.

"Name's Tina."

"Brandi." She introduced herself and wondered why the girl was still holding her hand. At this range Brandi could tell Tina's dark blue eyes were dilated. She'd had quite a few drinks already.

"Come dance with me, Brandi." It wasn't a request.

Tina turned and pulled Brandi into the throng of dancers. The crowd pulled them along in its frenzy of kinetic energy. Tina danced with a freedom and grace contradicted by her gothic image. The dark makeup around her eyes was doing nothing to disguise the brightness of the girl within. Brandi was actually having fun for the first time in a long time. Tina danced closer when a slower, more rhythmic song began to play.

"I'd like to dance with you. May I touch you, Brandi?"

Tina spoke into her ear as she moved her hips in a sensual flow and pulled back to look into her eyes. It was an invitation to play a new game. Tina was on the prowl.

"I don't . . . I'm not really what you're looking for, Tina. You're beautiful, don't get me wrong, but I don't play for that team," she said with an embarrassed flush.

Brandi liked Tina and didn't care if she liked girls or not. That didn't matter, but she couldn't fulfill Tina's needs. Tina just smiled and moved closer.

"I'm not asking for sex. Though I have to tell you I had hoped after the way you shot down those guys. I just want to dance. Let me?" she asked sweetly.

Brandi just nodded and tried to relax. The feeling of being that close to a female was so different. Tina was all soft curves and warm caresses. It made Brandi understand why some women went to strip clubs with their men. It was kind of hot. A thought crossed her mind and she tried to bat it away, but it kept resurfacing. Brandi actually could give Tina what she needed for the night and get her needs met in return. The bite of a vampire could be very sexual if he or she wanted it to be. Brandi could give Tina pleasure while she drank the heat pulsing through her lithe body.

"Let's go for a walk," she told Tina, adding a bit of compulsion to get her moving.

Brandi had to do it before she lost her nerve. Tina linked their fingers when Brandi left the floor. Hell. If she was going to go girl, Tina would be the perfect girl to go with. Tina smiled at her and gladly followed without question. Brandi had enthralled her into a feeling of safety and comfort. She would make Tina feel really good and leave her with no memory of the event.

On the sofa in Chase's studio apartment in the back of the club, Brandi allowed Tina to kiss her once, before it began to feel too much like cheating. Even if it was with a girl, cheating was cheating, and she was with Greyson. So, she enthralled Tina more deeply and projected the feeling of pleasure building toward release she experienced when Greyson manipulated her body. Tina would be enveloped in those intense sensations while she was under Brandi's influence. Tina moaned and rubbed against Brandi's leg, grasping at her sides while Brandi drank deeply of the beautiful blonde. This could be an option for Brandi. Feeding on a girl felt somehow better to her than embracing a man who wasn't Greyson.

Once Brandi sent Tina back to the club and went to check her appearance, the alcohol in Tina's blood began to creep up on her. Suddenly she felt overheated and wanted to strip out of her dress. Her head was spinning and the room tilted just a bit, causing her to bump into the dining room table. This was not the silly high she had experienced in the past. This was a sticky, thick-headed feeling that made her limbs feel heavy and her skin overly sensitive. *Oh, shit!* Tina hadn't been drunk. She was high.

Brandi staggered out of the club in search of a cab. She had driven there, but no way was she driving home. Even if she didn't care for her own safety, which she did, she'd never endanger others by driving under the influence. Taking a cab was her best option, because she didn't want to hear the lecture she'd get from her parents on the evils of drinking from impaired humans if she called for a ride. Brandi walked toward the corner feeling as if her feet were sinking into the sidewalk. Her limbs didn't want to work and all she wanted to do was stop to rest. The streetlights were making strange trails as she passed them and Brandi couldn't resist the urge to reach up, trying to touch the light with her tingling fingers.

"Well, well, look what we have here, boys." An ominous voice startled her just before she was hauled off her feet.

Brandi recognized the voice and knew she was in big trouble, but she couldn't work up a good scream. It was Nick. She suddenly found herself over his shoulder, staring at the pavement of the alley behind the club. His fingers dug roughly into the flesh of her thigh entirely too close to her ass. Swinging and bouncing limply as he strode down the alley, Brandi had a sickening thought. This is how she would die. She had survived multiple gunshots and a painful rehab just to be raped and murdered in an alley. She should have called her dad.

"This is a really bad idea, Nicky," Jason tried to reason with Nick.

"You can't just snatch a girl off the street. We're all gonna go to jail, man!"

"Stop being such a girl." Doug pushed Jason into a Dumpster.

"Screw this. I'm leaving. I get that you're pissed we got kicked out of the club, but I won't watch you hurt her." Jason began to storm down the alley but Nick called out to him.

"Stop, Jason. Come back and help me teach Brandi here a lesson." Nick had laced the command with a strong compulsion that even Brandi felt. Something that strong would render Jason mindless until Nick released him from it.

Jason stopped and returned to Nick's side. Doug looked at Jason, trying to figure out what had changed his mind so quickly. Jason trudged along beside them, staring forward in a silent trance.

"Don't worry, boys. Brandi had some fun with a friend of mine. Tina kindly shared her drug of choice with Brandi. Brandi won't be remembering what happened here. It's too bad, really. I wanted to share in the fun between the two girls, but Brandi is a greedy little bitch." He smacked her ass with his free hand. "I bet it was hot, too."

Nick propped Brandi against the brick of a building two blocks from Thirst. It was quiet and deserted in this part of town at night. No one would see them. A satisfied gleam lit Nick's eyes when he looked her over, and it made Brandi feel dirty. She shouldn't have pissed him off. She should have just danced once with him and quickly slipped away afterward. She could see the seething anger behind his eyes. Now he would take what he wanted.

"Take her arms. Hold her up for me," Nick ordered. Jason blindly followed his instruction.

Doug now hesitated. "You're not really going to rape her, are you? I thought we were just going to scare some respect into her." He reached across Brandi and snapped his fingers in front of Jason's unblinking face.

"Hold her up, Doug." Nick forced his will on him. Brandi tried to shake the guys off. They were human; she should be able to get away easily, but she could barely hold her eyes open. She was screaming in her mind but nothing made it past her numb lips.

———————◆———————

Abel watched in male fascination while the two women danced shyly but provocatively in the middle of the floor. Damn it. It was every guy's dream, but he was disturbed, even a little jealous. He wanted to be the one touching her skin and rubbing against her curvy body. This was the first time in the five months since he was released from his cell at the Nest that he'd been able to get more than just a glimpse of the girl who haunted his every waking and sleeping moment. His informants at the Enclave had assured him that she had survived the shooting. It had been close, but she made it. Her name was Brandi Vaughn and he couldn't have picked a worse girl to lose his shit over. She was the daughter of a prominent Councilman and the sister of the girl he had helped kidnap. If she ever saw him, she would likely have him arrested. She would hate him for what he'd done, for what he continued to do, but he just couldn't stop himself from checking up on her. He needed to know that she was safe and healthy.

Several times he'd made his way to her family estate and tested the security, looking for weak points. He'd actually made it onto the property and right up to a rear entrance, but he stopped there. What would he do if he got inside? How would she react to finding him in a dark corner of her bedroom? She'd think he was there to take her back to the Master. Why wouldn't she think the worst of him? He was a man who had done many evil deeds.

"Holy shit," his friend Nate hissed from behind him. "Is that the girl you've been panting over all these months? No wonder, man. If you'd told me she was into girls too, I would have understood."

"That's her." It was all Abel could get out.

He was hypnotized by the sway of her hips and the shimmer of her short black dress. Nate was a good friend and a fellow prisoner of the Master. Just like Abel, Nate did the Master's bidding to protect a parent. Nate's father wasn't helpless, but mentally unstable. Nate's dad had been lured into the Rogue's web by talk of a new nation of vampire-controlled freedom. Nate's father believed in the Master, but he also believed an alien invasion was imminent and figured they had better stake out claims on the human cattle before the Martians snatched up all the food. Nate felt an obligation to look after his father since the rest of his family had written him off.

"I don't think she's into girls. She doesn't look very comfortable. She's probably just feeding," Nate commented. "Damn shame, too."

Abel grinned and looked down at his partner in crime. Nate was shorter than most vamp males he'd met, but solidly built. His thick biceps stretched the fabric of his T-shirt and the dark goatee on his face made him look older than his twenty-four years.

The two girls disappeared into a back room, and before too long the blonde reemerged looking tousled and sated. Brandi followed shortly after and staggered out of a side exit.

"Do you mind if I check out the blonde? She looks like someone I'd love to make friends with." Nate's eyes had shifted from hazel to black while he continued to watch the girl dance on the edge of the crowd.

"Have fun. I'm going to make sure Brandi gets home safely. She looks trashed."

"Why do you keep torturing yourself, Abel? Get it into your head that you have no future. That's what I've done. I'll never have a mate or a life of my own with the Master's foot on my neck," Nate chided. Abel knew his friend was really trying to convince himself.

It made it easier to live the way they did and settle for nothing more than an occasional one-nighter with a human if you believed it was the only choice.

Abel wished he could return to that way of thinking, but it was impossible. He'd tried, but something happened to him in the entryway of the country club all those months ago. Something inside of him shifted and clicked into place. He should have killed her. She had swung a golf club at him, nearly taking off his head. If the other girl hadn't screamed, Brandi would have completely taken him off guard. He'd moved in the nick of time, taking the blow to his shoulder. The rage building in him had fizzled out when their eyes met and held. He then tried to disarm her instead of killing her. When her body pressed back to front with his, the contact had burned and left an indelible imprint. It felt like she belonged right there in his arms. Then, she'd actually burned him. He knew pyrokinetic vamps had existed in the past but he'd never met or heard of one in the present day. She was amazing and stunningly attractive. The deep blue of her eyes could drown a man.

It still tied his stomach in knots when he thought of Darren witnessing her ability. To this day he didn't know if Darren had seen her throw the fireball that incinerated their van or not. They'd been wrestling over Darren's gun at the time. Abel believed that Darren would have traded that information for another dose of the Hypnovam in order to trap his estranged mate if he'd known where the flames had come from. But, it was too late for that now. Soleil Danielle Vaughn had blood bonded herself to another, leaving Darren to suffer for his sins.

Making his way to the street, Abel hopped on his bike, but stopped before turning the key in the ignition. The sweet scent of honey and wood smoke wafted to him on a breeze just before the faint whimper of a female reached his ears.

The skin of her back was being rubbed raw. Brandi's bare shoulders were stinging. She wanted to scream. She wanted to fight and scratch Nick's eyes out. Brandi tried to stoke the flames in her belly and burn his ass, but she couldn't. She couldn't even spark an ember. His hands were all over her body. He had enthralled the other guys, who held her roughly against the wall.

"I should take you here in the alley like a common whore. Maybe that will teach you to behave as a female should. But I wouldn't do that to my mate." He smirked. "You shouldn't be out hunting in a club. Don't your parents provide for you up on that hill? Aren't they watching out for the interests of your future? This is exactly why our society is going to shit. You're a female with too much freedom. When I broke up with you before I left for college, you were supposed to beg me to come back to you. You were supposed to keep yourself pure and clean for me, not run off and find another guy, you slut. Your parents should have accepted the bonding proposal my parents offered them. You are a female." Nick snarled in her face, "What the hell do you need a college degree for? Your mate should be providing for you while you putter around pregnant and obedient."

He grabbed her jaw, slamming the back of her head into the brick wall. Brandi prayed he would do it again, because she didn't want to remember this if he was going to do what she suspected. She had no idea what he was rambling on about. They had decided together to end their past relationship, and she had never been told of a bonding offer from him or his family.

"Did you enjoy my friend Tina? I gave her a little something special to help you relax. I wanted to share her with you, but you were a greedy girl. Just like a Vaughn."

Closing her eyes tightly, she put everything she had into heating the core of her soul. Normally she fought to contain her fire.

Now she wrestled to set it free, but it was useless. Nick lowered his head to inhale deeply at her neck. He ran his tongue from her collarbone up to her ear.

"It's not too late, Brandi," he practically purred. Nick's entire demeanor had changed between one second and the next.

"I've decided to keep you after all. I think I'll bond you to me right now. I will take your blood and give you mine. Then we can work on teaching you to be a proper female. My mother could instruct you on the finer points of caring for your mate and his home." Nick kissed her, forcing his tongue into her mouth. It was revolting and she wished for the strength to bite him.

Suddenly both Jason and Doug released her arms. "What the hell?" Nick cursed. Brandi knew there was no way they should have been able to disobey him. He leaned to catch her weight and just as quickly as the heat of his body touched her, it was gone. She found herself on the ground with something sharp poking her in the ass cheek. She fell to the dirty asphalt. Her head lolled to the side and landed on Jason's shoulder. Doug was sprawled out in front of her, the back of his head resting in a puddle of questionable liquid, since it hadn't rained in a week.

Just as suddenly as she had been dropped, Brandi was scooped up and cradled tightly against a firm chest. Her champion was walking quickly away from the scene of her assault. She struggled to place his familiar scent. Lifting her head to look him in the eye wasn't working. She inhaled deeply and it all came back. She'd dreamt of him for months. She'd done everything in her power to erase the warm citrus aroma from her memory, but it still haunted her. How many times had she caught the scent on the wind and followed it, only to be disappointed when it faded to nothing? It was her dark-eyed obsession in the flesh. Holding her and murmuring nonsense sounds of comfort.

Six

Brandi was clutching at his chest. Abel tucked her more tightly into his body. The feel of the supple, bare skin of her thigh contrasted sharply with the way the sequins on her dress scraped against his chest. He could simply hold her away from his body, but having her close felt too good to let the opportunity pass. He might not get another chance.

Brandi pulled weakly at his shirt and gave a whimper. Damn it. She was probably frightened to death. She was incapacitated and he knew exactly why. She smelled of Hypnovam and it pissed him off. He was this close to her, and the sweetness of her was diluted by a drug she shouldn't have come into contact with. That was a huge problem he was going to have to get to the bottom of.

The asshole in the alley had laced the blonde from the club with a drug meant to take out vamps, but he hadn't been anyone Abel knew from the Nest. How the hell had he gotten his hand on the Hypno? Too bad he'd choked the bastard out in a blind rage and left him unconscious in a puddle before he could beat some answers out of him. When he'd found the man covering Brandi's body with his own and the two enthralled humans holding her down, it was all over. He had snapped. Abel would have to catch up with the loser another time.

It seemed like Brandi had had just enough Hypno to weaken her and make her easy prey, but not enough to take her out completely. Now that she was safe in his arms, he had to find Nate before he also sank his fangs into the pretty blonde.

Abel stopped in a doorway and sat on the stoop to balance Brandi in his lap while he called Nate. He called several time before Nate answered the phone, sounding harassed.

"What, man? I'm busy here," Nate huffed. A female voice in the background complained about the interruption.

"Do not drink from that girl, Nate. She's laced with Hypno. I have Brandi and she reeks of it."

"What? You mean the blonde? I'm not with her. She was too polluted for my taste. I found an alternate menu." Nate paused a moment and Abel could practically hear his warning sink in.

"What do you mean she had Hypno? How?" Nate asked.

"I don't have time to explain now. I have to get Brandi off the street. All I need is to get caught with the daughter of a Councilman, unconscious from Hypno. No one would believe I didn't intend to take her to the Master. I can't take her to the Nest and I can't take her home like this," he explained while absently stroking Brandi's back.

"Why can't you just drop her at the gate of her family's estate? They'll take care of her. Just don't get caught."

"Are you kidding me? Their security is a joke. I've slipped by them numerous times. She is completely defenseless. I won't leave her until she is able to defend herself." He had to think of a safe place to hide with his precious burden. "Cover for me if I'm missed at the Nest?"

"You know I will, but this a bad idea. You already have an issue with this female. Spending time with her, conscious or not, won't help you, my friend." His tone had softened to that of a concerned older brother.

"I know, but I can't leave her," he confessed. "Not yet."

Abel disconnected the call and looked down to find Brandi staring up at him. Recognition lit her eyes. Her head lolled on an unstable neck, but she held on to his shirt.

"I won't hurt you, Sparky. I swear it. I'm just going to keep you safe until you're able to defend yourself."

He gave her the most reassuring smile he could muster and slid a finger down her flushed cheek. He tried not to think about the fact that her ass was cradled between his thighs. Brandi looked deeply into his eyes before blinking at him in what seemed to be acceptance and leaning into his chest. Abel felt that damn shifting in his chest again. She relaxed against him and trusted him not to hurt her. She'd just been drugged and assaulted, but somehow she'd looked into his eyes and found someone she could trust. Why hadn't she seen the things he had done in the past and the things he was still capable of doing?

"Let's get going, Sparky. I didn't find your purse so I'm going to steal your car. I don't think it would be safe or inconspicuous if I strapped you to my bike."

He stood and headed for the little silver Jaguar he had followed around town so many times, and hoped she had really good insurance, because he was about to do some damage.

She seemed to have drifted off by the time they reached their destination. He hoped his friend wasn't in town so he could slip in and out without involving anyone else. Silently he performed a one-handed break and enter at the back door while propping Brandi against the doorframe. Then he scooped her up and silently pushed open the door. Once inside the dark kitchen he let out a relieved sigh. He had found a safe hiding place. That was what he thought until he found himself face-planted on the floor with a knee in his back. It happened so quickly he didn't see it coming. Abel began to struggle violently. Brandi had gone flying when he was struck from behind. Was she hurt? Had he been followed?

"Don't move, asshole! That's my Beretta against your thick skull." He received a tap on the back of the head to emphasize the statement.

"Damn it! Let me up, Candy!"

He remained still. His friend wasn't afraid to use that gun, and she was very territorial. He had trespassed in her home and she would defend it to the end. She loosened her hold and turned his face into the dim light shining down the hallway.

"Abel? Jesus! I almost capped you. What the hell are you doing? If anyone saw you, I'm kicking your ass! And stop calling me Candy!" she hissed and smacked him in the back of the head.

Candice was the closest thing to family he'd ever had, besides his mom. She'd taken him under her wing and trained him to fight. She was a petite spitfire with a head of deep red curls, the biggest blue eyes he had ever seen, and a smart-ass mouth. She was also a cop on the human police force. That made it difficult for them to see each other anymore. He was a criminal and the worst sort of vampire. She was a defender of justice and humanity.

After her run-in with the Master years ago, Candice decided to be more than just another vampire debutante waiting for her fanged Romeo to come and sweep her off her feet. She became a cop, because females weren't accepted in the warrior ranks. If it hadn't been for Candice's training, Abel would have died long ago.

"Come on, Candy. You know I'm smarter than your brothers in blue." She finally let him up, but gave him a swift kick in the ass to send him sprawling again before she backed away.

"My name is Candice. Officer I'll-kick-your-ass to you, boy. Do I look sugary sweet to you? No! So stop calling me Candy!"

She was in rare form. He must have really freaked her out with the B and E. Abel looked around the dark room and found Brandi wedged against a cabinet on the other side of the kitchen. The force of Candy's attack must have launched her across the room.

"I'm sorry I broke in. I was hoping you wouldn't be home. I needed a hideout." Quickly he began checking Brandi for injuries. She appeared to be sleeping, but he was worried that she'd hit her head.

"And you thought the home of a police officer was a great place to take cover. Do you know what will happen to my career if you get caught here?" She was still fuming.

It was unusual behavior for her. He had snuck into her place many times when he needed a place to crash at night and he hadn't wanted to wake her. This was the first time he'd had a gun pulled on him.

Abel swept Brandi up and carried her to the spare bedroom before he began to explain his predicament. He briefly explained that he'd found Brandi being assaulted, leaving out their history and who she was, as well as the reason why he had to hide with her. Candice smiled broadly and shook her head.

"You've got the hots for Miss who-needs-panties-that-actually-cover-my-ass in there. I can't believe it. After all these years of hiding and protecting your secrets from our people, you are risking it all for a girl who can't be bothered to cover her ass before she gets high. What was that, dental floss?" She didn't try to hide her disapproval.

"Screw you, Candy. We'll just leave. She's not like that, and I won't listen to you talk about her like she's one of your perps. I told you she was being assaulted. That's all I can say."

He couldn't explain to her the Hypno situation or his involvement in the kidnappings. Candice still had strong ties to the Enclave. Abel couldn't risk testing her loyalty. They had an understanding. Whatever she didn't know wouldn't hurt her.

"No. Don't go." She sagged into the corner of her sofa. The warm golden light of the lamp shone through her red hair, making her look as if flames were curling around her heart-shaped face. "I'm just on edge. There has been a rash of missing person reports and it's got me snapping at everyone. I'm sorry."

Abel had to tread carefully. Candice knew he hung with bad people and kept lots of secrets. She knew he did what he had to do to survive and protect his mother. She was freaking out because she had witnessed both the recent attacks by his Master and the ones years ago before he was born. Both times it had started this way. First the humans go missing and then the vampires. He could never tell her he worked for the man who had killed her best friend and sent her into a life of public service. He also knew about the missing humans and could tell her exactly where they were. He had helped capture half of them.

"I'm sorry," she mumbled from behind the hands that were covering her face.

"Look, Candy. Just let me keep an eye on her until she comes around. Then we'll go." Without looking up, Candy nodded her agreement.

Abel went to look in on his patient. Brandi was stretched out on the bed with a blanket tucked under her arms. Her chest rose and fell reassuringly. Though he knew for his own sanity he shouldn't, Abel climbed in next to her. He watched her sleep for over an hour, enjoying the chance to be close to her before he dozed off. When he slept he dreamt of her. In his dreams Brandi knew his real identity and didn't care. In his dreams she took him into her heart and her body. In his dreams he was the kind of man she deserved.

Abel woke to find Brandi snuggled against his side. She was still groggy, but awake. His heart thudded in his chest while he waited for her to realize who she was in bed with. He waited for her to rail at him in disgust that he would touch her.

"Mad at you," she murmured sleepily. "You're bad. Really bad." She softened the rebuke by snuggling closer.

Abel finally allowed himself a deep breath. She was obviously still under the influence, but she knew exactly who he was.

"I know, Sparky. I'm the worst of the worst." He stroked her arm. Brandi's nose wrinkled and she shook her head slightly.

"No. That's not true. You could have shot me in the chapel. You could have let Darren take Dani without a fight. You could have walked away and ignored what those guys were doing tonight. You didn't. You did what a good man would do." She paused. "What is *sparky*?" she asked.

"You are Sparky. You're a little fire starter, aren't you?" He immediately wished he hadn't mentioned it when she stiffened. "Don't worry. I haven't told anyone and I won't."

"I won't snitch on you, either. I . . . I've worried about you." She played with the button on his shirt. "Are you okay?" she asked.

"Don't worry about me. I can take care of myself. You need to be worrying about staying out of dark alleys." His tone was too harsh, but her concern made him uncomfortable. He was still waiting for her to scream and curse at him.

"Not my fault." Brandi's lower lip began to tremble and she began to pull away.

"I know, damn it!" Abel snapped.

He just didn't know how to deal with her. He had wished so many nights that he could hold her, and now that he had her in his arms, his brain was telling him to push her away. He couldn't afford to care about anyone. So why the hell had he been following her around for months? He looked down to find her peering up at him through a dark sweep of lashes.

"Thank you. I promise not to tell anyone who you really are. I won't tell them you save damsels in distress and warn people when they're in danger," she whispered.

Brandi reached up and pulled his face down to meet hers. She brushed her lips against his softly once, twice, again. Abel closed his eyes and breathed in the sweet purity of her. She stilled, and when he opened his eyes, she was asleep again. It would take some time for her to sleep off the Hypnovam.

The kiss had been so delicate, but the continued shifting in his chest had been violent. He had to get away from her to rebuild his walls. She had cracked them with her gently searching fingers and warm lips that tasted of cherry-flavored lip gloss and forgiveness.

———•———

Griffin sat on the curb outside of the Council chamber and fumed. He had finally laid his eyes on Tessa after more than six months of searching for her and pleading with her through the bond they shared. The Council had sent a request through Chase Deidrick that she appear and give them her account of the events that had led to her injuries and the recovery of two of his daughters after the kidnapping attempt. They needed to know if she had seen anyone or heard anything that might lead them to the identity or hiding place of the Rogue. She hadn't, of course, but she gave them her account of the evening with a respectful tone he knew she didn't feel. She hated them all, and while they thought of her as a human trespasser in a world where she didn't belong, she desperately wanted to tell them what she really thought of their Council. He could see it in her eyes, but she wouldn't do that. This was their daughter's world now, and Tessa wouldn't do anything that would make the transition any harder for Soleil.

When she spoke in the Council chamber he'd watched her mouth. Those bow-shaped lips that he knew would taste like warm vanilla and hot woman made him hungry for a sip of her sweetness. It had been so long since he had felt true desire for anything or anyone. Just being in the room with her had him panting.

As usual the Council hadn't entered the chamber until everyone was assembled and waiting for them. So, he hadn't seen her arrive. Once the hearing was over and they had dealt with disputes between several vampires, everyone was dismissed. Griffin had been surprised Soleil hadn't escorted her mother to the hearing. She didn't need to because when the crowd dispersed, Doc Stevens stepped up to take Tessa's arm and lead her from the chamber. The familiar way he touched her and leaned in to whisper words of praise for having controlled her temper told Griffin exactly where she'd been hiding. He had never thought to ask Doc if he knew where Tessa had gone after her release from his care. It seemed as if Doc was still taking very good care of Griffin's mate. Jealousy bubbled up in his gut.

Griffin quickly made his way to the parking lot in an effort to corner her before she disappeared again. They were halfway to Doc's SUV when he caught up with them. Tessa looked pale and too thin. Griffin had always loved her lush curves and full hips. She had been temptation itself and always would be. The cream-colored suit she wore hung a bit too loosely and gave a sallow cast to her skin. It seemed as if her recovery was slow going. He knew his jealousy was unwarranted, but there it was. He couldn't have her but he loved her still. It looked as if she was still in need of treatment and that worried him. Griffin would be sure to send a healthy donation to Doc's clinic in gratitude for his services.

"Tessa, love. May I have a word with you?" Not waiting for an answer to his request, Griffin took her arm and tugged her toward his vehicle. Doc followed closely with a defiant frown.

"Griffin, I need to get Tessa back home. She's not well." Doc tugged on her other arm, pulling her back toward his vehicle. Being pulled in two different directions, Tessa sighed and turned to force them both to release her. Griffin and Doc stared at each other over her head. She sighed again and walked back toward Doc's SUV. Doc grinned smugly and followed Tessa.

"Tessa, please. Just give me a moment of your time," Griffin pleaded.

"Griffin, she really isn't in any condition to deal with stress. She's still very weak and her immune system was compromised. We've been fighting illness and infections, one of which is still plaguing her," Doc explained.

"I'm okay, Reilly." She patted his arm and his whole body softened when he looked down at her. Doc nodded his understanding and strode off to wait by his vehicle. He watched tensely and waited for her to need him

Reilly? She called him by his first name? Funny, but Griffin had never thought to ask the man's first name. He had always just been Doc. But Griffin knew he needed to focus. He only had a moment to try explaining his position. Tessa didn't turn to look at him.

"Go ahead, Griffin. Say whatever it is that will make you feel better. Tell me you're sorry and that you had no choice. Tell me you love me, but your people and your *family* were more important than my life. Tell me a worthless human wasn't worth saving. Go ahead. I'm listening."

Then she turned and pierced him with the ice-blue force of her eyes. Griffin said the only thing that came to his mind. "I do love you. I still love you."

Her eloquent silence and absence of expression told him everything he needed to know. Griffin had let her down for the last time. Tessa shook her head and walked away. When she reached Doc, he wrapped an arm around her shoulder and led her to the passenger side. They drove off, and Griffin stood frozen to the asphalt until the weight of his heart forced him to the curb.

Brandi was going to be late to her martial arts class, again. Her trainer, Karrie, was going to rip her a new asshole. It really wasn't her fault this time, but she couldn't very well walk into the dojo and spit out the truth. She could just imagine looking up into the no-nonsense expression Karrie would be wearing when she tried to explain that she had fed from a drugged human. Dani would be listening while Brandi explained that she had been saved from a possible forced bonding.

Never mind that the man who had saved her was the very same man who had helped to drug and kidnap Dani, ruining her bonding ceremony and causing the life-threatening injury that had nearly killed Dani's mother. Brandi was sure it wouldn't please them to know that she had spent the night in the arms of a man who had assured her that he hadn't been the one who had shot her twice in the back. No, it had been his partner for the evening, Darren. Yes, Darren. The guy who sold Dani out to the Rogue in order to force a blood bond she would never have agreed to. Yeah. That conversation wasn't going to go in her favor.

She entered the dojo and Karrie turned from her conversation with Kayden and Dani to scowl at her. Karrie had an intimidating presence. She was taller than most women at five foot ten inches. She had the perfect balance of feminine curves and muscle tone. She scared the shit out of Brandi when she looked down at her with angry, dark eyes that were just slightly slanted at the corners. Brandi would suck it up and take her licks. No way was she going to explain the events of the night before, especially not with Kayden in the room. Kayden eyed her thoughtfully and leaned over to whisper something to Dani. It was still a little weird seeing Kayden and Dani together again after he'd rejected her, ending their relationship over a year ago.

Dani and Brandi had decided that they needed to be able to defend themselves in the event of an attack in which their extrasensory powers were rendered useless. She could have used what they'd learned the night before if she hadn't been drugged out of her mind.

She'd have to be more careful about feeding at the club. Whatever Tina had ingested had put Brandi down for a good twelve hours.

"Look, *Princess*, if you're not going to take this seriously, stop wasting my time," Karrie growled down at Brandi.

Brandi started to respond that she was sorry and did take it very seriously when Karrie cut her off. "Don't give me any excuses. I don't want to hear it."

As they went through their stretches and some cardio to loosen up, Brandi noticed Kayden watching her intently and so did Karrie. Brandi felt as if Kayden knew her secret and was just waiting to expose her. Karrie seemed to believe he was checking her out with male interest. If Karrie only knew that she and Kayden had grown up together, she would just see brotherly concern on his face.

"Are you enjoying the view, Paris?" Karrie barked at him.

Kayden snapped out of his inspection of Brandi as if he hadn't realized he was staring. You could always tell when Karrie was pissed at Kayden because she used his last name to address him. Karrie had been raised on the Enclave. Her father was a Wrath leader and her two brothers were both warriors. It was a constant source of agitation for her that women weren't permitted to be warriors. She'd trained alongside her brothers and had learned everything they learned from their father. She was as skilled as most warriors, and Brandi admired Karrie's ass-kicking skills when she wasn't using them to kick her ass.

"Shut up, Karrie. Something is wrong with Brandi. Something is odd. I'm just trying to figure out what it is." He dismissed Karrie's jealousy and continued to watch Brandi.

"I'm fine, Kayden. I'm just a little tired. I went out last night. You know how that can be." Brandi decided it would be better to take some shit for hitting the club alone, when they all knew they were under orders to only go out to feed in groups, than to have Karrie beat her ass over an imagined slight.

Karrie and Kayden had a thing going on that Brandi wasn't sure was entirely healthy for either of them. Karrie had always had a crush on Kayden. What sane single female wouldn't? Brandi would be attracted to him if he weren't already the big brother she never wanted. Kayden was a strong warrior with the face of a Greek god combined with the physique of a body builder. Kayden had never paid any attention to Karrie until after his fallout with Dani and Chase.

After a hard workout including a mixture of martial arts and other hand-to-hand tactical training, both Brandi and Dani fell to the floor. They lay there sweating and breathing hard.

"I can't believe we signed up for this shit," Dani panted. Long strands of sweaty sable, white, and red hair from her ponytail stuck to her face and neck. Brandi just laughed. Kayden walked toward the door and stopped dead when he got closer to the two women stretched out prone on the floor. He reached down and plucked Brandi up off the floor. He held her at eye level with her feet dangling in the air and examined her eyes, breathing deeply all the while. Karrie was hissing in the background.

"I know what's wrong with you." He brought her closer to smell her hair and neck. "You smell like that damn drug. You smell like Dani did after she'd been stolen away from me," Kayden cursed. He placed her gently back on her feet and waited grim-faced for an explanation.

Greyson stalked around his lover and waited for answers. She was so small and fragile looking, propped up on the warrior-size exam table in the infirmary. Kayden had marched her into the Enclave and called for Doc to come check her out. Greyson's team had just returned from a deployment that had taken them to a southern Enclave for several weeks when he was informed of her arrival.

When he found her she had been stripped, poked, prodded, and her parents had been called. It really screwed with his head that he was dating a woman who still answered to her mommy and daddy.

The doc wasn't forthcoming with whatever she had confessed to him, citing doctor-patient confidentiality. Greyson thought that was total bullshit. This wasn't a human hospital and they didn't live by human laws. But, the doc wouldn't budge. So Greyson was forced to try to pry the information out of a stiff-lipped Brandi.

"I need to know what happened, Pixie. Your blood came back positive for the paralytic used by the Rogue." He stopped and rested a hand on her trembling fingers. "Do you trust me, baby?" She nodded and threaded her fingers with his. Her deep blue eyes filled with tears.

"I'm ashamed. I made a mistake. I know better than to go out alone," she whispered miserably.

The sight of her fear and the pain tore at his protective instincts. He lifted her from the bed and crossed the room to the chair. He held her while she cried and explained the events of the night before. The last thing she remembered was being slammed against a wall. She woke this morning in the alley with nothing worse than a few bumps and scratches. She had been more concerned about the theft of her car than the possibility of a rape. She was sure that she would have known if she had been violated, but the fact that she had no memory for approximately twelve hours did nothing to reassure him.

The door opened and Doc entered. He looked at Brandi for permission to speak in front of Greyson. She nodded and Doc began. "I will assume you have seen fit to inform Greyson of your misadventures. So I will be blunt. Rape was a big concern for me given your lack of memory of events, so we ruled that out first. By exam there were no obvious signs of an assault, but I performed a rape kit anyway. It was negative for the presence of semen."

Doc paused to allow that bit of good news to sink in. Greyson took the first deep breath he'd allowed himself since hearing of her condition. The thought of another man touching her made him sick. He didn't know how he would have dealt with that situation and was glad he wouldn't need to find out. She was safe and relatively uninjured.

"Kayden made inquiries with a friend in the local police force but there were no calls to the area or reports of suspicious activity. He searched the area around the club and found your purse in an alley." He arched an eyebrow at her. "I don't know how you got out of this with just some scrapes and bruises, but I thank God you did. You are lucky not to be a guest of the Rogue. The only reason I can come up with for your release is your lack of an extrasensory power." He glanced up from his clipboard.

"Thanks, Doc. When can I go home?" She didn't want to be there any longer than she had to.

"You can leave whenever you're ready. I'll go so you can get dressed. If you want to avoid your father, I'd be quick about it," he suggested before shutting the door behind him.

"I'd like you to stay with me tonight." Greyson nuzzled her neck and held her tightly. "I have a few days off. What do you think?"

Brandi snuggled closer and gave him her mouth. This was the welcome home he had been hoping for when he unloaded his bags and gear earlier. Greyson had dreamt of his pixie loving him to exhaustion every night he'd been away. Tonight he would bask in the fulfillment of those dreams.

Seven

Brandi had been in Greyson's bed for three days making love, talking, sleeping, and just being together. He'd been doing a fabulous job of making up for the time they were apart and making her forget how lonely being the girlfriend of a Wrath guard could be.

"What are you thinking about, Nymph?" Greyson asked as he entered the bedroom with a tray of food and drinks.

"Nothing important. Just woolgathering," she lied. He eyed her suspiciously. "What time do you report for duty?"

"In about two hours. Once I get situated and I receive my assignments for the week, I'll text you. I'd like to see you again as soon as possible." He climbed over her on the bed. "I hate being away from you. You've ruined me." He smiled and nibbled on her throat.

"Ruined you?" she asked indignantly.

"Yes. I'm ruined," he huffed. "I never needed anyone before you. Now I'm a hopeless puppy nipping at your heels and hoping for some attention."

"You are so full of it!" She rolled over him on the bed to look down on him.

Greyson's expression turned serious and it scared the hell out of Brandi. He always seemed to be making a great effort to keep things light between them. She assumed that was because he didn't want her to take their relationship too seriously. Brandi wasn't blind to the fact that her age was still an issue for Greyson.

"You think I don't care? You think I don't miss you when I'm gone? You think I don't know there are tons of guys out there who would love to keep you too busy to think about the guy who's always away?" He held her face gently in his palms and kissed her softly.

Brandi couldn't do this. She didn't want him worrying about her and stressing out just before a long shift. He needed to be focused to stay safe.

"You want my attention? You've got it." Brandi lowered her mouth to his nipple and bit gently.

Greyson reacted the way she expected. Using teeth with another vampire was dangerous business. If she broke the skin, his blood on her tongue would bond her to him forever, but he liked it a little rough. It was almost a game for them, and the game was called *How far will you go?*

She nipped and nibbled her way down his belly, using her teeth to excite him while keeping her sharp fangs under tight control. When she reached his boxers she released her fangs and looked up into Greyson's shocked eyes. To see your lover's fangs during sex was a huge turn-on. It was dangerous but beautiful to know that you affected your partner so deeply. Brandi lowered her head and used one fang to slice his boxer-briefs down the front.

Usually Greyson was in control. He liked to teach her how to please him. He loved showing her what a man of experience could do to her body. But today she was going to show him what she liked. She intended to take her pleasure from the old guy and show him what naughty little girls were really made of.

Greyson clawed at the sheets when she applied herself, demonstrating the skills he had taught her. She teased, licked, and inhaled him. She stroked him in time with the motion of her mouth and he seemed to grow impossibly larger. When he pulled on her hair to stop her she knew she had taken Greyson very close to completion. He growled at her, a deep rumble of longing and desire.

"I need you. I want to be in you," he pleaded.

"Do you?" she purred. "How badly do you want it?" Brandi crawled up his body and rubbed her wet heat against his length. "Will you beg me for it, Greyson?"

His eyes flashed dark and dangerous. Brandi feared she might have pushed him too far. After a few tense moments of her torturing them both with the slick friction and leisurely searching strokes of her tongue, she retracted her fangs and began to nip at his neck, careful not to draw blood but hard enough to feed his need. Greyson moaned a deep, pained curse before looking her in the eye.

"Please, baby. Please let me in? I need to feel you surrounding me. Please, let me in," he begged.

Brandi felt dizzy with the realization of her feminine power over such a proud man. She gave him his reward and claimed her own by granting his request for more. When she began her slow, purposeful ride, Brandi didn't want to miss a moment of his surrender, so she watched him while their bodies joined. Greyson seemed fascinated by the sight of his length disappearing into her body.

"You're so beautiful, baby, and so damn sexy," he praised her and tried to encourage her to move faster, but Brandi refused. Keeping up the rhythmic pleasure-pain had sweat trickling down her back, but she maintained the pace. Greyson nipped at her breasts, using his teeth to punish her and then his tongue to soothe the hurt. He promised to repay her for the game she played so sweetly.

Finally Brandi saw what she had been waiting for. Greyson's face was breathtaking when he looked up at her with fangs bared, black eyes, and an expression of utter torment. It was time. She gave in to the pounding need of her body to possess the man beneath her. Brandi rode him hard and fast. He clasped her hips and guided her movements in time with his upward thrusts. Her climax rippled through her body, and Greyson bellowed his release to the rafters when she dragged him over the edge with her.

———•———

Tessa watched Reilly—Doc Stevens, as everyone else called him—when he went to lock the front door to the clinic. He'd asked her to stay with him for observation until he cleared her to return home. That was fine with her, because it kept her close to Danielle. Her daughter was a married woman who didn't need her mother to care for her anymore, but Tessa was having trouble cutting the apron strings.

Over the past few weeks Tessa had become so bored in his guest room in the private apartment over the clinic that she had begun following him to the clinic to find things to do around the office. He had a receptionist and several nurses, but it was a busy practice and there was always something to be done. Tessa wondered how Reilly made time to do all the house calls required by the vampires. The majority of his patients were human with a few vamps mixed in. The vamps were mostly pregnant women who needed the specialized care of a vampire doctor for their deliveries.

Every day Tessa got stronger and she knew she should have been released by now. She had no idea where she was going to go when it was time to go home anyway. Tessa had put her house in Perry Hall on the market. It wasn't a safe place for her anymore. She'd photographed a wedding one weekend and had been home working on a set of proofs for the client when a swarm of vampires had raided her house and hauled her off to the Rogue. He knew where she lived now and could use her against Danielle the way he had before if he caught her again. She had no home to return to now.

"How are you feeling?" he asked, looking concerned. Reilly had come to check her for the return of the fever that had plagued her body off and on over the last months. "You look so sad, honey."

He did that all the time now. They would be having a normal conversation and he would slip and call her a pet name. He had worked hard at first to hide his attraction to her, but now that she was quickly healing, Reilly seemed to be making a gentle effort to cross the line between a doctor-patient relationship into something more personal. It scared the shit out of her. She liked Reilly and thought that if she had a heart to give, he might have a chance at stealing it. He was an attractive man in an English professor kind of way with his average height, brown hair, and brown eyes. But Tessa knew from living under his roof that the firm, toned body of an athlete lurked under his business attire and white doctor's jacket.

Reilly was a doctor who cared deeply for his patients. He made her laugh. He made her feel comfortable and at home in a way she hadn't felt since her ill-fated relationship with Griffin. All she had to do was convince her heart that Griffin wasn't out there waiting for her to love him again. After over twenty years of waiting, the stupid thing hadn't figured out that she wasn't good enough for him or his people. A whole nation of people who believed humans were lesser beings stood between him and her. Griffin had proved over and over again that she wasn't worth the loss of his reputation. That made her wonder why Reilly behaved the way he did. Why didn't he seem to mind having a lowly human contaminating his home?

"Why are you so nice to me?" she asked. Reilly's eyebrows rose toward his hairline and he looked puzzled by her direct question. "I'm serious. Why don't you treat me like the rest of the vamps do? With the exception of my daughter's new family, most don't care for me or the fact that I'm aware of your people. Why are you so kind?" She needed to know.

Reilly took her hand and led her down the hall to his office. The warmth of his larger hand surrounding hers seemed intimate and familiar now that he had made a habit of touching her whenever possible. He stopped in front of a wall covered in pictures of family and friends. He pointed to a picture of a gray-haired couple who smiled at the camera. The man had his arms wrapped around the woman in a way that spoke of a long-standing love.

"Those are my parents, Bob and Bonny Stevens." He smiled wistfully. Tessa was shocked. She had never seen a vampire who looked older than fifty.

"But, they're . . ."

"Old? I know. They're both gone now. They lived into their eighties and died within six months of each other." He touched the picture once before moving on to a picture of himself and another slightly older guy.

"This is Bruce. When I started college he was a junior. He took me under his wing and showed me the ins and outs of college life. He said that I should enjoy my college years, but be sure to keep my eyes on the prize. He was constantly riding me to pick a major. By the end of my freshman year I still had no idea what I wanted to do with my life. I was just coasting by, taking general classes and happy to be getting good grades. As long as my parents were happy, so was I. Bruce graduated the next year and went on to law school. We still kept in touch and he still rode me to make some solid choices, but I was happy the way things were." He paused, seeming to be looking back through time. She was confused and decided to just wait for him to continue.

"I was walking to class the first week of my junior year when I had a massive seizure. I had been having some issues with missing time over the summer. I would be doing yard work one minute and wake up on the porch swing the next. Things like that. I had started getting these monster headaches but I ignored it. Like most twenty-one-year-olds I thought I was invincible. I was diagnosed with an inoperable brain stem glioma. In layman's terms, I had a tumor on my brain stem. I was given about four months to live. My parents were devastated."

Reilly went to sit in his high-backed leather chair and rocked back in his seat while Tessa tried to steady herself. How would she go on if Danielle were diagnosed with such a horrible disease? Her heart broke for Reilly's parents.

"Are you telling me you were human?" Tessa asked incredulously. "Because my understanding is that vampires don't get those kinds of human diseases."

"Yes, honey, I was human." Tessa went to his side of the desk and leaned back, crossing her arms, waiting for the rest of his incredible story. "I went home with my parents to wait for the end to come. The seizures began to come more frequently. The headaches got worse, and one day I just couldn't walk anymore. That was when Bruce showed up. He was irate that I hadn't called him. He couldn't believe I was going to go and die without clearing it with him first. He was bossy that way." Reilly laughed. "Anyway, he told me this unbelievable story about him being a vampire who could save my life if I were willing to have a lifelong connection to him and begin to supplement my diet with a healthy dose of human blood. He explained that according to his research not everyone survived the transition from human to vampire, but if I was going to die anyway it was worth the risk. After he did a few tricks to convince me of his sincerity, I agreed. We told my parents, which by the way is seriously against the rules, and they were willing to do anything if it meant they didn't have to watch me die without a fight. We started the process that day. It took a few days to complete because Bruce didn't want to overtax my body. It was a lot like having a fever. I was sweaty and hot with fever-like dreams while the vampire blood basically infected every cell in my body and converted it to replicate itself."

"You are bonded to another man?" Tessa asked shyly.

"No, honey, but I do have a blood bond with Bruce. I took his blood but he didn't take mine. I was human when I took his blood, and that makes a difference, as I'm sure you know from experience. It's a very interesting topic that I would love to do a study on. The way vampire blood reacts with humans and other vampires in their family is different from the way it reacts in the bodies of other vampires. I get faint impressions of Bruce's emotions from time to time. Even that has reduced since he took a mate." Reilly pointed to a picture of Bruce and a cute little brunette wearing glasses.

"That's Liz. She's human, too. They want to try having a baby before he converts her, much the same way you and Griffin did. It scares the shit out of me. They want me to attend the birth. Anyway, back to my story. After I was turned, I returned to school with a new view on life. I thought about all the people in the hospital, from the doctors to the nurses to the ladies who brought me my meals. That's what I wanted to do. I wanted to make a difference in the lives of others. I wanted to be the strong shoulder my doctor had been for my parents and the gentle hand of comfort my nurses had been to me." He cleared his throat.

"Listen to me waxing poetic. The point is I had finally decided what to do with my considerably extended life. I became a doctor and have never regretted the choice."

Tessa tried to stop the tears from running down her cheeks. She wanted to keep a stiff upper lip, but his story was so touching, her heart had squeezed out the tears. Reilly finally looked up from his contemplation of the past.

"Tessa, please don't cry. I didn't mean to upset you." He pulled her closer until she found herself resting in his lap. He rubbed her back soothingly while she got herself under control. "You asked me why I'm so nice to you. You want to know why I treat you so well. It's because I was born and raised just like you. I'm a bit of an outcast myself because I was made and not born this way. I don't have a problem with humans, honey. Especially not one so beautiful I want to be everything she needs." He wiped a tear from her cheek and their eyes met.

Tessa didn't know who moved first but they were kissing before she took her next breath. Reilly was gentle when he searched her mouth. He took long moments to explore her lips before parting them to taste her tongue. It was wonderful and awful in turns. It felt so good to be touched and feel desired by another person after so many years of loneliness. Tessa hadn't kissed a man since . . . No. She wouldn't think about him. Why couldn't she have a life? Why didn't she deserve love? Even if it wasn't the love of her life. She was sick of her heart wasting away over a man it couldn't have. Tessa threw herself into the kiss and hoped she wasn't too rusty to please him.

Griffin had gone totally ape shit. Kayden stood in the doorway of Griffin's study in his dusty black fatigues and surveyed the damage as it continued to spread across the room. Griffin was in the far corner of the room using a golf club to dismantle a lamp. He either hadn't noticed Kayden enter the room and shut the door behind him or he didn't care that he was there watching.

Kayden had been patrolling the grounds when a call came in from the house. He had been surprised to find Sarah on the other end of the line instead of Griffin. She was in a panic. Sarah explained that she had heard what sounded like a struggle coming from Griffin's office and had called security. When the warriors entered Griffin's study he had roared at them to mind their own business and return to their posts. She didn't know what to do. Mason had taken Debbie and their baby girl, Sydney, away for their safety until after the Rogue was dealt with. She didn't know whom else to call.

Griffin and Kayden had formed a friendship over the last year. So there Kayden stood, watching the man he had come to think of as a friend destroying a very expensive-looking leather chair with his bare hands. Kayden approached slowly.

"Good evening, Griffin," he said as if nothing were at all odd about the situation.

Griffin was the most controlled man, vampire or human, Kayden had ever known. For him to lose his shit like this was a big deal. Something was very wrong in Griffin's world right now. All Kayden could hope to do was return the favor Griffin had done for him. He could be there to listen when the man was ready to talk.

"Kayden. What is it? Is Danielle in trouble?" Griffin's calm tone was totally at odds with the black wildness of his eyes and the condition of the room.

"Dani is fine. The last I heard she and Chase were headed out of town to babysit. Mason is taking Debbie away for the weekend and the newlyweds are on baby duty." Kayden smiled weakly. They both knew Kayden had a mountain of regrets when it came to Dani and Chase.

"Good. Good. Debbie needs a break." He nodded and ran his hands through his disheveled hair, making the pure white highlights stand on end.

Griffin turned to flop down in the chair he had just been busy relieving of its stuffing. Kayden located the chair that was normally opposite Griffin's chair. It had been hurled to the other end of the room. He dragged it back to sit facing his friend and just waited with one booted foot resting on his knee. After several moments of silence Griffin began to speak. "You go through life wishing you could have some time to yourself. Your life is so full of people pulling you in every direction and you just want to be left alone—until one day you are alone. And then you sit alone, in the silence, and you choke on it."

Kayden mulled that over. He understood what Griffin was saying, but that was not what had caused this explosion, and Kayden needed to get to the trigger.

"So. What happened here, Griff? Because I don't believe this was an epiphany for you. What has you so pissed that you feel the need to destroy shit while disrupting everyone in your household? Sarah is about to call your parents, her parents, the Council, or anybody who might be able to get close enough to talk you down."

"Sarah doesn't care about me. She just doesn't want me to make a scene and embarrass her. She's probably fretting over the servants and the guards telling their friends about my animalistic behavior." Griffin rolled his eyes. "You should be glad you didn't let Soleil trap you into a blood bond."

The memory of his rejection of Dani stung a bit. He had regretted the mistake every moment of every day since that night. Kayden knew that what happened to Darren might have happened to him. It could have been a one-sided bond because of her human blood, but he chose to believe that they would have had a bond like Griffin had shared with Tessa. He loved Dani and he knew she had genuine feelings for him too. That could have been the difference between a loveless bond and happily ever after. But it was too late for that now. He made his decision and now he had to live with the consequences. Griffin must have seen him wince because he apologized.

"I'm sorry, Kayden. I know very well you and Soleil would have been nothing like Sarah and me. I'm just venting."

"Are you going to talk about the problem or just let it simmer until it boils over again?" Kayden asked.

Something dangerous flicked behind Griffin's eyes just before everything in the room with the exception of the chairs they sat in began to levitate. The force caused the heavy wood furniture to explode into toothpicks; everything flew through the air and crashed into the opposite wall. *Holy shit!*

Kayden stood his ground and continued to sit calmly across from a man he knew could crush him, in spite of his strength and training. Griffin was older and had incredible telekinetic power. He waited for Griffin to calm and continue.

"He's touching my mate, Kayden. He's kissing the lips that belong to me. She has been blocking me for months. Once I realized that the soft, warm buzzing in the back of my mind was Tessa, I began to constantly work on strengthening the connection. The more you use a blood connection the stronger it gets. I don't know if my bond with Sarah has always been so weak because of my bond to Tessa or if it's because neither of us ever bothered to nurture our own bond." Griffin paused, lowering his head to his hands. A loud crack splintered the silence and half of the solid granite mantel over the fireplace fell to the carpet.

"I don't know how she is blocking me, but the warmth and the love that always hummed reassuringly in my soul is now gone. It has been, since she almost died. She finally gave up on me. It must take concentration to maintain the separation between us because now that she is thoroughly distracted with another man's tongue down her throat, she isn't able to hold it in place. I can feel her better now than I could even just after we bonded. My efforts to strengthen the connection worked. I can feel her unease at having him touch her. I feel her discomfort at touching him, but she's determined to move on. She's been lonely too. And she has lived through this pain for all these years. She had to have felt this and been witness to every night I have spent in the arms of another woman." Tears began to fall from Griffin's downcast face and splash onto the carpet. Kayden held his silence. What could he say?

"She doesn't understand. I didn't know she was alive. I didn't know she was waiting for me. I never would have intentionally hurt her this way. I never wanted this pain for her. I love her so much. We didn't need a damn blood bond. We loved each other more than

any bond. I just didn't know she was still alive and waiting for me."
Griffin was practically sobbing. Kayden said the first thing that
came to his mind.

"Bullshit. That is such a load of bullshit."

Griffin's head snapped up and he glared at Kayden. Kayden put
his hands up as if he were trying to calm a snarling beast.

"Hear me out before you start disassembling me from the inside
out. I believe that you want to believe you didn't know she was
there. I believe that you never wanted to hurt your mate or cause
her pain. I also believe that somewhere in your subconscious you
hoped that if you couldn't really feel her that she couldn't really feel
you. You're an educated man who lived for years without that buzz
in your brain until after you met Tessa. My understanding is that
you were only bonded for two or three years before you were separated. It's not like the bond had been in place for so long that you
didn't remember what it was like to live without it. Even now, after
over twenty years of being bonded from a long distance, you can
feel the absence of her presence when she pulls away from you."

Griffin began to pace like a caged animal. He wasn't enjoying
hearing an outside point of view. Especially since Kayden refused
to toe the line.

"I thought she was dead, Kayden. They told me she was dead
and they had proof. Both Tessa and our baby died in the hospital.
I still have the damn death certificates. Human hospitals don't rou-
tinely issue death certificates for living people," he snapped.

Kayden left his seat to approach Griffin before delivering his
final thought on the subject. Griffin was going to have to deal with
this internally before he could move on with his life. There was
nothing Kayden could do to help him. So, if Griffin needed to
destroy his entire house in an effort to find the truth in his own
heart, Kayden wouldn't stand in his way. Hell, he was still wrestling
his own internal demons.

"When I look back on all the time I spent with Dani, I begin to see all the things that made her different. I see all the things that at the time I had decided to ignore. Her thoughts and feelings on humanity were unlike any vampire. Her blood scent drove me crazy in a way that it shouldn't have. Her physical weakness and lack of speed. All these clues I chose to ignore. For God's sake, she told me several times that she wasn't what I thought she was. Why didn't I demand an explanation? Why didn't I see what was staring me in the face? I'll tell you why. Because it was easier not to. It was easier to pretend I didn't know. It was easier to blame ignorance than to admit my own mistakes after I hurt her the night we almost bonded. I claimed to be the one who loved her the most. In the end I was the one who delivered the rejection and prejudice she had expected from our people all along. Why? Because it had been easier for me to turn away from her than to take the prejudice and shame that would come with her onto myself."

Now Kayden fought back stinging tears.

"It took me a while to figure out what went wrong that night. I wasn't strong enough. I wasn't man enough to stand by her side and be proud of her for exactly who and what she was in the face of our people. So this is my question to you, Griff. Did you really not know that Tessa was there, loving you and waiting for you to come back to her? Or was it just easier for you to believe what you were told? Was it easier for you to live the life your parents had laid out before you than to rebel and live a life without the comforts and advantages afforded to a man of your station? Tessa already knows the answers to these questions. I wonder how long it will take you to confront the truth of your own weakness."

Kayden turned to leave, but Griffin stopped him with a question before he reached the door.

"When did you grow into such a wise man, son?"

Kayden didn't have to think about the answer to that question.

"It was the moment I realized that I'd had it all twisted. It wasn't that Dani wasn't good enough for me. It was that she was so far above me I couldn't see all the ways I wasn't good enough for her. At least not until it was too late."

Eight

Griffin sorted through what was left of his study in search of the Rolodex. His cell phone had gone missing in the mess he'd made, and thanks to the age of technology he couldn't reach anyone without it. Who memorized phone numbers anymore when they were all programmed into your phone? As much as it galled him, Griffin needed to call Doc Stevens. Tessa had changed her number when he refused to stop calling to check on her after her injury.

A short time ago he had sensed a serious shift in Tessa's emotional state. He didn't believe she realized that her shield against him had fallen, so Griffin had been receiving a steady stream of feedback. If he had been feeling this depth of emotion from her all these years, he would have definitely known she was out there. Griffin wasn't sure yet if his work to strengthen the bond between them was going to be a blessing or a curse. It had gone a long way to calming him when Tessa made the decision to pull back from her make-out session with Doc.

Hours later Tessa seemed to have been sleeping, her energy calm and quiet, when suddenly it felt as if she were frightened. Maybe even terrified. It was probably just a bad dream, but until either the feeling subsided, or he spoke to Tessa or Doc, he wasn't going to be able to relax. He felt as if his heart were pounding in his chest, but it wasn't. Physically he was calm and steady, but mentally he felt on edge. Understanding that the emotions were Tessa's and not his own helped him to deal with the onslaught.

An odd noise, like a whimper, distracted him from his search. The house was quiet. It was the middle of the night and everyone had gone to bed hours ago. Griffin paused to listen more closely. Something hit the floor in the room above his study. J. R. had been having bad dreams since the night of his sister's abduction. Unfortunately, the boy had been standing in the entryway when Greyson had carried Brandi's lifeless body into the house. The dreams were coming less frequently with the passage of time, but it hurt Griffin's heart that his boy had witnessed something that had affected him so deeply. He left his study and swiftly climbed the stairs to comfort his son.

J. R.'s bedroom door was slightly ajar and it was unusually dark when Griffin peeked into the room. Normally J. R. slept with his bathroom light on and the door cracked. Griffin pushed the door open and crossed the room to flip on the bathroom light. He nearly tripped over a miniature racetrack in his path. Before he was able to straighten from his stumble, Griffin was tackled to the ground. He struggled against several pairs of restraining arms. All Griffin could think of was his son. They were here for his son and he couldn't let them harm another one of his babies. J. R. was literally just a child at eleven years old. He wasn't old enough to show any signs of extrasensory power.

He had just enough time to pull on his telekinetic strength for a single volley of objects in the room to pummel his attackers before one of them jabbed him in the side with a syringe. The world spun away from him and Griffin knew he had lost. He was powerless to lift his head within five seconds. His power was completely out of his reach. He now understood the feeling of helplessness two of his daughters had felt when they had come for them. Now they would take his little boy. J. R. hadn't stirred or made a noise during the fight, so Griffin knew he had already been drugged before he entered the room.

"Two-for-one deal tonight, boys. Looks like there will be more money to split than we originally estimated. Congrats," a gravelly voice whispered. "Now let's get out of here before anyone comes to check on the kid. Dad here made quite a bit of noise."

"I think we should leave Mr. Vaughn. We weren't told to bring him." This voice was vaguely familiar to Griffin even through the fog of his retreating consciousness.

"Shut up and do as you're told. Do you want to spend the rest of your life sitting in a gatehouse? Do you enjoy being on rotation at the homes of our esteemed Council members? Because that's all you're ever going to do in this backward society. Now grab his feet and get moving. The Master is going to pay us well for the extra work."

The guardhouse was empty. Just as she knew it would be. Tessa drove straight through the gates, which had been left open. She had never been to the Vaughn estate before, but her dream had told her right where to go. The premonition had been heart wrenching. She had to get to J. R. as fast as her human legs would carry her. The cost to her for this mission of mercy would be huge, but she couldn't let the boy die.

Thinking of her brave daughter and all of the lives Danielle had saved with her selfless acts helped to steel Tessa's spine. Tessa jumped the curb and drove across the manicured lawn that was surrounded by a circular driveway. The element of surprise would be her only ally tonight. Tessa drove her car to the left of the large stairway that led to huge red double doors she knew would put her right where she needed to be. Tessa grabbed the gun Mason had given her all those years ago and the lifesaving items she had stolen from Reilly's clinic on the way out the door. With any luck the alarms she triggered when she exited the clinic had Reilly right on her heels. His skills would be sorely needed.

Tessa turned the knob the intruders had left unlocked for an easy escape and drifted into the shadows. The windows above the doors shone on a set of marble staircases. Damn, the place was beautiful. An enormous crystal chandelier hung above the entryway, casting little rainbows of light over the walls and the landing that branched off in two directions at the top of the stairs. An antique-looking mirror that was as tall as Tessa took up residence on the wall between the twin staircases and opposite the front doors. Tessa moved quickly to stand against the wall next to the mirror. They wouldn't see her until it was too late. She removed a syringe from her pilfered black doctor's bag and tucked it into her shirt pocket. With her pistol in hand she waited for the players to move into position. Tessa's heart pounded so loudly she was surprised it hadn't given her away yet. When a group of men made their way down the stairs to her right, she held her breath. It was playing out just as she had expected. She said a silent prayer that the shooting lessons she had taken when Danielle was an infant would come back to her in a hurry.

The men reached the bottom of the stairs and Tessa took aim. Without warning she put a bullet through the thigh of the man who was carrying J. R. The man fell to his knees while the cacophony of gunfire echoed off the walls and ceiling. She only wanted to disable the men, not kill them, but a leg shot was too dangerous to take on the man holding Griffin by the shoulders. With Griffin's body hanging between the two men trying to balance the weight of his long body, she risked hitting him if the bullet went straight through the bad guy's leg. So she raised her aim and hit the guy in the shoulder, causing him to drop Griffin to the floor. The guy at

Griffin's feet released him and ducked into the hall at the right of the entryway. Tessa knew he would get away so she didn't give chase.

Right on cue the lights blinked on in the entryway and there she stood when Sarah came to the landing at the top of the stairs. Tessa had a gun in one hand and a syringe in the other. The two guards who should have been on duty at the guardhouse were bleeding from wounds she had inflicted and Griffin and J. R. were both out cold. Shit. Tessa had to admit it had to look pretty bad from Sarah's point of view.

"You bitch! What have you done?" Sarah cried out.

Three things happened simultaneously in the next few seconds. Tessa had to get to J. R., so she ran for him. Guards began to pour in from a hallway that led back into the center of the house, and Reilly busted through the front door. Right on time. Tessa was still running and Sarah was screaming that Tessa had killed Griffin and J. R. Tessa leapt the distance between her and J. R. to jab the needle into his leg. He didn't move, but she could hear him wheezing when the guards tackled her to the ground.

"She stabbed my baby! Oh God, save my baby! Did you see her stab my baby? There's a needle hanging out of his leg! Oh God! There's a needle hanging out of his leg! Doc, help my baby!" Sarah was wailing, but she didn't move to descend the stairs. Brandi appeared behind her mother and ran for the stairs when she saw her brother on the ground, but Sarah held her back.

The men she had shot were members of the warrior class on duty at the Vaughn estate. So when they agreed with Sarah and stated they had been shot in an effort to save the Vaughn men, they were believed.

Reilly was struggling against several warriors who had been restraining him until Sarah ordered him to help the boy. Tessa was being roughly held to the ground with her arms behind her back in an awkward position and with what she believed to be a boot on the back of her neck when Reilly knelt in front of her to reach J. R. He pulled the needle from the boy's leg and rolled him over to get a look at his face. The boy's eyes were swollen nearly shut and his lips were twice their normal size. A shuddering hissing sound came from his throat. Tessa tried to speak with what little air she had in her lungs due to the pressure being applied to her back.

"Allergic. He's allergic," she whimpered. Reilly looked down at the needle.

"It's an EpiPen. I think Tessa was trying to save your son's life, Sarah. His airway is still closed. I need a knife. I'll have to perform an emergency tracheotomy to reestablish an airway." The guards all pulled out their knives.

Sarah flew down the stairs. "Why? What's wrong? Is he still breathing?"

"Reilly! Bag! Black bag!" Tessa got out just before he cut the boy's throat open. Reilly scanned the hall and found the bag. When he came back the light in his eyes was breathtaking.

"Tessa, you are a genius and a savior," Reilly praised.

Tessa had taken the time to grab an extra EpiPen and the smallest intubation kit she could find in the clinic supply closet. Reilly began the work of feeding the tube gently down J. R.'s throat after tilting his head all the way back to open the airway as much as possible. Reilly had the tubes inserted and the bag attached faster than Tessa would have thought possible. He squeezed the bag at regular intervals to provide the much-needed oxygen to J. R.'s young body. Sarah knelt by his side, weeping over her son.

Tessa relaxed against the floor and let the rest of the evening play itself out. She had done what she had come to do. Even if the men had gotten away with the abduction, J. R. wouldn't have made it past the gates. The boy was allergic to something in the drug he had been injected with. Anaphylactic shock had a tight grip on him by the time they made it to the bottom of the stairs.

"She shot me when I caught her with the boy. She's no savior. She's a human piece of trash out to kidnap another one of our children," the guy with the hole in his thigh shouted. The other guy had passed out without putting in his two cents.

"I want her arrested. Take her straight to the Council chamber. I want this bitch executed by sunrise. Call the available Council members now," Sarah hissed at the group of warriors.

Reilly's back stiffened. "Sarah, you have no authority to make such demands and you know it." He turned to the warrior who was in charge.

"How much sense does it make that she shot one man in the back of the leg and the other in the back of his shoulder if they were coming at her? Trying to capture her would be very difficult while running away." This seemed to give the warrior just enough plausible doubt to make him pause.

"We will detain her at the Enclave until Mr. Vaughn is able to shed further light on this mess. I have a feeling his statement is going to make all the difference." The warrior commanded that she be loaded in a van and cuffed to the floor.

Reilly was still working on J. R. but shouted to her, "You did good, honey." That was all there was time for before she was hauled bodily out the wide red double doors and stuffed into the back of a van. To her surprise, Brandi climbed in after her.

"What are you doing?" Tessa asked. "You should be with your family."

"You are my family. You are my sister's mother. I'm going to stay with you as long as I can. J. R. is in Doc's capable hands and my dad will be fine when he wakes up. That could take anywhere from hours to days, depending on the dose he received. You, on the other hand, are in the custody of people who are unsure of your guilt and some who hold a grudge against your daughter. I'm just going to ride along and keep an eye on things."

———◦•◦———

"No way, man. No way in hell are we getting in there," Nate said from behind Abel.

Abel had been losing his mind since the news came into the Nest the night before. A three-man team had been sent to apprehend the youngest of the House of Vaughn. The intention had been to trade the kid for Danielle. Somehow these idiots had bungled the job by trying to walk out with Griffin Vaughn as well. Only one of the warrior traitors had returned from the mission, and he hadn't lived long after he gave the Master his report of the events that had led to the capture of the two other men. The Master had executed him painfully and publicly for deviating from the mission plan given to him.

Abel knew that Brandi had been home at the time of the debacle because he had followed her from a martial arts studio she had been attending regularly until she disappeared up the driveway to her family's palatial home. According to the undercover Shade warrior, several shots had been fired. Other sources at the Enclave reported that six people were transported to the Enclave. The two females were identified as Brandi Vaughn and another unknown human woman. Abel needed to see with his own eyes that she was in one piece.

"No way, man," Nate repeated. "They have this joint locked down. I've seen at least one man on the roof and several others circling the house."

"You don't have to go, Nate. I'm going in with or without you."

Abel checked his weapon and tucked a shot of Hypno in his belt, just in case. He would always disable a man before he killed him, if given the choice. As if on cue, the man on watch at the rear entrance used for deliveries and employees left his post to take a little stroll. Without warning, Abel left the tree line he and Nate had been hiding in and strode across the lawn like he belonged there. Nate was left to catch up.

"You could have told me one of our guys was letting us in," Nate hissed when they made it inside undetected.

"It was too much fun watching you sweat," Abel whispered back.

The two men moved quietly through the silent house, unhampered by anyone. Abel began to wonder if the reports from his contacts had been incorrect. Maybe Brandi was still at the Enclave. Maybe she had been injured. Getting into the Enclave to check on her would be much more difficult than a trip to the Vaughn estate.

He reached for the doorknob he'd been told led to Brandi's bedroom and was surprised when Nate slammed into his back and the door opened, allowing him to fall face-first on the floor with Nate on his back.

"If either one of you moves, I will blow a hole through your chest. No heart, no life, boys. Do you understand?" a husky female voice calmly asked from the doorway.

They both nodded in understanding. She collected their guns. "You got your gun ready, B? Don't hesitate to shoot his ass. He came into your room with a gun."

B? Her room?

"Sparky, it's me. This is my friend, Nate. Remember I told you about him?" Abel needed to look up. He needed to see her face but wouldn't move until he was sure Brandi felt safe.

"You told her about me? Are you trying to get me killed? Shit, Abel!" Nate complained.

"Let them up, Karrie," Brandi said as her feet moved away from him and a dim light was switched on.

"You can take the one who seems to know you, *Sparky*, but this bastard has too many hidden weapons for my peace of mind." Karrie instructed Nate to roll over slowly with his fingers laced behind his head. He did her bidding and she promptly straddled his chest, putting the barrel of her gun directly against his forehead. Brandi rushed to shut the bedroom door.

"Abel?" Nate said.

"Yeah, man. I'm sorry about this," he apologized.

"I think I'm in love." Nate smiled up at Karrie. "Do you think this is an odd way to meet your mate? Damn, man. This one is really hot. I really think she would kill me, too. Is it sick that that turns me on?"

Karrie tried unsuccessfully not to smile at Nate's antics. Nate gave her a wide smile in return. "Baby, if you don't have a man, you do now. And if you do, well, I hope you're not too attached to the bastard."

"Please let him up," Brandi said before turning her attention to Abel. "Abel, huh? May I point out that you never told me your name? What are you doing here?" Brandi was pacing a hole in the floor. Abel stopped her by wrapping her up in a tight embrace. For the first time since he heard the news about the failed mission, Abel felt as if he could breathe.

"I heard about the attempt on your brother. I knew you had been transported to the Enclave. It scared the shit out of me. I had to see you. I needed to touch you," he confessed quietly against her ear. Brandi wrapped her arms around his neck, allowing him to bury his face in her hair. "God, you smell so damn good, Sparky. I haven't been able to think of anything but you since that night at Candy's place."

"I'm fine. I wasn't anywhere near the action until it was over," she soothed while stroking the hair at the nape of his neck. "I'd like to know how you knew I was at the Enclave, though," she asked.

"Yeah. I'd like to know the answer to that question as well," Karrie piped in, but Abel gave no response to either woman.

"How did you girls know we were coming?" Nate asked.

"There've been too many unexplained breaches lately. The guards have been doing regular rounds for the past twelve hours. I knew something was coming when the warriors missed the last round. We just sat back and waited for you to creep into our web," Karrie explained. "I'm going to be staying with Brandi for a while. The security around here sucks. I snuck in myself, just to prove a point to her."

A noise from the hall alerted Karrie and Nate. They both started giving hand signals to Abel and Brandi to communicate an approaching threat. Brandi waved them all into the bathroom, but Abel refused to go. He scooped up his gun and stood behind the door waiting. It was just a warrior resuming his rounds. Abel and Nate hadn't been there long enough for that to have happened unless his contact on the estate was having trouble. He stood with Brandi at his back and listened to the warrior slowly ascend the stairs and walk down the other end of the corridor before returning to pass Brandi's door and continue walking down the hall toward the servant stairway without stopping. He would circle back around and then they would have fifteen minutes before the next round.

"Let's get out of here. We have fifteen minutes," Abel whispered against her ear and hoped she would agree to leave with him. The uniquely warm and smoky feminine scent of her crept into his brain, causing his pants to feel way too tight.

To his relief, Brandi nodded and went to free Nate and Karrie from their hiding place in the bathroom, but she stopped and gave him a stern look before opening the door.

"I'm going with you, but I will expect some solid answers to all my questions. If you aren't willing to talk, you should just leave now. Leave now and don't ever come back. I deserve the same trust I am giving to you."

She glared at him and dared him to argue with her conditions. Abel knew he could be making the biggest mistake of his life, but he had to take the chance. He needed just a little more time with the woman who haunted all of his waking and sleeping hours. He finally nodded in agreement.

Brandi opened the bathroom door and stood in stunned silence for a moment. Abel leaned around the door to see what held her unwavering attention. In the few moments that Abel and Brandi had been listening for danger from the hallway, Nate had talked Karrie straight out of her panties. Only a night-light lit the bathroom. The counter was covered with weapons of various types from guns to knives and even what Abel suspected was a garrote. He couldn't help wondering whom that belonged to.

Nate had Karrie nude from the waist down and was pressing her against the opposite wall. Karrie's long legs were wrapped around Nate's waist. Her head was thrown back in ecstasy. Nate was whispering against Karrie's neck, telling her what a dirty girl she was, while he thrust into her body. Abel thanked God that Nate had managed to keep his pants on, only lowering them enough to work himself free. Abel did not want to have the image of his friend's bare ass seared into his memory. The couple didn't seem to notice they had an audience. Brandi quietly shut the door.

"We may have to wait until after the next round passes before we leave."

A moan of pure pleasure escaped the bathroom, causing Brandi's cheeks to heat beautifully with color.

"Or maybe the one after that." Abel chuckled.

Nine

It was a really bad idea and Brandi knew it. She should have called for security the moment the two men came crashing into her bedroom, but she just couldn't. He—apparently his name was Abel—had spared her life months ago and had saved her from a forced bonding more recently. He had protected her until she was able to protect herself. There was something different about her dark intruder, and Brandi needed to get to the bottom of her obsession with him, once and for all.

Abel had become a distracting shadow that cast its shade over everything in her life. She thought about him constantly and worried for his safety. She knew he worked for the Rogue and she needed to know why. How could a man capable of saving lives, a man capable of risking his life to sneak into her family home just to see if she was safe, be capable of doing the things the Rogue would expect of him? How could she be so attracted to him after what she and her family had suffered at the hands of the Rogue? The fear in her said yes, he was capable of really bad things. He had helped to kidnap Dani, after all. Brandi stuffed that thought down. Freaking out wouldn't help her now. If nothing else, she could prove to herself that he was an evil minion of the Rogue and put him out of her mind. She might even be able to gather some valuable information for the Wrath.

They bobbed and weaved through the corridors and the servant stairway of her home and exited through a rear delivery door. Brandi followed Abel across the wide expanse of moonlit lawn behind the house. He led Brandi to a wooded area of the Vaughn estate where she had spent many long days romping around as a child. It amazed her that Abel knew exactly where he was going, as if he had been there many times before. They entered the woods with Karrie and Abel's friend Nate bringing up the rear. Nate held Karrie's hand tightly grasped in his own while he practically dragged her behind him. Karrie was whispering something to the mulish, angry man, but he ignored her.

Brandi had the feeling Nate was serious about the mating business he had been spouting back in her room, in spite of his joking demeanor. Nate stopped and whistled like a bird to get Abel's attention. A few hand signals passed between the men. Karrie watched the exchange and began shaking her head in denial. Brandi had no idea what they were saying, but it was obvious Karrie did and she was not in agreement with the plan they were devising. When Nate turned to stride away, dragging Karrie in his wake, she struggled to free herself. Brandi enjoyed watching Karrie's performance only because she knew Karrie could easily free herself if she really wanted to be free. After a few staggering steps Nate halted his forward motion to turn and sweep Karrie's wriggling body up into his arms.

He said nothing, but his hazel-green eyes sparkled with determination and possession. His mouth was a stern line surrounded by a well-trimmed goatee when he lowered his head to claim her mouth. Karrie sagged in Nate's hold and returned the kiss. When he finally lifted his head, Karrie sighed and followed obediently. She turned back to give Brandi a look of apology for leaving her. It was the damnedest thing. It seemed as though the stern, demanding woman had met her match and she knew it. Abel and Brandi both smiled, watching the other couple disappear into the darkness.

———————•◦•———————

Abel placed his hand on the small of Brandi's back to swiftly led her toward the edge of her family's property. He had a vehicle waiting a few blocks away from the supposedly secure perimeter wall. It was dark and quiet with stray beams of moonlight filtering down through the trees. When they passed through a clearing, Abel took the time to look down at his willing captive. The tension in her body was palpable and he knew Brandi had every reason to fear him. She had no reason to trust him; for all she knew he was leading her to her death, but she followed him into the night and away from the safety of her family anyway. She trusted him and wanted to hear his side of the story before summarily passing judgment on his life. Not that anything he said to her would matter once she realized that he would never leave the Master's service as long as his mother was a prisoner.

Brandi looked up at him, and the midnight blue of her eyes reflected the light from the moon, which seemed more like a disco ball hanging low in the sky. She was breathtaking. His arms ached to hold her close and feel the warmth of her acceptance.

This was a Brandi he had never had the pleasure of seeing before. Gone were the designer clothes and stiletto heels. Brandi was garbed in an outfit that seemed to fit her more naturally than all the flash she usually wore. She wore a simple pair of jeans, a snug T-shirt that bore the logo of the local college football team, and a pair of classic black Vans that made her look at home in her skin. He couldn't help it; Abel stopped and wrapped his arms around her lush, petite body. He had been dreaming of holding her ever since the night he'd spent watching over her in Candy's spare bedroom.

After only a moment's hesitation, Brandi returned the embrace, going up on tiptoes to tuck her face into the hollow of his throat. Dear God, he wanted this woman. He wanted to taste her, claim her, protect her, but more than that, he wanted to be the type of man she would allow to do those things and proudly claim him as her man as well.

"I think this is a bad idea," Brandi whispered, lifting her head. "I'm going back to the house. I can't . . . I don't want to be with you, Abel. I can't trust you." Brandi tried to look away, but he held her chin in his hand, forcing her to look him in the eye when she lied to him.

"Don't lie to me, Sparky. I know you feel the pull, the same way I feel it." Abel smiled weakly. Brandi blushed.

He knew he should let her go, but for just a moment Brandi was in his arms, and that had been all he wanted since the first time their eyes locked on each other so many months ago. This might be new for her, but he had been tracking her every move and doing everything in his power to protect her from the Master and his machinations ever since he'd been released from the dungeon after he and Darren had failed to capture Danielle. He was unable to stop himself from brushing his lips against hers. There was barely a whisper of contact before he placed one of her hands on his shoulder and took the other hand in his own to lead her in the first strains of a waltz only he could hear. Abel loved to dance. His mother had taught him that any man worth his salt could woo a woman on the dance floor. But that was a long time ago.

"There isn't any music," Brandi whispered with a sheepish smile.

Brandi was also an accomplished dancer. He had watched her dance at several formal functions. She was trying not to enjoy the dance and failing. He spun her in a turn at the end of the clearing and pulled her a little closer to his chest for the return trip.

Abel looked into her exquisite, upturned face and the slow shift in his chest that had been occurring every time he saw Brandi finally snapped. She made him want more and she made him dream of the impossible. He had to acknowledge the feelings he was experiencing for the first time in his life. He was falling for Brandi. It was time she recognized her attraction to him also.

He knew all about her surfer boyfriend and all of the Wrath guard's heroics, but he also knew Brandi was curious about him too. It was odd that when her *hero* accompanied her to the various balls and charity functions, he acted like more of a bodyguard. He never danced with her or made the social rounds. In his opinion, if Malibu Ken were doing his job, Brandi wouldn't be thinking about other guys. She wouldn't have followed him blindly into the unknown. Yes, she was very curious, and Abel would use that curiosity to keep her with him for as long as possible.

"There is music if you listen," he finally replied. "Do you hear the wind rustling the leaves in the trees, the branches swaying to the beat of the night? I hear the flapping of wings, an owl singing us a song, and the distant hum of passing cars. Can't you hear my heart thudding, trying to catch up with yours?"

Abel kissed her, licking his way into the heat of her beautiful mouth. He lifted her from the ground to rest against his chest when her steps faltered. He continued to dance but Brandi struggled to pull away. He wouldn't release her. Abel needed this chance to explain his life and his feelings to Brandi. He had to make her listen. Even if she hated him afterward, she had to know the truth. He wasn't the Master's willing soldier. He was a victim, too. But she likely wouldn't see it that way. How could he expect her to understand and forgive him for things he couldn't change? He would continue to be the Master's lackey.

"Let me go. I'm going home." She tried wrenching her arms free, but Abel held tight.

"Please, Brandi, you said you wanted answers. I want to give them to you." She shivered under his hands.

"Giving me answers has nothing to do with the kissing and wandering hands," she stuttered and looked ashamed. "I have a boyfriend. I'm in a serious relationship with a man who would be hurt by my behavior. He's a good male, a Wrath warrior. When they discover I'm gone, he will be the first person they call before they even contact my parents."

"A serious relationship, huh? That's funny, considering how much time you spend alone," Abel challenged.

Abel jerked her against him and laid siege on her senses. He stroked her back with his hands and claimed her mouth with his. He surrounded her with his arms and the mingled scent of their bodies until she allowed his tongue entrance. He let Brandi feel the effect she had on his hungry body when he rotated his hips, pressing his length into the softness of her belly. This was his specialty and one of the many reasons the Master valued Abel's services. The human girls were drawn to his vampire nature, foolishly flocking to the predator, while the vamp girls longed to get closer to that elusive scent that pulled them in like eager little lambs to slaughter. It was the human in his blood that drove them crazy with the need to feed, but his vampire blood confused them into believing it was the need for the purely carnal pleasure he promised. Sometimes he actually gave it to them and slaked his own lust before resigning them to their fates as fodder for the Master and his men.

At the moment he did what he had to do in order to gain Brandi's compliance. He pulled back, peering deeply into her astonished, almost confused, eyes. His heart beat wildly. She wasn't the only one affected by the soul-rending kiss.

"Can your man make you feel like that? Can he make you forget I exist the way I just made you forget his name?" Abel taunted.

Abel tried to keep his grip on Brandi when the skin under his hands became hot and searing. He might have gone too far with that last comment. Brandi was pissed. He had wondered what it would take to push her into using her secret talent. Her deep blue eyes had shifted to a glassy onyx and her skin became molten hot. With a hiss he was forced to release her or suffer burns that would take him much too long to recover from. The massive power contained in this sweet little spark of a woman amazed him and only made him want her more.

"I'm not the kind of girl who cheats, Abel. I'm done with this shit. Thank you for helping me in the past, but you need to leave now. Please don't come back." Brandi began to walk back toward her home.

The sadness that flashed in her eyes made Abel regret pushing her. He had made her feel dirty and that was the last thing he intended to do. It felt like the secret flames in her body reached out to him, igniting a need for her every time they came into contact and making him act like a letch.

"I'm sorry, Sparky. I get close to you and all my good intentions go up in flames, so to speak. Please don't go. I promise to behave like a gentleman." He held his breath and watched her continue walking away from him. If she left, he wouldn't pursue her tonight, but he'd be damned if he would stay away as she requested.

At the edge of the clearing she paused, sighed deeply, and turned around. Abel's mouth fell open when she raised one hand to him. The air between them began to heat up. Brandi's body began to ripple as if he were looking at her across a field of hot asphalt instead of grassy clearing. Her image shimmered and waved like a desert mirage.

Shit.

She was going to attack him. He wasn't sure his half-human body could survive the damage of the fireball he knew she was capable of producing. He had seen one scorch a path of earth and trees through the woods. There was no sense in running. He was stronger than most vampires but not as fast. He couldn't outrun her rage.

She stared at him, looking anguished. He waited silently for her judgment. Maybe it was for the best. His forced life of crime and depravity would end at the hands of the only woman he had ever longed for, the one person who had been able to make him feel real shame for his deeds. No matter that his evil deeds were all in defense of his mother. It was fitting, after the things he had done to so many innocent girls.

Brandi lowered her hand and a tree stump halfway between them, completely covered in debris from the forest floor, burst into flames. It was an instant campfire. Wow. She must have been practicing. There hadn't been a fireball or a path of destruction. Brandi had merely pointed at the stump and up it went. The flames cast a warm glow over the area between them. Abel took a deep breath, realizing her intent hadn't been to hurt him.

"You have one hour, Abel. Stay on that side of the flames and I will listen."

Kayden eavesdropped with keen interest from the canopy of trees above the couple eyeing each other over the flames. Brandi had created a brilliant blaze. Kayden was shocked and amazed at Brandi's pyrokinetic talent, though not surprised that she'd kept it hidden. It would have made her an immediate target for the Rogue.

He'd been on guard and secretly watching the Vaughn estate for the last two days since Griffin was taken to the infirmary. It had been warriors, his own brethren, who had tried to deliver the Councilman and his son to the Rogue. Kayden decided to stay hidden and watch over the family until Griffin was able to come home and protect them himself. The last he heard when he checked in with his father, Gage Paris, the captain of the entire warrior class, Griffin still hadn't awakened from the drug-induced sleep caused by the Rogue's flunkies.

The bastard was still after Dani. Kayden clenched his fists in anger and struggled to keep his breathing even. Dani had told them all the truth. There were spies and traitors in their midst. All it had gotten her was banishment from the Enclave and the distrust of most of the warrior class. Now she had to live a life of restriction, hiding from the Rogue to protect the entire vampire nation from the power that lurked in her petite body. If the Rogue were ever able to drain the life from Dani and steal that power, he would be unstoppable.

Kayden was glad he hadn't immediately taken out the intruders when they made an unauthorized back-door entrance at the Vaughn estate. Now he had the identity of at least one traitor, the one who left his post and cleared the way for two unknown vamps to creep inside. He wouldn't apprehend the traitor yet. It would be more beneficial to follow him back to his friends.

He hadn't panicked immediately when the house was breached because he had seen Karrie sneak in, without the aid of the spies, early that morning. He knew Karrie would protect Brandi. Karrie was impressively trained and able to defend against any threat, so long as she wasn't drugged by the intruders. It hurt Kayden just a little when Karrie had walked off with another guy, but he had no claim on her. She'd tried to develop a more serious, exclusive relationship with him, but Kayden just wasn't ready. He was still nursing the self-inflicted wounds he'd suffered after losing Dani to his best friend. Kayden knew he couldn't expect Karrie, with her long, sexy legs, beautifully tilted, deep brown eyes, and strength of body and mind, to wait for him to get it together. The only surprise was that it had taken this long for her to move on. The fact that her new guy was possibly another minion of the Rogue was something he would have to deal with, though. Somehow he just couldn't believe Karrie, the daughter of a Wrath team leader from a long line of warriors, would literally be sleeping with the enemy.

Kayden held his position and watched over Brandi and her new friend instead of storming in to take him down, and his patience had paid off. The unknown vampire male had spent the better part of an hour explaining his history and how he became an unwilling minion of the Rogue. Kayden pitied the guy. He didn't know what he would do if it were his sweet, gentle mother in the Rogue's clutches. To the guy's credit, and obvious detriment, he confessed all of his various sins to Brandi, explaining that he didn't want her to learn of it later and believe he'd lied or purposely kept secrets from her. Brandi sat silently listening to the man, who was clearly in love with her, speak of past deeds that included drug distribution, kidnapping vamps and humans, theft, and fights to the death organized by the Rogue. He swore that his many and various sins were all done in the name of love for his mother. Apparently he was such a successful fighter the Rogue used him as a weapon to discourage his other minions from attempting a mutiny. The situation with the Rogue had grown well past the scope of the Enclave's understanding.

Now was the time, while the stranger was distracted by Brandi, to sneak in and apprehend him. If he were as close to the Rogue as he claimed to be, the stranger would have valuable information, such as the location of the Rogue's hideout. They could end this nightmare. Dani could finally live free, and his people wouldn't need to live in fear of their children disappearing without a trace.

Kayden slowly descended the tree and hit the ground on silent feet. He made his way through the shadows of night to come up on the other man's blind side, but by the time he got into position, the vamp had made his way around the flames and was holding Brandi in his arms. She was sobbing.

"I'm so sorry, Sparky. Please, tell me you can try to understand the situation I'm in?" Kayden heard him say.

"We can end this together, Abel. Can you help my people catch this bastard?" Brandi sniffed. Silence. More sobbing.

"My mother would never make it out alive. He would torture her to bring me back under his control. You may not believe that one life is worth the price of many, but she is my mother. She is all the family I have. I can't leave her at his mercy. Can't you try to understand?" He stroked Brandi's dark hair. Brandi shoved at him and came to her feet.

"What is it that you're asking me for? I don't understand why you're here. Do you expect me to leave a good man, a warrior who protects and cares for my people? Should I forsake my family and my race to run off with you? Did you plan on dragging me into your sick little world so the Rogue can use me against you too? Did you imagine that we would share a cell in the dungeon he locks you in? What do you want? Why are you telling me all this shit?" She was screaming in his face; the air around her began to wave with the heat of her temper. If the guy wasn't careful, he would find himself charbroiled.

"I had to see you, to know you weren't hurt. I'm sorry I came. I just wanted you to know I'm not evil at heart, only in actions. That doesn't seem to really matter in the end. No matter what the reason for your actions, you are still responsible for the results. I understand that." He sighed and tried to get closer to Brandi but he was forced back by the heat of her emotions.

"I care deeply for Greyson. I don't know what you expect from me but I can't deliver. I will never betray his trust. I'm sure that's not a concept a criminal would understand."

The guy looked like she had punched him in the gut. He stepped back, putting more space between them.

"You need to leave. I don't want to see you again. If you ever come back here, I won't be so friendly. Again, I thank you for stepping in and saving my life. Now get off my family's property and don't come back." Brandi stomped off into the trees. The guy just stood there looking forlorn while he watched her disappear into the trees.

He saved her life? Kayden would like to know when and how. Brandi was going to have a lot to answer for when they got this guy into custody. Kayden crept forward while the other vamp was still distracted. Now that Brandi wasn't in the line of fire he could take the guy down without getting too close. He raised his sidearm and aimed for the vamp's knee. He wouldn't get far on only one leg. As he pulled the trigger a huge weight fell on him, forcing his shot to go wide and miss its target. Kayden struggled but couldn't move, and the vamp in the clearing took off like a spooked animal, escaping into the forest.

"Calm yourself, son. I'm not here to hurt you," the deep timbre of a huge male informed him from behind. How the hell had this guy gotten the drop on him? Kayden hadn't heard or smelled a thing. He struggled against the steel hold of the stranger but failed to get even one limb free.

"We need to talk, son. We can't do that until you calm yourself. I don't want to be forced to knock you out and carry you off over my shoulder. I know you wanted to capture Abel, but there is far more at stake here than you can possibly understand. You can't see the whole picture, yet. You need to understand the situation from all angles before you can conquer your enemies. That is why I am here. We will be allies in this war if you are willing to keep an open mind."

"Who the hell are you? Let me up! Where I come from, friends don't blindside you," Kayden growled.

Finally the scent of the vamp invaded his senses. It was just slightly off and Kayden recognized the difference immediately. He had become very familiar with the confusing aroma in the past. Kayden had been closer to Dani than any other person when she first arrived in his society. They had been a couple and had spent many hours snuggled up next to each other before she was fully turned against her will. Kayden froze. The vamp's chuckle was a deep rumble in his chest.

"You can sense the difference. I knew you would. You have the most experience with my kind. I was hoping your past would help us come to a mutual understanding. I am hoping you are unprejudiced enough to see me for who I am, instead of how I was born."

The vamp loosened his hold and leapt away from Kayden before he could strike out. Kayden got to his feet and stared at his would-be ally. The man was huge even by warrior standards. He stood several inches over Kayden's six-foot-four stature and outweighed him by at least fifty pounds of ripped muscle. Thick biceps protruded from a short-sleeved black shirt that seemed to strain against the pressure of containing the vast muscular plain of his chest. He had dark, shoulder-length hair and eyes of undetermined color in the darkness. The vamp stood on guard and allowed Kayden to take in the sheer size and power he possessed.

"You are half human." It was a statement, not a question.

"I'm actually only a quarter human. My grandmother was human, my grandfather a vamp. My father, who was half human, mated with a pure-blood vamp who loved him no matter his race. So I am technically only a quarter human, but who's counting? Your illustrious Council would still consider me a mongrel."

"Shit." Kayden's head was spinning.

"I understand it's a lot to absorb, son, but I need you to give me the benefit of the doubt here. There are things I want to share with you, but not here. Come with me and it will all become very clear." The demi-vamp stood from his defensive position and extended a hand to Kayden.

"They call me Hawk."

Ten

It had been two damn days. Griffin woke up confused and ready to fight in the Enclave infirmary after being unconscious for two damn days. The last thing he remembered was the crushing devastation of knowing he had failed his son. Those traitorous bastards had come for J. R. and all Griffin could do was lie there uselessly while they carried him away.

Griffin woke to find his twins, Brandi and Samantha, at his bedside. They were surrounding him, one girl on each side holding his hands. Once his confusion cleared, the girls assured him that J. R. would be fine, but he was being observed due to an allergic reaction to the drug used by the Rogue's minions. The story Brandi relayed to him was incredible. Once Brandi began to praise Tessa for her bravery and using her incredible psychic talent to save not only J. R.'s life but Griffin's life as well, Samantha got up and left the room. There didn't seem to be anything Tessa or Soleil could do to erase the anger Samantha harbored against them. His mate, Sarah, only made the situation worse by fanning the flames of Sam's resentment. Before Brandi could finish her story, Sarah stormed into the room dragging Greyson, the reluctant physician turned warrior, behind her. Sarah chased Brandi from the room. The one good thing that had come from the situation was that Griffin had proof of Soleil's claim that the Rogue had infiltrated the warrior class. The vamps who had perpetrated this crime were guards from the gatehouse.

That much he remembered overhearing before he fell unconscious. Griffin hadn't yet decided what to do with that information. He had to find a way to bring the traitors to light without alienating the entire warrior class.

Greyson gave him a thorough physical and basic neurological exam before proclaiming him fit to be released and retreating to give Griffin privacy to shower and change into an Enclave sweat suit for the ride home. They had cut his clothes off of him. To Griffin's surprise Greyson returned looking disturbed and uneasy.

"Griffin, about Tessa?" he started to ask but Sarah cut him off.

"That's not something he needs to worry about right now, Dr. Drake. I need to get him home." Sarah literally pushed Greyson out the door.

That had been two days ago. Griffin had spent the last two days hunkered down in the remains of his office. The sofa was still in mostly one piece and that was where he had been sleeping. Only the maid who brought his meals and carried away the dirty dishes had disturbed his solitude. The phone had been destroyed and he still hadn't located his cell phone.

He used the time to look back over his life and contemplate all the wrong turns along with the right ones. He regretted deeply the loss of the life he would have lived with Tessa, but he couldn't regret the births of the three children who came as a result of his life with Sarah. He loved all of his kids and wished there was a way to bring them closer together. Soleil deserved to be a part of his family, and the other kids needed to know their long-lost sibling. Griffin believed in that moment that it would take an act of God for Sarah to allow that to happen, so he prayed for one.

He also wondered how Tessa was doing. Again she had found a way to build her psychic walls and block him out. He could still feel her out there, but the only real feeling he could decipher was a kind of sad resignation. He needed to find a way to contact her and give thanks for her selfless intervention the other night. Not just anybody would brave the danger she had to save the man who had ruined her life. But his Tessa wasn't just anybody.

Finally, he dragged his tired bones up off the warm, coffee-colored leather sofa and began to sort through the debris. He'd need to rent a Dumpster to haul out the mess he had made of his office. Griffin had just located his cell phone buried under the remains of his desk when the office door flew open. Soleil stomped in, black-eyed and furious, nearly running in his direction. Everything in the room from the large chunks of debris to the matchstick-size pieces of furniture began to levitate. Even her long, dark hair rose as if caught in a strong wind, the snow-white and red highlights dancing like flames. Chase ran in after her and wrapped his arms around her waist. Together they also lifted from the ground and continued to float in his direction.

Damn!

His baby girl was strong . . . and pissed off. It made him proud to see the strength of her fury, but he wondered what he'd done to be on the receiving end. Suddenly the sound of Sarah cursing and screaming for help from the hall reached his ears.

"Lovely, please calm down. This isn't helping anyone. Hanging Sarah from the chandelier isn't going to endear you to her." Chase held tight to his mate while Sarah continued to scream.

"Screw her; I hope she falls and breaks her jaw so we don't have to listen to her lying mouth!" Soleil growled and turned her attention to Griffin. Chase gave him a sympathetic look. Griffin could only imagine what it would be like to have a mate with power like that angry with you. Chase's expression said he completely understood.

"I don't give a damn what she says, Griffin!" Dani screamed. "How could you believe my mother would ever hurt you? How could you believe she would even think of injuring my brother? She saved your sorry excuse for a life and your son's. He would have died before they got him off the property if it weren't for my mother! How dare you let her sit in jail for days while they charge her with treason against a government that she isn't a party to?" Soleil took a few calming breaths.

"Chase, release me, please," she asked her mate, but judging by the look on Chase's face as he gently floated back to the ground, he hadn't done it voluntarily. She had used her telepathic power to force his compliance. Griffin knew that wasn't something she ever did lightly because she considered it a violation of trust.

Chase rushed to explain the situation to Griffin before Soleil could do anything she would regret when she calmed down. "They are transporting Tessa to the Council Hall. You haven't stepped forward to refute Sarah's claim that Tessa drugged you and J. R. in an attempt to kill you both. Sarah claims it was an act of vengeance against her because you chose her over Tessa, and also a strike against the Council for being prejudiced against humans. Tessa is being given a trial but the two warriors who corroborated Sarah's story are missing, so they can't be cross-examined. You aren't speaking up and no one has been able to reach you for days. Sarah has turned away anyone who came to speak with you. We just got back into town from babysitting for my parents. Dad is on his way back now and I called Donovan, as much as it pained me, because he was a great deal of help with Lovely's trial."

Griffin was shocked into silence, his mind trying to work through the ramifications of his absence since the night of the attack. Tessa would be executed without his testimony. Sarah's odd behavior at the Enclave and her willingness to let him brood without complaint for the last two days since he arrived home began to make perfect sense. Chase continued.

"Dad hadn't heard a thing about a Council session being called. We weren't even informed there was a problem here. We had to force our way into the house to speak to you." He glanced at Soleil, indicating that she had done the forcing. "Your phone has been off. When we arrived, Sarah was leaving to go testify against Tessa. That's why she's hanging in the entryway."

Griffin looked down at the cell phone in his hand. "I just found it. It's dead," he replied lamely, his head spinning with news of Sarah's betrayal. Tessa had saved their son. How could Sarah do this? She had gone out of her way to keep him in the dark, figuring by the time he got his head out of his ass it would be over.

"The only evidence they have are the statements given by the missing warriors and Sarah's side of the story. She will be executed, *Father!*" Soliel said *father* as if it were a curse. "You had better stop them or I will do the same to you."

It was a promise from the heart of a girl who loved and believed in her mother.

"Lovely, please don't say things you will regret. I'm sure Griffin had no idea this was happening." Chase pulled her into his arms again and she began to sob on his shoulder.

Griffin felt sick. He had been hiding from the world while Tessa paid the price for protecting one of his children, once again. Sarah must have been very proud to have manipulated the situation to her advantage.

"I'm leaving now." Griffin stepped around the embracing couple. "I swear to you that I was clueless of the happenings outside this office. I was told by Brandi that Tessa saved our lives. I had no reason to think anyone else believed otherwise. I will make this right, baby girl. I swear it."

<hr />

Tessa was cold, hungry, and ready to get the show on the road. She had been stuck in a cell with no visitors since she had been hauled off the Vaughn estate in shackles. The only person she had seen was a warrior who brought her food and a fresh pitcher of water twice a day. Using the facilities right out in the open had been a new and unwelcome experience for her, but at least she didn't have any guards or other prisoners standing around to watch her shame. Every once in a while she would hear voices from somewhere down the corridor but they never came any closer.

Tessa knew Reilly must be losing his mind. Unbidden, a smile spread across her face—poor Reilly. He had seen the rough way she had been handled by the warriors. He was likely imagining broken bones and black eyes.

The jeans and T-shirt she had been wearing when they tossed her into a cell at the Enclave hadn't been much of a barrier between her skin and the cold metal of the slab they were calling a bunk. There weren't any sheets or a mattress, just solid steel to rest on. Her new, short-term home in a holding cell outside of the Council chambers was much the same, only colder.

Tessa had known when she decided to go all superhero that it wouldn't end well for her, and she had been correct. She had been informed by the warrior who'd led her to the van for transport to the Council Hall that she was being charged with treason against the vampire nation for the attempted murder of a Councilman and his son.

"Wow." That was all she had been able to say to the man's ridiculous statement of her supposed crimes. Well, if they were calling it attempted murder, at least she knew both Griffin and J. R. were still living. She had done what she set out to do and that was to save their lives. Unfortunately for her, the punishment for both of the crimes she was being accused of was immediate execution, and if that were the Council's intention, Tessa really wished they would get it over with. She was tired of her self-imposed life of lonely despair.

She had lived day to day, hiding her pain for the sake of her daughter. Some days had been harder than others, but she got through them, and her daughter had grown into a happy, well-adjusted young woman. Now that Danielle was twenty-one years old and a married woman, Tessa had no purpose in life. She spent her days helping out at Reilly's clinic and longing for the man who'd crushed her so many years ago. What kind of life was that really?

Her only hope for redemption was Griffin, and she honestly had no idea if he had been awake to see who had drugged him or if he had been in bed and drugged in his sleep. If the latter were the case, there would be no one who could testify to her innocence. Tessa refused to probe her psychic link with Griffin to verify his state of mind or well-being. So there she sat, clueless as to what her future, or lack thereof, would bring.

A door down the hall swung open but she didn't move from her position on the slab. Tessa remained curled in a ball, tucked in the corner to conserve her body heat. Two male voices rumbled from the room beyond.

"Kayden has been watching the house and grounds surreptitiously. The boy is really good at staying hidden, but I'm beginning to worry. It isn't like him to miss his daily report. It's been more than two days since his last call." Gage's raspy voice was full of concern.

"I will have a look around the grounds myself. If he's out there and he sees me, he will approach. If he isn't aware that I've been home, it's likely that he's simply still on guard," Griffin responded.

Oh God, no.

She couldn't deal with him. Not now. Just the sound of his voice made her hurt. She was tired, and after days of very little sleep and the stress of worrying and waiting, her defenses were not at their strongest. The men came closer and Tessa tried to make herself smaller. Maybe they would just pass by her. She avoided any situation that would bring her into contact with Griffin. Just listening to him speak made her want to cry. All her heart and soul wanted was for him to hold her, and she knew that if she asked him to, he would, but for how long? Not long enough to make up for time lost.

He would never leave his family, and for that she couldn't bring herself to blame him. She just wished he would stop trying to contact her. It made her nuts. She had to change her number because he would leave her messages, and would she just delete them? No. She would play them over and over again, wistfully listening to the sound of him begging for her attention. He would plead with her to speak to him, let him visit her, give him a chance. A chance for what, he never said.

Gage was speaking again. "I have a meeting with a female who lives outside of our society. She is an officer on the local human police force. She wanted to be a warrior but was denied because she is female." Gage paused a moment. "I have to tell you, Griffin. I think it is long past time we reconsidered that antiquated law. I know many strong women I would be proud to lead."

"That is something we can surely debate, but you know the old school will protest. I'm having a hell of a time fighting arranged marriages. Most vampires like things the way they are. But let's leave that for another day, my friend." There was an uncomfortable silence before Gage continued.

"Anyway, the female officer—her name is Candice Hughes—has concerns that a recent rash of missing persons may be related to our missing vamps. She believes there is a pattern wherein first the humans start disappearing, then the vamps. She wants to consult with us as a liaison of sorts. It's an interesting idea. We monitor human police radio traffic but if we had someone on the inside policing our own troublemakers, it would be easier. Normally, if one of our young gets out of hand, the police get a call, and this female would know what to look for."

They were just outside of her cell now but Tessa refused to turn and look at them.

"It's certainly worth looking into. If you think it will be a beneficial partnership, you will have my support," Griffin replied.

Tessa thought it was kind of funny that she was waiting for the end of her life and they were calmly discussing the ins and outs of vampire politics. *Assholes.*

———◆———

Griffin just wanted Gage to shut up and open the damn cell door. It had taken him several hours to convince the rest of the Council that he had been of sound mind and was well aware of who had attempted to take his son. Given his uncharacteristically unkempt appearance after spending a couple of days hiding in his office, it had taken a little extra convincing. He requested a closed session, which was highly irregular, but Griffin felt it was necessary to explain that the warriors who had been on duty at the gatehouse were the perpetrators. The Council didn't need public scrutiny on top of the threat of an attack from within. The Rogue had infiltrated their ranks, just as Soleil had tried to tell them.

But that was over now, and the Council as a whole, including himself, had decided to call Sarah to the carpet to explain her acts of perjury. The lies she'd told would have made them a party to executing an innocent person, no matter that she was human.

He turned his attention to Tessa, who seemed so small, curled up on the bunk. Griffin had a strong sense of déjà vu. He had visited Soleil in a similar situation. Until she turned around, the only physical difference between mother and daughter was the color of their hair. At present, the dark honey blond of Tessa's hair called to his fingers, daring him to stroke it.

Gage unlocked the door and swung it wide open. "Tessa, it is my great pleasure to inform you that all charges against you have been dropped. You are free to leave whenever you are ready. I would like to personally apologize for your imprisonment and also, as a friend of Griffin, I'd like to thank you for the risk you took to protect his family."

Tessa acknowledged his heartfelt statement with a nod.

Gage addressed Griffin, "I've got that meeting, so I'll head out." He then retreated down the corridor and out the door that connected with the Council chamber.

Griffin stood there like an idiot, not knowing what to say. How did you thank a person for all the things she had done for him and his family? How does a man apologize effectively for the deceitful actions of his mate? Tessa still hadn't moved an inch. She looked like an injured animal trying to hide from a predator. Tessa finally broke the tense silence but she didn't turn around.

"How is J. R.?" she asked. "I haven't had any visitors to give me news. I've been worrying about his reaction."

"He is doing well. You saved his life. I'll never be able to repay that debt."

Griffin could hear the tears in her voice. Giving in to his body's need to touch her, Griffin lifted her stiff body from the steel of the bunk and sat to deposit her on his lap. She didn't struggle, and nor did she relax when her head rested against his shoulder, so he began to stroke the honey gold of her hair. Her breath against the skin of his neck sent chills coursing over his body. The warm, slight weight of her petite body made him long for the past, when she was his to have and to hold. She began to tremble against him and he knew he wasn't the only one affected by their contact. The starch went out of her spine and she melted into his embrace.

"I'm so sorry, baby," he whispered against her forehead. "I'm sorry for everything you've been through. I wish I had been there for you and Soleil. I had no idea what Sarah was telling people until today. I know it doesn't correct the wrong done to you, but I am sorry it took me so long to get to you."

They sat there for a long moment while she allowed him to hold her. It felt so good after all the years of heartache to just be able to touch her, to smell the warm vanilla scent that had driven him crazy. The world felt right for the first time in many years. It was like all the missing puzzle pieces fell into place.

"I love you, Griffin." Tessa began to quietly sob.

Griffin's heart soared and ached all at once. He hadn't heard those words since the day he left her with their newborn baby, but the tone in her voice said it wasn't a good thing.

"I love you, too." He kissed her brow. "Can we go someplace and talk for a while? I can get a room somewhere and we can talk without interruption." He prayed she would say yes. Griffin knew if he got her alone they could come to some understanding about the future.

"Are we going to talk about you and me? Are we going to talk about being together as a family? Are you planning on getting a divorce? I know you're mated to Sarah, but I understand that you also gave her the honor of a legal human marriage for your human public image. Is that what you want to talk about?" She sounded calm but he could see the storm on the horizon. Tessa lifted her head to look him in the eye for the answer she plainly knew was coming.

"Baby, you know it's not that simple. I wish you would give me the chance to explain. When our people agree to an arranged marriage it is legal and binding. Our reputation as a family, as well as a fortune, is at stake. We contract agreements that link two families financially and socially for a lifetime. I'm not just Griffin Vaughn. I'm Councilman Griffin Vaughn, heir to the House of Vaughn, leader of an entire species of people. I have to live by the rules I expect our people to follow. I wish I knew how to make you understand my position."

Tessa seemed to take in this new information and swish it around in her brain for a minute. He resisted releasing her when she tried to pull away, until he heard footsteps rushing down the corridor. She got to her feet just before Doc Stevens burst into the cell. He wrapped his arms around Tessa in a manner that was entirely too familiar for a doctor-patient relationship. Griffin was no fool. He knew it was *Reilly* who had been kissing his mate just days before when he lost his temper and destroyed his office.

"I have been sick with worry." Doc kissed her temple, seeming not to even notice Griffin sitting there watching the exchange. "They were so rough with you when you were apprehended. I wanted to examine you for injures, but they said you weren't allowed visitors. Not even a damn doctor." He pulled back to examine her face and then swiftly went to his knees and attempted to lift her shirt. "The way they tackled you, I was concerned for broken ribs."

Tessa pushed her shirt down, but not before they got a look at her black-and-blue rib cage and hip.

"Reilly, could I have a few moments alone with Griffin? I promise to allow a full exam when we get back to the clinic." She smiled wanly at his concerned grimace. "Just give us a minute, okay?"

Reilly Stevens got back to his feet. He looked directly at Griffin when he answered her. "I will be waiting right down the hall to take you home." He kissed her temple again and walked away.

Griffin was ready to rip that pushy bastard apart. Tessa did not belong to him, and nor did he miss Reilly's taunt about taking her home. To *his* damn home. Griffin stood then and crowded Tessa. He wanted to get closer but he didn't believe she would welcome his touch right now.

"I love you so much," she admitted sadly, and he couldn't stop the smile that tugged at his lips. Hearing those words warmed the empty places in his heart. "I would have done anything for you. I suffered years of loneliness and fear. I raised our child alone. I hoped, I prayed, I begged, and I pleaded with you for years to hear me, to love me in return. You ignored me. I knew you could hear me. I guess that was easier for your binding financial agreements. Not to mention the embarrassment you have endured due to my humanity."

Griffin tried to interrupt but Tessa was on a roll. She put space between them and gave him a look of warning.

"I have often wondered if you wished that Danielle hadn't come back into your life."

"That is a cruel thing to say, Tessa. Whether you choose to believe it or not, I suffered when I lost you and our baby. I don't care how much drama it has caused. I want you both in my life—"

She cut him off. "Really? So what do you want from me, a fling on the side? Will you continue to treat me like the dirty little secret I've been since the day you met me? Will you put me up in a suite somewhere so you have easy access to your pet human?" she hissed.

"It wouldn't be like that again," he argued.

"Wouldn't it? What exactly did you want to get a room to talk about?" She arched an elegant eyebrow and waited for an answer.

Griffin felt sick. That was exactly what he was going to ask her for, minus the pet human part. He had always loved her, humanity and all. Tessa softened and suddenly her eyes filled with tears. He tried to hold her but she swatted his hands away.

"I have a chance at a real relationship and I intend to take it. Please don't approach me again with offers to be your whore. There is nothing left for us to talk about." She turned away, but Griffin grabbed her and pulled her back against his chest, his arms wrapped around her trim waist. The vanilla heat of her body swamped his senses. He loved her. It couldn't end this way. Tessa lifted one hand and stroked his arm soothingly. She began to speak softly.

"We all choose our own path in life and make our own mistakes. We hurt people or we help them, one way or the other, whether it's intentional or not. Eventually everything we do in life comes back to us, and we're confronted by our triumphs and our tragedies, our loved ones and the ones we lost. The hearts we injured along the way will always make the round and show up again. I prayed for so many years that you would hear me and come back. I would have forgiven anything, everything, to have you love me again." Tessa paused and lowered her head. "I hope you have enjoyed seeing me again, hurting me again, and destroying me, again. Because the next time you cross my path it will all be different. I still love you, Griffin," she whispered. Tears tracked down both her cheeks.

Relief continued to flood Griffin and he was finally able to breathe. If she still loved him, Griffin refused to believe it was over between them. As long as she still loved him, he had a chance.

Tessa continued. "I would have done anything for you. I would have died for you, Griffin. But I can't live for you anymore. I'm moving on with my life, blood bond be damned, the same way you have done. I have nothing left for you, Griffin Vaughn, my husband, my mate. You are *unforgiven*."

Eleven

Candice had been working with a Wrath special task force for a week. Her meeting with Gage Paris had gone far better than she had expected. Honestly, when she approached the warrior chief, she'd expected him to dismiss her out of hand solely because she was female. Then she would have told him to kiss her feminine and quite firm ass. What a pleasant surprise to find the leader of the warrior class to be more than willing to not only work with a female, but to actually listen to her opinions and take them into consideration.

The chief approved her request to shadow a Wrath team that was making frequent trips to the southern states because of organized and well-armed pockets of revolutionary-minded vampires who wanted to overthrow the human race. Idiots. They claimed to be tired of living in the shadow of their prey. The leaders were spouting bullshit with what sounded suspiciously like the same vampire supremacy drivel they heard from discontent vampires locally. In the same areas they found these troublemakers, there seemed to be a high rate of missing persons, mostly humans, but a few vampires, too.

The task force was on a mission to locate the cells of fanged terrorists and shut them down before they could cause enough trouble to reveal the vampire nation. Candice was going to be looking for connections between the missing humans and vamps in both areas while the task force members would work on tracing the pockets of discontent back to the Rogue.

Gage was convinced that the influence of the Rogue was further reaching than they had initially believed. The only way to prove or disprove his theory was to get the bad guys talking, find out where they got their ideas, and who was financing their operations. Most of the cells consisted of underprivileged vampires who were sick of scraping by in life, who were led by one or two well-organized ex-military types. The pattern was repeated over and over. A pocket of trouble would pop up and be reported to the nearest Enclave, and then they would attempt to track and apprehend the perps on their own. When the human and vampire missing person reports began to cause panic and threaten to expose the local vampire population, it was reported to the Wrath.

When the Wrath made the scene, it seemed as if the perps were always one step ahead of them. They tracked the perps to a home base that always contained a few heavily armed, but untrained, lackeys the warriors believed to be sacrificial lambs. They would fight to the death to defend their stronghold, but when the warriors breached their defenses, they would find nothing worth defending. They would always find provisions and accommodations for plenty of people but no perps to interrogate. It looked like the perps had forewarning and evacuated, leaving behind a few men to distract the warriors while they slipped farther away. They often found cages and sometimes they would find dead vamps and dead or dying humans. It was a nightmare.

A knock at her back door made Candice jump and pulled her from her morbid musings. She knew exactly whom she would find on the other side of the ruffled curtain covering the window on the kitchen door. Only one person ever found it necessary to make a sneaky rear-door entrance.

"Hi, Candy. Have you missed me?" Abel kissed her on the cheek when he slid past her and into the kitchen. He walked to the fridge and started pulling out the fixings for a sandwich. Well, hell.

There went her lunch for the rest of the week. She didn't mind. There had been many a night, when Abel was a teenager, that he would show up at her back door looking for food or a friend to talk to, but she drew the line when he attempted to drink straight from her milk container, snatching the carton and pouring him a glass before she responded.

"No, I can't say that I have missed having a sharp pain in my ass," she teased before she slid onto the stool next to him at the counter. There were crumbs and a trail of mustard running across the black granite surface. Abel leaned over and left a mustard-smeared kiss on her cheek.

"Come on, Candy. What would you do without a mooching criminal to brighten your day?" He chuckled and resumed devouring his first sandwich. She knew he would eat at least two.

When she really thought about his question, it made her heart heavy. She had no family. They had disowned her when she left the life of the socially elite to pursue a more fulfilling existence. Abel had been the only person she allowed close to her heart. What would she do if she didn't have his sporadic visits to look forward to? When she didn't come back at him with a cutting retort, Abel stopped eating.

"What's going on with you, Candy? You seem . . . sad. It's not a good look for you." Abel poked her in the side. "I know I'm just a sharp pain in the ass, but you can talk to me about anything."

<hr />

Abel had heard through the Shade grapevine that a vampire who chose to be a cop for the humans was going to be partnering with the Enclave to figure out the missing person problem and apprehend the perpetrators. He knew it had to be none other than his adoptive big sister, and he hated it. He had come to investigate and see if he could get her to talk about what information the Enclave already had on the subject. None of his contacts were high enough on the food chain to get any solid information from the Wrath. The Master charged him with getting the information by any means necessary. Abel knew the consequences of failing his mission—he and his mother would both pay dearly.

He knew it was underhanded to use her love for him to get information, but he had to do what he had to do, just like he had to in any other situation. Candy was the only person who had ever made him feel like he had a home and someone to turn to when things got tough. When he needed a shoulder to lean on or a meal that didn't involve tapping a vein, Candice had always been his girl. She'd stood between him and insanity more than once. Some of the things he'd done in his life for the sake of his mother had been horrific. So now he was trying to convince himself that this was nothing. It was just a little harmless information gathering, right? Candy wouldn't suffer for it at all either way.

Abel was doing his best to pretend this was a visit just like any other when Candice's behavior began to seem odd to him. She hadn't fussed at him for making a mess or made any comments about him eating her lunch provisions. She hadn't even smacked him in the head for trying to drink from the milk carton or for purposely getting mustard all over her when he swooped in to kiss her cheek. Something was wrong. He just hoped it was the stress of working and dealing with the Enclave and not anything more serious.

If nothing else, it was a good opening for him to ask her what she'd been up to. Abel decided to finish his sandwich before beginning the inquisition. It would seem odd to her if he didn't worry about his stomach first and the rest of the world last.

"What's going on with you, Candy? You seem . . . sad. It's not a good look for you." Abel poked her in the side. "I know I'm a sharp pain in the ass, but you can talk to me about anything." He held his breath, waiting for an answer, but Candy just stared off into the distance.

Abel pulled Candy off of her stool and dragged her into the living room, where he flopped onto her recliner and pulled her onto his lap. She snuggled into the comfort he offered, but ignored his question.

"You might as well spill it, Candy. I'm not leaving until you tell me what's wrong." He kissed the top of her head. Her silence had him worried. This was about more than just stress from work. She would have admitted to that and told him to mind his own business.

"I really hate it when you call me that." She humphed.

"I know." He smiled and waited.

"I'm lonely," she confessed. "Sometimes I miss having a big family and lots of friends. I was just thinking about the fact that you are my family and the only true friend I have." She snuggled a little closer, petting him like she had when he was much smaller and she would hold him in her lap, giving comfort when needed.

Damn. That made what he was doing so much harder. They were family, and he was pretty sure you weren't supposed to manipulate your family members, but for his mom he would do anything. He could take a beating and survive. His mom was human and fragile.

"I thought you hated other people. You only tolerate me so you have someone to beat on when you need to release your pent-up rage. Don't think I don't know you just keep me around for the sparring matches. It's not like you can really let loose on your weak little fellow officers," he joked, trying like hell to lighten the mood. She giggled.

"Well, that is about to change. So, watch out, kid. I have lowered myself to offering assistance to the Enclave. They need help with a few things."

Abel wanted to laugh. He knew how bad she had wanted to be a warrior, and working with the Enclave would be a dream come true for Candy. But he let her believe he had no idea she had approached them. It was good for her ego.

"I can't say I'm surprised. I knew those idiots would wise up and see what an asset you could be, once they pulled their heads out of their asses." He smirked.

She laughed out loud. "Yeah. It was just a matter of time."

Abel was quiet, trying to think of where to go from there. How was he going to get Candy talking? Candy broke the silence first.

"I met a guy, a really hot guy who acts like I don't exist. It pisses me off. The arrogant bastard just treats me like one of the guys."

Here was the real reason for her pouting. After he talked her through this, he could steer the conversation back to the important matter at hand.

"Really? Where'd you meet the asshole?"

"At the Enclave. They're allowing me to shadow a Wrath team that is working on the same thing I'm researching. He is one of the Wrath guards on that team. They're about to go on a field trip, so to speak, and I'm tagging along. I took some leave from the force to do this. Anyway, he's the low man on the totem pole, so he's been assigned the loathsome duty of helping me prepare and making sure I understand their procedures."

"I'm sorry, but I thought you wanted to be treated like one of the guys? I thought you hated that they thought a female couldn't perform the duties of a warrior?" he asked.

She leapt up off his lap and began to pace the hardwood floor. "I do want that, but not with *this* guy. I don't want him to see me as a soldier. I want him to look at me like a female. Damn it!" she shouted. "I'm hot! Men love redheads. Redheads are wild and sexy. I have to bludgeon the human guys to get away from them." She collapsed onto the couch. "I flirt and smile and give the jerk every chance to reciprocate, but he stays completely professional. I just don't get it. We are close to the same age. We have a lot in common since we both work in law enforcement. Yet, he ignores me."

"Aw, Candy. I think you should forget about this dude. He can't be worth it."

"But he is! He's smart and sexy. He used to be a surgeon, a combat surgeon even." She looked at him wide-eyed, as if that should impress him. It didn't. He knew exactly whom she was talking about. Greyson Drake. Abel was so tired of hearing about him. Oh, but this put a new twist on the situation. It was perfect. Candy wanted Captain America and Abel wanted his girlfriend. It was a win-win situation. Now he just had to push the right buttons. He could wait for the information he had come for. Now he would try to help Candy get some much-deserved happiness with a guy whom he suspected could handle her fiery temper.

"You know, it's too bad you never let a man get close to you, Candy. There is no need for you to be lonely. I'm sure if you didn't hide yourself away in the human population you would have a mate and a couple of kids by now. Hell, as old as you are, you might even have grandkids." Abel tried to keep it light. Candy just humphed at the crack about her age. He knew if he encouraged her to stay away from the warrior, like a rebellious teen, she would only strive to get closer.

"Now that you're working on the Enclave you'll have the chance to meet lots of guys who will appreciate a female with a need to protect others and serve the way they do. I bet you'll find Mr. Right by this time next year. Don't worry about that guy."

She said nothing for a while but he could see her fuming. She was not a quitter.

"I didn't understand his reason for ignoring me until today. It was almost lunchtime and the guys were splitting up. A few were going to find blood; the others wanted a burger. One of the guys said to Greyson—that's his name—'*I heard you have a lunch date. Are you going for burgers, or do you plan on using the time to tap that sweet ass?*'

"Greyson lost his mind. He obviously didn't think it was funny. He tackled his teammate to the ground and they rolled around throwing punches and cursing until Gage happened to pass by and broke it up. Of course he has a girlfriend. Why didn't I think of that? A man like that cannot be at a loss for female attention. Not only is he beautiful, strong, and intelligent, but he's loyal, too." She just shook her head. "He's the perfect male."

Abel was seething inside. After having Brandi reject him for Greyson, listening to Candy made him sick. He really couldn't compete. If he played fair, that is.

"The fight was just breaking up when this kid walks over. She's a cute little thing with short, dark curls, designer heels, and a shirt that didn't cover nearly enough skin. I'm wondering whose daughter had come to meet them for lunch. She runs over to Greyson and starts fussing over him. She wiped away the blood on his lip with a hankie from her little beaded purse and kissed his face. I couldn't believe it. This kid was even younger than you, Abel. And the twit has a man she can't possibly handle."

"Well then. If you're really that into the guy and you're going to be going on a field trip together, why don't you use that time to show him what a full-grown female with the heart of a warrior is like?"

———— • ————

Brandi was in the Council Hall library doing some research on Greyson's family name, starved for anything that would help her relate to her secretive lover. She had loved to come here and soak up the history and knowledge when she was in school. When her father had meetings or work at the Council Hall, Brandi would always beg to go with him. Sometimes she would hang out in the library all day. The warm, wood-toned panel walls, polished tables, and the smell of dust and paper always made Brandi feel at home. When she entered today, Brandi felt like a guest in the home of a stranger instead. She hadn't been here in ages and the rows of books that had been her friends didn't seem to recognize New Brandi.

She came hoping to find a family tree for the Drake family or maybe even some reference to Greyson himself, considering he was old enough to have been counted in the last several censuses. Vampires kept track of their population the same way humans did. She hadn't found anything yet, so she decided to head toward the back of the library where the census records were housed.

She had just turned the corner at the far end of the huge, quiet room when a pair of hands reached and snatched her right off her feet. She didn't even have time to scream before a large hand covered her mouth and she was forced against the wall. A hard body pressed into her back.

No. This couldn't be happening. Had Darren seen her first effort at self-defense when she tossed the fireball at him? Had he told the Rogue? There was no way the Rogue could get her in the Council Hall.

"Shhh . . . hush, Sparky. I won't hurt you," Abel whispered into her ear. Damn it! Was there anywhere he couldn't sneak into? Obviously the Rogue could get her in the Council Hall if his henchman had a back door key. He loosened his grip and let her feet touch the floor. As soon as his hand moved from her mouth she growled.

"You scared the shit out of me. What the hell do you think you're doing? How did you get in?"

He slapped his hand back over her mouth. "You need to lower your voice and calm down, or I will take you out of here whether you are willing or not. I would be killed if the Master found out I was here, and if I get apprehended, he will know. Do you understand?"

She nodded.

He moved his hand again and allowed her to turn in his arms. "Please come to the upper-level storage with me. It's private. Neither one of us will have to worry about being seen."

"I thought I asked you to go away and never come back." Brandi scowled up into his bottomless sable eyes. Damn, it was hard to stay angry when he looked so crestfallen.

"Yeah, well, I asked you to give me a chance and you didn't do that. And I haven't been back to your house so, technically speaking, I did as you asked."

"I'm not doing this with you. I told you I'm with . . ."

He slapped his hand over her mouth again. Brandi wasn't sure because the natural color of his eyes was very dark, but she suspected that his eyes had turned black with rage.

"Don't. Say. His. Name." He spoke slowly so she couldn't misunderstand. "I never want to hear that name on your lips again. It's an insult."

Okay. He had lost his mind. Brandi decided that going along with Abel's request for privacy was her best chance of not being abducted, because she was sure he had a shot of the Rogue's poison on him somewhere. If she didn't comply, in his current mood, he might force her. She wouldn't address his absurd demand that she not say the name of the man in her life. She just nodded until he moved his hand.

"I will go to the upper level with you."

Abel silently led the way, checking around every corner before proceeding. He opened a door in a far-flung corner of the library Brandi had never visited before. She was pretty sure she could scream her head off and still not be heard once the solid door was closed and locked. Not a very comforting thought.

A dim light shone on a desk in the left corner of the room, which looked more like a conference room or a study hall than a storage room. There was a large table consuming the center of the room and various desks spread out sporadically against the walls around the perimeter. The white walls and overhead fluorescent lighting fixtures made the room look much more utilitarian than the rest of the library.

"Okay. You have me here. What do you want, Abel?" She couldn't look at him. It would be too easy to sink into those soulful, dark eyes.

"First off, I was concerned because I was shot at on your property. I worried that you hadn't made it back to the house safely."

"I don't believe that. Not that you were shot at, because I'm sure the warriors on patrol would shoot first and ask questions later after what happened to my dad and brother, but that you didn't know if I was safe. I have the feeling you keep a close enough eye on me to know I was fine by the following day. So that's not the reason you're here."

He smirked at her and stalked slowly closer as she backed away. Before she knew it, he had corralled her into the back right corner, where a blanket was spread on the floor.

"If you think I'm going to let you screw me to keep you from taking me away from here, you have lost your mind!" She was angry and insulted. Before she could blink, he was on her, pinning her shoulders to the wall, glaring down at her with black eyes.

"Do you think I would try to take what you didn't freely offer me? I may be many things, Brandi, but a rapist isn't one of them," he growled.

"Why not? You kidnapped my sister. You broke into my house and the Council Hall. You threatened to take me if I didn't follow you. Why wouldn't I believe you would demand what you want in exchange for my freedom?" she hissed back at him.

Abel's expression melted from anger to defeat. He backed away and sank to the blanket on the floor before reaching under the nearest table to pull out a small cooler.

"I had planned to find a public place like a park or something to do this so you would feel more comfortable. You know, so you could scream for help if I scared you. I just wanted to see you. But I couldn't get you alone long enough to ask you to come on a picnic. It was stupid. I should know better." He ran his large hands through his dark, wavy hair. "You will never see me as anything other than the Master's minion. That is, after all, exactly what I am. And instead of talking to you, I acted like the animal I am and man-handled you. I'm sorry. I just . . . you make me crazy." He rose to his feet and walked to the door before turning to look at her with suspiciously wet eyes.

"Don't let the food go to waste." He paused. "Damn, this is hard. All I want to do is walk over there and wrap my arms around you." He turned away and cracked the door to be sure the area outside was clear. "I won't bother you again. I'm really sorry if I scared you, Sparky."

The reminder of the nickname he had given her was what did it. He was one of only three people that knew about her pyrokinetic power. He knew, but he had never told anyone. She bet the Rogue would reward him handsomely for that information, but he hadn't told.

"Wait. Abel, don't go. You just scared the shit out of me. You have to admit after the last couple of years I have good reason to be jumpy." He looked back at her, not convinced she really wanted him to stay. She wouldn't beg. She sat down on the gingham blanket—yes, he had actually found a red-and-white-checked blanket for their picnic—and she began to dig in the cooler.

"Let me do that," Abel said from just behind her. He moved so silently she hadn't heard him approach. He made them both paper plates of chicken salad, fruit, cheese, and crackers. He offered her a choice of diet or regular cola before settling in to devour his food. They ate in silence but he kept stealing furtive glances at her.

The food was delicious and she actually cleaned her plate, not something that happened often anymore. After the meal was finished and the cooler tucked away, Abel stretched out on the blanket like a contented cat. Brandi settled herself against the wall to watch him.

"Tell me about your mom," she said. His body stiffened. "Not the bad parts. I mean the stuff from when you were young, before the Rogue."

Abel relaxed and began to speak. His mom's name was Sheena. He loved the unique name, and as a kid he imagined one day his own daughter would have the same name. He told her about the smell of tart apples and summer rain that always reminded him of his mother. He spoke of days playing in the park with his mom and picnics with plain peanut butter sandwiches because he didn't like jelly. He recalled early memories of what life had been like for the son of a single mother.

Having always lived in a family of means, Brandi couldn't imagine what life would be like if you had to do without. He told the story of the great love his mother claimed to have for the father he didn't know. At some point his hand had come to rest on Brandi's bare foot, which lay on the blanket. He continued to tell her little snippets of memories he could recall from his life before the Rogue. He had been eight years old when they went to live under the Rogue's influence. Somehow, before he finished speaking, Brandi found herself resting her head on his arm.

They fell asleep like that, relaxing in the quiet support of someone who wanted you around, someone who wanted to hear your stories and tell you his or her own. She drifted off with the aroma of sun-dried laundry surrounding her.

Hours later, the sound of a phone vibrating brought them out of their sleep. She was wrapped in his arms with a leg resting over his hip. The position was so intimate and his body so warm, she forgot he was not the man for her. She forgot to be wary of his intentions, to fear his past and his future. He was looking at her like a gift he knew he couldn't keep. She felt cherished, wanted.

His scent pulled her in to him. He smelled delicious and warm, making her crave him like the purest blood. It was disorienting and thrilling. Her body felt overheated and hungry after hours spent resting in his arms, surrounded by him. Brandi kissed him. His lips were stiff and shocked at first, but he quickly relaxed into the kiss. She vaguely remembered that this wasn't their first kiss. They had kissed that night in his friend's guest bedroom. She'd made the first move that night, too.

Brandi's tongue teased the seam of Abel's lips until he allowed her entrance into the dark sweetness of his mouth. His taste was intoxicating and confusing. She needed to get closer, search deeper for the source of her need. The light from across the room cast a warm glow over their tangled bodies and the beauty of his face. His irises flashed to midnight, his face flushed with heat and need when his gaze roamed over her body wrapped around his. He met her stroke for stroke in a duel for supremacy she suspected he'd let her win. She knew he didn't want to scare her after his behavior earlier, preferring her to take the lead.

One hand twined through his hair to hold him right where she wanted him, the other roamed over his hard male form, from shoulders to waistband, exploring every inch of his washboard perfection while she reveled in the flavor and strength of him. Abel was as perfectly formed as any runner or swimmer would be. His long, lean muscles and narrow hips called to her. She wanted to taste it all. Feel his skin pressed against hers. He still didn't touch her, and she wanted him to, needed him to caress her body. Her hand lowered again to his waistband, pulling at the fastening. He tasted so good, felt so right.

His phone buzzed again. "Shit. Sparky, I have to get that."

The fog lifted slightly with his words. Then she remembered. This was wrong. She was wrong to want him. He wasn't her man. Shame and embarrassment had her running for the door before he could reach for his important call. It was likely a new assignment. Brandi wondered if she was just an assignment for him. When she raced out of the Council Hall and peeled out of the parking lot, she wondered if he would take her in if the Rogue demanded it. She knew he would do it for his mother. Or the memory of whom his mother had once been.

⎯⎯◆⎯⎯

Temptation was a bitch. Greyson and his team had just spent over a week in close quarters with a fiery redhead who'd made it very clear she wanted to try him on for size. The entire week he spent preparing Candice Hughes for the rigors of deployment with a Wrath team had been a test in patience for Greyson. She had flirted, smiled, and teased, but he had kept everything aboveboard.

Thankfully, once they were deployed, Candice was all business, but God almighty she was hot. It wasn't like Greyson was in need of sexual release. Brandi was a handful in bed. He had trained her well in the art of lovemaking, and what an eager student she had been. She knew how to build him up to towering heights of need. Brandi would pleasure him to near pain before she rocked his foundation to watch him crash at her feet. She had also learned to submit to his need for total domination when that was his inclination. His nymph could be a demanding temptress, a sweet little submissive, or an equal partner in pursuit of ecstasy.

So, no, he had no reason to stray, but he was also not a blind man. Candice had a body that had the guys on the team begging for mercy every night when she stripped down to her little boy shorts and tank top at lights out. Because she insisted on receiving no special treatment, Candice bedded down with the men, which had actually become a bit of a problem. The team seemed to be getting a little restless from lack of sleep, or, more likely, lack of release.

Candice was a magnificent woman. She could handle a weapon as well as any man, and hold her own in a fistfight. What she lacked in size and strength she made up for in tactical knowledge and street smarts. She had the whole package. Beauty. Strength. Intelligence. Confidence. And she was old enough to have earned those character traits the hard way. Greyson had to respect Candice. He could also admit to certain chemistry between them, but Candice just didn't compare to his Pixie.

No one had ever made him burn the way Brandi did. She was well muscled from years of athletic training, but there was a delicate femininity to her form that made his protective instincts flare to life. He loved the way she made him feel needed and missed her terribly when he was gone. No one had ever really needed him or clung to him trustingly like Brandi did.

Greyson knew the nymph would steal his heart the first time she smiled up at him from her sick bed, sleepy and kittenish. She had touched his face and told him what she thought of him with one word.

"Beautiful."

That moment would live in him forever.

"Greyson, may I have a private word with you?" Candice called to him.

He'd finished unpacking his gear from the mission they just completed after a tedious debriefing with Gage and a few other Wrath team leaders. All he wanted to do was go home and fall face-first onto his bed for about twelve hours of uninterrupted sleep.

"I'm kind of in a hurry. What's up?" He didn't want to be rude but his weary brain was beyond social niceties.

Candice's face fell a bit and he felt like an ass. He was assigned to be Candice's contact on the Enclave. If she had a problem or needed information, it was his job to provide it or find someone who could, thanks to his status as low man on the team. Babysitting, or in this case cop-sitting, was getting to be a real chore.

"What? Do you have a date at the mall or something?" was her snide retort.

"Excuse me? I'm sorry, Candice, but what in the hell are you talking about?"

"Nothing." She blushed all the way to her roots. "I didn't mean to snap. I'm just tired."

Candice was nervous when she stepped into his personal space and placed a small hand on his bicep. It was an odd look for the confident woman.

"I would like to take you out to dinner. Like a date." She blushed again. Greyson was dumbstruck.

"What do you think?" she asked hopefully.

"I'm sorry, but I have a girlfriend. I have to decline," he replied politely.

"Is she really your girlfriend? Or are you just dating? I can see why you keep her around, but if you're only dating, I don't see the problem. I mean, what could you possibly have in common with the kid? I don't even think her fangs are sharp yet." Candice blurted the insult and seemed to immediately regret it.

Greyson shook off her hand and walked away. He wouldn't stand there and listen to anybody try to tear his girl down. If Candice had been a man, Greyson would have laid her out on the pavement.

Twelve

Abel made a hasty retreat from the Council Hall library, leaving behind the blanket and cooler. Nate had called and interrupted what promised to be the hottest sex of his life. Brandi looked on the outside like a woman who would be content to let a man take the lead in bed, but that was a part of her fabricated image. She had been hot, controlling, and sexy as hell. Abel knew the scent of his human blood combined with her sleepy mind had contributed to her easy acquiescence to the needs of her body, but he didn't care. He had wanted her so badly for so long that he was willing to take all the help he could get. In those quiet moments of loving, the shifting in his chest that started the first time they faced off snapped, and everything fell into place. Brandi was meant to be his, no matter that he didn't deserve her. It just felt so right, like she was fixing all the rips and tears inside him. She felt the pull too. He would do his best to win her and let her decide the rest.

Brandi had all but melted into him. It was beyond sexy when she demanded control of their kiss by grabbing his hair and holding him in place for her possession. Her small, inquisitive hands had explored the plains of his chest and shoulders until his length throbbed with need and ached to be buried in the darkest, sweetest place on her curvy little body. She writhed and rubbed her heat against him but he never touched her. Afraid to startle her back to her senses, Abel let her do as she wished without interference. His eyes had crossed when Brandi began unfastening his jeans. That was when Nate's second call broke the spell clouding Brandi's mind. She took off but he couldn't chase her. He was late for his monthly visit that the Master allowed him to have with his mother. It wasn't a kindness, but the proof of life the Master knew was required to keep Abel in line. Every month he was given a mere few hours to have dinner and talk to his mom. Sometimes she would be perfectly lucid. Sometimes she would rant and rave at him for causing trouble. Sometimes she would just sit there and stare out the window as if he didn't exist. But, she always believed wholeheartedly in the imaginary love she shared with the Master. He was her everything, and Abel needed to behave and do as he was told to keep the Master happy because his behavior reflected on her.

Abel was well aware that his weak-minded human mother was deeply under the influence of mind control. She lived in a state of constant enthrallment and he feared what would happen to her fragile psyche if it were lifted and she realized how many years she'd spent in the dark.

He snuck in the rear entrance of the Nest and went to his room for a quick shower before heading to the Master's quarters. He was loath to wash the arousing aroma of his little flame from his skin, but Abel didn't want to take the chance the Master would catch it and find it interesting. He knocked on the heavy oak door and waited for permission to enter. His mother wasn't kept here at the Nest on a regular basis. She was hidden away so Abel didn't have a chance to break her out. She was brought in for their monthly visits only and updated on his recent behavior before he was allowed to see her. Fortunately, he hadn't done anything to raise the man's ire lately.

"Come," the deep male voice he had hated for years called out. When Abel entered, his mother was resting on the Master's lap, petting him and purring.

"Sheena, love, your son has come to visit." He let his fangs graze her neck in a blatant show of sexuality that turned Abel's stomach.

"Who? Send them away. I have missed you so much, Master. I need you," she moaned.

Oh, damn. This was going to be one of those visits. She would be angry with him for interrupting her playtime. Gross. Just gross.

"No, love, you want to see Abel, remember? You want to talk to him," he encouraged.

"Abel? My baby? Is he here?" Her head finally lifted to search the room for him. When their eyes met she seemed embarrassed and lucid for a moment. She leapt off her Master's lap and straightened her clothes. The Master laughed at her awkward behavior.

"Sweetheart, I have been waiting so long to see you. Where have you been?"

She crossed the short space between them to fold him into a motherly embrace. She was still as beautiful as she had been in his childhood. Her large, fathomless chocolate eyes looked up at him from a fine-boned, creamy white face. Her long, wavy hair was the same sable shade as his, cascading down to her hips and draping over his arms when he hugged her. She was tall and lean like him, nearly able to look him in the eye.

The Master gave her his blood to tie her to him, and that maintained her youth, but he never took her blood in order to complete the bond. It was the one-sided blood bond that had driven her to near madness. The man she called Master was not a faithful lover and she would know it, would feel it every time he took another into his bed.

"I'm sorry I was late, Mom. I was on duty," he lied.

"Oh. Okay, baby. I understand. You must do as the Master orders." She patted his cheek. She released him and went to the table that was always set for three, but the Master never stayed.

"The Master was kind enough to get the cake I requested. Your birthday will come before I see you again, darling."

The Master smirked at him from his seat. He would play the loving patriarch in front of Abel's mother. "Of course I did. We can't let the boy's birthday pass without recognition, can we?" He rose and went to kiss his half mate on the cheek. "Sheena, love, I have an important meeting to attend but I will return soon." Her hand fisted in the tablecloth, angry that he would never have a meal with his family. "You may spend the night with me." She beamed up at him. "It will be your reward for explaining to your son the role he must play in the coming strike."

The Master wrapped his hand around her neck and looked into Abel's eyes. It was a threat. He could snap her neck with ease. "You must make him understand his place at my side. Isn't that right, Sheena?" he purred and kissed her.

"Yes, Master. Abel will do his duty. He is a good boy."

———————◆———————

Tessa just couldn't seem to find her center. After so many years of loving and missing Griffin, it had been heaven to be in his arms, but now nothing she did would wash away the feel of his arms wrapped around her or his breath on her neck when he pleaded with her to understand his position. She did understand, but she couldn't give him what he wanted any more than he could fulfill her needs.

She had lived a half-life since she was twenty-four. The only good thing in her world had been her baby. It was time for her to live and try to love again. Tessa had a bone-deep need for affection that she couldn't ignore any longer. She was sure Griffin would be plenty affectionate if she let him, but all he could give her was a few hours here and there when nobody was looking, and a condo in the city, rent-free. She really wondered just how he planned to explain his sexcapades to his mate, who would surely feel it. Sarah had tried to have Tessa executed for saving the lives of her son and husband. God only knew what she'd do if Griffin had an actual relationship with Tessa.

But that was all over now. She had to look to the future. Tonight she would give in to her need for sensual touch and attempt to seduce Reilly. It wouldn't take much, because she knew he wanted her. He accepted her for who she was and was attracted to her. They had a certain chemistry that she was sure would burn brighter if she could stop thinking she was cheating on Griffin every time she kissed him. That was partly because every time they got close, her connection to Griffin would spark to life and Tessa would feel his hurt and anger. His pain was a living thing in her chest that haunted her at night. She supposed she should feel vindicated after all the years she'd spent living his sex life with his mate along with him, suffering a broken heart over and over, just to forgive him in the morning because she had to. Their bond demanded it. Tessa could never take pleasure in inflicting the kind of pain she had endured, but she would not let the bond stop her from living the life that she deserved.

She'd taken extra care with her beauty regimen and was sure every inch of her body was smooth and hair free. Her usual cotton nightgown was replaced by a pair of barely there panties. She was nervous as hell and she knew Griffin could feel it. He was buzzing around the back of her mind, looking for a crack in her armor, but she ignored the attempted intrusion.

Reilly had gone out on a house call and should be home at any time. When he came down the hall to his room, Tessa planned to invite him into the guest room he had put her up in since her injury. The butterflies in her stomach took flight when she heard the clinic's rear door open and shut before heavy footsteps made their way up the back stairs. She reached over and flicked off the light. This was going to be hard enough without her worrying about her body image. Maybe the lack of light would help her this first time. Griffin always loved having sex with the lights on so he could look at her body.

Damn!

She could not think of him right now. She needed to be in the moment with Reilly. As the footsteps came down the hall, Tessa took a moment to strengthen her mental defenses against her mate. They were solid and he was now strangely quiet. She was getting better at blocking him, thank God.

Her bedroom door was open and she stood in the darkness wondering why she had invested in the skimpy negligee. Then she remembered his excellent night vision. The hallway was pitch-dark and so was her room, but the veil of shadows gave her a measure of confidence.

When Reilly reached her door, he stopped to look at her. She knew his vision was just fine when a low growl crept out of the darkness. He could see her, but to her he was a towering dark form in her doorway.

"Come on in." Her voice cracked. Reilly said nothing, only stood staring down at her.

"I . . . um . . . I was hoping you would spend the night with me?" Damn it! Did that have to come out sounding like a question? It sounded more like a plea than an invitation. She was so pathetic.

He growled again. This was not looking promising. Embarrassment had Tessa floundering about for the words that would allow him to reject her without feeling bad about it. Reilly would never want to hurt her, and the last thing she wanted was a pity screw.

"I . . . I know you've had a long day, so it's alright if you just want to go on to bed." Tessa reached for the door to quietly push it closed. That way she could dissolve into a pathetic heap without an audience and he could walk away without the discomfort of knowing she was watching him go. Once the door was closed she pulled the negligee over her head and hung it on the back of the door before retrieving her standard cotton gown from the hook next to it. She tried to hold back the tears. If her own mate hadn't cared enough to come back for her, what had made her believe an attractive, single guy like Reilly would want her?

Before that thought was finished in her mind, the door flew open and a large shadow lunged for her. Startled, Tessa dropped her cotton gown and braced for impact. She was lifted off the ground and propelled across the room to be pressed against the far wall before she could blink. Damn, vampires were fast. She was still trying to catch her breath when strong, angry lips descended to claim hers.

Her lips were none too gently coaxed apart and her mouth was invaded by a marauding tongue. His flavor was dark and strangely familiar, sending elated shards of euphoria to her brain. Tessa was shocked and pleased. Reilly had such a docile personality that she feared he wouldn't be able to give her the touch of manhandling she enjoyed in her lovemaking.

She clutched his shoulders, and her palms burned at the contact. Her body tingled with insatiable desire. She needed this like she needed her next breath. Reilly continued to claim her mouth with luscious urgency while his hands manipulated her breasts. Her nipples burned when he pinched them just the way she liked. It felt so right. So good to be pinned to the wall with her legs wrapped around the hips of a man who wanted to possess her body.

That thought made her freeze. He could possess her body, but that was all she could ever give him. Even now with her body ablaze, begging to be taken, she was worried about Griffin. She was searching her shields for cracks in an attempt to protect him from the pain she would inflict on him. She suddenly felt selfish because she not only would hurt Griffin, but she would also only be able to give Reilly a small piece of herself. He would never take her heart. Even in bed she would always be thinking of Griffin. It wasn't fair. Tessa jerked her mouth away.

"Stop, Reilly. Stop," she panted. "I'm so sorry. I can't. I'm . . . I just can't."

Reilly's chest heaved while he struggled for control. Tessa dropped her legs but he didn't back away to release her. He lowered his mouth to her throat and nibbled. Chills shot over her body. He lapped at her neck from collarbone to earlobe and bit down while he rotated his hips, nestling his erection against the apex of her thighs and brushing maddeningly against her most sensitive spot. He moaned and sank his fangs into her flesh.

Oh God!

He continued to grind into her as a climactic tide of euphoria crashed over her mind. The bite of a vampire sent the most intense pleasure echoing around one's brain and doubling back over itself again and again, until the resulting completion threatened unconsciousness. Heat spread from her neck, causing every nerve to fire and every muscle to tense and strain for more. Tessa couldn't help searching out the friction she needed so badly. Moisture coated her thighs and she held on tight while he fed. She rode out the rough waves of ecstasy he provoked. It had been so, so long for her, and it felt so good. Tessa's touch-starved body basked in the glory of the contact. He was working on removing her wet panties while he licked at the bite on her neck to close the wound.

"Please. Stop. I can't," Tessa panted. "You have been so good to me and that felt so incredible, but I'm never going to be capable of giving you what you need, what you deserve."

He groaned and rotated his hips, causing shock waves to reverberate through her.

"Please put me down, Reilly. I'm leaving. It's time I go home," she pleaded, her heart in her throat, tears in her eyes. This would hurt Reilly, but he was worthy of so much more.

Tessa heard the guest room door creak slowly open. She couldn't see a thing in the darkened room and Reilly was absorbed in nibbling her collarbone. Her ears rang with sudden fear. What if the Rogue had come for her again? Would he hurt Reilly, take him too?

She pressed her mouth against his ear and whispered, hoping the intruder couldn't hear her, "Someone just opened the door." He stopped instantly and pulled back just as the light flicked on. Tessa stared into the deep blue eyes of the man she still loved and her heart sped even faster. He'd been kissing her, holding her, making her come. The shock of seeing him there in Reilly's home quickly cooled her heated blood. Everything she'd said and done in the last few moments replayed in her mind and brought color to her cheeks. Griffin held her to the wall, his stiff length pressed into her softness and one hand on her breast. He stayed in that position, shielding her nudity. Tessa looked over Griffin's shoulder and found Reilly standing in the doorway looking very angry.

"Walk away, Stevens," Griffin commanded.

Reilly ignored Griffin and spoke to Tessa. "You'll forgive me for eavesdropping in my own home, since it was actually me you thought you were speaking to. I can't imagine how difficult losing your mate has been for you, honey, but I want to be the man who takes away your pain."

"She hasn't lost me. I'm right here. Now. Go. Away." Griffin snarled each word. Reilly continued to ignore him and a knot tightened in Tessa's belly. Reilly was completely sincere. He really wanted to be with her. She was speechless.

"What if I changed you, Tessa? Or what if we bonded? What then?" Reilly asked seriously.

Griffin hissed and set her on her feet, but he pushed her back into the corner behind him, shielding her body when she attempted to get away.

Reilly growled at him. "Let her go, Griffin. You are my friend and I'd like to keep it that way."

"Get out, Stevens!"

"Do you want me to leave, Tessa?" Reilly stepped farther into the room.

"No," she answered. Griffin growled again.

"Tessa, honey, I know this isn't the best time to talk about this, but I think I'm in love with you. I know you care for me too. We could have a good life together, even if you want to remain as you are. I would never leave you or forsake you for anyone else." He eyed Griffin accusingly. "You don't intimidate me, Councilman. So you can drop the caveman routine," Reilly calmly told the vibrating Griffin.

Tessa was still trapped in the corner but she was able to peek around Griffin's arm to look at Reilly when he spoke to her. "Reilly, I just can't sentence you to a life like that. You need a woman who still has a heart to give you."

"I would bond with you, Tessa. We know it can work because Griffin did it. It would loosen if not break his hold on you. It will be your choice to be turned or not. I want to love you, Tessa. I want to be your husband and your friend. Please consider it. I will treat you like the angel you are until the end of time. Please, honey, just think about it."

"I will," she whispered.

"Over my dead and rotting corpse, Stevens!" Griffin interjected.

"That can be arranged," Reilly snarled. Tessa had never seen this aggressive side of Reilly. It was sexy as hell.

"Are you challenging me?" Griffin's tone sounded as if he relished the chance to fight.

"If that's what it takes to get you away from my girl."

"Your girl?" Griffin roared.

"That's right. She's my girl. She hasn't been your mate for years. You left her to die, twice. Now she belongs to a man who will give her what she needs." He smirked at Griffin. "*Everything* she needs."

In a couple of long strides Griffin was in Reilly's face, but Reilly didn't budge.

"If you ever touch her again . . ."

"What will you do? Will you sneak into my home and impersonate me? Will you force yourself on a woman who has repeatedly denied you?" Reilly hissed coolly, disgust dripping from every word.

"She is my mate! Mine! I love her!" Griffin was losing his shit, big-time.

Reilly remained calm in the face of this snarling madman.

"You don't love her enough to be with her. You never did." Reilly looked Tessa in the eye while she struggled into a pair of pants.

"You don't love her as much as I do, Griffin."

Oh shit!

Tessa tried to get around Griffin and get between them, but it was too late. The two men flew at each other.

<hr/>

Brandi shuffled around Greyson's kitchen, silently hunting up the ingredients for a vinaigrette to go with the salad she had just finished preparing for their lunch. Every once in a while she would catch Greyson eyeing her suspiciously from the stove where he was expertly cooking them both a steak that could feed a small village. As usual, she would eat about a quarter of her steak and he would polish it off for her. Brandi knew he wondered about her lack of conversation, but, really, what else was there for her to say? She had spent the last two days in his home trying to talk to him about his life, trying to figure out what made him the man he was, to no avail.

Greyson was about to head out on another mission down south. That was the only detail she could get out of him. She tried to accept his assurance that it was a confidential matter he wasn't permitted to discuss, but she knew there was more to it than that. She had become friends with several women on the Enclave and they always knew where their men were going and had vague details of their missions. Brandi was always surprised at how much Karrie knew about the comings and goings of her father, who was a Wrath leader, and her two older brothers, who were both Wrath guards, like Greyson.

Greyson refused to talk to her about anything to do with his work or his past. She knew that he came from an Enclave in California, but she didn't know where he was born or anything about his family. She knew he had gone to medical school and had become a trauma surgeon, serving in Vietnam, only because of the work he had done on her after she had been shot. He hadn't even told her that tidbit. Greyson had confided it to her father, who relayed it to her in passing conversation. Griffin had a great respect for Greyson, partly because he had saved Brandi's life and partly because he had volunteered to use his knowledge in service of others. Greyson continued to use the combat skills he had learned in the US military, and since then as a warrior, to serve his people. Brandi suspected that was the only reason her father had accepted her relationship with a man so much older than herself. Greyson had around thirty years on her father, but they both looked to be about in their late twenties. That was how vampire genetics worked. Once you hit your midtwenties, the aging process slowed down to a crawl. If they took care of their bodies, they could keep their youthful appearance for a few hundred years before age began to creep up.

Brandi assumed that the fifty-some-year age difference between them was the source of most of the problem. Greyson was either trying to protect her from the ugliness of life, or he just didn't think a person her age could relate to the life he had lived. It really was unfair considering Greyson worked side by side with men who weren't more than five to ten years her senior. She had to find a way to break through the barrier Greyson had built between them. What she really needed was to find a way to erase Abel from her memory. When she and Abel were together, they talked. He shared things with her that Brandi was sure he had never told another living soul. He made her feel trusted and wanted for more than just her body. The fact that she had this secret from Greyson was eating at her and she wondered what secrets Greyson was keeping from her. Who was he confiding in, if not her?

Every time she tried to have a serious conversion with Greyson, he would distract her with sex. They had a relationship of convenience, in her opinion. They were nothing but available, warm bodies, ready to use each other for sex, but never really letting the other get too close.

"If you don't want a real relationship, tell me now," Brandi heard herself say through the fog of her thoughts. She paced to the other end of the kitchen.

Her plan had been to spend the day, before he left for God only knew how long, trying to get closer to Greyson. They needed to bond on more than a physical level, but he wouldn't give an inch. Just like always, Greyson held himself away from her. It did nothing but reinforce her belief that he saw her as nothing more than a kid, good for nothing but a piece of ass. Greyson froze and turned to look at her in confusion.

"Where exactly did that come from, Pixie?"

"It came from your don't-give-a-shit attitude. You have no interest in my life and refuse to tell me anything about yours. It comes from the feeling that our 'relationship' is nothing more than a sexual outlet for a man who's too busy to put any effort into finding someone he really wants to be with!" Brandi began her unrehearsed and completely unthinking speech calmly and ended it yelling.

While Brandi was getting louder and louder, Greyson seemed to be growing, his posture straightening and his broad chest expanding with his anger. He put his tongs down and turned off the flame under his pan. He turned and took a few aggressive steps toward her before he stopped. Greyson stood with his legs spread in a defensive stance, his arms crossed over his broad chest, and his normally jewel-green eyes glistening an obsidian black. He was pissed. Brandi was sure he had actually gotten bigger, and she could well imagine the fear he must inspire in the enemies of the vampire nation. But she refused to back down or say anything to placate him. They would have this out today, before he left town again.

"I'm not a child in need of your protection, Greyson. I'm a woman in need of a relationship built on a foundation sturdier than just sexual attraction."

The breath froze in Brandi's lungs while she waited for Greyson to reply. She cared deeply for him but it wasn't enough. It certainly hadn't been enough to keep Abel from taking up residence in an unknown corner of her heart. A corner that seemed to be reserved for people who could get her killed, or worse, disowned from the family she loved. They might be crazy, but they were her family and she loved them all. Greyson needed to help her pull Abel out of that corner and banish him . . . she needed him to give her just a fraction of himself. It was sad that she'd uncovered more about Abel, the real Abel, in the few times they'd been together than she had learned about Greyson in the months they had spent together. If Greyson wouldn't let her love him, if he wouldn't love her back, they were doomed. It was over before it could start.

Finally Greyson came to life, crossing the room to stand over her. They faced off like enemies, but all she wanted was to wrap her arms around his waist and hold him, clinging to his strength until he understood how badly she wanted to be with him.

"I treat you like a child when you behave like one, Brandi."

Greyson spoke in a calm tone that belied the tension in his body and the black of his angry eyes. The fact that he had called her Brandi instead of Pixie or Nymph was also telling. Brandi felt as if Greyson had slapped her with his harsh statement. He thought she was acting like a child?

"It's just like a child to expect to be given what you aren't willing to return. Our relationship is purely sexual because that's the only time you're ever honest with me."

She was outraged. "I have never lied—"

Greyson cut her off. "Haven't you, though? I have no idea who you are, Brandi. The only time I ever get a glimpse of the strong woman lurking behind the insecure mask you wear every day is when we are making love." Greyson looked deeply into her eyes. Brandi tried to talk over him but he shushed her.

"You said your piece without me interrupting. Now you will act like an adult and listen to me," he snapped.

Brandi sputtered for a moment before swallowing her protest.

"You want me to confide all my deep, dark secrets? You want to know how I came to be the man standing before you? I'm sorry but I can't give that much trust to a woman who hasn't earned it, a woman who doesn't trust me enough to let me see who she really is inside." Greyson turned and strode a few paces away from her before returning to pluck at the strap of her designer tank top. It had cost more than one should spend on an entire outfit including the shoes.

"You think I don't know this is a costume?" He looked down at the bejeweled peep-toe pumps that adorned her perfectly pedicured feet. The bubblegum-pink polish on her toes stared back up at her in accusation.

"I spent quite a bit of time in your home when I was caring for you. I saw the pictures in the family room and in your father's office. I saw all the trophies you won for every sport imaginable. I read the diplomas and awards of honor and excellence hanging on the walls." Greyson paused to touch her cheek and once again search her eyes. Brandi was stunned to silence. She couldn't have argued with him if she had wanted to.

"That is the woman I was looking forward to getting to know. I haven't seen her since the day you left your sickbed. Do you think I haven't heard people talk about how much you've changed? Your old friends wonder why you've forsaken them, and your new friends are glad you finally stepped out into society because trying to be friends with your sister was too much damn work. Everyone wants to be associated with the mighty House of Vaughn, even if it is only through the lowly imitation of the legend that is Samantha Vaughn." He shook his head as if ashamed of her.

"You see, people don't mind talking in front of me because they believe I'm just another warrior there to protect the best and brightest. Why else would you lower yourself to being in my presence? But you never really made it known to your society circle that we are together, did you, Brandi?" Greyson spoke quietly.

Brandi's eyes burned with unshed tears. Greyson's words, bouncing around in her head, continued to sting her. She had believed that people really liked New Brandi. She had believed that she had finally stepped out of Sam's shadow. Greyson must have seen the pain in her posture and continually blinking eyes. She was trying to hold back the tide. His eyes had bled back to a beautiful emerald. He looked sad, disheartened. He seemed to deflate and his tone became gentle and pleading.

"I haven't shared myself with you because we haven't even been introduced yet. I've been waiting for you, hoping that one day soon you would trust me enough to let me in. I know you're in there somewhere, hiding from the world, but I don't know why. I need you to uphold your end of this relationship because I refuse to carry it for both of us. Until you grow up and learn to love yourself, to not be a slave to what you think others expect of you, I can't give you more than we have now. I need a female who wants to be my equal partner, not a debutante, not a girl who plays dress-up every day of her life." Greyson held her by the shoulders. His eyes beseeched Brandi to see the truth of his words, to understand his point of view, and she did.

Brandi just stared up at him. All this time she had believed he was holding back because he didn't want anything serious with one so young. In actuality, it hadn't been her age but her own false behavior that had held him away from her. She needed time to think, time to regroup. The piteous expression on Greyson's face was more than she could handle. She refused to stand before him and cry like the little girl he accused her of being. Without another word, Brandi turned to leave, picking up her purse on the way to the door.

"Don't go, Pixie. Please stay and we can work this out like adults," Greyson called to her.

It was another slap whether he'd intended it to be or not. He thought she was running like a frightened child. Maybe she was.

Thirteen

That unfaithful bastard!" Sarah fumed.

Did Griffin really think all of his recent mental construction would shield his infidelity? He could build all the walls he liked, but nothing would hide his uncontrolled lust for that filthy, home-wrecking human slut! Sarah had refused to sleep with him until he purged his unfortunate and embarrassing past from their lives, but that did not give him permission to go elsewhere. It was a punishment Griffin needed to suffer through in order to teach him to make the right decisions, but it didn't seem to affect him at all.

It made her sick knowing she had birthed the children of a male who had lain down with humans before her. Apparently very recently before her, given the closeness of his children's ages. She had known when they bonded he didn't want her, and nor did she want him. Being the male of the species, he was allowed to wander the streets and live as he wished. He had hunted and screwed to his heart's content while she was hidden away from the world waiting for him to decide he'd sown enough wild oats. She was home-schooled and was only allowed to feed on the donors her family provided because she was being preserved for the future Council-man, the only son of the mighty Lloyd and Adele Vaughn. Sarah had been raised from birth to be his perfect mate.

By the time Griffin finally came to claim her, Sarah was twenty-two and she hated him. But that was all supposed to change after the bonding. They would bond and all would be right in the world. He would forget all the other women before her and she would forgive him for dragging his feet. It hadn't worked out that way. Their bond had always been shaky at best, but they got along and the resentment did fade. He took excellent care of her and always made her feel loved, but it wasn't enough. There was always a shadow in the back of his mind, a place she couldn't reach that he guarded and somehow cherished.

Now, over twenty years later, he had the nerve to flaunt his past in public and degrade the life they had built together. Did he believe she would stand by while he made a mockery of her family? Doing her best to remain calm and not give away her knowledge of his whoring, Sarah made a phone call. Her new friend would help her teach Griffin a few lessons. He answered on the second ring.

"Well, hello, Mrs. Vaughn. To what do I owe this unexpected pleasure?" His smooth baritone voice made her shiver. It was a shame she hadn't been a few years older. Life might have been different for both of them if he had been her mate. She knew the identity of the elusive Rogue after physically running into him the night Griffin revealed his bastard child to the world. She couldn't endure the public slap in the face when Griffin informed her at the Gala that he had a child he would be introducing to all present, whether she liked it or not. So she'd come face-to-face with the Rogue and his minions when she made her way to the rear of the building to fetch her own vehicle. The valet was nowhere to be found. But no one would believe her if she confessed, and the Rogue knew that.

"I did not appreciate the attack on my family. My son was nearly killed."

"I told you I would do what I had to do to get what I want, darling. If you help me toward my goals, it will benefit us both, don't you think? The last time you fed me information it nearly worked, didn't it? Too bad your daughter got in the way. That's the problem with girls today. They have no discipline, no morals, and no fear of their parents."

He had a lot of nerve to speak of morals. Sarah gritted her teeth. It was people like him who would have the females in their society raised just the way she had been. No way would she watch her daughters suffer as she had for men they didn't want, men who didn't want them.

"That was indeed unfortunate for my family. Thankfully she is fully recovered. Now to the point, I have information to share. I am willing to trade it for the safety of my children."

"You only care for your children's safety? You don't wish to protect your loving mate?" He chuckled, taunting her.

"Do we have a deal or not?" she pressed.

"That depends of the quality of your facts and the outcome. If it's worth the lives of your brats, I will leave them be. None of them are of any use to me except as bargaining chips."

"That's not a fair trade." She could tell him what she knew and still lose her children because of Griffin and his filthy bastard.

"Well, what would I know about being fair?"

———•———

Candice looked up into the darkest, most breathtaking green eyes and waited for a response. He said nothing for a long time, maintaining the same cool, aloof expression he had since she'd let her mouth run away from her and insulted Greyson's playmate. Since then he had been very professional and didn't hesitate to provide assistance with anything Candice needed, but that was it. It was almost as if his personality had been surgically removed.

Candice couldn't apologize for what she'd said to Greyson, because frankly she wasn't sorry. If she had it to do again maybe she would have held her tongue in an effort to get closer to Greyson before giving her opinion on his relationship with a neophyte.

"Come on, Greyson. Can't we just start over? I realize that I insulted you, and that wasn't my intention. I hate this tension between us. We are going to be working closely together for a while and I'd hate for every moment to be uncomfortable because I put my foot in my mouth."

There. That was as close as she would ever get to an apology. Some of the steel seemed to melt out of Greyson's spine and he looked off into the distance, contemplating her request for a do-over.

"I get it that you're not attracted to me. We were becoming friends before. That's all I'm asking for, just a chance to go back to where we were."

Greyson shook his head and went back to stowing his gear in the truck. They would be deploying in just over an hour and it was going to be damned miserable if this was his attitude. Fine then. She'd be damned if she would beg any man for anything. If he wanted to be an ass, that was his prerogative. Before she made it to the door, he spoke up. "It's not that I'm not attracted to you, Candice. I sometimes find myself a little too interested. I don't want you to think I declined your invitation because you're lacking in any way, because trust me, you're not. The issue is that I'm in an exclusive relationship and I want to keep it that way. End of story. I hope you can respect that and let it go."

"As much as I may hate it at the moment, I do respect the fact that you're a loyal man and I think that your . . ." *Hold your tongue. Do not say anything like tart, or playmate, or arm candy, or infant.* " . . . girlfriend is a lucky lady. I'll go so you can get this wrapped up."

"Don't go too far. We roll in an hour." His tone was decidedly friendlier.

Candice just nodded and went to fetch her duffel and gear from her SUV.

———•———

Abel was hiding in the backseat of Candice's truck. He had purposely spent the night before at her place. He knew from a previous
conversation that she would be leaving on a *field trip* with the Wrath
in the morning. He needed to get into the Enclave and she was his
ticket.

He'd enjoyed his evening with his adoptive big sister because
he feared it would be his last. If she ever found out that he had used
her this way, Candice would never forgive him. It would be the end
of the only real loving relationship of his life.

Abel had quizzed her the night before, hoping to hear that she
and the warrior were getting closer. "So, tell me about your Wrath
crush. Have you made any headway with him yet?"

Abel knew damn well Brandi was still seeing Malibu Ken. He
had followed her to the Enclave a couple of days ago and she never
came back out. According to Abel's contact, Greyson had some time
off before this trip. Abel's stomach turned. Ever since he had tasted
the sweet perfection of Brandi's kisses, it tore him apart to think of
her sharing them with someone else. He wanted them to be his
kisses.

"No." She turned away to hide her dejection. "I actually
screwed up good. After the last trip I asked him for a date. He
turned me down because he has a girlfriend. The word *girl* is the
key in that sentence. I kind of implied that she was just a kid, so it
really didn't matter to me because he is surely just with her to get
in her pants anyway."

Abel winced. If anyone had talked about Brandi like that in his
presence, he would've made sure it never happened again. Just pushing Candice at Greyson would not be enough to bring the big man
around. Further intervention would be needed.

"Alright. That was bad. Do you want my advice?" he asked.

"It can't hurt. He only speaks to me if he absolutely has to now."
She reached into the fridge and came back with a quart of Chocolate Overload and two spoons.

"I think you should apologize . . ."

She raised an imperious eyebrow.

"Apologize to the best of your ability. You don't have to actually
be sorry, but if you want to get back into his good graces, you have
to start somewhere."

She shrugged and dug into her chocolate therapy.

"Once you are on speaking terms, you can do what I told you
before and show him what a real woman can provide. Act like you're
just being friendly and include the whole team in your conversa-
tions so he doesn't feel like you're cornering him until he's ready to
relax around you again. Do they go out for drinks after shift change
the way cops do?"

She nodded. "Sometimes."

"I'm not suggesting you need it or anything, but maybe if you
all go out as a group and you find him something a little tipsy to
suck on, it would loosen up his strictly loyal moral code. I bet just
one kiss from you and he would forget that girl's name. It's just a
thought. I personally wouldn't continue wasting my time on the
bonehead."

Candice humphed and dug around the ice cream container.
"I've actually thought of seeing if he'd loosen up in a more social
setting. I swear there is some definite chemistry between us. He just
won't give in to it. I was thinking if I could get him out on the dance
floor his body would take over for his brain. It just seems a little
desperate to me. I'm out of my depth here. I've never had to pursue
a male before. It sucks. I really like him a lot."

Abel pulled her to him and crushed her in a bear hug. Then they
played a few hands of gin rummy before turning in for the night.
During the game, Candice had confessed to having trouble sleeping

while she was on assignment. Being in close proximity to her crush while he slept shirtless in a pair of boxers had her mind spinning in circles and her body aching. She feared the lack of rest would slow her reaction times and leave the team at risk. So Abel gave her the small vial of Hypno he kept in his backpack, with instruction to use only one single drop and no more in whatever she was drinking before bed. It would guarantee her a solid six to eight hours of uninterrupted sleep. He knew. He used it from time to time when the guilt of carrying out his missions wouldn't let him sleep.

When she questioned him, Abel explained that his doctor had found an all-natural formula for anxiety relief in humans that acted as a good sleep aid for vamps. Candice was aware of Abel's long history of nightmares and insomnia. She seemed to buy his story and accepted the *medication*. He didn't want her making mistakes in the field and getting her head blown off simply because she was exhausted.

In the morning after Abel said his good-byes, he hopped onto his bike and drove around the corner. Sneaking back with the spare key he'd lifted from the key rack by the front door, he climbed into the floor of the backseat of her SUV and was thankful Candice owned a larger vehicle. He pulled the blanket from her emergency kit and covered up with it. Candice loaded up her things in the rear of the truck and drove to the Enclave, never checking the backseat for intruders. She unknowingly smuggled him into the center of the warrior population. He hated the things he had to do, but in the end he had no choice when it came to the Master's demands.

———◆———

After riding around for hours, Brandi parked and went to see the only person she believed might understand her. The fight with Greyson had rocked her. She had been so sure New Brandi was the girl Greyson would want and equally sure he had no idea she had ever been any other way. Brandi had been certain all her new friends truly liked her and enjoyed the company of her new persona. She was wrong. Brandi knew Greyson would never lie to her. He might not tell her everything she wanted to know, but he wouldn't lie.

She also had not made the conscious decision to leave Greyson out of her social circle, but she had. He would never be accepted in her circle because of his low breed status as a warrior. What a snob she had become if taking a date to an event with her and refusing to introduce him to her friends had become acceptable. They actually believed him to be a bodyguard. And why not? She had never said otherwise. It was amazing Greyson had stayed with her this long. He was a strong, proud man and she had relegated him to being her babysitter instead of her lover in public. She needed help sorting all this out.

Brandi wanted to talk to Dani about her man troubles, but just before she entered the building that housed the downtown condo Dani and Chase shared, Brandi had a horrible realization. She couldn't talk to her half sister about Greyson without thinking about Abel. As much as Dani strove to control her telepathic power, she would surely pick up more than Brandi could safely tell her. Dani had told her several times that people tend to broadcast their thoughts and feelings when they're under stress. Her half sister would be crushed if she knew Brandi was involved with Abel, the man who'd helped ruin her bonding ceremony.

Brandi beat a hasty retreat back to her car to find a tall, thin female in jeans, ballet flats, and a dark hood pulled over her head leaning against her hood. Brandi immediately went on the defensive. She felt relatively safe on the bustling city streets, but she also felt safe at home, and that was where her brother and father were attacked. The thought of her baby brother being snatched from his bed while the rest of the family slept just down the hall still made her blood boil.

Brandi stopped on the curb with the car between her and the stranger. "Can I help you?" she asked.

The female turned around and the shock nearly felled Brandi. Samantha pushed the hood off her head and glared down at her twin. It was impossible. She hadn't seen her sister like this since they were kids, not even when Samantha was sick. Her clothing alone made her look like a stranger. Her platinum hair was pulled back in a messy knot. Her face was scrubbed clean of makeup but just as beautiful as ever in spite of the dark circles under her eyes. Her scowl was so fierce it pulled wrinkles into her forehead. Sam must have been really upset to allow her face to show expression. She rarely ever smiled, in an effort to avoid laugh lines.

"Yes, you can help me," she snapped at Brandi. "We need to do something about Mom, and J. R. is a mess. Dad buries himself in his office if he comes home at all, and you haven't been there in days."

"What's wrong with J. R.?" Brandi's heart skipped. She had worried about his experiences over the last year or so affecting him adversely, but when she tried to talk to him, he just gave her a half smile and said, *I'm good,* in his best *Hey man, I'm not a baby* tone.

"He's having nightmares again. He refuses to sleep in his own room so you never know where you will find him. He could be in the hall bathroom sleeping in the tub or in the coat closet in the family room. This morning when I went to breakfast, I fell over a pile of tablecloths. When I opened the sideboard doors I found him curled up in there. He had emptied the shelves and removed them to make room for a sleeping bag and a camping light. I don't know if you have noticed, but at eleven years old, J. R. is on his way to being as big as Dad. It was not a comfortable fit in that cabinet."

She took a deep breath and turned her face away, tears glistening in the warm brown eyes she had inherited from their mother.

"He's terrified, Brandi." She sniffed and stepped up onto the sidewalk. "He doesn't believe we can protect him anymore, and who can blame him?" Sam shook her head. "Don't even get me started on Mom. She is so self-absorbed. She's so focused on the *shame* Dad has brought on the family and her, especially as his mate—*Oh, woe is me*—that she hasn't even noticed anything is wrong with J. R." Sam imitated their mother perfectly. It was actually kind of creepy.

Okay. This was all bad news but something else was happening here. Nothing she said explained Sam's appearance. Not that anything was wrong with how Sam looked. To the contrary, as always Sam was beautiful, but she had the look of your average fresh-faced college student. If there was anything Sam never wanted to be, it was average.

Brandi took the chance of getting her eyes scratched out, stepping close to her twin and wrapping her arms around her in a tight hug. Sam was a bit shocked and her face showed it.

"What's going on with you, Sam? You alright?"

"I . . . it's nothing I can't handle. I'm just going through some changes." Sam wriggled out of the embrace and looked down at Brandi, scowl once again in place. "I'm not good at dealing with emotional bullshit, so you need to get your ass home and help me out. I am not the best person to be counseling a preteen male. If our parents are going to be slackers, we have to step in and look after our brother."

It was amazing. Sam had never shown anything more than mild interest in J. R. when he was a baby and as he grew into a rambunctious child. Sam treated him like an annoyance she was forced to bear because selling children was illegal.

"I'll be home later," Brandi promised.

"Don't make me hunt you down again," Sam growled and walked away.

As Brandi hopped into her car she wondered exactly how Sam had "hunted her down."

Needing some time to herself before heading home to help Sam, she decided to drive out to a piece of property owned by her father outside of town. It was partially wooded and very private. It was the spot she always met with Doc Stevens to work on controlling her fire. Maybe if she let it fly for a while it would help clear her head.

<hr />

Fear that Griffin or Reilly had found her had made Tessa jump when the rap came at the door to her suite. After the altercation at Reilly's house, she had packed her things and left after making a last-minute call. The men were both bloody and snarling like wild animals with black eyes and fangs by the time they tired of beating each other. Griffin's presence in her mind and Reilly's proclamation of love were too much. She had to get away.

She crept toward the door and peeked through the peephole to see the top of her friend's head.

"It's only me. They haven't tracked you down, yet," Debbie Deidrick teased.

Tessa threw open the door and embraced her partner in crime, being careful not to wake the dark-haired baby girl sleeping with her cheek resting on her mother's shoulder.

"Come in. Take a load off, for goodness' sake." She ushered mother and child to a comfortable chair.

"I have to tell you, when I said I needed a place to hide, I didn't expect to find myself in a luxury suite. You may have gone a bit overboard," Tessa chided.

"Don't be silly. Nothing but the best is good enough for my family. If it's the cost you're worried about, don't be. Seriously, Mason takes care of everything for our family and gets perturbed if I use my money to buy things for myself. When we bonded, I came with a sizable dowry that Mason refused to accept because he was wealthy in his own right. So all that money is mine to do with what I please. It has been sitting in a bank earning interest for twenty-five years. Mason will never know it's missing, so no one will be able to track you through me. They may suspect that I know where you are but they won't be able to prove it."

"No offense intended, Debbie, but I never will understand the way you people barter your children for position and power. A dowry? That's some old-world shit right there."

Debbie just shrugged. "It's just how things are. When it's all you've ever known, you don't expect anything different. The old ways are falling to the wayside now. I will regret trying to hold Chase to the bonding agreement we made with the Vaughns to the end of my days. He had true love without the aid of a bond and we tried to deny him that gift." Debbie sniffed. Tessa went to hug her again.

"It all worked out. Please stop beating yourself up about it, Deb." Tessa took the seat across from her. "I asked you to come over for a reason. We have to talk, and doing it over the phone would have been wrong. I need you to look into my eyes and see the truth," she confessed.

"Oh, man. This can't be good. Let me put the baby down so I can get comfortable." Debbie shuffled into the bedroom.

Tessa looked out over the city outside her patio door and breathed deeply to dispel her fear. Some things just had to be done. She reminded herself that fear did not equal cowardice. Bravery meant doing what needed to be done even when you were afraid.

Debbie returned and settled in to listen to Tessa's tale. Debbie sat slack-jawed when Tessa was finished. There was nothing she could say, but Tessa saw belief and acceptance in Debbie's tear-filled, hazel-green eyes.

"Mason is going to kill me." Debbie sighed.

"Will he know you're keeping a secret? I really hate asking you to do this, but I don't trust anyone else. It won't be forever. When the time comes you will need to tell him everything."

"That is why I'm not freaking out about that part of it. He'll know I'm up to something but he won't know what. Neither of us is telepathic. Our bond helps us feel each other's emotions and sometimes pain, but we can't read each other's minds." She smiled at the thought of her mate.

"Does that mean you'll help me?" Tessa was hopeful.

"I will, but I don't like the implications. I think you should tell me the entire plan so I don't lie awake at night worrying," Debbie pleaded.

"Can you accept that you are better off not knowing?" Tessa prayed Debbie would understand.

"You know once you do this you'll have to go into deep hiding. We'll have to have your meals delivered. You can't go out and I won't be able to visit. If you're spotted, or Mason follows me here, the jig will be up." Debbie paced a nervous circle around her chair.

"I'm prepared for that. I won't take the chance of being seen. I just need you to promise to keep the secret until the time is right."

Debbie nodded her understanding.

"I'll make some calls and be back tomorrow with friends." Debbie did her best to smile. Tessa understood the burden she had just laid on her friend's heart and mind, but in the end, the lives of the people they both loved were worth the extra weight.

Fourteen

Beads of sweat popped out on Brandi's brow. Focusing her energy was hard work that still required intense discipline on her part. Brandi couldn't wait for the day to come that it would all be second nature. She'd been meeting Doc in this spot to practice controlling her pyrokinesis for over a year, but today she was alone. She had come a long way from the days when she had to keep spare clothes in her car in case she lost control and flamed out, ending up nude and pissed off. If she lost control of her emotions, her grip on her growing power would slip, too. She'd lost a lot of cute outfits that way.

Brandi had gone from avoiding everyone in the early days because she never knew when she'd burn up her clothes, to containing the fire in her hands instead of letting it spread across her body. Then she progressed to a point where she held the heat without allowing actual flames to appear. She went from throwing fireballs with no skill or real aim to forcing waves of angry heat out from her hands. With a lot of practice and encouragement from Doc, she had learned to focus the heat into a controlled beam instead of walls of blistering energy. Her goal was to think about an object, completely focus on only that object, and burn it. She could do it to a point, but she had to be really close to the target. If she learned that skill with confidence, she wouldn't have to worry about harming innocent bystanders if the need to defend herself arose.

The night of Dani's bonding was the first time Brandi had directed the flames outward instead of trying to contain them within. Since then, she and Doc realized that her power needed to be vented from time to time. She had to be especially careful in times of stress or the pressure would build up and eventually bubble over. After her fight with Greyson, and Samantha's unexpected visit, she needed to let off some steam.

Brandi focused herself on the target she created across the clearing. It was much farther away and a larger target than she had attempted to ignite thus far in her training. She dug down deep into the bottomless pit of flames in her belly and willed it to consume the pile of wood.

❖

Abel watched Brandi from the tree line. What in the hell was she thinking, coming out here to this secluded spot on her own? He wanted to put her over his knee. What if he wasn't the only one watching her? The situation at the Nest was getting tense. Things were coming to a boiling point and the Master was gearing up for a strike. This was not the time to be out in the woods playing fire starter.

He had watched her for over an hour while she practiced tossing fireballs accurately and sending waves of heat rushing out ahead of her. She concentrated fiercely on a target she created out of a pile of fallen tree limbs at the opposite end of the clearing. Sweat trickled down her face and the deep blue of her eyes slowly bled to the deepest black. He was amazed when the pile began to smoke without Brandi lifting a finger to lob a fireball or send out a heat wave. First it smoldered and sparked, until suddenly orange-and-red flames shot up into the darkening early evening sky.

Brandi was so powerful and so beautiful it made his chest ache with the need to protect her. He knew from experience that he could eventually pay for his attachment to Brandi. The last time he dared to have even a friend outside of the Nest without a purpose set forth by the Master, he paid dearly and so did the girl. She was just a friend whose company he enjoyed and occasionally fed from, but someone had reported his interest in the girl to the Master. So the Master took her, to teach Abel a lesson. Even now she was locked in a cell awaiting the Master's pleasure. It made him sick, and he couldn't decide if it was a good thing she had become one of the Master's favorite playthings or not. Would she be better off dead than living to please a monster?

The thought of losing Brandi that way was more than he could bear. Brandi was more than just a girl whose company he enjoyed. She was the only thing he wished for in life, the only person other than his mom who had ever been able to breach the walls of defense around his heart and mind. He had resolved time and again to stay away from her. He should let Malibu Ken look out for her safety. He really did try to forget her, but before he knew it, he would find himself watching her again. The sight of her was an addiction. The taste of her haunted him constantly.

Abel didn't think Brandi knew he was hiding in the woods until the tree concealing him from view burst into flames. His jacket caught fire and he had to execute a classic "stop, drop, and roll." He didn't realize the danger he was in until he found himself surrounded by a blistering wall of air that shimmered and undulated like a desert mirage in the distance. Brandi rushed through the trees with her hands up, ready for a strike. With nowhere to go, he put up his hands in surrender and prepared for the hit. Brandi walked right through her molten cage and glared at him.

"What the hell do you think you're doing?" She pushed him. The ring around them dissipated. "You scared the shit out of me!"

"I scared you? Jesus, you nearly roasted me. This jacket is toast." He smiled in spite of himself. Brandi was so damn cute when she was angry. Her hands were propped up on her hips and she glared up at him from eyes of darkest night. His grin just made her even angrier.

"I was keeping an eye on you, Sparky. You shouldn't be out here alone. What if I had been a bad guy?"

"The last time I checked you *were* a bad guy." She smirked.

It stung. He really hoped she would learn to understand his dilemma. "I've never hurt you, Sparky."

"What do you want, Abel? I asked you to stay away from me. I don't know why you keep popping up like this. I have Greyson and—"

Abel tried to speak over her. The sound of the other man's name on her lips pissed him off. "Don't say his name—"

"And Greyson is all—" she continued.

He spoke over her again, getting angrier by the second. "I said, don't say his name, Brandi." He growled.

"And I said *Greyson* is all I need. So you can just . . ." She was goading him.

That was it. He stalked toward her. If she wouldn't shut that sweet mouth, he would do it for her by giving her something far better to do with that sharp little tongue.

"If you're gonna burn me, do it now, Sparky." He didn't stop advancing as she backed away, wide-eyed. "Do it now because I'm about to give you a reason to need more than that old man of yours."

She just gawked at him with a strange mixture of curiosity, fear, and challenge. She retreated until a tree hit her back. Abel caught her around the waist and lifted her to eye level, wedging her between the tree and his body. He used his arm to prevent the rough bark of the tree from rubbing her back. He moved in slowly, giving her the chance to stop him if she wanted to. Brandi looked at his mouth, watching his lips get closer. She licked her lips just before he claimed them. She tasted like warm honey and smelled like a bonfire on a cold night. He leisurely caressed her tongue with his own, searched out every bit of flavor he could capture, and did his best to brand her with his own flavor. No matter what she claimed about her relationship with the ever-absent warrior, Brandi responded to Abel and gave him as good as she got. The temptation of her soft warmth pressed against him was sublime.

Abel lowered her slowly to her feet. He was holding on by a thread to the last bit of his control. She clutched at his arms and held him close to her body. He had to get away from her. If he made love to her, it would all be over. His whole life, all of the suffering he had endured and inflicted on others, would have been in vain. His mother would die and he would live with that guilt forever. If he stayed and Brandi allowed him to take her, he would never return to the Nest.

"You don't need to burn me anymore, Sparky. You've already branded yourself on a part of me that no one else will ever see." He kissed her forehead and backed away.

"Where are you going? I thought you said it wasn't safe out here?" She followed, challenging him, breathlessly.

Abel looked over his shoulder. He let her see the fierce need for her that was riding him. "You're in far more danger if I don't walk away. I'll stick around until you're gone." He faded into the trees and watched, waiting patiently until Brandi gathered her things and climbed into her car.

On his way back to the Nest, Abel contemplated his life and cursed the course it had taken. Brandi was the best thing that would ever happen to him and he knew it. Something deep in his gut said she was the one who could change everything for him, but what could he offer her? Nothing. The Master would use her against Abel to control him. If the Master ever learned of her pyrokinetic ability, it would become another tool in his arsenal of stolen power. In the end he would lose both his mother and Brandi. It was hopeless. He was hopeless.

The last couple of weeks had given Brandi the time she needed to evaluate the state of her life. The time she spent at home with J. R. had grounded her and helped her remember what it felt like to be in her own skin. She couldn't bring herself to regret the transformation she put herself through in an effort to find her place in the world.

When she was younger her entire focus had been on education and sports, with a passing guy thrown in here and there for entertainment. Brandi had totally missed the experience of being young and carefree while she pushed herself to continue her education. The pressure of completing her bachelor's degree at eighteen had made her mature beyond her years and unable to relate to others her own age, but she couldn't regret that either.

Now that she had forced herself to slow down and live the life of a nearly twenty-year-old for a time, Brandi had a new outlook. The day New Brandi came into being, she had bagged up all her old clothes with the intention of donating them, but she had never been able to actually let them go. She was glad for that now. First, because she was sure some of her jerseys would fit J. R., and, second, because the time had come for her to find a balance between being an educated wallflower who could run rings around anyone on the playing field and a trendy socialite. It was time to be comfortable in her skin again. Brandi dragged several large bags from the rear of her walk-in closet and started to dig around for the one that contained the sports gear.

"Do you really think I could play? I'm not very big, or coordinated," J. R. asked from the doorway.

"Absolutely." She smiled up at him from her seat on the carpet. "You're plenty big enough, and coordination is something that comes with practice and exercise. Maybe you should think about taking some kind of martial arts as well as football."

J. R. smiled, and it warmed a place in her heart that had been cold for quite a while.

"I'd like that." He came to his knees and helped her search.

After Samantha's cry for help, Brandi had come home to find a kid much changed from the sunny boy she knew and loved. J. R. was skittish and stressed out. He refused to sleep in his own room and his grades were looking like crap. So Brandi devised a plan. First she set up a schedule of daily chores, homework, bedtimes, stuff like that. She had taken a psych course in college and she'd learned that kids needed a routine and boundaries. It helped to keep them centered and on task. She had never had any chores but she had also learned that kids who had such tasks learned responsibility. She'd always been responsible so she didn't feel bad about skipping that part of childhood.

The next item on her to-do list was to help him feel safe in his home again. She took J. R. around the property and introduced him to all the various warriors on duty. He didn't seem to realize exactly how many guards were on the property at any given time. There were more than usual since his attack. The next task was figuring out how to get him back into his own bed.

It started out like an adventure. They went camping in the woods on the property one night. The next night they moved closer to the house so J. R. could see the patrolling warriors moving about the grounds. The night after that they camped in the kitchen. They spent two nights in the dining room before she could get him to go upstairs and sleep in her room. Then they camped in the hall outside of his bedroom door, much to their mother's annoyance. Finally, after a week of talking about what had happened the night he woke up in his bed surrounded by strangers, and reassuring him that he was safe now, they camped together in his room. The next night he slept in his bed and she camped alone in the hall. He had come to the door several times in the night to check on her. Seeing her safe and alone in the hall seemed to reassure J. R. The night after that she slept in her own bed, going to check on him several times, but he slept through the night.

Now they were working on his confidence. He tried on various jerseys and kicked a soccer ball around her bedroom. Brandi thought he needed some self-confidence to feel like he could defend himself. He wanted to play football and take some tae kwon do. It was a perfect mix of self-defense training and a full-contact team sport. J. R. was going to be fine, and she felt confident that his experiences would make him a stronger person now that he had conquered his fears. Now that she had her baby brother straightened out, it was time to do the same thing for herself.

Candice tossed her duffel into her truck and unobtrusively peered at Greyson and the other guys over the car parked next to her. They were all laughing and Greyson was looking kind of sheepish.

"You are so whipped, man. You can't even take a victory lap with the team before you run off to the little woman?" Garrett teased Greyson.

"Don't give him a hard time, Garrett. I'd hate to see little Greyson here get into trouble or anything," Troy joined in.

"You're right, Troy. We have Candice now anyway. At least she doesn't have a curfew," Garrett replied. Ray, Mitch, and Linc all made a show of searching for Greyson's "man card" so they could revoke it.

They hadn't yet invited her to go to The Tap, a local vamp-owned bar frequented by off-duty warriors and thirsty humans, but now that her name had been mentioned, it was less awkward for her to join the conversation.

"I heard my name. What did I do now?"

She smiled at the team and did her best not to look directly at Greyson. It had been that way the whole three weeks they were deployed. She listened to Abel's advice and included the whole team in almost every conversation they had so that Greyson wouldn't feel she was stalking him or continuing to pursue a personal relationship. It had been pure hell bedding down near him every night. She had used the sleep aid Abel had given her almost every night, but she had to use more than he suggested. Just one drop made her feel high instead of sleepy. After the first time she used it, the guys had made fun of her because instead of going to sleep she had talked and talked about God only knew what because she couldn't remember a thing.

"We were just going to give you Greyson's man card because your balls are bigger than his." Linc was looking back and forth from her crotch to Greyson's and nodding as if he could verify the size of her nonexistent testicles through her pants.

"What did I miss?" she asked innocently. Greyson shook his head good-naturedly and tried to speak but couldn't get a word in.

"Greyson has to check in with his momma—I mean girl-friend—so he can't go to the bar with us tonight. You're coming along, aren't you, little red?" Garrett asked.

"I'd love to go. A little bar food sounds great."

They all laughed because they knew she didn't mean wings and french fries but slightly intoxicated humans. A good buzz might do her some good. She could sleep in a guest room on the Enclave so she wouldn't have to "drink and drive."

"It's too bad you can't come, Greyson. I guess I'll see you around."

Candice did her best not to pout but didn't think she had suc-ceeded. After spending so much time with him, it was hard to walk away not knowing when she would see him again. Her training was over so she had no real reason to be on the Enclave until they allowed her to tag along again.

Greyson took a deep breath. "Fine, I'll go, but only for a few drinks. I need to feed anyway. I'm exhausted. I must be getting old because I can't keep up with you whippersnappers."

The guys laughed at the self-deprecating remark about his age. He was at least twenty years older than the rest of them but he didn't look a day over thirty, and he ran circles around them all most days.

As soon as they walked into The Tap, one of the local barflies Candice had seen the guys with before approached them. The woman immediately singled Greyson out and steered him toward the dance floor. She was intoxicated and looking for love in all the wrong places. Greyson danced with her for a bit. She pressed her value-size breasts into his chest and groped his ass. Greyson made eye contact with the bartender, who nodded and smiled his approval.

They had a few hidden spots in the bar meant solely for the use of vamp clientele to discreetly feed, but you had to have the approval of the bartender on duty to partake in the bar. The owner of the bar cared for his human patrons as well as the vamps. So, if the person was too intoxicated or had already been fed on recently, the bartender would deny the request to use their secluded areas.

Greyson left a healthy tip on the bar in thanks, as if he'd actually just purchased a meal, and led the busty blonde away from the crowd. It was a while before he returned, looking disheveled and noticeably more relaxed. The blonde made her way to the door. It was typical of Grayson to compel the women he fed from to go home afterward for their own safety. Over-imbibing after blood loss could be harmful, and Greyson would feel responsible for the human's welfare after his or her gift of blood.

Garrett was ordering their second round by the time Greyson pulled up the only open stool at the bar, which just happened to be next to Candice's. She had already found a meal of her own and made her way back to the guys in half the time it took Greyson, and she wondered if he had screwed the woman while he fed at her neck. Candice hated the uncomfortable feeling of jealousy Greyson was so easily able to inspire in her.

Conversation flew freely around Candice, but she was lost in her own thoughts. The longer she sat next to him, the more she remembered he didn't want to be there. He wanted to be at home in bed with his fledgling. He smiled at her and lifted his glass to hers.

"To bar food," he toasted and swallowed a mouthful of amber liquid.

No longer in the mood to hang out with the guys, Candice decided to walk the several blocks back to the Enclave instead of waiting for one of the guys to leave. She knew she had a long night of tossing and turning ahead of her while she imagined Greyson's reunion with his girlfriend. Candice swore to herself that she was done with pining after the man. He was off-limits and that was that. So many men had hit on her during her time at the Enclave and she could have her pick. Why in the world was she torturing herself over the only one who wasn't interested?

Candice pulled the sleep aid out of her pocket and put several drops into her drink. It might have been a bit much, but she didn't want to think anymore. Candice figured she had just enough time to make it back to the Enclave before it kicked in and put her down for the night. The bartender cleared the empty glasses and gave her a disapproving look. She missed her pocket and dropped the bottle. It rolled away and she was forced to chase it across the floor. She returned to the bar just in time to see a tipsy Greyson reach back, without looking away from his animated conversation with Garrett, and empty her glass, instead of his own.

Fifteen

Greyson was so damn tired he collapsed onto his bed. The California king embraced him like a long-lost friend. He realized with a shrug that he was drunk. Really drunk and really tired. He knew he should have gone straight home when he got off duty, but the team had so much to celebrate. It had been a grueling three-week deployment, but they'd made a huge dent in the southern uprising. The team had raided two strongholds and both had fallen before the enemy even saw them coming. Without forewarning of the coming siege, the primarily untrained vamps were easy pickings. Finding the Nest and keeping it quiet had been far more challenging than taking them down. With the help of the local Enclaves, the team wiped the minds of the enslaved humans they found, leaving them with happier, more reasonable explanations for their lost time, and they detained the perps with minimal bloodshed.

He'd planned to go see Brandi as soon as he was off duty but the team teased him about being whipped, and Candice pouted when he refused to go to The Tap. He agreed to a drink or two only because he needed to feed. With that out of the way he could focus on reuniting with his Pixie. That was hours ago and now he was too polluted to go anywhere. How in the hell had he even gotten home?

It had been weeks since he'd last seen Brandi, weeks since their first big fight, and he hadn't been able to contact her in all that time. They'd parted with harsh words and hurt feelings on both sides.

Greyson would correct that injustice, just as soon as he could stand again. First he needed to sleep, because when he got his hands on his little Nymph, he was going to teach her to recognize his need for her. She would never again question his motives where she was concerned. Not after he used every trick he'd ever learned to brand her, mark her as his, so that she and everyone else would know whom she belonged to.

Greyson felt the bed dip next to him and warm little hands tugging at his shirt. He smiled. His Pixie had come back to him. They were meant to be, and Greyson was glad Brandi recognized it too. She'd searched him out in his bed, ready to start over with him. He chuckled, imagining how much fun makeup sex would be. His hand brushed her backside and found it blessedly devoid of clothing. Greyson wanted to lift his head. He wanted to look at her sweet little body, bare and pink and ready to make love, but his head was heavy and his eyelids refused to rise. She pulled and he helped her remove his shirt. The scent of her arousal filled the room with an unfamiliar tang. He breathed more deeply, searching for the warm honey aroma he craved. She rubbed her tight nipples against his chest and moaned, nibbling and tugging at his earlobe before raising herself off of him.

Greyson must have drifted off for a moment because he was unaware of his pants being removed until soft little hands wrapped around him and began to stroke him again and again, up and down. Her tongue joined in, teasing, kissing and licking while she stroked him with her hand until he couldn't take it anymore. He would embarrass himself if she kept up her erotic torture. One hand pinched a tender nipple between his thumb and index finger just the way Brandi liked it. She jumped as if surprised by the rough treatment.

"That's right, Nymph." He chuckled. "You'll have no tender lover tonight." He tweaked the other nipple and she jolted again.

"You'll never question me again after I'm done with you." Greyson pulled her mouth to his with a firm grip on her neck. He nipped and licked at her, demanding entrance until she opened for him and welcomed his intrusion. She tasted oddly of alcohol and mint. The flavor distracted Greyson from his task. Greyson enjoyed having a beer or two after all the years he'd spent drinking to keep up the appearance of humanity in the military. Brandi never drank alcohol because she said it tasted like shit and was a waste of time. She hadn't even fed on an intoxicated human since her close call at Thirst. He wondered if their fight and the long separation had upset her to the point of feeding on a drunk. He hadn't even tried to contact her while he was away. He was such a jerk sometimes. But he would make it up to her. Now he had his priorities in order. Brandi would work through whatever had her hiding behind the mask of a stranger, and Greyson would love her through it.

"Let me show you how much I want you. I needed you, baby. I have to be inside you, surrounded by your heat." Greyson flipped her over. He rose to his knees and the room spun, the world tilting wildly on its axis before he got his bearings. Once steady, he placed her hands on the top rail of the black wrought-iron headboard.

"Don't let go," Greyson demanded, pushing her legs farther apart. Greyson bent her to his liking. He let Brandi feel his thick length resting against the round globes of her ass. She moaned and pushed back into him, trying to find relief, but he wasn't quite ready to give it to her. His fingers crept down her belly to the apex of her thighs, seeking out her humid flesh. He circled the hidden pearl he found there, slowly spreading around her silken cream until she quaked with need, panting and thrusting her hips into his hand. She was so close he could feel her muscles quivering.

Greyson positioned himself at her entrance and thrust home in one long stroke, hurling her into a climax that bowed her back and had her screaming his name. Her heat rippled around him as she took her pleasure and tested his control. Greyson gritted his teeth against the urge to follow her. He shook his head again. The fog was so thick around him even her voice sounded distorted. He was exhausted and drunk but he wouldn't stop until Brandi lay replete in his arms.

Greyson rotated his hips, alternating between short digs and deep drives into her body. She was close to bursting again when his fangs descended. Greyson leaned forward to graze her shoulder with the sharp tips. It was a sexual game of chicken he liked to play with Brandi. The adrenaline released by the risk they both took when they bared their fangs in the heat of passion made the climax all the more intense.

Greyson brushed her hair aside and lightly grazed his fangs over her skin. She bucked beneath him, causing him to slice her tender skin. Blood smeared across Greyson's lips. Two very disturbing things occurred to him at once.

Number one, Brandi would expect his fangs, and it would turn her on but she would not jump. Number two, Brandi's hair hung slightly past her chin. He had never had to push it out of the way. Greyson struggled to clear the fog from his mind. Still buried deep in her body he grabbed the chin of the woman under him and turned her face toward him, because this was not Brandi. The hall light popped on, casting the bright light of awareness over the bed and into Greyson's brain. Head spinning, heart pounding, he looked into the passion-filled eyes of Candice Hughes. They stared at each other while he tried to sort through what had just happened. It was like he came fully back to himself between one sobering thought and the next. He watched a ribbon of blood trickle down her back while she took in his blood-stained mouth and chin. Greyson waited for any sign that he had bonded himself to Candice.

A horrified gasp echoed around the silence of the bedroom. Both Greyson and Candice turned toward the sound. Brandi stood shamefaced in the doorway.

"I'm so sorry. I didn't mean to interrupt your ceremony, Greyson. I thought . . ."

Fat tears rolled down her suddenly flushed cheeks. "I don't know what I thought. I'll leave my key by the door on the way out." Brandi fled back down the hall.

Greyson wiped the blood from his face and withdrew from Candice's body. He rushed to rinse out his mouth. He didn't taste blood but rinsed twice to be sure. Staggering back into the bedroom, he grabbed his pants from the floor, wrestling them on with effort so he could chase after Brandi.

"You bit me," Candice said, watching him from the bed.

"How the hell did you get in my house? Why did you come here?" Greyson wanted to berate Candice, but he didn't have time.

"You asked me to come." She pulled the sheet up over her body. "You said you needed me. You said you had to have me. So I brought you home," she reminded him.

Fuzzy memories of the evening began to filter back through his consciousness. The bar, the inebriated girl he fed on, Candice in his arms, the dancing and the kissing. He'd made it home but not alone. How had he gotten so wasted on a few swallows? The girl had to have been high. He was suffering from more than just the effects of alcohol. He could sort it all out later. Now he had to catch up with Brandi.

Greyson staggered out into the cold, rain-soaked predawn. He followed the stares and stunned expressions of his fellow warriors. They must have seen Brandi pass. She had to be devastated by the scene she'd walked in on. The pain and shock that lit her eyes when she walked in on him tangled up in his bed with another woman would be burned into his memory forever.

His bare feet slapped on the wet pavement and rain pelted Greyson's face. He continued to follow the astonished faces of males who had stopped in the middle of their morning routine to stare. When he finally caught up with Brandi, his mind was at first unable to process the sight of her.

Brandi was walking across the Enclave in the rain . . . nude. Her entire body was engulfed in flames that silently roiled around her in spite of the heavy rain. His steps faltered and fear choked him. At first he thought she was on fire. Her clothes had been eaten away by lapping tongues of scorching heat. But Brandi wasn't on fire. She was the flame. It wrapped lovingly around her limbs, caressing her hips and teasing her sable hair like wind.

She trudged on, passing the gawking warriors, and she made no move to cover herself. Greyson called out her name. When she turned to face him he met her agonizing black gaze. The tear tracks on her face were like miniature rivers of fire licking at her skin but not burning her flesh. Brandi's body seemed to be glowing from within. Greyson followed the scorched footprints she had seared into the grass when she left the sidewalk until the heat from her body stopped him from getting closer.

"Pixie? Baby?"

Greyson reached for her, confused but not caring if he was burned. She stepped back; the flames shot higher, heedless of the rain. She shook her head. Greyson looked around; they were drawing a crowd.

"Let me try to explain. I . . . I didn't know. I thought she was you."

God, that sounded so lame. Brandi shook her head again and looked past him.

"Greyson?" Candice walked up behind him wrapped in only the sheet from his bed. She was rain soaked and beautiful, but she wasn't his Brandi.

Earlier . . .

Brandi was resting peacefully when her cell phone jolted her into wakefulness. She peered at the glowing numbers on the alarm clock. It was four in the morning. It was never a good thing when someone found it necessary to wake you at this hour. Cautiously, she answered the phone.

"Hello?"

"Hey, it's Karrie. I'm sorry for calling so early, or late, depending on your point of view."

"It's alright. What's going on?" Brandi had sudden visions of an injured Greyson being dragged back to the Enclave. Her stomach dropped.

"My brother dragged me out of bed early this morning for PT. He says there are rumors of the possible training of female warriors. If the rumors are true, he wants me to be ready and . . . I'm rambling. That's not why I called."

"Okay?" Brandi waited.

"I thought you'd like to know that Greyson is back." Then silence. It didn't bode well that the usually straightforward Karrie was hesitating.

"He didn't look good when we ran past him. He had to have help getting into the house. I think you should get over here and check on him," Karrie finished.

"Was he injured?" Brandi was out of bed and sliding into a pair of shoes. She didn't have time to change; her pajama pants and tank top would do.

"I don't know." Karrie lowered her voice, presumably to avoid her brother overhearing her words.

"I just knew that I would want someone to call me if it were Nate. We are going to need to talk about him and your friend Abel very soon. I can't believe you didn't at least give me a heads-up about his profession," Karrie hissed.

"I know." Brandi groaned. "Can we talk about that later?"

"Yeah, I'll see you soon."

Karrie's brother bellowed her name in the background.

"I gotta go." She disconnected the call. Brandi was already running to her car.

The drive to the Enclave gave Brandi time to organize her thoughts. She had a plan of action. Greyson's deployment had given her time to come to grips with the problems that existed in their relationship. She'd thought long and hard about the argument they had the day he left. Everything Greyson said had been hurtful but true. She was deceiving him by pretending to be someone she wasn't. He couldn't be expected to carry their relationship and she did have issues to work out within herself.

The problem was that she didn't really know who she was anymore. She wasn't the girl she had been before her power came into being, and she wasn't New Brandi, the snobby socialite, either. She was on the brink of, once again, reinventing herself, but not in the image of what was expected of her.

Brandi took the two distinct and separate personas and forced them both down into the bottomless cauldron of flames in her soul. Now began the arduous task of finding the woman who would emerge from the fire. It would take time and she would make mistakes, but Brandi was ready to move on.

Greyson would have to decide if he could wait for her to become whoever she would be or cut his losses. He might not even like her when it was all said and done. After her recent run-ins with Abel, she didn't really like herself. She told him to stay away but when he showed up, Brandi couldn't stop herself from provoking him.

Abel made her feel wanted in a way that Greyson hadn't been able to. Brandi felt she had learned more about Abel and herself in the short time they'd spent together than she knew about anyone else in her life.

Greyson and Abel were two sides of a coin. The differences between them were like comparing a laid-back day with warm sun on your skin to the cool light of a full moon bathing you in an alien glow. The dark and the light. The good and the bad. The warrior and a criminal.

Brandi couldn't build a life around the shadowed existence that was Abel's life. He'd made it clear that he had no choice but to continue his service to the Rogue, and that was not something she could abide by. He was protecting his family and she had to protect her own. It was an impossible battle she couldn't win.

She hadn't really been unfaithful to Greyson, but she was cheating in her heart. To Brandi, that was just as bad as the physical act of sex. Now was the time of reckoning. After she assured herself that Greyson was healthy and uninjured, Brandi would tell him the truth and explain her need for time to learn about herself and let him decide if he could forgive her indiscretions. If he still wanted to be with her, Brandi thought they should start over from the beginning. She knew virtually nothing about Greyson and he only knew the facade she put forth. They had a chance if he was willing to risk his heart this time.

Her key in hand, Brandi took the five stairs to Greyson's front door in one long running leap. Before she worried any more about the future, she had to find Greyson. What if he were hurt or ill? Then she would wait until he had time to get better before she put any more stress on him.

Her heart thudded wildly in her chest. She had missed him so much. That was the worst part of dating a warrior. Brandi wanted to kiss his face and hold his big body in her arms. Everything else could wait.

The door opened on the darkened interior of Greyson's house. If he was sleeping, she would crawl in bed behind him and hold him all day while he rested. Dropping her key on the entry table, Brandi hit the light switch and hurried down the hall to his bedroom. The door was open wide and the lights from the hall spilled over his huge bed.

Brandi found herself standing in the middle of a nightmare when she entered the bedroom. It seemed as if her ability to be at the right place and the right time to learn things people didn't want her to know had resurfaced after a long absence. It was too late. She had played a part for too long and Greyson was obviously tired of waiting for her to grow up. The future with Greyson she had hoped for shattered on a moan that escaped from the woman he held in his arms. Their bodies were intimately joined on the sheets that she had slept in the last time she and Greyson were together.

Greyson had taken a mate to his soul. The couple was frozen in the rapture of the mating bond forming between them while she watched. The stunning redhead's blood was still glistening wetly on his lips and she stared in fascination at the proof of her mate's acceptance. As the shock began to fade, Brandi gasped in burgeoning horror. The sound was like a shotgun blast in the silent reverence of Greyson's bedroom. She was trespassing on their private union. The sound brought the couple's heads whipping about in her direction. Greyson looked into her eyes, and the force of his rejection and the wordless dismissal of the time they spent together crushed her.

"I'm so sorry. I didn't mean to interrupt your ceremony, Greyson. I thought . . ." Tears rolled down her suddenly flushed cheeks. The heat was beginning to build in her body along with the embarrassment. "I don't know what I thought. I'll leave my key by the door on the way out."

Greyson made no reply. Brandi doubted he was able. She had to get out of his home and fast. She was losing her tenuous grasp on the flames in her belly, and the clothes on her back were starting to smoke by the time she made it out the front door. She had to head for the woods. It would be a long time before she could handle the spare clothing in her car or the vehicle itself without setting it ablaze.

She walked quickly, but the flames were faster. Warriors gaped at her in either awe or revulsion; she wasn't sure which. Her pajamas floated away like little embers. The shoes on her feet melted away within a block of Greyson's house, and she walked naked, completely exposed to the prying eyes of the Enclave. The sky opened up and seemed to echo her misery. Gone was her veil of privacy. Everyone on the Enclave would know her secret by breakfast and it would spread from there. Brandi wondered how many of the open-mouthed males she passed were the Rogue's undercover minions. How long would it take the news of the only known pyro in existence to reach the death dealer? The wet grass hissed and crackled under Brandi's feet. She looked down and cursed. She had completely flamed out. Her clothes were gone.

Of course Greyson had moved on after all of her theatrics. Shit. He had probably been seeing his new mate for some time. It wasn't as if he had ever made any mention of a commitment to her. For all Brandi knew, the redhead had been dating him the whole time. She foolishly believed that he hadn't been able to contact her over the last weeks. It was more likely that he just hadn't had anything left to say to her.

Brandi halted when Greyson's voice called to her from a distance. She couldn't believe he had left the bed of his mate to come after her. The pouring rain couldn't reach her skin but Greyson was soaked. His hair matted to his face and rain dripped from his nose.

It was like Greyson was seeing her for the first time as he gazed into her eyes, and truthfully, he probably was. She could only imagine what he saw lurking behind the flames.

"Pixie? Baby?"

He reached for her and she backed away. Brandi didn't want his pity.

"Let me try to explain. I . . . I didn't know. I thought she was you."

Brandi looked past him to the beautiful female huddled in nothing but a sheet from his bed. Brandi recognized her now. She was his new teammate. There was the reason he hadn't called her in weeks. The woman had heard his declaration and looked injured by it.

"Greyson?" the woman asked. Her huge blue eyes filled with misery and the red of her long, curly hair glistened in the rain. Greyson looked at the woman briefly before returning his eyes to Brandi.

"I can explain. Or I will find a way to as soon as the bar opens. Brandi, I think I was drugged. Come with me to the infirmary, please."

She looked at him disbelievingly. He was trying but failing to look at her face instead of the fire coursing around her body.

"I see. You thought it was me because I suddenly have long, red hair and look suspiciously like your new civilian teammate?" This was also the female she'd seen in pictures on the walls of the home Abel had hidden her away in when she'd been drugged, but she would keep that to herself. She'd never met the female in person, so the one time she'd seen her with Greyson's team Brandi didn't make the connection. Now she wondered what, if anything, Abel had to do with this situation.

Brandi saw Gage Paris, the captain of the warriors, approaching, and she used the opportunity to head for the trees.

"Wait. Brandi, let's just calm down and talk this through," he pleaded. When he attempted to follow her, a sodden Gage halted Greyson's motion. Karrie ran past them, doing her best to shield from the rain the towels and clothes she carried.

"Report to the infirmary, Drake," Gage demanded. "Now."

"I'm off duty, sir," Greyson replied respectfully. "I have a personal situation I need to deal with."

"Off duty, huh?" He looked from the dripping Candice Hughes to Greyson and out to where Brandi had disappeared into the tree line.

"Not anymore. Maybe some manual labor will help you work off the stupid."

Hot, flaming tears tracked down Brandi's cheeks and the reality of the past fifteen minutes sank fully in to her skin. Something inside of her died in that moment. It was almost comical. All this time she imagined herself as a glorified phoenix who had risen from the ashes of social retardation to become a powerful force among her people. What a joke. This pain in her chest was a real death. These feelings of abandonment and useless fury were the death throes of her discarded dreams. She would come back from this, and when she did, Brandi planned to live her life her way. No more hiding and no more regret.

Sixteen

Abel walked in through Candice's unlocked back door. She was expecting him so he didn't worry about being capped in the ass or pistol-whipped this time. When the rumors of a pyro on the Enclave spread to the Nest, he cursed his fellow minions for being so efficient. Fortunately none of them were eyewitnesses and the female's identity was being protected. Obviously the Enclave knew his Master would love to have the only living pyro. They were keeping it under wraps for now, but it was only a matter of time before Brandi was outed. His master was already hunting. Abel had to get to her first. He contacted Candice under the guise of wanting to come for a visit after her long trip, as soon as he could get away.

He had to find out what had happened to set Brandi off. She was very careful about concealing her growing talent and she'd done an excellent job so far. If she lost control in public, there had to have been an earth-shattering event in her world. While Abel didn't like the idea of Brandi hurt in any way, he couldn't help hoping Candice would verify his suspicions.

Candice had a serious thing for Greyson. She'd been working with his team out of town for several weeks. Abel hoped the time together had given Candice and her crush some much-needed time to get to know each other. It was entirely possible the warrior had fallen for the lovely Candice Hughes. She was closer to his age and they had a lot in common. Candice was in law enforcement and could relate to the rigors of his position.

He knew in his gut that the warrior wasn't the male for Brandi. If he were, she wouldn't respond to Abel the way she did. He told himself this was the best thing for both of the females, but guilt ate at him as he entered Candy's kitchen. He was a selfish prick to want a female he couldn't provide for or love openly. He'd spent his life among the worst males their people had to offer. Abel began to believe he was no better than the rest of the minions his master ruled over. He began to believe he might be as manipulative as the Master himself.

Abel found Candice on her sofa. She didn't look happy and her eyes filled with tears when she saw him.

"Candy, what's wrong?" He knelt in front of her. "Why are you crying?" This wasn't good. Candy did not cry, ever.

"I'm in trouble. Big trouble," she sniffled.

"Okay. We will have to get you out of it then. What kind of trouble are we talking about?"

"I need to know exactly where you got the sleep aid you gave me."

Oh shit.

"I told you I got it from a doctor."

Candy didn't look convinced. "Where did you get it, Abel? Don't lie to me." Angry tears filled her eyes again. "I think it's time you told me exactly who you work for. Now," she demanded.

"Who I work for doesn't matter. You know I don't have a choice. Why are you so angry? My line of work shouldn't be a surprise after all these years. What does it have to do with the sleep aid?"

"I'm being accused of spying for the Rogue, Abel. Because I had a vial of the drug he uses to subdue his victims. They think I approached the Enclave with the intention of breaching the ranks of the Wrath for the purpose of recruiting them."

"That's total bullshit! You'd never work for such a monster and you certainly wouldn't encourage others to. Shit, Candy! How did they get the vial? You were only supposed to use a drop at bedtime."

"I accidentally poisoned a Wrath guard when he drank from my glass. He was already intoxicated and the alcohol didn't mix well with the drug," she confessed.

"I don't care how drunk he was; one drop would not have hurt him. Hell, it wouldn't hurt a hundred-and-twenty-pound woman," —he eyed Candice's small frame—"much less a man the size of a Wrath guard. I use it myself. There's no way."

Candice looked sheepish.

"Candy, I know I was very specific when I gave you the vial. I said only one drop."

"Yeah, well, it didn't work!" she snapped. "It only made me feel drunk and out of control. So I was taking a few drops. The other night I wanted to be sure I slept through the night and hopefully the next day as well. So I doubled the dose I was taking. Only I didn't drink it. My glass was on the bar and Greyson picked up the wrong drink."

Abel tried to remain calm. This was getting worse by the minute. If Greyson had hurt Brandi in his drunkenness, even if it wasn't his fault, Abel would kill him. He was beginning to see red.

"Where is Brandi? Did he . . . ?" Abel couldn't say the words. It would be indirectly his fault if anything had happened to her. Candice stared toward the doorway and her eyes widened.

"How the hell do you know my girlfriend?"

Abel spun around, gun at the ready, and faced a wall of armed Wrath muscle. Greyson was standing front and center.

"Ex-girlfriend," the black-clad mountain to Greyson's left stated plainly.

Greyson shot the man a look that should have eviscerated him.

"Shut up, Linc," the other giants grumbled in unison.

"What? It's true," he defended.

"Put the gun down, Abel." Candice put her hand on his raised gun arm. "You'll never make it out of here."

He already knew that.

"You set me up? You led me into a trap? Candy?" He had to know. Had she turned on him?

She cried openly and pulled the gun from his grasp. There was no sense in fighting. He was now surrounded.

"I had no choice, Abel. I needed you to verify my story and we need to know where the drugs are coming from. They're showing up in the hands of our youth. The kids are passing it around at parties and in clubs. They're calling it Hypno. It's the same drug they found in Brandi's blood after her attack at Thirst. This is not a recreational drug. It can kill people and ruin lives."

She patted him down and came away with another gun and his blade. Luckily, he didn't have any Hypno on him.

"We will be getting to the bottom of your previous knowledge of Brandi," Greyson snarled at them both. "If you purposely drugged me, Candice, I swear I will . . ."

A male Abel recognized from pictures to be the captain, Gage Paris, stepped over the threshold and cut off Greyson's threat. He cuffed Abel as he spoke. "Greyson, you and your team are dismissed. You're too close to this case for you to remain objective. Everyone return to the Enclave. I'll take it from here."

Greyson tried to argue but his teammates dragged him away.

Abel only had one more question before his life and that of his mother came to a screeching halt. Because he knew as soon as one of the rogue warriors was able to get close to him, he would be dead. Abel knew far too much about the Master's operations for him to be allowed to live for long. His mother would be of no further use to the Master. He would rid himself of the burden of caring for the mentally unstable human at his first opportunity.

"Candice, did he hurt Brandi? What happened to her?" He pleaded for the truth with his eyes.

"He hurt her but not the way you are thinking. And nobody knows where she is. She took off early yesterday morning and hasn't been seen since."

———◆———

Abel was surprised it had taken this long for the Shade executioner to make an appearance. He'd been locked up for most of the day and into the night. The sound of quiet footsteps entering the corridor outside of the cell he occupied in the Council Hall surely heralded his end. Abel wondered why he'd been taken to the Council Hall instead of the Enclave, and the only reason he could think of was that he would be quickly executed. Maybe they'd figured out his involvement in Danielle Vaughn's attempted abduction. Along with possession and distribution of Hypno to Candy, it would be an open-and-shut case. The Council did not abide lawbreakers, but it seemed as if one of his brothers-in-arms was going to save them the trouble. Finally, in the middle of the night, they had come for him.

It was almost a relief to know his life was coming to an end. What kind of life did he really have anyway? The only things he regretted were not being able to protect his mom and not having the chance to spend more time with Brandi. If he had a chance, Abel would tell Brandi that she had changed his world from a dark and lonely place to one where he dared to dream. He would tell her how hard he'd fought falling for her in the beginning, but he was no match for a sparky little brunette who smelled like honey and warm campfires. He'd been a goner since the first time she'd burned him. Abel smiled at that memory. It seemed like so long ago. He would also apologize to Candy if he could. He'd never meant to hurt her. But it was too late for his confessions now.

There was no sense in trying to hide. In the barren cell there was nowhere to go, so he sat upright on the steel bench and waited. It would be like shooting a fish in a barrel. When Gage Paris had taken him into custody, Abel was sure he would be dead within the hour. His Master would not let him live long enough to give any secrets away. The steps slowed and stopped in the darkness outside of his cell. He watched the shadowed figure digging around in a pocket. When the figure silently unlocked the door to his cell, Abel's heart sank. They wouldn't kill him here. No. He would be taken back to the Nest to be made an example of in front of the other minions. The barred door swung open.

"Are you just gonna sit there and stare at me or are we getting out of here?" a vaguely familiar female voice came out of the darkness. "We don't have all night," she pressed.

Abel didn't ask any questions. He followed the tall feminine form out of the Council Hall through a rear exit and straight into a waiting car. Abel jumped in the back and his rescuer ran around to the passenger side. They pulled away from the curb before the doors were even shut. The wide grin of the driver who peered at him in the rearview mirror had Abel shaking his head in astonishment. He hadn't seen or heard from Nate since the day he woke Abel from the best sleep of his life with Brandi in his arms on the floor in the Council Hall library.

"Where the hell have you been, man? I thought the worst." Abel patted his friend's shoulder. Nate looked at the stern face of the woman to his right.

"I've found better things to do with my time. Abel, you remember Karrie, don't you?" He glanced over his shoulder and smiled even more widely.

"Of course I remember her. How could I ever forget the woman who beat us at our own game? She nearly blew your head off." Abel smirked.

"Nate, I want both of you off the streets and this car returned to its rightful owner before they know it's missing. Do you know where you're going?" Karrie's face bore a look of total shame and guilt. She licked her dry lips and scanned the nearly abandoned street.

"Sweetheart, I know this goes against the grain for you, but we had to get him out before he ended up dead." Nate reached over to lay a hand on her thigh.

"I know that, Nate, but I didn't do this for him. If I didn't know what was coming, I would have let him rot. This is for Brandi and Danielle. They will need him and so will we," Karrie snapped.

"What do you mean when you say you know what's coming? And where is Brandi? Where are we going?" Abel was getting nervous. Karrie was not a fan of his.

"I was contacted by a friend who insisted we help you. We're taking you to her so she can explain the rest. I don't know where Brandi is now. The last time I saw her, she was in the woods surrounding the Enclave, literally burning with shame and hurt because of your stunt with that damn drug. As far as I know, no one has seen her in two days."

Abel laid his hand on Karrie's shoulder but she didn't turn to look at him. This was a friend of Brandi's who had protected her and taught her to defend herself. It was no wonder she was unhappy with him.

"I know you have no reason to believe me, but I didn't have anything to do with what happened, other than the fact that I gave the drug to Candice for her own personal use. I had no way of knowing anyone else would have access to it. I meant no harm and I'm sure Candice didn't either." He hoped she would believe him.

"Candice may not have meant to drug Greyson, but she took advantage of the situation once it was done. She could have taken him home and let him sleep it off, but that's not how it played out, is it? No. She made sure everyone in the bar knew they were leaving together and she crawled into his bed as soon as she got him to his house. Then, instead of letting Brandi and Greyson speak privately when she caught them in bed, she chased him through the rain in a sheet. I can't imagine how mortified Brandi must have felt."

While they drove, Karrie filled Abel in on the drama that had taken place at the Enclave. It was no wonder Brandi had lost her cool. Whether he liked it or not, she had genuine feelings for Greyson. He didn't believe she loved him but she definitely cared for the warrior. Walking in on him and Candy must have been mortifying for her.

Nate informed him that he was leaving the Master's service to be with Karrie. He needed to be worthy of her attention or her father and brothers would kill him. Nate had snuck back into the Nest a couple of times to check on his father but no one seemed to notice he was missing yet. They assumed he was with Abel. So when Nate showed up, everyone assumed Abel was around too and he went along with the story. Therefore Abel's absence wouldn't have been noticed unless the Master had summoned him. From the looks of things, the Master was busy monitoring Darren and his preparations with his army of flunkies.

They pulled up to the side entrance of a luxury hotel by the park downtown. Abel looked at Nate, who just shrugged. "I'm only following orders. Good luck, man."

Karrie handed him a small envelope that contained a key card. "Use the card to get in to the building's side entrance. It's better to avoid the main entrance. Go to the room number on the envelope. The card will unlock the door. She's waiting for you. That's all I know."

Nate gave him a new cell phone and some cash. They made plans to meet up when the time was right, whatever the hell that was supposed to mean.

Abel did as directed, but he stood nervously outside the hotel room he was supposed to enter. The door opened and he looked down into a lovely and oddly familiar face. This was the human mate of Griffin Vaughn, Danielle's mother. She held out her hand.

"My name is Tessa Vaughn. It's a pleasure to meet you, Abel. Please come in. We have a lot to talk about."

⸱⸱⸱

An hour later Abel sat on the sofa in Tessa's suite with his head in his hands. He didn't know why he believed this human woman, but he did. Maybe it was the human in him that wanted to trust her. She needed his help, and for him to help her she had to get him out of lockup. The amount of detail she knew regarding the coming Rogue offensive was startling. He thought she had a contact feeding her information, but she claimed that she had dreamt it all. If her predictions were correct, much of what was to come was riding on Abel's shoulders.

Whichever side he chose to fight for would reign. He had choices to make and they were going to be the toughest of his life. Only one of the two women in his life could survive the coming storm; which one was up to him. Did he protect his mother and continue to be a cog in the Master's machine, or cling to the woman he had come to love? Could he let Brandi's world fall apart so that his mother could continue to live safely with her delusions? Abel felt sick. A knock at the door startled him out of his musings.

"It's okay," Tessa soothed him. "I have a surprise for you."

The door opened and a petite woman with the most beautiful hazel eyes strolled into the room, stroking the back of the infant resting on her shoulder. Her eyes shot straight to Abel's and he had the oddest sensation of being a bug under a microscope. She examined his face closely and smiled before looking to Tessa. "I'm sorry I ever doubted you, friend," the woman said to Tessa. "I'll send her in and wait for you in the lobby."

Abel had no idea what to make of the woman or her comments. Tessa grabbed her coat and purse before heading for the door. Was she just going to leave him there? What was he supposed to do next? How the hell was he going to sort all this shit out on his own?

"That was my daughter's mother-in-law, Debbie Deidrick. She can be very protective. Remember that everything we spoke of is between us. I'll call you when the time is right." She smiled.

He heard hushed female voices in the hall. Abel knew before she stepped into the room that Brandi was in the hall. The warm honey aroma of her tickled his brain, and his heart leapt. Tessa saw the recognition in his eyes.

"I think it's time you showed her there's more to you than what the Rogue has tried to make you. I won't be back until late tonight, so feel free to stay as long as you like." She winked at him and walked out.

Brandi stepped into the doorway and stood there looking confused and beautiful. She was wearing a borrowed sweat suit that was rolled a few times at the ankles. Her skin was too pale and her eyes looked bruised from lack of sleep. Tears filled her eyes when she saw him but she didn't move. She looked so lost and unsure.

Taking charge of the situation, Abel walked slowly to her. He guided her gently into the room and locked the door. She turned to look at him, and the tears running down her face shimmered and flickered with the heat of her pain. Little flames hit the carpet and Abel had to step on them to prevent a fire. He was lucky she wasn't too hot to touch. Her mouth opened to speak but nothing came out. He wiped the hot wetness from her face, wincing when it burned his skin. She was exhausted. Everything else could wait. Right now Brandi just needed to rest.

"It's alright, Sparky." He pulled her to him, and his heart soared when Brandi immediately wrapped her arms around his waist and held on tight.

"You don't need to say anything. I don't need any explanations." He kissed her lips gently and pulled away quickly when she turned her face up to him.

"Did you know?" she asked. "I need to know if you knew your friend was sleeping with my . . ."

Now he knew what had sent her over the edge of her control. Candy must have achieved her goal of stealing the warrior. "I knew that Candy was working with the Enclave on some secret project, and I knew she had a thing for Greyson, but I didn't send her to the Enclave."

She stepped away from him, looking hurt. "There has to be more to it than that, Abel. It's too big a coincidence."

"Are you really going to blame *me* for what they did?" he asked.

She blinked and took a deep breath that seemed to calm her a bit. "I don't know what to think anymore. What's done is done. I'm just so damn tired."

"Let's get you into bed. I think some sleep will make a world of difference. We can figure out everything else later." He opened his arms again and to his relief she came to him without protest. Abel led her to the second of the two bedrooms in the suite. She stood where he placed her by the bed while he turned down the blankets. Like a child, she allowed him to undress her. Abel's breath caught in his throat when he realized Brandi had no underwear beneath her clothing. Dear God, she was perfection. Every creamy inch of her lush body was on display when he tucked her into the bed. Her ample breasts sat up and begged him to lick their dusky peaks. The notch in her waist that flared out to the luscious curve of her hips was made for his hands to grasp and hold tight while he rubbed himself against the firm globes of her ass.

Abel shook his head. This was not about sex. The fact that her sweetly arousing aroma called to him and her soft pink heat could be seen through the neat curls at the apex of her thighs did not mean that he had to act on his lust. His mouth watered. She needed rest and they needed to talk. They needed to spend what little time he had getting to know each other better. The rest of their lives depended on it.

He pulled the blanket up, more to block his view of temptation than to warm her body. She was already warm to the touch. He was enjoying the sight of her tightly peaked breasts and that flawless skin entirely too much.

Abel leaned over the bed and brushed another glancing kiss across her full lips. He wanted so badly to delve in and taste her again.

"Sleep, Sparky; I'll be here when you wake." Abel backed away from the bed.

"No," Brandi spoke for the first time. "Don't go. Please stay with me, Abel. Hold me. I don't want to be alone."

She pushed back the covers for him to climb in, baring her hip to his hungry eyes. He wanted her, but he didn't want to take advantage of her emotional state.

"I don't think that's a good idea." His voice was husky and kind of pained. She was tempting him beyond his ability to refuse her.

"Please? Don't leave me."

The look of need in her steel-blue eyes undid Abel. He pulled off his shirt and kicked off his shoes. He approached the bed and Brandi glared at his jeans when he tried to climb in.

"You're killing me, Sparky," he growled, but she gave him a little smile when he tugged them off and crawled in behind her in his boxer briefs. He pulled her back against his chest and Brandi sighed contentedly. His best efforts at keeping his arousal from rubbing her ass were foiled when she insisted on tucking herself closer and closer into the curve of his body until her hips were nestled tightly against his. There was no way he would be getting any sleep.

Seventeen

Greyson sat stone-faced in his recliner. The game was on but he stared at the door. He waited in vain for Brandi to come sweeping through the door in a pair of sparkly heels and a designer smile. His heart ached for the sight.

Memories played out around him like reruns of his favorite show come to life in his home. He could see Brandi sitting on the living room floor in her underwear, painting her toenails while he complained about the smell until she left the room. She'd put that sofa cover over his beat-up old couch and it made a big difference but he'd complained it was too girlie. She would make them a salad with every meal, except breakfast because she usually skipped it, and he always teased her when she did eat it and mostly ignored the pile of protein he'd put on her plate.

Brandi had a habit of tidying up behind him as he moved through the house, leaving debris in his wake. His clothes always ended up magically in the hamper and the shower curtain he left perpetually open would be inexplicably closed when Brandi was around. She made the bed as soon as he climbed out of it and never left a dish in the sink. For a woman who'd grown up with maids and servants, Brandi was extremely self-sufficient. Greyson had accused her of mothering him on several occasions.

If she would just walk back through that door and into his life, Greyson would never complain or make fun of her good habits again. In the days that had passed since she'd walked away in a flaming fury of pain and embarrassment, he'd had time to think about their relationship as a whole. Brandi had done everything possible to get closer to him and solidify them as a couple, with the exception of publicly introducing him to her peers as her man. That still chapped his ass since he knew it was because he fell below her on the societal food chain.

Brandi would lie next to him in bed and ask him endless questions that he never really answered. During their first argument, which turned out to be their last, he accused her of keeping secrets and being dishonest about whom she was inside. In hindsight, Greyson realized that he never bothered to ask her about herself. She would bombard him with questions that he would swat away because he didn't know her well enough to answer them comfortably. But he never made the effort to get to know her better. She was right. He'd shown no interest in their relationship except in the bedroom because he'd been too tired and stressed out from work to bother doing the hard work required of a partnership. Greyson had refused to carry their relationship, but maybe if he had at least hauled his own weight, things wouldn't have ended the way they did. He had never even asked her to be with him exclusively. It was no wonder she believed herself to be nothing more than a plaything to him.

Looking back, he realized that all the little things she did in his home were quirks of her true personality. Her behavior when she was alone with Greyson was at total odds with the socialite persona she wore outside his home. Brandi had been giving him little pieces of herself when her guard was down. He was too self-absorbed to see it at the time. Those true glimpses into the real Brandi were the things he complained about and made fun of. Why was he so blind when it mattered most?

Greyson believed they could have gotten past anything—except the scene Brandi walked in on the other night. He would not have been able to forgive her if he caught her in bed with another man. The memory would have haunted him every time they were together until he could no longer look at her. Still, he wanted to search Brandi out and try to explain the extenuating circumstances of his infidelity, but he couldn't. He'd been ordered by the captain to stay away from Brandi unless she came to him. Her father was aware of the situation and he had people hunting for her. Her new ability would make her a sure target. Griffin Vaughn had made it clear that he would not tolerate his daughter being harassed while she worked on getting over him and concentrated on controlling her ability. Her father had heard every detail of the scene that played out that rainy morning several days ago and he wouldn't be forgetting it.

How the hell could he harass her if no one even knew where she'd gone? For all they knew the Rogue had already heard of her amazing pyrokinetic ability and snatched her off the street. But that wasn't supposed to matter to him because he'd made a mistake and fallen into bed with the wrong woman? To hell with them! They could expel him if they didn't like it. He could always go back to medicine if his career in the Wrath came to an end.

Greyson jumped up from his chair and began to gather his things. He was going to search until he found Brandi. Then he would find a safe place for them until she at least gave him the chance to explain things. He wanted to give her his proof from the infirmary that he had been under the influence of the same drug that had knocked her out for a day. What she did after that would be her decision, but at least he would know Brandi was safe and she would have all the facts before she condemned him.

Greyson was stuffing some things in a duffel bag when someone rapped on his front door. He ran to the door and wrenched it open, praying that Brandi would be on his doorstep ready to give him another chance. But it wasn't his blue-eyed pixie at the door. It was his teammate Garrett, and judging by the sympathetic look on his face, Garrett knew he wasn't whom Greyson was hoping to find.

"I'm sorry, man. I tried to call but your phone is going straight to voice mail."

"It's cool. I turned it off so Candice would stop calling. What's up?"

"We've been deployed, my friend. We leave in an hour. I hope you can get past your aversion to Candice quickly because she's coming along." Garrett patted him consolingly on the shoulder. "You'll be our driver this round. It will keep you busy and away from trouble-making redheads."

Garrett walked down the front stairs before Greyson got up the nerve to ask, "Has anyone heard from her?" He didn't need to specify which *her* he was asking about.

"I asked Gage when he gave me the assignment. He said she had contacted someone to let them know she's safe but she isn't ready to come home. That's all he could tell me."

<hr />

Her body felt heavy with sleep. The light of the midday sun seeping into the room through cracks in the drapes told Brandi that she had slept for quite some time. She stretched against the muscled body pressed to her back. His hot skin smelled clean and intoxicating. This close, he always made her drunk with hunger and need.

Abel. He made her feel small and protected. She felt sheltered from the world outside, resting in his arms. Brandi arched her back to press against the heavy erection prodding her bottom. He placed kisses along her bare shoulder and climbed her neck to tease her earlobe with nibbling little bites and kisses. She moaned. Chills chased each other down her body.

His arm pulled her more tightly to his body and wedged his length between her ass cheeks. Abel murmured his approval of the fit while gently kneading her breast and palming the ridged nipple before tugging with his thumb and forefinger. Brandi slowly ground herself against him.

Lazily, he loved her. His hand made an unhurried path south, stroking between her breasts, over her ribs to her belly. He traced her hip downward until finally he cupped her wet heat. She waited in an agony of anticipation for the touch she needed. The touch he wanted to give her. Parting her curls with one long finger, he began teasing and circling her clit. Brandi squirmed while he patiently teased her until she pressed into his hand, searching for more. Another finger joined the first and delved deeper, pumping slowly into her body. Brandi tilted her hips backward, panting silently, begging to be filled. He chuckled and tsked.

Abel rolled until his back rested on the headboard and dragged Brandi with him so that her legs spread wide and rested high on his thighs, straddling him backward. He grinned over her shoulder and she saw them in the mirror across the room. The blankets slid away and cool air teased her heated skin, tightening her nipples further. Holy shit. She was watching him play with her body while he watched her, his expression intense and absorbed now.

The hand between her legs shifted, thrusting and massaging the spot inside where she needed him so badly. Her moans filled the room. The sight of them together on the bed was erotic beyond anything she'd ever experienced.

"Do you like that?" he asked.

"Yes. More, please," she begged.

"Do you like watching me finger you?" he growled. She didn't want to answer. Her cheeks burned. She did like it, a lot. Abel's fingers stilled and his reflection scowled at her. "I asked you a question."

"Yes! I like it," she said quickly and tried to circle her hips. He grinned then and gave her three fingers. Stretching and probing deeper, he hit that perfect spot with every pass, making her grind against his hand, pleading for him to fill her. She could see his erection standing tall between her legs. It was larger than she'd expected, given Abel's solid but lean frame. His other hand continued to pinch and flick the taut peaks of her breasts. She watched him pleasure her and her climax grew closer with every stroke of his fingers. It felt so good. So close, but not quite what she wanted.

"Please, Abel. I . . . I need you. All of you. I've wanted you for so long."

He froze and she feared she had said something wrong. Would he leave her when she needed him this way, this intensely?

Finally he moved his hands to her hips and lifted her over his length. He entered her slowly while she watched every thick inch of him invade her sex. It was tight and the stretching burned just a bit. He worked himself in slow circles until he was able to seat himself entirely. Brandi had been sure for a moment that it wouldn't work. She looked away and tried to relax. He petted her and whispered praise in her ear while he let her body adjust to the width of him.

"I love you, Brandi. Do you hear me?" He slowly moved out of her and steadily pushed back in. "Look at me," he demanded, and she pried open her lids to meet his eyes in the mirror. "If you believe nothing else, believe in that. I love you and I'm about to show you, the only way I know how." He kissed her neck and went to work making her believe him.

She wanted to answer but the slide of flesh against flesh stole her words. He filled her so completely she could hardly breathe. Abel guided her hips, setting up a steady rhythm. Before long his hips were slamming against hers and all Brandi could do was hold on for the ride.

———◆———

She was so hot and so wet. Brandi's body was milking him with little grasping ripples. He couldn't watch them in the mirror any longer. The sight of her spread out and accepting him would end his struggle to hold off. Her head thrashed back and forth on his shoulder while she repeated his name over and over. She writhed in pleasure, her nails digging into his thighs, egging Abel on. He wanted to go slower and savor this experience, but the months of watching her and wondering what it would be like to slide into her eager heat were nothing compared to the reality of being buried inside of her.

He was close. Too close. One hand slid down into her folds and circled the sensitive nub of her clit. She gasped and struggled to escape the overwhelming sensation but he held her to the spot. Pounding and rubbing, he bit firmly with his blunt teeth into the spot where her shoulder flowed into her neck. Abel wanted nothing more at that moment than to let his fangs drop and sink them into the delicate column of her neck. Brandi cried out his name and shattered.

"Abel! So good! Can't . . . it's too much!"

Flying apart, she came screaming his name and took Abel with her. He held on tight, riding out the heated waves that sucked at his shaft, pulled him under, and drained him completely. He knew then he'd never let her go. Not now. Not ever. He had to find a way to make this work. He had to.

He rolled them to their sides and tucked her in next to him, grateful he still had the strength to do so. Brandi purred and snuggled down until the little electric aftershocks faded into a sated sleep.

They drifted in and out of sleep, making love twice more during the early evening hours until they both knew it was time to leave their drowsy haven and face the world. Brandi ordered room service and they ate in companionable silence. Neither of them wanted to taint the reverent atmosphere created by their loving. It was Brandi who began. "You should know what happened with Greyson—"

Abel cut her off. "Don't say his name." He hated the sound of his name on her lips. Brandi smiled, likely remembering a similar argument in the woods. "And I don't need to know. We both have pasts. Right now let's focus on the future." He smiled at her.

Abel pulled Brandi onto his lap and held her. He wanted to tell her all of the things he promised himself he would if he ever had another chance. "I don't need to know what happened unless it will make you feel better to talk about it. All that matters to me is I love you and you now know it. I fought it so hard in the beginning. I have nothing to offer you and the fear of rejection still weighs heavily on me. But my fear is no match for the intense need I have to be near you."

Brandi stroked his face and kissed his eyelids when they drifted shut under her caress.

"I know you are trying to be understanding of the situation with my mom, but that doesn't undo all of the wrongs I've done. And there are so many things I just can't tell you yet."

They held each other and he knew Brandi was gathering her thoughts. He knew she wanted him too, but that didn't mean he had it in the bag. There would be conditions to their starting a real life together. Conditions he couldn't comply with until he played his part in the coming struggle, but how could he make her understand without breaking Tessa's confidences? His gut said he had to keep the things he learned from Tessa a secret until he was free to be with Brandi.

"I guess we both have some things to work out, huh?" she asked.

"Yeah, I need some time to try to get my mom out. I don't even know where he's keeping her, but I have to try. I can't just leave her behind. If I can find her, I'll walk away, Sparky. I'll do anything to be like this with you forever."

"Of course, I understand that." She paused and looked away. "What will you do when he sends you for me, Abel?"

"He doesn't know who you are. He only knows there's a female pyro on the Enclave." He tried to reassure her. She smiled grimly.

"It's only a matter of time and you know it." Brandi rose from his lap to pace the floor in front of the coffee table. "Your lack of an answer is answer enough for me. I understand. If it comes down to me or your mom, well, enough said."

"I think you're assuming too much. Did you know Nate left the Nest to be with Karrie?" She looked surprised. "He did. I saw them. I can't be absolutely sure, but I think they're already mated and keeping it a secret." He smiled. "I want that for us. Not the secret part but the mated part. I want to share my life with you. I just don't know what kind of life I can offer the daughter of a Councilman. Hell, I don't know what I could offer the daughter of any man."

He shook his head. Brandi crawled back into his lap.

"I'll likely be disowned anyway." She shrugged.

She rested her face against his chest. Abel hadn't even considered the consequences Brandi would pay to be with him.

"Let's not get ahead of ourselves. I have to go to the Council and admit to my power now that it's out in the open. My parents are probably worried sick. They're gonna want to lock me away for my own good. You can't do anything but go along with things on your end until you find your mother."

She was quiet for a minute, drawling circles on his chest while he stroked her hair. "I have a question. Does he keep your mother drugged? Why doesn't she leave on her own?"

This was not a conversation he could have without being partially dishonest. He hated giving her half-truths but Brandi deserved what he could give her.

"Mom is half-mated to the Master."

Brandi's head snapped up and she gasped.

"Yeah, I know. It's screwed up. It's a lot like the bonding between Darren and Dani. The Master's ability to drain other vamps' power by drinking from them has a downside. He can't bond to anyone. It fades in a matter of hours. She is devoted to him, but to him she is no more than a tool. My mother swears he loves her and it's not his fault he can't be faithful. It's disgusting."

"So you're telling me that not only do you need to break her out, but you need to convince her to leave with you? You have to convince her to leave her mate? Darren hasn't given up on Dani yet and she's bonded to another man. Why would your mom be any different?"

Brandi's eyes were wide and sad. She didn't believe he would ever get out and Abel couldn't really blame her. She just shook her head and climbed off of his lap again.

"I'm not stupid, Abel. I know there's a lot you're not saying. I still haven't figured out why I found you with Tessa and Debbie." She looked defeated. "Secrets and lies. How do you build a life on secrets and lies? It's the reason I was clinging to Greyson. You give me no reason to hope for a future. I didn't love him but I wanted to. I cared a lot for him. At least I knew where I stood with him, or at least I thought I did." She laughed a little hysterically. Abel growled. There was nothing he could do and only one more thing left to say.

"Well, I do love you. For now I can't give you any more than that."

———————— • ————————

She loved him, too, but Brandi couldn't say it. Somehow it felt like admitting defeat. It would be like rewarding him for breaking her heart. And he *would* break her heart. Brandi had just spent the most amazing day of her life with a man who was the absolute worst choice she could have made. Abel was a minion for the Rogue. He lied and cheated and he hurt people for a living. It would be forbidden. She would lose everything that made her Brandi Vaughn, including her family, if she chose to be with him, whether he left the Rogue or not.

But that didn't stop her from wanting to run into his arms. It didn't stop her foolish heart from falling for him, or her traitorous body from craving his like an addict, after only one day in his arms. He crossed the room and wrapped his arms around her. Again his scent made her hungry and hot but she denied the need. Damn, she needed to feed. How long had it been?

"I have to go. I'll be missed soon," he stated flatly, resignation in his voice.

"Me too. I need to see my father. He's working in his chambers at the hall. According to Debbie he's practically living there to avoid my mother." She smiled. "But that's a story for another day."

Together they left the hotel and exited the building. Abel hailed her a cab and faded back into the shadows. That was where he lived, in the shadows of life. Brandi remembered what life was like when people never saw you because the shadows swallowed you whole. She would try to remember that in the future.

Eighteen

Griffin watched with annoyance as the other Councilmen questioned his daughter. He knew it was necessary to get information from Brandi, but the urge to grab her and run to a safe place where the Rogue would never find her was making him edgy. She'd been hiding for days. Now that he had her back he wanted to keep it that way.

"How long have you been aware of this mutated power, Ms. Vaughn?" Kane Stafford asked Brandi. She sat with her spine straight as a rod in the chair across from Griffin's desk in the Council chambers.

"I experienced it for the first time the other day," she responded.

Griffin knew it was a lie and so did Kane. She couldn't look at anyone when she said it. Brandi had never been able to lie successfully so she didn't try. Today, though, for some reason, she was dissembling, and Griffin had every intention of finding out why, as soon as he got rid of the other Councilmen. Mason, Kane, and his own father, Lloyd, were hovering around his office.

"And you claim to have no idea how the blaze in the park started when you disrupted your half sister's abduction last year?" Kane wore an expression of utter disbelief.

"This isn't an inquisition, Councilor Stafford. Why are you badgering my granddaughter?" Lloyd asked from his position leaning against the wall.

"The girl hasn't done any harm, Kane. It's not her fault she's gifted. It may be a destructive gift that will scare the shit out of people, but it's a gift, nonetheless. Let's leave her with her father and go home. We all have our own families to tend to. Griffin will protect her from harm," Mason, ever the mediator, piped up from the sofa.

"Hasn't done any harm? You say she hasn't done any harm? She's been walking around for God knows how long with the power to wreak destruction on us all and she didn't think we should know? What if that monster had found her before now?"

"My daughter says she didn't know until recently and I believe her. The Rogue could not know of her ability because her singular episode occurred on the Enclave. And we all know after your vehement defense of the Enclave and its warriors that it isn't possible that there are any spies in their ranks. Though you have no problem allowing the power contained in my other child to roam the streets freely without so much as one guard to watch her back."

Griffin was on a tear and ready to lay into Kane for the way he chose to wave double standards to promote his own causes. Kane hated the fact that the House of Vaughn and the House of Deidrick were united by marriage. He had been pressing for an arranged bonding between their families for months. It was lunacy, considering Griffin was trying to abolish the laws that held people to the contracts made by their families without the consent of the individual. Now Kane thought he would whisk away Griffin's youngest daughter for the purposes of "protecting" her. The conniving old vamp would love to get his hands on a powerful member of either his or Mason's family. Luckily for Mason, his daughter was just a baby. Griffin's girls, however, were ripe for the picking.

"You will not use my—"

Griffin's tirade was cut off by shattering glass and an explosion accompanied by blinding light and dark, suffocating smoke. A projectile of some sort had been thrown through Griffin's office window. He leapt from his perch on the corner of his desk and tackled Brandi to the ground, taking her chair and table next to it out as well. Similar explosions and screams could be heard from other areas of the Council Hall.

Mason grabbed Brandi's shirt and dragged her toward the door. Griffin followed, giving cover to his daughter. Brandi struggled to turn over so she could crawl instead of being hauled out of the room. Griffin could only imagine this was the strike they had all been waiting for. They knew the Rogue hadn't disappeared. He was just lying low. Striking the Council Hall itself was a huge tactical risk. Warriors patrolled the building and grounds around the clock. An invading force would have to strike hard and fast, taking out everyone quickly before backup troops arrived. The Enclave would send an army to aid their leaders and protect the home of their government and history.

Griffin realized his mind was wandering. He'd struck his head when he hit the ground with force. Brandi looked over her shoulder to make sure he was following and slowed when he wasn't keeping up the pace.

"Go!" he shouted over the blaring smoke alarms.

Brandi pulled on Mason's arm, and he looked back just as more windows shattered, heralding the arrival of several fully armed men in black fatigues and full face masks.

Two sets of hands reached out and pulled Griffin through the door just before a line of bullets was laid in the floor where he'd been creeping along the carpet seconds before. The room spun and nausea threatened to overtake Griffin. The door to his office slammed shut. Lloyd and Mason carried him by his arms and Kane was opening the hidden door under the Oriental rug in the assembly room. When it was closed, the boards were so cleverly laid that the door blended seamlessly into the surrounding hardwood floor. There was a door in the office of every Councilman that led to this room. The room was used for closed meetings and entertaining guests in the hall.

In the days when the hall was built, there was a greater fear of being discovered by the human population. So an escape route was established for the Councilmen in order to preserve continuity of government in the event of an attack. It was still a concern, but in today's world of popular vampire fiction, if a person claimed to have seen a vampire, people would just assume he or she was either crazy or had seen someone in a costume. To Griffin's knowledge this was the first time the tunnel had ever been used.

He realized that his mind had wandered off again because in the blink of an eye he was being carried down the tunnel beneath the building. He watched Kane lock the hidden door. They hustled along the long corridor that ended at a storage building far enough from the main facility that most people didn't realize it was part of their property.

Mason immediately called Gage. He put the call on speakerphone.

"What the hell happened over there?" was Gage's greeting when he answered the phone. "I've got men heading your way. Did we lose anyone?" Gage's baritone came through the speaker loud and clear.

Griffin listened to Mason explain what had happened but that wasn't much information. They'd gotten out as fast as they could.

"They used flash-bang grenades. Damn thing landed right next to Griffin on his desk. I think it rung his bell pretty good. He may have also taken a blow to the head when he took Brandi to the floor. I'm pretty sure he was the only injury in our group."

Mason looked around the room and froze. Griffin knew something was very wrong.

"They didn't use live grenades? Are you sure?" Gage sounded puzzled.

"Yes. Shots were fired but no real explosives."

"Then why is the entire rear of the hall in flames?" Gage wanted to know.

Mason met Griffin's eyes and swallowed hard. "Brandi isn't with us."

Griffin struggled to his feet with his head spinning and his stomach ready to revolt. He headed back down the mile-long tunnel to look for his little girl, with Mason and Lloyd on his heels. Kane continued on to safety. Smoke was filling the tunnel and the building above them creaked and groaned. They could see the door and knew the safety bar was engaged from the inside, but it was so hot they couldn't even get near the door. It was too late.

Griffin sat on a fallen tree watching the remains of the Council Hall smolder hours after the strike ended. Soot covered his face and blackened his clothes. His usually crisp white dress shirt hung open, the sleeves rolled to his elbows, his jacket long gone. Samantha sat at his side, silently weeping for her fallen twin. Sarah stood behind them, fixated on the embers that continued to glow orange in the dark of the night. Ribbons of smoke rose into the air as if to carry the souls of those who had died in the battle to heaven on a soft wind.

"This wasn't supposed to happen. This wasn't supposed to happen," Sarah repeated time and again.

Griffin couldn't agree more. He was surprised he hadn't been arrested for assaulting his elder Council member. According to Kane, Brandi began to lose control of her power during the melee and her clothes were on fire. She backed away from the door and told him to get Griffin to safety while she diverted their attackers. Kane agreed, reasoning that her uncontrolled temper would kill them all if they were to get stuck with her in the tunnel. Not only did he leave her behind without telling the others, but he also locked the hidden door so she couldn't follow them to safety. By the time they realized Brandi was missing, the back of the Council Hall was engulfed in flames.

Six warriors had been lost in the fighting and fire, along with an unknown number of rogue invaders. The heart of a father beating wildly in Griffin's chest took over for his mind and demanded retribution when he overheard Kane explaining his part in all of this to Gage. He knew the attack wasn't Kane's fault, but he needed to destroy something and Kane was the nearest target.

To save his own ass, the elder had blocked Brandi's only escape route out of the destruction. Griffin had beaten the man until he begged for mercy. It had taken Gage and three of his men to bodily carry Griffin away from his target.

When they finally set him free, Griffin entered the still-burning building to search for Brandi, but he couldn't get past the point where things had started to collapse. Warriors swarmed the building to put out the fire and shore up the parts that could be saved. The front of the hall, including the chamber room where public sessions were held, and the library survived the fire with minimal damage, but the rear of the building, which contained the offices and the holding cells, was a total loss.

His baby girl was in there somewhere among the rubble and he couldn't reach her. It was unlikely there would even be a body left to claim. Griffin gave in to the misery and cried with his daughter. There was a ripping pain in his chest that nothing would assuage. The place in his heart his children occupied throbbed from the loss. Sobs racked his body and tears ravaged his face. Samantha leaned into her father's embrace to hold him while the grief had its way.

Bile rose in Abel's throat and he choked it back. This shit came out of nowhere. Darren had commandeered a troop of the Master's lackeys and raided the Council Hall. Abel's absence from the Nest had left him out of the loop and scrambling for answers. Brandi had been on her way to the hall when they parted, and not knowing where she was now had his gut twisting.

"If you could have been found, you would have participated," the Master had told Abel when he asked why he hadn't been included in the planning of the raid. "Darren believes we have a double agent making the rounds. Therefore our plans are of the utmost confidentiality until the last moment."

How could he protect Brandi if he had no idea what was being planned until it was too late? He couldn't. Abel needed to find his mother and get her out before Darren took everyone in the Nest down with him. His personal mission to reclaim Danielle Vaughn would get them all caught or killed.

"I'd like to know where you've been, boy," the Master demanded.

"I was looking for information on the pyro reported, but the Enclave is closed up tight. Nobody's talking." That seemed to appease the Master. He wanted the pyro.

By the time Abel reached the Council Hall, the battle was over, but the fire burned on. All but one of the vamps Darren had taken with him were killed in the raid. Darren had to have known that would happen. He was an ex-Wrath guard. There was no point to the exercise other than to cause death and destruction. What tactical advantage could come from attacking a mostly unoccupied government building? What could be gained by burning offices and empty holding cells? Hell, maybe Darren thought Dani would be there for the taking. Who knew what was going through Darren's head? After witnessing his mother's decline and Darren's particular brand of crazy, Abel believed he had found a new form of mental illness. If a vamp tied himself to another and they were separated for long periods, it would result in a sort of mania that could only be relieved by contact with his or her mate. He had been told that most vamps who lost their mates chose to wither away and follow their mates to the grave rather than live on without them. He supposed that was also a form of the madness.

The scene at the hall was bad. Dead minions and warriors alike bearing large holes and severe burns littered the ground. Large-caliber rounds had been used in the battle and the evidence of their effectiveness covered the ground and dripped from the remaining walls. The area smelled like a funeral pyre. Warriors crawled over everything, searching for timber to shore up the collapsing building.

Night finally fell and Abel crept out of the trees. He pulled his hat down low and tried to blend in while he made his way around the property in search of Brandi or news of her whereabouts. A battered-looking elder vampire was lifted into a truck for a ride to the infirmary. Abel ducked behind a truck to listen while the vamp denied all responsibility for the death of an uncontrolled child.

"She wanted to stay behind," he told Gage Paris.

"She died a noble death in defense of her father and the Council. Griffin should be proud of the girl. It's just a shame no one had time to teach her to control the flames. That was not my shortcoming, you have to admit, Captain. I only did what was best, just as she did."

Abel fell to his knees in the dirt. It couldn't be true. He couldn't lose her. No. He'd just found her and convinced her to give him a chance. He loved her. He refused to believe Brandi was gone. Somehow he knew if she were dead he would know. If she were gone from this world, he would feel the loss. She was not his mate, but the madness would have taken him too if the spark that lit his world was gone.

No longer caring if anyone saw him or not, Abel began to circle the smoldering building. She was still here and he would turn over every ashen timber until he found her.

———◆———

Buried alive. Buried alive. Brandi was buried alive. It was dark and hot in her little cubbyhole. The flames never burned her anymore. It was a part of her now. The heat wouldn't kill her but the weight of the collapsing ceiling could crush her.

Time seemed to have slowed to a crawl just before the ceiling caved in on her and her adversaries. She'd planned to block off all six entrances to the assembly room while the Councilmen, including her dazed father, made their way to safety. After all, the bad guys were after her, not the others. They would assume she and the Councilmen were trapped in the burning room while, in actuality, they would be slipping out right under their feet. It was a simple, last-minute plan that had failed miserably.

Everyone but Brandi had been in the tunnel when she explained her plan to Councilman Stafford. While she spoke to him he watched her hands in fascination. She was still learning control and the stress of the sudden attack had her nerves frayed. When she looked down at her hands, they were bright with rising heat that set her shirtsleeves on fire. She took a deep breath and pulled the heat back into her body, while someone was attempting to kick in the heavy wooden door to her father's office.

"I will cover the entrances to the room. They're here for me. I'll distract them long enough to give you time to get away before I follow. Please get my father to safety. He doesn't look well," Brandi explained. She expected an argument but didn't get one.

"I will keep your father safe." He nodded crisply.

Councilman Stafford ducked into the floor and the door dropped into place. If she hadn't seen it was there, Brandi never would have suspected the floor opened into a concrete tunnel that went on for nearly a mile. She hadn't expected to hear the clank of a lock being engaged under her feet either. Brandi hit the board that would release the locking mechanism but it held tight. It was sealed from below. She was trapped.

Panic flared and her hard-won control slipped. Instead of wasting the surge, Brandi decided to improvise. Another hard boot landed on the door and the rogues were nearly on her. Her fangs dropped painfully and the room came into sharp resolution. Brandi let loose a wave of hot energy that pushed them back. Fire began consuming the area around the door.

The vamp in front was badly burned but he didn't seem to notice. It was the blast that moved him, not the heat. He landed inside the room instead of the outer office with his friends. He came at her again, even though the only visible skin around his eyes was blistering. Mindlessly, he barreled down on her, his blank eyes locked in on his target. Brandi put out her hands defensively. She didn't want to kill the vamp but he left her no choice. Another door crashed in, admitting two more vamps who looked as stony and distant as the first. Their clothes bore charred patches from their first attempt.

That's when it dawned on her. These men were trapped just like her. They weren't in control of their own minds. An outsider was pulling their strings. Flames snaked across the carpet and up the papered walls. The fire crawled along the ceiling while they fought to subdue Brandi. She struggled to reach one of the doors not yet engulfed, but they held her back as if her capture was their mission. Unfortunately, their zombie-like minds were not able to see the danger to their own safety. If Brandi were a normal vamp with no extra-elemental ability, they would have easily subdued her and carried her away.

But she was not normal and it was far too late to save the men dragging her to the door of her father's burning office. Her body was a living flame. Her clothes had long since burned away. The smell of burning flesh and hair made Brandi gag, but the vamps still foolishly held on to her. If these men survived, they would quickly wish they were dead.

The building moaned in protest before part of the ceiling crumbled to the floor. Loud cracking noises preceded a larger failure. In the doorway, Brandi held on to the frame. The massive burns caused the vamp's bodies to weaken without the permission of their minds. When the floor above finally collapsed on them, Brandi found herself wedged into a pocket created by the door frame and a large piece of fallen ceiling. The inferno raged around her but Brandi felt no pain.

Up until that point, Brandi had considered her power something she had to fear. It was a separate entity living inside of her. The power had control of her life and she had no choice but to see where it would lead. The strength that surrounded her now was not an enemy to be feared, but a vital part of herself she hadn't been able to accept. She was the fire, and the flames came from the pain, stress, or joy of her soul. She accepted the flames and held on to them tightly for the comfort and protection she desperately needed. She winced when pain suddenly seared its way up her leg and across her back. Maybe her body could only withstand so much heat? Brandi breathed through the pain until it slowly subsided. She had a second to be grateful she was still alive before her body gave in to an exhausted sleep while the arms of her power cradled and protected her from the hell storm.

She woke long after the fire abated. A smoldering pile of rubble and ash now weighing down on her body, Brandi took inventory of her situation. Eventually one of two things was going to happen, because, after several attempts, she was not able to move even an inch from her current position. Either the remains of the building would crush her or she would starve from lack of blood.

She would die there along with the vamps who had come to fetch her and gotten caught in the blaze. It was a fitting end for her to die next to the men she'd killed. The guilt on her shoulders was heavier than that of the pressure crushing her body. Those men might have made a bad decision when they signed on with the Rogue, but it was obvious they had been forced to fight and die that day. There was no callous intent in their eyes. The three vamps had worn masks of emptiness as if their bodies had no souls. Like flesh-and-blood robots. Knowing they had no control only made her guilt grow. They were young guys with possibly hundreds of years of family, friends, and better decisions in front of them, but now, all their tomorrows were gone at her hands. Her burning hands. She deserved to die with them.

Mason was correct when he assumed people would fear her when they learned of her extra-elemental ability, especially after they learned she'd burned down the Council Hall and killed God only knew how many people in the process. She wouldn't have to worry about people liking her only for her family connections anymore. She wouldn't have to stand in her twin's shadow anymore. Everyone in the vampire nation would recognize and respect her for her power and for being the first pyro in many generations. But, she would be feared above all things.

Thinking of the destroyed building above her brought vivid memories of Abel flooding in around her. Unbidden, a smile spread over her dirty face. She remembered fearing him when they entered that secluded room on the upper level of the library what felt like years ago, but it had only been a month.

Abel had the potential to be a good man, if he only had someone to love him through it. He was the kind of man who'd survived being abused and neglected from a young age, but didn't allow the memory of it to twist his mind. He lived a solitary life of crime to protect the mother who'd led him into that life. He went out of his way to protect the people he cared for, even if it meant punishment for him. There was so much she didn't know about Abel, but she did know that he had the core of a great man in spite of his upbringing. It was a shame Brandi would never get to see the man he could become in time.

Her smile faded. What would happen to him now? Would he blame himself for her death? Would he remain with the Rogue after she was gone? Would Abel end up like one of the vamps who lay dead and buried around her? Abel had professed his love for Brandi just hours ago and she knew he would hold himself responsible. He would stay with the Rogue as punishment for not protecting the woman he loved. He would end up dead or worse after she left this world. Brandi couldn't let that happen. She loved him. It was crazy and impossible, but she knew Abel was going to be her life, her love, and the best of friends.

She struggled to free herself from the wreckage but nothing she did helped. Every time she moved, the rubble moved in more tightly around her body. Brandi fought for every breath. She had to find her way back to Abel. He belonged to her, and Brandi wasn't giving up on him, or the life they were meant to live together, without a fight.

Dani straddled Chase's lap on a dining room chair. She fought to suck air into her lungs while she came down from a shattering climax. Chase lapped at her neck to close the vein he had opened in the heat of passion. Dani shivered and held on tight to the mate of her heart.

"You will kill me one of these days, Lovely. But I will die a very happy man." Chase sent the praise telepathically because he was beyond words at the moment. Dani giggled. He hadn't seen anything yet. Chase was still firm inside her body, so she wiggled and had the satisfaction of hearing him groan and feeling him harden further.

"I've decided we should die together," she told him through their mental connection.

Dani lifted her body to slide back down Chase's length and he hissed. She giggled. He groaned. She sank her fangs into his shoulder and let the connection between them open wide. They shared each other's ecstasy. He felt the pleasure of her heat wrapped around him and her rapture at being filled by him. The bite was a hot point of bliss, and with Dani's mouth sucking and licking, Chase's mind and body blew like a fuse. He threw his head back and screamed her name. Dani ground herself against her mate and followed him over the edge.

She didn't remember getting into bed, but sometime later she woke there, wrapped in Chase's arms. Dani looked around the room. A sound in the darkness had pulled her from sleep. Chase slept on when she climbed out of bed to stand at their bedroom door. If there was an intruder in their home, she would destroy him before he touched her sleeping mate. Dani stretched out her telepathic sensors in search of a mind that didn't belong. She felt nothing. Just when she started to believe she had imagined the sound, a scream of unimaginable sorrow ripped through her mind. Dani fell to the carpet, gripping her head. She fought to narrow the telepathic path she'd opened in search of an intruder.

Chase leapt from the bed, disoriented and furious. His bond with Dani allowed him to hear the scream on a muted level. His first thought was someone was launching a telepathic attack on his mate. She was crumpled on the floor, sobbing. Chase lifted her from the ground and forced his way into her mind. He gave her his strength and together they focused on fighting the scream back out of her sensitive psyche. The sound was heartbreaking. The sheer misery of the source dug at his gut.

When Dani was able to open her eyes, the crystal blue he loved so much had been swallowed by the blackness of the sorrowful wail echoing between their heads.

Dani's voice shook when she told him, "Call Mason now. I need every telekinetic he can find to meet us at the Council Hall."

Nineteen

A bel watched Brandi's family climb into the back of a long, black car. The driver ran around the car and climbed in behind the wheel. They had given up on finding Brandi alive but Abel refused to believe she was gone. It was obvious that Councilman Griffin Vaughn had no idea who he was when Abel strode up and tapped on the window. When it rolled down Abel informed him that he was Brandi's mate. Okay, he was her future mate, and he knew she was still alive. Mr. Vaughn looked surprised, but he listened. He wanted to know exactly how Abel knew she was alive.

"Are you telepathic?" Griffin asked while getting out of the car.

"No. I have no extrasensory ability, but I can still feel her." Abel laid a hand over his chest. "I feel her here."

Griffin gave him a sympathetic nod and wrapped an arm around Abel's shoulder. "I don't know how you knew my baby girl. I was under the impression she had a boyfriend that I know wasn't you." Tears filled Griffin's already red-ringed eyes. "To be honest I've seen so little of her lately I have no idea what was happening in her life," he sniffed, "but it's obvious you cared for Brandi."

"I didn't just care. I love her. Not past tense, I still love her and I know she's still in there," Abel interrupted.

Brandi's sister eyed him suspiciously. She had seen him the day he helped Darren abduct Dani. It was only a matter of time before she recognized him and blew his cover.

The tears in the Councilman's eyes spilled over when he looked at the destroyed remains of the building. He patted Abel on the back. "Yes, son, Brandi is still in there." But he meant her body was still there. Not the person she had been.

Dani'd had quite a few surprise revelations in the last hour. What she first believed to be a telepathic attack had actually been her half sister crying out for help. The mournful wail had brought both her and Chase to their knees. It wouldn't have been so bad if she hadn't opened her senses wide just before it hit full force.

The pyrokinetic ability Brandi had hidden for over a year was now a front pager in the black-eyed freak tabloid gossip mill. Something catastrophic had happened at the Council Hall and the ensuing fire had been caused by a trapped Brandi. Dani got all of this information through her telepathic connection to Brandi. Normally Dani could find a way to communicate with others telepathically, but Brandi was so mired in her own thoughts and fears that Dani simply couldn't get her attention.

Dani had learned a lot about her half sister's life of late through her thoughts, and not all of it was good. It was obvious that Brandi had built up a successful shield in her mind for Dani to have never seen the stress and loneliness before. Brandi was in a serious relationship. That wouldn't have been a shock, but the man's identity was. He was a minion of the Rogue. She was in love with a rogue, but he wasn't a willing accomplice to their enemy. He was protecting someone else.

A large part of Brandi's current pain was a direct result of her fear for the life of the man she loved. Brandi seemed convinced that he was on the scene and searching for her. That put him in danger of capture again. Well, Dani would be doing some serious fact-finding as soon as her sister was free and safe. She was also going to have a talk with her father and father-in-law regarding the fact that she and Chase were being left out of the loop on important events. She was furious that no one had bothered to call and inform her that they believed Brandi was dead. Mason claimed they'd feared it was a trap to bring her out in the open, and if it was, it had worked because she was surely not going to sit at home and wait for news. She was trying to get a feel for exactly where in the rubble Brandi could be. Like Brandi, Dani feared the smoldering building would crush her at any moment. She had to move quickly before the pocket that protected Brandi's body collapsed.

Dani stood near the destroyed back side of the building with three low- to midgrade telekinetics behind her. Dani was a midlevel telekinetic but she wasn't very controlled in her talent. She'd spent her time honing her telepathic gifts. She feared moving material from the wrong place and causing the remaining debris to crush Brandi. Griffin was on his way back to the hall as fast as he could get there. Dani believed between her and her father, they could lift Brandi out.

A vaguely familiar guy stomped by wearing a fierce scowl and carrying a crowbar and what looked like drapes from the Council Hall library. He was attempting to wrap a curtain around one of his hands. Dani started to follow him, but Chase caught her around the waist and pulled her back against him.

"Do you know him, Lovely? He doesn't look like one of ours. There's no uniform and he's a little too rough around the edges to be one of Gage's boys," Chase whispered in her mind.

"I think we may be looking at Brandi's mysterious new love. She is convinced that he is here. If she has that kind of attachment to him, I think we should follow him to see where he thinks she might be," Dani responded telepathically. Chase was privy to all the information she was getting from Brandi through their bond because she hadn't put any walls between their minds. Chase was helping Dani filter the

emotions screaming out of Brandi so she could concentrate on finding a direction.

"We will follow at a distance. It isn't clear if all of the rogues are gone," Chase agreed and motioned for the other telekinetics to follow.

On the opposite side of the building, they found the brooding, dark-eyed guy attempting to lever a huge beam off the mass of rubble. He had the fabric around his hands to protect them from the pressure of the bar and the heat of the smoldering beams. Dani threw her telekinetic strength in with his muscle and the beam was removed cleanly. It wasn't until he spoke that Dani knew exactly who this man was for sure. The sound of his voice still rang in her dreams some nights. Darren wanted her, and this man had stood between her and insanity. It was his vehemence that Darren not touch Dani that had given Brandi time to step in and carry her away. If not for him and Brandi, she would likely be unwillingly bonded to Darren today instead of Chase.

The guy gave her a grateful look and continued digging while he spoke. "Thank you. You're Brandi's sister, right? I need to move the debris from this area. I'm sure this is where she's pinned."

Just then, the building started to collapse further and crush the area while they watched in horror.

"Where? Exactly where should I focus?" Dani coaxed the man, who had fallen to his knees.

"There." He pointed. "I think close to the middle. It will take hours of careful digging."

Dani attempted to lift the weight of the falling building with the help of the other telekinetics. Her vision sharpened. Dani was waving her black-eyed freak flag. She could hear Brandi scream in her mind. She was being crushed.

"More. Now." Dani fell to her knees and mentally pushed up on the heavy weight with her arms like that was going to help. But it was barely budging.

"Everything is so tangled. We will need to lift the whole thing at once. I'm sorry but we can't do it," one of the guys said, panting.

"Don't quit," Dani grunted. She felt wetness on her lips and knew her nose was bleeding from the strain. Chase held on to her from behind, sending her waves of support and belief in her ability. Just when she thought the weight would crush her along with her sister, the weight disappeared and she fell back into Chase.

It was impossible. The falling building seemed to be floating in chunks, with individual pieces some twenty feet above where they had just been. The entire thing flew en masse into the field behind the Council Hall.

"It's your dad," Chase told her. "He's running this way with Gage."

Dani could feel Brandi more clearly even though she still couldn't see her. She locked on to Brandi's unique mental signature and willed it to rise above the rubble. She focused every cell in her body on pulling her sister out alive.

Things shifted and fell. The guy on the ground next to her held his breath when Brandi's naked, soot-darkened form began to rise out of the ash.

"I've got her! Great job, kid," Griffin's deep voice came from behind her. "I never would have been able to find her in there."

"It wasn't me." Dani gasped for air. "Him." She pointed to Brandi's new love. "Her man knew where to look."

Dani watched as Brandi's body rose higher. At first she seemed to have some rubble wrapped around her arms and one leg, but as she rose above the ashes it was clear that the partial remains of other vampires were still clinging to her. It was a morbid sight. They must have been holding on to Brandi when they died. Brandi came floating over to them with the skeletal arms of three people still hanging onto her limbs. Dani searched Brandi's jumbled thoughts for some understanding of what she was seeing until she found it. The rogues who'd been sent to retrieve Brandi had held on to the very end, never releasing her, even in death.

Chase stepped in to remove the dangling remains. Brandi's man was out of his shirt and waiting there to catch her when she drifted gently down. Abel settled cross-legged on the ground with her in his lap while he maneuvered her into his shirt and buttoned it up. Brandi stirred and cracked her eyes open to smile up at him.

"I knew you were here." Her voice was a raspy whisper.

"Does anyone have any water?" Gage yelled to the gathering crowd. Several bottles were passed forward and Griffin knelt in front of the couple. He held a bottle for her while she drank greedily.

Brandi's new love held her to his chest. "You scared the absolute shit out of me, Sparky! You smell bad but I love you anyway," he joked.

"You smell wonderful. I'm sorry." She kissed him and tried to wipe away the black marks she left on his face. Griffin tried to take Brandi from the guy but she clung to him.

"No, Daddy. I want to stay with Abel. You can't protect me. Look what I'm capable of. You're all in danger around me. It will be safer if I go away until things settle down," she pleaded.

"You can't be serious about this guy, sweetheart. He's some kid off the streets who has a drug problem. I recognize him now. He was in a holding cell for distributing Hypno. I will not allow you to waste your life that way." Griffin looked at Abel with disdain. "You will hand over my daughter or I will take her from you the hard way."

Oh, shit. This was going downhill in a hurry. Chase pushed Dani behind him and she peeked around his side to watch the action. She was still receiving thoughts from Brandi. Daddy was about to be put in his place. Brandi struggled out of Abel's lap when it didn't look like he would release her. She put herself between Abel and her father and they glared at each other. It was a standoff. Dani was waiting for the tumbleweed to blow by.

"I guess that's what your parents said about Tessa, huh?" Brandi cocked her head.

Griffin looked like she had slapped him. Brandi was beginning to glow with anger.

"Babe, if you toast that shirt, we're out of luck. It was the only one I was wearing," Abel reminded her. Brandi turned, for the first time noticing that Abel was shirtless. She breathed deeply and pulled the heat back in.

"Much better, Sparky." He placed a hand possessively on her hip. Griffin did not miss the subtext: *She's already mine.*

"You know nothing about Abel or the life he lives. I'm not you, Daddy. As much as I love you and Mom, I will not allow you to make my life decisions for me. You will not take him from me because he doesn't meet your expectations. I can't believe you of all people would even try."

Brandi grabbed Abel's hand and walked off with her shirttails flapping in the wind.

* * *

Abel took Brandi to Candy's house. It was the safest place he could think to go for the night. Candy was out of town and he still had the keys he'd swiped the last time he visited. They would find another hiding place in the morning.

When Brandi had a chance to look around, she was none too happy to be in the home of the woman who had caused her public embarrassment. She was almost green-eyed. Abel had to laugh at how angry Brandi became at his involvement with Candy, but she settled down when he explained his relationship with her nemesis. He liked her being possessive of him. If he hadn't known how she felt about him before, he did now. Her behavior in front of her family and the jealousy she displayed reassured him that she loved him even if she wasn't ready to say it yet.

He took a good look at her and frowned. She wore only his black button-up shirt hanging to her knees, and every inch of visible skin was dark. He wondered how she'd managed not to lose her hair in the fire but he didn't ask. He assumed it was as fire-resistant as her skin.

Abel steered Brandi to the bathroom and turned on the shower while she watched. He thought of running her a bath to soak in but she was too dirty for that. The water would be black by the time she settled into it. He hoped the shower would help wash away the remains of her traumatic day. He laid out a fresh towel and unbuttoned the shirt covering Brandi's filthy-but-inspiring skin. He had to work at not staring at all of her more interesting bits when he guided her to the cleansing spray. Brandi looked up at him hopefully. She wanted him to join her, but Abel believed she needed some time alone to process the day and all of its ramifications. He left her to bathe and unwind in privacy.

Before today, Abel never understood the concept of life-affirming sex. The thought of sex after the death of someone close to you or after a close call with your own life never made sense to him. But today, for that moment in time when he believed Brandi could really be gone, his world had come to a grinding halt. He had never known pain so deep or all consuming in his admittedly difficult life.

He'd looked into the deep sapphire blue of her eyes and he had to have her. He wanted to sink himself into her body until the fear of losing her stopped and he was sure that Brandi was safe and alive in his arms. He wanted her in his arms and in his bed so often that they would forget they were separate beings. Their first time together had only intensified the sureness of the voice in the back of his mind that screamed to him that they belonged together. He was sure he needed Brandi on a soul-deep level to survive. It begged him day and night to claim her and make her his mate.

Abel made his decision. He would fulfill his promise to Tessa. Then he would try to free his mother. If she refused to leave, that would be her decision. Abel had a life to lead and a mate to claim. He couldn't spend the rest of his life protecting his mother if she didn't want his protection. He wanted a family of his own, and Brandi was the only person, vamp or human, he wanted to have that life with.

Brandi crossed the hall and entered the room almost shyly, clutching the towel that covered her. Her hair had grown out a bit and dark locks curled damply around her slender neck. In the quiet refuge of the small spare bedroom, Brandi twined her arms around Abel's waist and turned her face up, in silent request for the same reassurance he needed. She wanted to know they were both alive and together no matter the consequences.

He took her mouth with a gentle control he wasn't aware he had in him. This was the single most important night of Abel's life. He had to get it right. Brandi opened for him and he swept inside to explore the soft offering. The lush taste of Brandi's lips never failed to make an impact on him. Abel took his time searching out all of the places he might have missed the last time they held each other.

Brandi molded herself to his body and rubbed herself enticingly along his frame. The towel fell from her freshly washed body and he groaned. How was he supposed to take his time and seduce her if she kept trying to tantalize him? Abel slid his hands down her smooth curves to pull her closer to him, but he stopped when the texture of the skin on her left hip surprised him. He pulled back to look into her eyes.

"I know. I didn't notice it until I was washing. I felt when it happened in the fire but I forgot about it. It doesn't hurt. You can touch it." She looked down at her lower body.

Abel knelt in front of her to examine her. He was at a loss to explain the odd impression that wrapped like a vine around her thigh several times and up over her left hip. Abel turned her to get a look at the healing burns that crossed her back and ended in a curl around her right shoulder. The skin was smooth and a little pinker than the rest of her creamy complexion, instead of being a twisted, shiny scar like you expect to see in burns. This new decoration to her already lovely body was beautiful and haunting. The scars looked like climbing vines of flames dancing over delicate flesh. He looked up to see her watching him. She smiled and shrugged. Abel kissed the pink skin of her hip and took both of her hands in his. No time like the present to make his intentions known. He was already on his knees. Brandi might not appreciate the gesture, given her pure vamp blood, but his human heart demanded he show respect to the woman he loved.

"Brandi . . ." he choked. Emotions forced the words to freeze in his throat. He would have to explain his humanity but that could wait a few minutes. If she rejected him now, it wouldn't matter. He cleared his throat. Brandi tried to sink to the floor but he stayed her motion. "Please, let me do this, Sparky?"

She stood and looked down at him with fear and concern in her eyes.

"Will you be my one true mate, Brandi? Will you try to love me the way I love you? I know I have nothing to offer the daughter of a Councilman, nothing but my heart, nothing but my life. I'll give it all to you, if you'll have me. Please, say you want this too." He sounded like a total sap but every word was true.

Brandi gasped and fell to the floor in front of him as if her knees had given out. She looked dazed. He didn't see rejection in her expression as he had feared he would. It was more like confusion and disbelief.

"I know I can't provide the life you are used to, but I will work and go back to school. I'll do whatever it takes," he promised.

She tried to speak but he wasn't ready to hear the answer, so he kept talking. Why did it feel like he was giving her reasons to reject him? Shouldn't he be promising her the world? He should, but he wouldn't make promises he couldn't keep.

"I know I'm not what your family will expect in a mate. I don't want you to be estranged from them. Maybe in time they could accept our bond. I'm sure your father would come around once he sees how much I adore you."

She tried to answer again, but he kept rambling. Abel was so nervous the words were spilling out of their own volition. He stroked her face and fought the tears burning the backs of his eyes. This was it.

"I love you. That's all I can promise, Brandi. I will love you with all that I am from now until I take my last breath and beyond."

Abel took a deep breath and watched the tears track down Brandi's cheeks. She leaned in and kissed him softly, sweetly, and smiled against his lips. When she pulled away, her grin split her face from ear to ear. Abel released the breath he had been holding.

"I love you already, Abel. I don't need to try to love you. I don't need a bond to force the emotion. As far as my family is concerned, it's like I told my father today. I'm not him. I won't live my life to please him and my mother. I want them to love you too, but if they don't, I will get through it. I want you. I need you. I love you."

Abel's heart swelled in his chest. He let out the breath he'd been holding and leaned forward to take her full lips, but her expression darkened and she pulled away from him.

"I can't be mated to a man who is a slave. I can't respect a mate who does the things you do. I understand that the past is in the past but what about now?"

Abel had known from the beginning there would be conditions to her acceptance of him as her mate. "I'm not staying with the Master . . ."

Shit. He had to stop thinking of the man as his master. It was just that he had called him that since he was eight years old. The title didn't carry the meaning it should for a Shade warrior. It was just his name in Abel's mind but he knew it wasn't just a name to the rest of the world. Calling him *Master* meant that Abel was obedient and faithful to the man.

"The Rogue," he corrected. "I need to at least try to convince my mother to leave. That's the only reason for me to go back at all. She may not leave, but at least I will know in my heart that I tried to save her."

Brandi thought that over. She rose from the floor and paced around the small room. Her fingers brushed self-consciously over the new lines on the skin of her hip. Abel couldn't help enjoying the picture she made, walking around completely naked and thoughtfully considering his words. Her hand drifted down her leg to worry the newly pinked skin on her thigh. This was a serious discussion that deserved his full attention but all he could think of was licking every inch of the flaming marks to see if they would burn his tongue.

"We can go to my grandparents' summer home for a while until we get a place of our own," Brandi suggested. "They'll never know we're there and no one will think it's strange if they see me in town. I go out there sometimes just to get away. There will be plenty of room for your mom. I think we should hide out there until the Rogue stops searching for me. I may not be as wealthy as my parents, but I have an inheritance that should get us through until I find a job. There will be enough left to put a sizable down payment on a house as long as we're conservative."

She sat on the bed and reached out for his hand.

"Wait, what?" Abel sputtered. He thought she was considering being his mate and she had moved on to where they would go to hide and how they would afford to live. As if she'd already decided they would mate. His heart began to pound.

"Well, I'm surely not staying here. I can't live with that woman and there isn't enough room for your mom," she explained.

"Are you sure? I mean about me?" He didn't want to give her the chance to change her mind but he did want to give her every opportunity to think it through.

She opened her mouth to answer but he stopped her by placing a finger over her lips.

"Wait. There's one last thing I have to confess before you give me an answer, because I don't think I'll be able to let you go if you change your mind. If you can live with it, we can be mated as soon as I find my mom."

Brandi kissed his finger and smiled. Slowly he moved his finger from her mouth and replaced it with his lips. Abel needed to know she loved him too and wanted to be his mate as much as he wanted to be hers, just for a little longer. His next words could be a deal breaker. She kissed him back and the heat between them built. His shaft tightened his pants and throbbed like a heartbeat. The sweetness of her mouth made him forget his purpose. He wanted to taste every inch of her perfection, starting with her mouth and ending with her honey-coated sex. Before he knew it he was laid back on the bed with her legs wrapped around his denim-clad hips. She tugged at the fastening of his belt.

"Wait. I have to tell you." Abel moved to sit on the edge of the bed facing away from Brandi. He didn't want to see disgust in her eyes when she looked at him.

"It's about my mother." He hesitated. "It's about my mother and me," he clarified. Brandi sat up to rub his back.

"You don't have to do this, Abel. I know the worst about you

already. Nothing you say is going to change how I feel about you."
She cuddled against his back and kissed the nape of his neck, sending fire licking through his veins. Her lips on his skin drove him
past all logical thought. "Just come to bed with me." She tried
coaxing him to lie back on the bed.

"No. I feel like I've been lying to you. I haven't lied, but I haven't
admitted the truth, either. It's a lie by omission. I . . . well, you see,
my mother . . ." He took another deep breath.

"I already know you're a demi-vamp. If that's what has you in
knots, you can relax," she informed him casually.

Abel whipped around and grabbed her by the shoulders. He
stared into her eyes, shocked and confused. "You knew? You knew
and you still made love to me?" He was floored.

"I've known you were human since that day in the library. I
have a sister who was very similar to you when I met her. Her scent
was always confusing and complex to me. She drew men like flies
because of the mix of human blood and vamp hormones. You have
the same effect on women. The smell of you when I'm close is
enough to drive me mad." She smiled and leaned in to kiss him.

"So you're not worried about ending up like Darren, with a half
bond?" He needed to know. It was possible that she would bond to
him but his human blood would interfere with his ability to bond.
It could go either way. Griffin's bond to Dani's mom had worked
but Darren's didn't.

"Do you love me now?" she asked.

"Yes, of course I do." He quickly kissed her again, afraid to hope
this would all work out.

"If I were human, would it matter to you?" she asked.

"No. Humans don't bond when they mate," he explained.

"Are you prejudiced against vampires? Because I demand equal
treatment." She was trying not to smile. "If I were human, you
wouldn't ask me these questions." She did smile then.

"I just want you to be sure, Sparky." Her happiness meant everything to him. He loved her so damn much. He wanted nothing more than to be worthy of her.

"I'm hoping for a complete bond, but if it doesn't work, we'll still be in love, right? Darren didn't have that and he's paying for it. My dad told me he was in love with Tessa. Maybe that's the difference?"

Abel leapt onto the bed and dragged Brandi over to lie on his chest. She squealed and snuggled in against him. He couldn't believe Brandi had known about his humanity all along and still she wanted to be with him. She said she loved him. It was a gift beyond measure and he would spend his life proving she had made the right choice.

"I don't want to wait. I think we should be bonded now," she told him.

Abel tipped up her chin with one finger.

"Now? But I still have things to do. I don't know how long it will take. I feel so unprepared to care for a mate."

"We want to be together. Does anything else matter?" She looked at him with those deep blue eyes, looking anxious. She was anxious? About his answer?

Abel couldn't argue with that logic. He wanted to bind her to him so badly it hurt. The voice in the back of his mind howled in triumph. His sweet little flame was just as ready to seal their vows as he was.

"I think you deserve a ceremony with family and friends, Sparky. Don't you want that? I can wait for you. I don't want you to have any regrets."

The voice in his mind kicked him in the ass. Brandi went to work on his belt again.

"I want to do this the old-fashioned way. Before our people started making the bond between two people a social and financial joining of power, the ceremony was a private event between two people in love." She had his pants undone and climbed down the bed to tug them off.

"We don't have any blades," he reminded her. He had never seen a bonding ceremony before, but he knew about the process and he was sure they used blades.

"We will improvise." Brandi smiled up at him as she tossed his pants to the floor. The glint of her sharp little fangs had him painfully hard. Oh man! It was so hot to think of Brandi sinking her fangs into him. She would be able to drink from him for the rest of his life. She climbed up his body and he watched the pulse point in her neck throb. Abel had to close his eyes or he was going to embarrass himself. The mere idea of his fangs in her skin and her blood running down his throat had him riding the edge of torment. Brandi was naked and delicious and everything he ever wanted. She nipped his chin. Abel steadied himself and opened his eyes. Brandi looked back at him through eyes as dark as the deepest night. She licked her lips and used her tongue to toy with one of her fangs.

She was teasing him and he was ready to play. Abel lifted his hips to rub his solid length against her slick sex. She hissed and pressed into him, coating him with her honey. He tried to control his breathing. Her smoky, sweet scent filled his head. She was already hot and ready for him. Their mouths came together and her fangs grazed his tongue. He hadn't realized his own fangs were on display until she stroked the sensitive points. Brandi was circling her hips in search of the pressure she needed. A slight adjustment of his hips would join them, but he wanted her fevered and eager for his possession.

He smiled against her mouth and sat up to press Brandi back onto her haunches so he could reach the dusky pink peaks of her breasts. She moaned her approval. Abel nipped and licked at her until she was again searching for the friction she craved. He chuckled. She purred and mewled like a hungry kitten. His hand explored the new, strange marks on her skin while his fingers made their way to the pulse of need at the apex of Brandi's thighs. He lightly massaged her little clit with two fingers and used his other hand to reach around to circle the entrance of her sex from behind without dipping inside. She panted and moaned into his mouth, rocking against his hand and circling her hips. Abel almost had her where he needed her to be. He adjusted his hips and let her feel how ready he was for her, how hard she made him.

"Please. Yes," she begged.

Abel continued to circle the sensitive nub of flesh with gentle fingers and pleasure her breasts with his tongue and teeth. She pleaded for release and bent her head to nip at his ear. Her climax was building and Abel was finally ready to let her have it. He adjusted his hips, positioning himself at her entrance. Her slick arousal helped him pull her down onto him in one deep thrust. Brandi screamed. Her body sucked at him while her climax claimed her completely. She shook and called his name. Abel guided her body and thrust in time to stretch out her orgasm. He had to grit his teeth against the urge to allow his own release.

When the violent waves subsided into small aftershocks of rippling heat, Abel kissed her neck at the spot he wanted so badly to taste, and then her lips.

"I love you," Abel whispered. She said something unintelligible.

He repositioned them on the bed so that she lay beneath him. He was still buried within her and reveled in the heat and complete acceptance she offered. Abel began a slow, deliberate joining of their bodies and souls. He invaded and retreated, alternating between deep thrusts and shallow digs into her core. She lifted her hips to meet each slow slide.

Abel didn't know the ritual words that were to be spoken but he knew what was in his heart. He was close to the precipice and didn't want this to end until Brandi was his mate for this lifetime and every lifetime that followed, if she would have him.

"You belong to me and I belong to you. I will never let go, bond or no bond. I will protect you until my last breath. I love you now and always, Brandi."

He took her mouth and his hips bucked faster without his consent. She was pulling him deeper under with every clenching slide into her heat. Their eyes met and Brandi replied, "I vow to love you for the whole of my existence. I vow to protect you to my last breath. I vow to cherish the gift of your returned love for all time. And I vow to always remain grateful for the man who will from this day forth be the one and only mate of my soul."

Abel waited for Brandi's bite. This had to be her choice. She had so much to lose in this act and he wanted her to take that step in her own time. He would not break her skin first.

"I love you," she told him, and she leaned in to plunge her fangs into his shoulder. The stinging pain was quickly replaced by a euphoric tidal wave. Every nerve in his body soaked up the pleasure overload. Brandi's mouth sucked and lapped at him and he was barely able to hold on to his release. Without another thought he plunged his fangs into the tender skin where neck met shoulder. Her blood welled and spread across his tongue. It was the sweetest honey sliding down his throat. Her blood was like nothing he had ever experienced. As he drank from her body, her soul crept into his. Her hopes and dreams became part of his dreams. He swallowed down her life and gave her his.

Brandi's muscles closed around him, sucking and demanding his release. She convulsed and shook in his arms. His will was snapped by the feeling of oneness that washed over him like a warm summer rain. Abel exploded, filling his mate with his seed and his blood. He was shattered by the intensity of the joining. He was no longer alone in this world. His mate would always be with him. The light of her pure white soul was like sunshine on all of the dark places inside of himself he could no longer hide. He floated for a while in that warm, new place in his mind before settling back down to find himself wrapped in love and contentment.

It had worked. He could feel Brandi's relief and joy. She'd pretended that it didn't matter if the bond didn't take, but it mattered greatly to her. She had been willing to sacrifice this incredible link to another soul in order to be with him. It humbled him.

"You undo me, baby," he told her softly. "Thank you for choosing me."

Brandi said nothing. She held him tightly, clinging to him with her arms around his neck. Abel lay down beside her and pulled her close. She snuggled there, kissing his chest before closing her eyes, but she wasn't asleep. Brandi and Abel were both in a state of awe, reveling in the discovery of their other half—like they had been blind in one eye their whole lives and were suddenly able to see clearly with both eyes. The whole picture was now in focus. He felt at home for the first time in the arms of his mate.

He was surprised at how insecure and lonely Brandi was at heart. He would do something about that. Brandi had no reason to feel less than complete satisfaction with her image and he would make damn sure she was never lonely again. He couldn't read her thoughts but he got a clear sense of her emotional state of mind. When they were both riding out the release at the end of the bonding it was nothing Abel had ever expected. He could nearly feel her ecstasy and it magnified his own.

Exhaustion eventually claimed them both, and for the first time in more years than he could remember, Abel had no nightmares. He dreamt only of the future and the life he would share with his sparky little mate.

Twenty

G age answered his cell phone, glad for the distraction from the embarrassment on Griffin's face. His daughter had just publicly put him in his place and rightly so, in Gage's opinion. He looked at the screen and didn't recognize the number. He'd been hoping it would be his mate, Koren. She was attending a wive's support group on the Enclave this evening, but she should be home by now. He'd been getting odd feelings of stress and something like panic from her for a little while now but she always got emotional when she was dealing with the newly mated females on the Enclave. Koren remembered clearly what it was like to sit by the phone and wait for your deployed mate to call. When the call doesn't come there's nothing to do but worry.

"Gage Paris," he answered with his standard greeting.

"Good evening, Captain."

He would have known the voice anywhere. The man had worked under him for decades.

"Darren." That got the attention of everyone standing around Gage. It became eerily silent.

"To what do I owe the dishonor of a call from the dark side?"

"I had information to share, but since you're already being an asshole I shouldn't tell you. I just figured since I saw that long-legged blonde of yours being herded away with the rest of the mates and children you might be interested. You're such a sucker. We cause trouble down south and you ship out the Wrath. We stir up a little trouble at the Council Hall and you just about empty the Enclave. You're so predictable. It was too damn easy. Have a nice day, Captain. Oh, and tell Danielle I'm coming for her."

Darren hung up. Gage made brief eye contact with Dani before the rest of what Darren said sank in. It had to be a joke. Everyone watched and waited for him to explain the call. He quickly dialed the gatehouse at the Enclave and got no answer. He called his secretary and got no answer. He tried the reception desk and got no answer. Then, when the fear began to sink in, he dialed Koren's cell phone. She picked up but said nothing. He could hear mumbled male voices and a woman crying. The soothing sound of Koren trying to comfort someone was shattered by gunfire and the phone disconnected.

"Son of a bitch!" Gage roared. He was seeing red. He had been taken in by a ploy to draw the Wrath away from the Enclave and now that crazy rogue bastard had his sweet Koren. His son had been MIA for weeks and now this? He would not live without his mate. He would not! He knew she still lived because he could feel her inside of his soul, where she belonged, but the Rogue had her and the rest of the mates and children. Darren's taunt made it sound as if the Rogue didn't realize Koren was his mate. Did Darren plan to inform the Rogue? He couldn't even think about what they would do to her if they did know. He had to get his mate and the rest of the families back.

Gage rallied the warriors and called back the ones who were returning to the Enclave. His house would be the command center. Griffin and Mason were informing the rest of the Council and following him to his house. He needed to get some men out there to do some recon while the Wrath warriors were on their way back to town.

———·—

Brandi buried her head under the pillow and cried. She could feel Abel's sorrow at having to leave her so soon, but it didn't make her feel any better. They'd spent the night making love and bonding on a deeper level, but as soon as his phone buzzed, he was up and out of bed.

"Now? I can't come now," Abel said to the person on the other end of the phone and listened to a reply.

"You don't understand . . ." He looked at her over his shoulder while the person spoke.

"Fine. Fine." He disconnected the call.

"What's going on? Who was that?" she asked.

"A friend. Things are coming to a boil and I have to go."

He was pulling on his pants. It really annoyed her that Abel had a closet full of clothes in the redhead's guest room.

"You said you were done with the Rogue," she reminded him.

"I said after I tried to get my mom out, I would be done." He came back to the bed, but she scooted away from him and pulled the covers to her chin.

"Sparky, please don't be this way. As soon as this is finished we'll leave. Hopefully I'll come back with my mom, but with or without her, we'll go," he pleaded.

"You're lying. I can feel it, remember? This isn't just about your mother. I want to know what's going on and when you'll be back. I'm not staying here without you." She knew her eyes had bled to black with anger.

"I'm not even sure what's going on. I just know that I have to go. I don't have anything to tell you other than the time is right and I need to go."

He ran his hands through his hair. She was pulling away emotionally and she knew he could clearly feel it.

"The time is right for what?" she asked.

"I don't know, Sparky! Damn it! Can't you just give me the benefit of the doubt? I have to do this but it has nothing to do with us. We will be together no matter what happens. I just need a chance to untangle myself from the mess I'm in." He paced across the small room and back.

"This is exactly why I wanted to wait to be bonded. I didn't want this resentment between us when I had to return to the Nest."

"Just go." She rolled away from him. Yes, she was pouting, but it was her bonding day and she felt she had the right to pout. "I guess I should have asked how long it would take to find your mom and do whatever else you're up to. I don't know where I'll be the next time you're available for a visit, but I won't be here."

Abel crawled onto the bed behind her and pulled her back to his chest. She didn't resist, but she didn't participate in the embrace either. They had been bonded for eight hours and already he was lying so he could run off and serve his master.

"I love you, Brandi. Your animosity right now is hurting me. Can't you feel that I'm doing this so we can stay together? Can't you feel how much I want to please you? This is just a step toward our goals." He kissed her nape and left the bed. His feet retreated to the door.

"Abel?"

"Yeah, Sparky?"

"I love you, too. I'd tell you to call me but my phone went up in smoke."

Abel came back to the bed and lifted her into his arms for a kiss that left her cross-eyed and mindless. Abel poured all of his love for her and his determination that they would get through this into his kiss. He laid her gently back on the bed and he was gone.

———◆———

Darren was tired of waiting for Danielle to realize she needed him as badly as he wanted her. He had given up the career he'd spent nearly a hundred years building to be with her and she'd just walked away. The day she left he should have stopped her, but he would have had to hurt her to do it. Her power had grown so much. She was devastated by his betrayal of their friendship and needed time to come to terms with it. He felt sure she would come back once she settled down. Then they would complete their bond and life would go on. His sacrifices would have been worth having Danielle as his mate. But she never came back.

Darren lived day and night with the intimate knowledge of just how much that puppy had enjoyed having Danielle in his bed for the last months. Chase Deidrick had dared to take her blood into his body and create a bond that dulled and quieted his own bond to Danielle. That was the moment Darren had made his first really big mistake. Out of anger he agreed to train the Rogue's Shade army to help him take over the Enclave. Darren was well aware that he was beginning to lose his grip, but he was still sharp as a tack compared to the male everyone—everyone but Darren—called Master. He had no interest in taking over the vampire nation or controlling the Council. He just wanted his mate back.

Darren thought having Danielle's thoughts and emotions invade his every breath was maddening, until he couldn't quite hear it anymore. He would catch whispers of happiness or feel echoes of stress and anxiety. He wanted to know what made her laugh or who was causing her discomfort. The not knowing was making him crazy. It was time to make a move.

Now that he'd fulfilled his agreement to get the Rogue into the Enclave, it was time to pull out the ace up his sleeve. Today he would get himself the appropriate bait to lure in his prize. He'd followed Abel and his lady love, Brandi, to a little house Abel visited often. When Abel rolled out, leaving the pretty brunette alone, Darren quickly formulated a plan to get Danielle back into his arms.

He found the girl curled into a sad little ball of misery in the middle of a full-size bed. Darren could surely empathize with her pain. His mate had left him, too. He would need to be careful with the little pyro or she would fry his ass. Darren stood far enough on the other side of the doorway so he could take cover if necessary.

"You and I need to talk, little fire starter."

The petite female bolted upright in the bed and clutched the blankets to her chest. This close to her, Darren could see the family resemblance between his Danielle and her half sister. It momentarily surprised him. If the girl's hair were longer and bore Danielle's distinctive coloring, he would have leapt on her. But the eyes were all wrong. Danielle's eyes were so clear blue it was like looking into mirrors. Her sister had the deep sapphire gaze of their father. The girl raised her hand defensively and a wall of heat sprang up between them.

"I see you've graduated from throwing fireballs." He smiled. "Very good. I'm sure the Rogue will appreciate your work on his behalf when he sucks you dry and wields that talent himself."

"Get out or I will burn this house to the ground with you in it," she threatened.

"I doubt we have time for that." He checked his watch. "The Shade will be here very soon. I suggest you get dressed, Ms. Vaughn. It's time to go. If you want your mate to see another day, you will move now."

"What? What are you talking about?" She hopped out of the bed and ran to the closet, keeping the searing wall of hot air between them.

The view had his heart skipping a beat. She did indeed resemble Danielle very closely. They had the same Coke-bottle figure with large, high breasts and a tucked-in waist that flared out to womanly hips and a round backside. Darren forced himself to look away and reminded himself that she was not his mate.

"You see, I'm not as stupid as your mate seems to think I am. I have been following him and watching him make a fool of himself over you since the night you dared to take my mate from me. I know all about your power and all the time Abel spent looking after you instead of doing his job. I wonder what his master will do to him when he finds out that he's been hiding you from his hunters and protecting you instead of bringing you in."

She turned to look at him, and Darren was sure if she had the ability to shoot fire from her eyes, he would be toast.

"You leave my mate alone or I swear . . ."

"Don't threaten me, child. I'm holding all of the cards here. This is what's going to happen. You have a choice. I've called the Shade and they are on the way. I'd say we have less than five minutes to be clear of this building.

"Option one, you choose to come with me peacefully and I keep my mouth shut about Abel's extracurricular activities for the time being. I trade you back to your family for my mate. You took her from me and you will help me get her back.

"Or, option two, I will detain you for the Shade and they'll take you to the Rogue, who is anxiously waiting to drain every drop of blood from that sweet little body. I will then inform the Rogue that Abel was harboring you and deceiving him as well. Then I will sit back and wait to see what kills Abel first, the Rogue or the loss of his new mate. And I do have a backup, so killing me is a bad idea. If I don't show up with you in tow or the Shade doesn't find you here, I have a friend ready to deliver a letter complete with photos to explain Abel's betrayal. Either way he will die. The choice is yours, but you'd better make it fast or it will be too late for both of us."

Brandi went peacefully for Abel's sake, but she knew her father would never trade one child for another. They would find another way to free her, or she would die. Darren was truly delusional to believe this would help him get Dani back. She would only hate him more. As soon as they reached his car, Darren stuck a syringe in her thigh.

"Sorry about that. I can't very well give away the location of my evil lair, though, can I?" He smiled.

She wasn't at all amused. The first few minutes after you're injected are hell. You're completely aware of your surroundings but your body no longer follows commands and your power is just out of reach. Then slowly the world fades to black.

Brandi woke in an unfamiliar bed. She had to wait for the cobwebs to clear before she could sit up and have a look around. She cursed Darren for drugging her. She'd had no choice but to go with the lesser of two evils. She had to do her best to protect her mate, and trust that Abel and her family would find a way to get her out. Chase would never let Dani go, so Brandi felt sure she was only buying time for them to come up with a plan of attack.

Now her head was pounding and she had no flipping idea where she was or how she had gotten there. Gingerly, so as not to jostle her throbbing brain, Brandi climbed out of the rather large bed. The room had no windows and the only light came from a small lamp in the far corner of the room. The room was large and well appointed with puffy couches and a desk. There was a fireplace and a small kitchenette.

"Well, if I have to be held prisoner, I guess the cell isn't so bad," she thought out loud.

"You may think that now. Talk to me in a few months." Brandi was startled by the distinctly feminine reply. "Are you his new toy? I wonder if he'll kill me now. I hope he kills me now."

Brandi spun around in search of the owner of the sad little voice. In a small alcove off of the main living area was a cozy-looking reading area. A table held a lamp and a book, but the woman sat in the dark with her feet tucked under her on a wide, cushioned chair.

"He who? The Rogue?" Brandi asked.

"The Master. I don't know any rogues."

The woman reached up and turned on the light. She was a breathtaking beauty. Her wavy blond hair wrapped around her like a blanket to her waist. She unfolded her tall, statuesque frame from the chair and promptly collapsed back into it. Brandi moved in to get a closer look.

"Are you alright? When was the last time you fed?"

"I don't like it," she confessed. "I don't do it until he makes me."

Okay, this was weird. On closer inspection Brandi realized that the woman's eyes weren't just dark but black with hunger, and the tips of her fangs were pressing into her lower lip. Vamps at this stage could be unstable.

"What is your name? I'm Brandi, Brandi Vaughn."

The blonde looked at her curiously. "I've seen you at the club before. Did they take you from the club?" Tears filled her obsidian eyes and Brandi began to put the pieces together. She was a made vampire and very recently made. It had to have been against her will, considering she was a prisoner. A gilded cage was still a cage. Her comment about being taken meant she was likely kidnapped. Humans who chose the change were usually in love with a vamp so they understood the process, having been fed on themselves, or they were humans with life-threatening illnesses. If given the choice between dying or a long life that included vampirism, most chose to live. They also knew that there was a fifty-fifty chance they wouldn't survive the change. Some bodies simply rejected the blood, treating it like a virus.

"No, they didn't take me from the club. I was born this way. They took me because they want my sister." Brandi opened the fridge and was grateful to find a stock of bagged blood along with other food items. She popped a bag in the microwave to warm it a bit. "It's kind of a long story I would be glad to tell you after you feed. Tell me your name. I don't really like *Hey, You.*"

"Lindsay. My name is Lindsay. I don't want to drink that stuff. It's gross." She shuddered.

"I know it seems that way now, but over time your palate will adjust and you'll start to think of it as food just like any other. If you don't feed, you'll die, probably after you attack and hurt someone else, though. Do you want the hunger to take over and force you to take what you need to survive?"

"No. I don't want to hurt people. I used to be a people, a person, I mean."

"You still are a person, Lindsay. You're just a stronger person with different dietary needs. You will likely live longer than most people, too."

The microwave beeped and Brandi pulled out the bag of type A. She swished it around while she searched the drawer.

"Yes! This is just what we need. I found a straw." She cut a small hole in the bag and inserted the straw. "I want you to put the straw toward the back of your mouth and suck it down fast. You'll feel much better when you're done."

Lindsay winced but followed directions. Her body wanted it but her human sensibilities balked at drinking human blood. As she drank the color of her eyes faded to chocolate brown with little flecks of gold, and her fangs receded. Now that Brandi didn't have to worry about being attacked, she'd get down to trying to figure out where they were and how they could both get out alive.

———— • ————

Abel walked across the Enclave in shock. The bodies of dead warriors lay haphazardly all over the grounds. Most of the warriors had been either deployed during the raid or they were out at the Council Hall fighting off the attack and fire there. Most of the men who stayed behind were traitors working for the Master. Those who weren't were either killed or escaped the carnage. So far, he had counted ten bodies. Darren had planned this entire siege with the Master, and Abel never saw it coming. He had been sneaking in and out of the Enclave with Candy to retrieve documents from rogue warriors and he knew things were coming to a head, but he never imagined the Master would attempt a takeover so soon.

Even if he had known, Abel couldn't honestly say he would have given up last night with Brandi to stop it. He only wished they'd had more time to strengthen their bond. He knew it would deepen with time and close contact, but at this distance she was barely more than a shadow in the back of his mind. He had feared his humanity would keep them from having a complete bond, but it hadn't. Now he hoped their connection would grow so he could feel her constantly, the way he had when they were close. After the experience of being able to feel how much she loved and needed him, this separation left him empty and cold.

Abel needed to focus. The Master's faith in him was definitely waning and his distraction wouldn't be received well. He wondered how much time he had left to find his mom. He entered the gymnasium where he'd been directed to report and was confronted with the accusing eyes of the women and children who lived on the

Enclave. They were being held prisoner and Abel had a good idea of what the Master would want in return for their release. Dani. Some of the women were terrorized after seeing warriors and friends mowed down in front of them and many of the younger children were crying. One woman in particular looked like she'd had the shit beat out of her. Her long, blond hair was matted with blood from her mouth and nose. Her eyes were swollen shut.

Abel approached a Shade on guard duty he recognized.

"Where is the Master? I was told to find him here."

"He went to get his little pet settled. If you ask me, it sets a bad example for him to keep a human around. But nobody asked me, did they?" the Shade commented. "Says this is gonna be our permanent home so he wanted his property close at hand."

The Master strode into the room and the females cringed. They knew exactly who he was and what he was capable of. Abel's mind struggled to work out what was happening here. Why had the Master put Abel's mother within his reach, unless he planned to use her as leverage?

The Master directed Abel to follow him into a private room. There was a map of the Enclave on the wall and he studied it while he spoke. "It's about time you showed up, boy. I have a task for you. Where have you been?"

"Darren sent me out on patrol by the docks," he lied. "I wasn't informed of this action."

"Yes, well, Darren disappeared just as soon as his duty to me was served, so it's up to you. I would have had to kill him eventually anyway. He holds too much sway with the Shade. They shouldn't hold anyone above me."

"May I ask exactly what Darren got out of this? He doesn't seem like the type to volunteer."

The Master chuckled. "He didn't; I assure you. When his deal with me was discovered and he had to hide or be punished for his crimes, Darren tried to run. The only problem was that all of his considerable savings were frozen in an account here on the Enclave." The Master looked over his shoulder at Abel. "Did you know they have their own bank here? It saves them from having to explain to the bank why they've had accounts under the same name for hundreds of years. That's how he ended up with us. You can't even get a hotel room for the night without a functioning credit card. So he agreed to train the Shade and get us into the Enclave in exchange for an ungodly amount of cash. I have to say that it was well worth it."

He shrugged elegantly and turned to face Abel. The man was a fool if he thought Darren was going anywhere without his mate. It was clear the Master didn't understand the mate bond. Abel was starting to feel a little out of sorts and edgy to get back to Brandi. He was now beginning to understand Darren's madness. No matter what deal Darren had stuck with the Master, Darren would be going after his mate now. Abel was sure of it.

"Now, back to you. Your mother sends her love. I've got her close at hand, just in case you decide to misbehave."

Abel expected his new mission would be to retrieve Danielle, the object of the Master's obsession, but if the Master thought Abel could get anywhere near Danielle, he had really lost his mind. They would be on high alert now.

"I have the identity of our mysterious pyro. I tried to beat it out of the woman who seemed to be in charge of the females, but she wouldn't talk. It was really too bad of her to let me mangle her pretty face." He looked contemplative. "Anyway, when I decided to drain her for making me break a sweat, one of the other females said she would give me the name if I would just let their matron live. I agreed. But I never said how long I would let her live. I'm getting hungry."

Oh, hell no! This could not be going where he thought it was?

"It seems the blood running through the House of Vaughn is particularly strong these days. I have contacted the Council and demanded Danielle Vaughn in exchange for the rest of their mates and children. It could go either way. Half the Council will want to sacrifice the one to save the many. The other half will argue that Danielle is too powerful to hand over. She will make me powerful beyond their understanding. The things that girl could do if she had the backbone to use her gifts.

"What I need is a backup plan, an insurance policy of sorts. You will go fetch me my pyro, Ms. Brandi Vaughn."

Abel had to back up a step to keep himself from strangling the Master. The need to protect his mate ran deep.

"Get her and bring her to me. If the Council doesn't want to give me my prize, I will offer Brandi up directly to Danielle. She may come out of hiding to save her half sister. If not, I drain the pyro. It's a win-win for me. Now be gone before I feel the need to show the men how strong I am. It will be much harder to catch your prey after I kick your mongrel ass."

The Master exited the room and Abel breathed deeply to control his need to kill the man. He would never let the Master touch a hair on Brandi's precious head. The only way he had ever kicked Abel's ass was when Abel submitted in order to protect his mom. Nobody wanted to tangle with Abel, but the Master had all of them fooled into believing he could take Abel down. It seemed even the Master had forgotten it was just an act.

Twenty-one

Dani leaned against the kitchen counter and watched the males standing around Gage's huge, heavy wood dining room table staring at a map of the Enclave. Gage's usual icy calm and steady control had melted into simmering rage that had everyone on edge. Something intensely painful had happened to his mate, Koren, and Gage was spoiling for a fight. Strategies and backup plans were in the making to take back the Enclave and, more importantly, their mates and children.

Several Wrath teams had arrived after being recalled from their deployments and Griffin was filling the men in on current events. A few of the team members had to be restrained when they were informed that their family members were being used as pawns. The Rogue wanted Dani and he was trying to turn her people against her again. She was sure that every warrior who had a loved one, mate, or child trapped on the Enclave right now would trade her for them without a second thought. That was as it should be, in her mind. Griffin asked them to put their anger to good use and come up with suggestions on the safest way to free their mates and children. The teams listened to Griffin as they watched their frazzled captain brood in the corner. They knew his mate was in danger too.

Once again, the map was reviewed and additional options were given and discussed. Dani looked out the window over the kitchen sink at the tent city that had sprung up on the large piece of property the Paris family owned. Several hundred warriors had made their temporary home as comfortable as was possible. Many warriors who lived out in the community had taken their friends and teammates home with them to clean up and prepare for the coming battle. Everyone was on high alert, waiting for the order to move.

Dani had a plan of her own. The execution was going to be difficult at best. As per her habit, Dani's mother, Tessa, stepped in just when she was needed most. Her mother was being particularly elusive of late and Dani didn't believe any of her lame excuses, but now wasn't the time to pry. Now was the time for action. So Dani didn't question her precognitive mother when she called, offering the opportunity to speak with the very man she needed to solicit for help but had no way of reaching. Her hope was that Tessa was in contact with Brandi and had arranged the clandestine rendezvous with her boyfriend.

She had to get out of the house and to the church in town without Chase or anyone else realizing she had gone. She looked over her shoulder and couldn't help smiling at the sight of her mate brainstorming and strategizing with the other males. He had gone from a vampire playboy to mated male and junior Councilman so fast that many people didn't recognize him anymore. Chase felt her eyes on him and looked up to give her a half smile. He could feel her pride in him and the love that poured through their bond wrapping around him. It was unfair, but she was using those very real emotions to build a mental wall between them. Chase was preoccupied and unable to focus on her. It wouldn't work for long, but it would give her a chance to slip away. She returned his smile and nodded toward the guest room they were sharing. Believing she meant to go rest, Chase went back to deliberation with the other males.

Once in the guest room, it was only a matter of opening the French doors to exit onto the lawn that now held a sea of multi-colored tents and camping chairs. No one looked her way when she walked calmly and purposefully to the front of the large house and hopped into Chase's Mercedes.

———•———

Dani made her way to the courtyard in the rear of the church and entered the open wrought-iron gate. She shot out a mental feeler and found a sad darkness hovering around the gazebo. Abel had some very strong shields. She attempted to catch any stray thoughts to gauge his receptiveness to the meeting, but all she got was a solid wall of sullen regret.

The dark deeds in Abel's past and the potential for even worse criminal behavior in his future made her fearful for Brandi. In the time they were connected during Brandi's ordeal at the Council Hall, Dani had learned a great deal about the male who was drifting around in the evening shadows. She knew he had the potential to be a great man with the right influences. His willingness to risk exposing himself to search for Brandi spoke volumes about his feelings for her. When they were together Dani hadn't felt the ominous cloud that surrounded him now. That also gave her pause to worry for her half sister's safety. No one had seen or heard from her since she'd walked away with Abel. If she wasn't hiding out with Tessa, where was he keeping her?

Dani had to tread carefully. Abel held the power to swing the advantage at the Enclave in their favor or against them. She wanted to try to relate to Abel on the only level she could, by using the most incredible fact that had leapt out of Brandi's mind in her time of stress. Dani would share her history of humanity to bridge the distance between her and Brandi's half-human love. She stepped into the gazebo, where he hid in the darkness, and prayed this would work.

"Thank you for coming." She gave a weak smile.

"Tessa said it was important, so here I am." He circled behind her in the shadows. It was against everything she learned in training not to protect her back but Dani felt like it was a test. So she held her spot and let Abel move as he pleased. Unfortunately for Dani, her anxiety had alerted Chase to her absence. He was pissed. She sent him love and apologies. Then she begged him to be quiet and listen so she could concentrate.

"We need your help, Abel. All we want at this point is the release of the women and children. But you and I both know that isn't going to happen without a huge loss of life." She wanted to turn and look him in the eye. Having him at her back was unnerving. This *was* the guy who'd carried her out of the chapel on her bonding day, but she was trying to think of him the way he looked in Brandi's mind.

"I think it will happen rather quickly if your Council hands you over. Apart from that, you're correct. Sadly, the innocent ones will be the first to suffer." There was real sympathy in that statement.

"So help us. I want you to smuggle the Wrath back into the Enclave with you. We need to sneak in and extract them quietly," she pleaded.

"Why should I help a bunch of power-hungry elitists? They wouldn't help me. They would turn up their prejudiced noses and move on," he scoffed.

"Being half human doesn't negate the fact you're also half vamp. I can help you through the transition into society. I know it won't be easy, but my family and I will stand behind you." She did look at him now.

Abel took a few steps back. She had surprised him. He took in the fact that his secret was out in the open and settled back into himself. "She told you about me, did she? I'm a little stunned by that."

Dani decided not to tell him Brandi didn't need to inform her of his humanity. Maybe if he believed Brandi trusted her, he would too. "Look, I understand your fear of the future. I know how it feels to be rejected by people you care about, people you want to love."

Dani turned her face away. She didn't want him to see her weakness. She had to be strong to encourage Abel to do the same. The memory of her experiences as a demi-vamp still haunted her dreams, the stress of constantly waiting for the other shoe to drop and waiting for someone to realize you're not who you pretend to be. She felt hurt when other vamps spoke of humans with disdain. The prejudice still stung her. Composing herself, she continued.

"I feared for my life. I ached to be me, myself, and be loved anyway. I wanted to be recognized by my father as his child. I wanted Chase to love me no matter what or who I was born to."

Dani turned back and saw him watching her with a cocky smirk on his face. She longed to knock the look from his arrogant mouth. The sable depths of his eyes mocked her pain and discounted her effort to make him feel welcome and understood. She had to make him understand the way he was raised was not the only way. There were people who wanted to help him. His actions could bring the world down around their ears if he couldn't be trusted. If he flipped on them, everyone would pay the price. Many lives would be lost. She had to pray that his need to be near Brandi, his wish to be a better man for her, would put him firmly in their camp.

She stepped into his personal space and the alarms in her head began to sound. She'd been doing her best to block Chase but since their bonding, it had become increasingly difficult. He wanted her to step away from the dark man looming over her. He wanted her to get out now. This had not been a part of the plan. He was totally going to kick her ass. She tried unsuccessfully to project her feelings to Chase. He didn't care about anything more than her safety. Abel might tower over her, and even with all of her power his darkness made her feel weak, but she knew in her heart he would never hurt her. Not without provocation. There was a light in his soul begging for release.

Brandi had begun the process of peeling back the frigid shell around his heart and now the edges brightened with the hope she induced.

Abel stepped away from her and began to laugh. Not an amused, happy laugh but a frightening, almost hysterical, laugh. It made the hair on her neck stand up.

"You think you know something about rejection? You think you know hurt and fear? You're a damn joke!" He spat the words at her. "I'm supposed to feel sorry for you because you lived a lie for a few months? Did you get your feelings hurt by people who didn't even know what they were doing? Should I feel pity for you because you're hiding from a hunter out to steal your power?"

He shook his head and turned away from her, taking deep, steadying breaths. Dani knew he tried to give the impression that nothing mattered to him and his life in hiding hadn't mattered, but she knew better. When he turned back to her, the cold, dead expression on his face scared her. This was the man who kidnapped their youth and delivered them to their deaths at the hands of the Rogue. The man stood up to vamps twice his size and took them out. He was an assassin and a dark warrior.

His voice was a hiss of contempt when he continued. "I have lived my whole life in the shadows. I didn't know the love and acceptance you lived with for the first nineteen years of your life, until I found Brandi. I starved when I was a kid because my mother wouldn't let me feed and my Master wouldn't let me hunt. My mother always believed what he told her. He said I needed discipline and I needed to be broken of my willful ways. I killed a man at ten years old in a mindless bloodlust. It had been so long since I was allowed to feed, I was overcome. To this day, the people I deal with daily think I'm just like them, and they make me sick! They hate humans. They treat them like cattle. Guess who helps them hunt the cattle they keep in cages? You want me to relate to your past because you were in hiding with the good guys watching your back?

I would die within moments if the vamps at my back realized I'm part human. My life has been day after day of lying, killing, hunting, and hiding in plain sight. So don't try to relate to me. You should be glad you can't."

He paused then and looked at his boots before returning his gaze to hers. Something big was happening behind his eyes. He was gathering himself like a thunderstorm on the horizon, lightning flashing in those dark eyes. Abel backed into the shadows of the churchyard. Maybe it was easier for him to speak in the dark, where his vulnerability wasn't so obvious. His words were no more than a whisper now and Dani ducked into the darkness herself. It felt like the right thing to do. It was like he was in a confessional and she was there to hear his sins without judgment.

"You want to talk about Brandi? Good, I do too. I love her. I wanted her and yes, it killed me to see her with that blond warrior from California. I know you think I gave the Hypno to Candy to purposely drug him, but I didn't." He smiled a wistful little grin and Dani knew he was thinking of Brandi.

"I didn't set him up, but I can't be sorry it happened. I need her too much to care about what had to happen to bring us together. All I can do is hold on and be thankful for every moment I get to spend in her arms."

"If you love her, why do you continue to serve the Rogue? What are your reasons, Abel? Why have you stayed when a man of your strength could easily get away? Why do you let him continue to blacken your soul? If you ask me, Brandi should be the only reason you need to help us."

A long, uncomfortable silence settled before Abel stepped into the shaft of moonlight again. His athletic form was backlit. She couldn't see his face, only the silhouette of a shattered man.

"He has my mother. If you know I'm half human, I'm surprised you don't know that tidbit."

Dani had learned from Brandi's inner thoughts that Abel had a good reason for his crimes, if there was such a thing, but she didn't know what the reason could be.

"He keeps her hidden away and I only get to see her once a month for dinner. I get all cleaned up and go to her as if nothing is wrong so she doesn't worry. He watches the whole time. I don't see him, but I know he's watching. As long as he keeps her happy and healthy, he knows I will do his bidding. As long as I do his bidding, he will keep her that way."

"Why you, Abel? It seems like a lot of trouble to go to when he could use one of his other henchmen."

Abel stopped to consider her question. He seemed to come to some decision before he continued.

"There are two reasons and in my opinion they both stem from my humanity. The first is that I am strong, even for a vampire. In the same way your human birth gifted you with off-the-charts psychic skills but little physical strength, mine lent me strength but no psychic skill, with the exception of enthralling my prey. I learned to fight at a young age, so I became his bodyguard of sorts."

"I don't even want to know how you found out about my weakness. It's not a publicly known fact." Dani shook her head. Chase was doing some mental cursing.

The Rogue knew more about her than she expected and that gave Dani a chill. Abel didn't answer the implied question but instead continued with his explanation.

"I'm sure in the past your demi-vamp nature did interesting things to the people around you. He needs me to bring in the vamps. They aren't stupid, but the human in me draws them to the elusive scent of prey. They don't realize it because my dominant vamp nature makes them want me for a lover or a friend. The humans don't have an instinctual fear of me and are attracted to my strength as well. My humanity bleeds through and distracts them long enough for me to herd them away from safety. So you see, I am honey to any fly he wishes to catch, be they human or vamp."

Abel backed up again. This was hard for him and she knew it. She could feel Chase in her mind, silently taking in the scene, and she knew Chase understood exactly what Abel was talking about. Her scent had made him want to make love to her and drink from her all at once. The one-two punch of a powerful vamp and tasty human brought Chase to his knees.

"I'm sure you're wondering why I would care so much for a woman who abused me. You should know that my early childhood before we were taken in by the Master was pretty good."

Another long silence.

"I'm about to let you in on the secret to end all secrets, a secret that I would be killed for divulging. I'll give you the short version. My mother fell in love with a vampire who supposedly loved her too. But she didn't know he was a vamp until the night he took her for his mate. Rather than risk her rejection, he bound them together knowing she would accept anything after his blood had been shared with her. They were happy for a time but then something went wrong. Her bond to him remained solid. His bond to her dissolved and faded as many human relationships do."

Chase was putting things together more quickly than Dani. He was becoming aware of something she hadn't considered yet. He wanted her out of there before the end of the story. It was indeed a big secret and it called Abel's loyalty seriously into question.

"My mother literally went crazy when he withdrew his love from her and put her out on the street. He was screwing anything that spread its legs and having a great time. As you know from your own mother's sad story, my mother felt it every time he bedded another woman. She suffered for two months until she realized she was pregnant.

"It took her another three months to find him and sneak into his office. He let her weep all over him about how she was carrying his child and she forgave him for his adultery. She wanted them to be a family. He told her he no longer loved her but said he would take care of her and the child after it was born. Of course he didn't mean it. He knew she would die in childbirth, if she made it that far, and the child would die along with her. Imagine his surprise when she returned, weak but alive, with a baby boy she didn't know how to feed. Vamp mothers have hemoglobin in their breast milk that provides for the child's nutritional need for blood. My mother was feeding me formula and her breast milk wouldn't have been any better. He told her to mix blood with the milk if she wanted me to live and again he turned her away."

Abel began to pace, odd for a man who seemed so controlled.

"Have you figured it out yet? I know you're too smart for the facts to elude you. The Master is able to control my mother because he is her mate. She would even neglect her only child to please him. The Rogue, as you call him, is my father."

Chase was still there in the back of her mind and he was doing his best to remain calm. He was trying to mobilize some men to search for her. He wasn't familiar with the church at all. Dani sent him soothing reassurance that a rescue wouldn't be necessary. She only hoped she was right.

<hr>

Abel watched shock spread across Dani's now ashen face. "What do you think Brandi will do when she finds out I'm the mongrel son of a crazy human and a monster?" he asked her.

"I think Brandi loves you whether you're a human or a leprechaun. She has seen you for the man you want to be instead of the deeds of your past. I think that has earned her the right to know the truth, don't you? I don't know how she will feel about your father's identity, but if you let me go with you, we can tell her together. Where are you hiding her? I hope she's not alone on the Enclave without protection."

Dani begged with her clear blue eyes for news of her half sister. Abel stared at her, confused, and suddenly filled with worry for his mate. She had not gone home to her family.

"I don't know where Brandi is. I had to leave her when the call came in to report to the Enclave. I thought she was with you. When Tessa told me to come here, I hoped it would be her coming to speak with me."

"We haven't even heard from her." Panic was spreading across Dani's features.

"She told me she wanted us to go hide at your grandparents' summer home. I think we should check there before we jump to conclusions. She probably just went on without me." Abel was doing his best to think through this calmly. Brandi was a strong pyro and a smart woman. She had to have found her way to safety. Dani reached for her phone to make a call but it rang before she had it out of her pocket. She looked at the screen.

"I don't recognize this number. It may be Brandi. Let me get it." She hit the talk button. "Hello," she answered.

Dani's face paled and the hand holding her phone began to shake. The male voice on the line was speaking nonstop. Abel's phone vibrated and he checked the screen to see Tessa calling again. He answered. "Yeah?"

"It's time, Abel. The choice is now yours to make. The end is near. Will you help us or not?" Tension vibrated in Tessa's voice.

He ended his call with Tessa and turned back to find a tearful Dani staring at her phone.

"That was Darren. He has Brandi. He wants me, or he's taking her to the . . . to your father."

Twenty-two

Griffin watched the split screen on the wall of Gage's home office. One of the tech guys had hacked into Enclave security and enabled the remote viewing options. They had an unobstructed view of the training facility where the mates and children of the warriors were being held, a large part of the barracks occupied by unmated warriors, and the front gates. There were guards who changed shifts every four hours in all areas with a heavier presence at the gates.

Their best guess from the available footage was that they were up against several hundred Shade warriors. That's what they were calling themselves. The Shade. Griffin agreed. They were certainly casting darkness over his people. At least half of them were known males who had turned their backs on the warrior class and the entire vampire nation. Every time Gage spotted one of his men, he winced. He had a piece of paper on his desk that was filled with names of the traitors.

Griffin prayed vehemently for divine intervention. A plan was slowly forming but it wasn't solid. They had to find a way onto the grounds without giving away their approach. Sneaking in would only be slightly easier than finding a back door to the White House without getting shot.

Chase was stalking the halls while he waited for Soleil to return. She had snuck off to work on helping get them into the Enclave but it hadn't worked out as far as Griffin could tell. She had gotten very good at building mental walls with the help of her grand-mother and she used those walls to slip out. It surprised Griffin that his mother, was taking an active role in training Soleil to control her power and protect her mind. He was afraid that his mother had only accepted his eldest child because of her power. After all, being the grandparent of such a renowned vamp wasn't so bad. He could imagine his mother bragging to her society friends about the power running in her family's blood.

On the other hand, Soleil's power wasn't such an easy thing for Chase to deal with at all. She was strong, but that made her a target. Griffin didn't envy Chase his lot in life. Just now he was muttering about kicking her ass for blocking him out. The girl was not the type to follow a man's lead. Chase would be forever running after his mate.

Chase was in contact with her for a time and began to gather men to go after her but Gage shot him down. He was still under Council orders not to aid Soleil. Even with the proof of her accusa-tions that there were traitors in the warrior class staring back at him from the screen on the wall, Gage was a male who did his duty to the letter. Until he got word from the combined Council, he would stay the course. So Chase paced and cursed because their connection was now limited to the normal connection between mated pairs. He could get a bead on her emotions but that was it.

"What are they doing?" Mason asked from his chair in the back of the room.

"It looks like they're preparing for something," Gage replied.

While Griffin was lost in thought, the Shade had begun to gather into clusters on the lawn in front of the training facility. On the screen they watched the males move from the barracks over to the lawn.

The double doors opened and a group of four vamps exited the building. They stood on the landing at the top of the eight or so stairs looking over the crowd. There was something odd about these vamps.

"Can we zoom in on those four? I want a better look," Griffin asked.

"I'm on it." The tech's hands flew over the keyboard. The screen switched to a single image and closed in on the foursome.

"What do you figure that's about?" Gage asked.

They looked calm enough but every one of the four had black eyes and fangs pressing into their lips.

"It's like they're ready to fight, or starving," Mason ventured a guess.

"Lovely's eyes turn like that when she overextends her extrasensory talents. I've even seen her nose bleed," Chase commented absently and paced away.

<hr />

Darren was starting to lose his patience. Time was ticking away and Danielle wasn't answering her phone. He wasn't the only one looking for her, but he had to get to her first. He didn't want to resort to calling her family to negotiate a trade. They would raise the alarm and Darren knew somehow they would hear the news that he was still in town and was in possession of the pyro. Danielle had a soft heart and knowing that her half sister was in danger would be wearing on her conscience. With any luck she would agree to come to him. Darren hit the speed dial again and finally got an answer.

"Yeah?" Abel answered.

It took Darren off guard. This was not good news. His chances of getting to Danielle just fell exponentially.

"Put Danielle on the line," he demanded.

"I can't do that. She's a little . . . sleepy just now."

"What are you up to, Abel? Why did you put her down?" Darren feared permanent damage from frequent overdoses of Hypnovam. Danielle was small and Abel was careless.

"You're too late, man. She's mine now. I'm sick of this shit. I'm trading Dani for my mom and my freedom."

"Did Danielle tell you I have your mate? It would be a shame for her to die for your mistake." Darren could only hope Abel wanted his mate more than his mom.

"Did she admit to being my mate?" Abel asked. "I'm surprised."

"I guessed and she confirmed my suspicions. She came nice and quiet when I informed her that you would suffer. I know all about your little affair and her ability to make trucks explode. I have a friend waiting to deliver the good news of your betrayal to your *Master* if I don't get my way. I want my mate, Abel, and you want yours. Let's trade."

"I'm thinking this way—I'm young. I'll find another female quickly after Brandi's dead. Once I trade Dani in, I won't have to deal with that bastard ever again. If I take Brandi and run now, I'll be running for the rest of my life. I'd rather negotiate my freedom while I have something to barter with. As for your snitch, well, I guess we'll see who gets to the Master first."

Damn it! The kid had called his bluff.

Brandi felt like a mother trying to explain the ins and outs of the world to a child who was about to leave her nest. Lindsay was aghast at the way upper-class vamps treated their women like commodities to be traded for gain. The idea that a person, male or female, would have to marry someone he or she didn't choose because the parents had a legally binding agreement was a prehistoric notion to the liberal-minded ex-human.

They'd spent hours talking about their lives and what had brought them both to this gilded cage. Brandi learned that Lindsay had gone to college with Dani and they had been good friends until

Dani withdrew from classes on campus and started getting her credits online. Lindsay was friends with a guy she wanted a more serious relationship with but he wouldn't give. He said sex would ruin their friendship and kept it platonic. She never knew more than his first name and she never knew when he might appear. He would be gone for weeks and suddenly have a weekend or just a night to burn. They would hang out and go dancing. They would see movies and go to dinner. She fell for him. He was just enjoying her company.

Then one night at the club she went to the ladies' room, and when she exited, this huge guy had grabbed her and stuck her with a needle. The next thing Lindsay knew, she was waking up at the feet of a man who sat in a large chair on a raised dais like he was a damn king or something. The room was full of men who looked at her like a juicy bone. Some of them looked normal and others had fangs and black eyes. They seemed to be bidding on her like a slave. Lindsay was horrified and tried to get away, but she couldn't move. Her body was dead weight. Then, out of the crowd stepped her friend, Abel. His expression was cold and uncaring when the man in the chair informed him that he had done well to find him such a tasty morsel. The men kept yelling amounts they would pay to have her. When Abel put in a bid, the man in the chair laughed and told the crowd that he would keep the pretty piece for himself. And he had.

Lindsay was his slave. He could make her do anything he wanted with a thought and she had no hope of resisting. He took her blood. He took her body. And he took her humanity when he decided he was in love. He claimed to have been waiting for a mate to share his life and his power with for years. He would talk to himself about how he was sure it would work this time. This time, he would break the curse. Lindsay explained that the Master displayed remorse and regret for his behavior during occasional moments of disorientation, and other times he would insist that she should be thankful he had saved her from her low-born human life.

He forced her to drink from him over and over. Whatever he expected to happen didn't happen, so he kept trying. All that came of it was her development of fangs and the need for a blood bank. The Master wouldn't allow her to feed from anyone but him. Good thing, because she didn't want to feed from anyone at all.

Brandi knew the mysterious Abel had to be her mate, and she was powerfully grateful to know he hadn't slept with the ethereal Lindsay. It would be hard not to strangle her, much less be friends, if the woman had touched Abel.

They were in bed and drifting off for the night when the door to the secured room opened wide and Darren stepped in. Lindsay shrank back into the headboard, and Brandi jumped up, ready to defend her friend. Lindsay was still afraid of her own shadow.

"Let's go," Darren demanded.

"I'm not dressed." Brandi was wearing nothing but a man's shirt she'd found in the closet. Her own clothes were less than fresh and no one had come to check on them since Darren had deposited her in the room.

"Get something on. We have to go," he barked.

Brandi grabbed her clothes from the chair and tried not to notice that Darren was watching her change.

"Where are we going?" she asked over her shoulder. Lindsay was weeping.

"It seems your mate and family aren't as fond of you as I had hoped," he informed her.

Darren hustled Brandi toward the door as soon as she was dressed. She back looked at her new friend before he dragged her from the room. Tears welled in Lindsay's two lovely brown eyes and Brandi prayed that wouldn't be the last time she saw her.

⎯⎯⎯◆⎯⎯⎯

Chase was pacing the front lawn of Gage's home after explaining to the gathered members of the Council and their varied relatives what he was able to observe of Lovely's conversation with Abel. The guy was the Rogue's son and somehow he had wriggled his way into Brandi's life. Lovely didn't believe he was a threat but Chase didn't agree. She was trying to convince Abel to help their effort to free the females and children.

They'd tried to keep from her the fact that the Rogue had made contact but she was very aware. The Rogue had sent word via a text message to Gage that he would trade all the captured mates and children for Lovely, or he would kill them all. His Lovely was overcome with guilt that so many people were suffering while she remained safe. That's why she'd snuck away. That's why she was out there risking her life.

She wouldn't let him into her consciousness but she sent him wave after wave of love. He felt every emotion from betrayal to guilt and heartbreak like a blow to the stomach.

Chase stormed back into the office. He fisted his hands and slammed them onto the desk in front of Gage. Gage stood and glared down at Chase.

"Something is wrong! I know it! We have to go after her! She's my mate! I . . ." Chase couldn't finish the sentence. If he gave voice to his fears, it would make them more real. Tears filled his eyes and his mother appeared to stroke his back.

Gage spoke calmly, but Chase could see the lightning flash in his eyes. "Do you think you love her any more than I love my mate? Do you think sending people out on a wild goose chase will do anything but make you feel better? I told you before that even if I had permission to take Danielle into my charge, I can't protect a girl who doesn't want protection. She left of her own free will."

"She left to give us a chance to save our people!" Chase shouted.

Voices on the TV distracted the room from the impending explosion between Chase and Gage. On the screen, a tall, dark-haired man in a suit began to speak to the crowd. He stood on the landing with the four fanged vamps, looking out at his subjects. He was praising their efforts and promising them all high-ranking positions in his new world order. This was the face of the mysterious Rogue. He was revealed to the Council without his knowledge and gasps of disbelief circled the room. Seleste collapsed into a chair and put her head between her knees.

"It can't be. It's a lie," Seleste stammered. Mason got closer to the screen and squinted.

"What the hell is this?" Griffin barked.

"I don't believe what I'm seeing. We were friends. He wouldn't do this," Donovan chimed in from the corner.

"I knew it!" Kane shouted.

Chase watched the charismatic vamp boast about his strength and wisdom and his plans for his Shade army once he took over the Council. He insisted he would have the power this very day to rule over all. Half of the crowd cheered wildly while the other half stared blankly at the vamp.

Chase looked at his father and back to the man. It was spooky. They looked very much alike. He looked around the room for an explanation but was greeted with open-mouthed horror all around.

"Who is it, Dad?"

"It's David. My brother," he whispered.

Seleste cried openly. It was her eldest son, the son who had killed himself to keep the Rogue from using him to get to his secret mate. David Deidrick and Leann Vaughn had been forbidden from bonding because they were both betrothed to other vamps by their parents.

"That son of a bitch," Lloyd hissed.

Leann was the oldest child of Lloyd and Adele Vaughn. Adele was also openly sobbing at the implications. Leann had committed suicide when the overwhelming experience of losing her mate swallowed her whole. The question now was, if David was still alive, what had happened to Leann? She would have known her mate was still alive when she ended her life.

"Didn't you see his body?" Chase asked.

Mason swallowed hard. "By the time he was found, he was unrecognizable. The body was the right size and he wore David's clothes and his ring." Mason looked down at the ring on his hand. Chase's father had worn the ring for as long as he could remember.

There was movement in the corner of the screen and Chase focused on the couple coming into view. A female was being roughly led up the stairs by none other than Abel, the son of the Rogue. Abel was his uncle's son—his own cousin.

Chase's heart froze in his chest and he screamed a keening sound of pain and disbelief. The hood was pulled from the female's head and a mane of dark hair, streaked with white and red, fell forward. His soul cried out to her. She cried back, begging forgiveness and understanding.

Mason reached out to touch her head on the screen and looked back at Griffin with tears in his eyes. Debbie squinted at the screen and moved in close to get a better look. She opened her mouth to speak but shook her head and closed it before the words came out. She returned to Chase and wrapped her arms around him and held on when he dropped to the floor.

"Not again. Not again," Adele moaned from the corner.

"The girl is making a noble sacrifice, if you ask me. One for the good of many," said Kane.

Donovan reached over and punched his grandfather in the jaw, knocking him out.

"Asshole!" Donovan cursed.

On the screen, David noticed Abel moving up the stairs and beamed at him. Abel leaned in and whispered something to Danielle. She jerked away from him and kept walking. Chase screamed at the screen as if she could hear him.

"Don't do this, Lovely! We can get them all out! I love you! Please, don't leave me! You can't leave me!"

Mason came to kneel on the floor beside his wife and son to encompass them both in his arms.

David spoke to the assembly. "Ah. Here is my prize. Finally." He held his hand out toward Abel and Lovely.

"You see. The strongest and most loyal of my Shade has brought me the power I need. Bring me the girl," David crooned.

"Damn it! Why Danielle?" Gage wondered aloud. "I know she's strong, but she doesn't have anything he can't get elsewhere. David is already telekinetic. Dani isn't the only strong telepath in the world. She has the ability to enthrall vampires as well as humans, but Lance proved she isn't the only vamp alive who can do that. The only thing that makes her special is that she's multitalented."

David grabbed Lovely by the hair and dragged her up the last few stairs. He put his nose in her hair and inhaled with a smile. Chase knew the exact vanilla-and-lavender sweetness that would be filling David's senses. The bastard had no right to touch her. He had no right to breathe in Chase's mate and smile. Chase searched his mind and dug deep in his soul for traces of her, but a quiet shadow, curled up in the back of his mind, was all he found.

David continued to speak. He had his hands wrapped tightly in her distinctive hair. She didn't struggle to free herself. Even if she had, there was nowhere to go but into the arms of the Shade army, who watched in fascination. The four fanged vamps stepped forward to enclose them.

"It isn't about Danielle anymore," Donovan answered Gage's question. "It's about the game. We have her and he wants her. She defeated him before. She embarrassed him publicly. He has made her out to be such a powerful icon to his men to explain away his defeat. To redeem himself, he has to have her. He has to prove he can beat the Council by taking their new toy and breaking it."

Half the room turned to look at him with raised eyebrows. He shrugged. "I'm a lawyer. I studied criminal psychology. He can't be the biggest bully on the block if he allows others to take his lunch money. The other bullies won't respect him."

"Why doesn't she do something? Why doesn't she fight? She should just kill him where he stands. I would force him to do it himself or have one of his men do it if I could control the minds of others," Lloyd mused.

"She isn't as strong as she once was." Adele sniffed. "She is riding a difficult line between telepathic and physical strength. Since she was turned, her power has teetered back and forth. The more she begins to feel physical strength, her telepathic strength wanes, and vice versa. Darren took more from her than just the humanity she held so dear. Her gifts were partially human in nature. He also weakened her considerably."

Griffin looked at his mother in stunned silence.

"She came to me for help because she said I had the best shields in town. We'd been working on strengthening hers against attack. Right now she could probably hold her own in a fight, but telepathically there isn't much fight left in her. She can probably pick up some thought from unshielded minds, but that's it."

Chase knew all this, but it had been a secret to everyone else but Adele. Lovely was also working with her friend Karrie to build her self-defense skills for the physically weak days. His Lovely had paid dearly for her change. She had been much healthier and happier as a demi-vamp. It was just one more reason to see Darren suffer before he died.

David finished his speech and looked down at Lovely. He pulled her closer by her hair and stroked her cheek. "This is your last chance, beauty. Will you join me, or do you die today?" He purred the question.

Lovely spat in his face and caught him with a loud open-handed slap. He roared at her and struck back. Abel stood nearby looking stone-faced and removed from what was happening in front of him. Chase roared when his Lovely's body went limp and fell into David.

"Now is the time!" David shouted to the crowd. "Today begins our new world order!"

He lifted Lovely's limp body from the ground and sank his fangs into her jugular. He drank greedily Chase struggled to his feet and went for the door, only to be tackled by Gage. He fought to get to his mate while Gage told him over and over that it was far too late. He would need to save his energy to avenge his mate now. It was the only thing left to do. Chase crumpled and turned to watch his uncle murder his one true love, his mate. He would need to remember this in the days to come when he wanted to lie down and die. He would need this memory to keep him alive long enough to make this bastard pay.

When David finished his meal, he lifted his head to look down with eyes the black of night at the female in his arms. Blood covered his lips and dripped from his fangs. The crowd cheered while David shook with energy. He released Lovely without a care, and her body tumbled end over end down the concrete stairs and came to rest in an unnatural-looking heap on the sidewalk. David shook his head like a confused animal and staggered into the building without a word to his gathered army.

The Shade looked around at each other and began to quickly disband, as if they were used to their leader's unpredictable behavior.

Chase watched Abel surreptitiously make his way down the stairs and scoop up Lovely's broken body. He moved quickly off screen.

The office had taken on the cold, sorrowful atmosphere of a mausoleum. The women sniffled and moaned. The men struggled to bear up under the heavy sadness. Across the room, Griffin stared blankly at the screen while tears ran down his face.

Twenty-three

Chase just couldn't wrap his head around the loss of his mate. He felt crushed into the ground. When the horror of seeing his only love murdered faded a bit, he expected to feel the loss of the warmth she brought to his soul, but the emptiness of her absence never came.

Griffin slumped back into a corner chair. A never-ending flow of tears streamed down his face. Chase's father and mother were taking turns going back and forth between Lovely's grieving mate and her father, but Chase wasn't grieving. He closed his eyes and prayed for the thousandth time. He heard Lloyd say to Adele that he was in denial. It was possible that his heart and mind refused to let go of Lovely. Maybe this was why vamps who lost their mates tended to go nuts. If he had to live without her but still feel that she was alive in his heart, Chase would never stop looking for her.

Chase closed his eyes and bowed his head. He searched every corner of his mind for any trace of his mate. He had just about given up hope when he felt the dark spot, where the presence of his Lovely had curled up and disappeared, begin to unfurl and warm the depths of his soul. His body moved of its own volition and he was completely unable to react. He rose from the chair and looked at his mother.

"I'm going home. I want to be alone. I'll call you tomorrow."

Chase's mouth said the words but his mind was not in control. His heart pounded. His mind screamed a joyous sound of relief. It was his Lovely. She was leading him to her without the others knowing. His body carried him toward the door but Adele grabbed his arm. She looked deeply into his eyes and the tightness around her eyes relaxed. The sorrow was fading. Chase had the feeling she was talking to Lovely instead of him when she spoke. There was more to Adele Vaughn than she ever let on in public. Adele knew that Lovely was there in his mind, controlling his actions, even if the others didn't.

"You will call me also. Won't you . . . Chase?" She smirked and released his arm.

"Yes, ma'am," his mouth said.

On the way out of the house he was greeted by dozens of warriors and Wrath guards who gave him condolences on the loss of his mate. Many of the warriors had been friends with Lovely during her time on the Enclave, and Chase felt the sincerity of their sorrow for a female many of them had considered to be one of their own. His mouth thanked them and his feet slowly took him out the door. His mind howled and wallowed in the glory of knowing that his mate was very near. Chase knew she no longer had the strength to do this total mind-control trick from a long distance.

As soon as he figured out how she survived the scene he had watched, Chase was going to put her over his knee. Then he was going to kiss it all better. He loved her so much and was so thankful for another chance at life with his mate. He was glad someone else controlled his limbs because his knees were weak. The last couple of years were a crazy roller coaster ride but the past hour had been the worst of his life. Watching his mate's lifeless body roll down the steps and come to an unnatural-looking rest would be a thing that brought him nightmares for years to come.

Gage felt a restless anticipation and couldn't figure out if it was his nerves or Koren's. In all of his years as a warrior, Gage never knew fear the likes of which he experienced when he knew for sure his mate, his sweet, gentle-hearted Koren, was in the group of females held prisoner on the Enclave.

He placed the blame for this debacle squarely on his own shoulders. When the Council Hall was attacked, he threw everything he had at it and left the Enclave undermanned and vulnerable. His careless judgment had cost the lives of an unknown number of warriors and he shuddered to think of what was happening to the females. Gage was certain Koren had taken a beating. He would spend the rest of his life making up for every scratch and bruise on her beautiful body if he ever got her back in his arms.

Every minute that passed had Gage more and more on edge. Something was definitely wrong with Koren. He had waited long enough. If he had to go in there alone and carry out every female and child on his back, he would do it. Gage got to his feet and went to his gun cabinet.

Greyson stuck his head in the room and instantly had everyone's attention. "We've got movement out by the access road, sir. Several teams are already scrambling to assess the situation."

"What kind of movement?" Gage asked.

"It looks like one of the travel buses from the Enclave hit a tree. How would anyone get off of the Enclave? It's locked down." Greyson looked oddly hopeful. "I think we've either got the females and children back, or there's a bus-size bomb out past the gates." Everyone started talking at once. Gage knew Danielle, and it was entirely possible that she would give her life for her people. It wouldn't be the first time. Only this time she'd succeed in getting herself killed.

Greyson continued, "Do you think Dani exchanged herself for the females' release? Isn't that what the lunatic wanted? I'm hoping the bastard actually kept his word."

A group of vamps in full battle gear hustled past the window and around the building. Gage was fastening his vest and holstering weapons.

"I'm coming with you," said a red-eyed Griffin.

"Griff, I know you feel the need to do something, but I can't have you in harm's way. Please, remember who you are, Councilman," Gage pleaded.

"I don't care. I need to see her." Griffin pushed past Gage and out the front door.

Gage swallowed hard. He couldn't deny Griffin the right to see the body of his child if that was his wish. Gage just hoped they were able to retrieve Dani's body.

The driveway leading from the main road was half a mile long. The house itself was blocked from view by a copse of trees. Gage picked his way through the trees to catch up with Greyson. His team took point and they were quickly moving in. When the men came out of the tree line, the bus door flew open and every warrior hit the ground with weapons drawn and ready to fire.

The females with children came pouring out of the bus. Greyson got to his feet and began to assign the females to warriors if their mates weren't on hand to scoop them up. The glad sounds of reunited friends and mates sucked the tension from the air. In a matter of seconds the bus was nearly emptied and Greyson boarded to check for stragglers.

Gage knew he should be moving to help his people, but his Koren had not left the bus with the other females. He approached the open door to find Greyson lifting a female from the front seat behind the driver. He expected to see the body of Danielle Vaughn but the light hair was all wrong. The woman's long platinum hair was matted with blood and her face was swollen beyond the point of recognition. Her arm flopped over Greyson's shoulder unnaturally. It looked to be broken in several places. Then he noticed her hand. The distinctive sapphire-and-diamond band of his mate adorned the left ring finger of the battered female. Gage roared and the female started. She opened one eye as far as she could and reached for him.

"Gage, carry her to the house and straight to your bed. I'll be right behind you. I think she's got some broken ribs. I don't want to jostle her now that she's awake so don't run. She's not critical at this point but she has to be in a lot of pain. I'm going to check the rest of the bus," Greyson explained while he transferred Koren into Gage's trembling arms. Koren moaned and weakly gripped Greyson's sleeve.

"Baby, Koren, I'm so sorry I didn't protect you." He gently kissed her swollen, battered face and she tried to speak. He couldn't hear so he turned his ear toward her split lips.

"Tessa," she said and pointed to the rear of the bus.

"Tessa?" Greyson asked to be sure he'd heard correctly.

"Go now while he's down. She fed him his own drug," she panted through the pain and tried to explain to Gage and Greyson.

"Tessa fed the Rogue? She was at the Enclave?" Gage asked gently.

Koren nodded. "It was Tessa, not Danielle," she clarified and promptly gave in to the pain and exhaustion now that her message was delivered. Tessa was on the bus. Greyson rushed to the back.

"Holy shit," Greyson cursed.

Gage gingerly carried his precious burden to the rear of the bus where Greyson stood with his mouth agape. On the bench seat a couple lay tangled together like lovers with their clothes on. It was Doc Stevens, and he held a petite brunette with distinctive white-and-red markings tightly to his body. She clung to Doc as if her life depended on it, and it seemed that it did. Gage thought Koren was mistaken and confused due to her injuries, until Greyson brushed the female's hair aside to reveal a black-eyed Tessa Vaughn, her lips and teeth stained red with blood. Doc had a deep slice across the wrist he'd used to feed Tessa, which was already healing, thanks to his vampire genetics. Tessa's transformation to vampire was already under way. She wasn't sporting any fangs yet. That would take a few days.

The resemblance between Tessa and Dani was startling, especially with the changes in Tessa's hair. Doc would have been forced to induce a rapid change to save her life if what Koren said was true and it had been Tessa, not Danielle, the Rogue had nearly drained and tossed down the stairs at the Enclave. Doc had nearly depleted himself to flood her blood with his blood. Tessa was sweating and shaking. It would be a painful experience for her while her body fought the change.

"It's a good thing I brought in a large supply of blood and medical equipment in case we had battle injuries. It looks like Doc and his brand-new baby vamp are both in need of sustenance." Greyson busily looked over Doc Stevens, checking his vitals, his pupils, and the condition of the cut on his wrist. Doc roused enough to kiss Tessa's head.

"My baby," Reilly crooned.

"Let's pray she survives the change," Greyson said somberly.

It was true that only about half of the humans who attempted the change survived the experience. In Tessa's case it was either give it a try or let her die. A noise from the front of the bus made Greyson reach for his gun. He lowered it quickly when a frantic Debbie Deidrick came barreling down the aisle of the bus. Gage realized then that Griffin had also been on the bus with them, silently taking in the scene. Debbie pushed him out of the way to get to Tessa. She brushed the hair from Tessa's face and breathed a deep sigh of relief. Tessa opened her eyes, which were no longer a clear blue but the onyx black of a vampire, and blinked up at Debbie. She was panting with her effort to breathe through her pain of the transformation. Griffin was still standing silently in the front of the bus, listening to everything and looking anxiously for his ex-mate.

"I didn't know if it was you or Dani. Chase is out of his mind with grief. I had to come and see for myself." Debbie's voice shook with the force of her emotions. She held Tessa in a tight embrace.

"Sorry," Tessa wheezed. She looked confused and the pain of her rapid change had her shaking. It was obvious that Tessa had planned this whole charade and was completely unaware that she'd had an audience over the security feed they had been monitoring. Her eyes drifted shut and Greyson reached out to check her pulse. He seemed satisfied for the moment so Gage decided to try sorting this mess out.

"You knew it was Tessa?" Gage asked Debbie.

"I knew she had a plan that involved me helping her get her hair dyed to match Dani's and stay hidden until the time was right. The right time for what, I had no idea. It was clear Tessa planned to impersonate her daughter. They looked so much alike once her hair was done, and their scent is very similar. When we saw Dani being led to the Rogue I couldn't tell who it was. So I kept quiet. I didn't want to give Chase false hope, and Tessa is convinced someone on the Council is feeding the Rogue information, so I couldn't voice my suspicions with so many present. If she was correct, the sacrifice she was making to protect her daughter and gain the release of our people would have been for nothing. If the news of an imposter imitating Danielle was carried back to the Rogue, he would keep hunting for her," Debbie explained.

"I was waiting for her," Reilly added tiredly. "Tessa called yesterday to tell me she was ready to be changed. She said she wanted to be with me. She said I would need to change her to save her life. I was confused. I thought she was sick but she wouldn't explain. She told me where to meet her and that I should be ready for anything.

I was ready and waiting. This has to work. I love her." Reilly reached up to stroke her hair.

The sound of a furious Mason could be heard yelling his wife's name in the distance. Debbie winced. She would have a lot of explaining to do to her mate and her son. Debbie kissed her friend's face and laid her back in Reilly's arms before leaving the bus to go face her worried mate.

"I'm going to need some help with these two." Greyson lifted Tessa from Reilly's weak arms.

Gage ducked into a row of seats with Koren held tightly in his arms when Griffin approached from behind. His expression was one of pure sorrow.

"Give me Tessa. You get *him*." Griffin spoke to Greyson and made the last word sound like a curse. Reilly leaned forward to reach for Tessa and nearly slid onto the floor in an effort to keep her away from Griffin.

"She's mine!" he hissed.

"I know," Griffin replied. His eyes glistened with tears. "I know."

Dani felt like the worst mate in history. After all the drama in their lives and the threats to their relationship up until this point, it was a real kick in the teeth for Chase that she hadn't been able to trust him with the plan her mother had conceived. He was being very understanding, but that was likely because he was still reeling from first losing her and then getting her back, all in the space of a few hours.

Dani couldn't imagine living through the rest of the day after watching Chase die. Her mother had no idea the entire performance was playing out for a portion of the Council, including Griffin and Chase, via a remote-view security system. Her mom was adamant that her death had to look genuine. The Rogue, who turned out to be Chase's dead uncle, needed to believe she was gone. Tessa believed someone on the inside was feeding the Rogue information. It had all happened so fast Dani's head was still spinning, but she never would have gone along with her mother's plan if she had known Chase would be forced to watch it play out.

Once Chase had her in his arms, he didn't want to let go. They made good use of a wall in her mother's hotel suite before he would even allow her to speak. Chase was in need of some serious proof of life before he could process anything else.

His mother, Debbie, secretly brought him to her after they found out that it had been Tessa, not Dani, who had confronted the Rogue. Debbie and Tessa were the only people who knew where Dani was hiding. Her death had to look real and they didn't know whom they could trust. So hiding was her only option. She couldn't explain much of her mother's plan to him because she didn't really understand it herself. Her mother had left her instructions detailing where and when she was to meet her mother's new friend. Tessa had been having precognitive dreams and Dani knew better than to doubt her mother. Chase, on the other hand, would never allow her out of the room if she told him who they were meeting. This was crazy but it had to work. She believed in her mother's gift and trusted that her mother wouldn't send her into anything she couldn't handle.

Dani kissed her mate one last time before hustling him out the door. She wanted to go without him but Chase wasn't having it. He would be nearby for whatever was about to go down. He went with her to the prearranged meeting point in the directions she'd been given by her mother. It was a secluded clearing in the woods that separated the Enclave from property owned by Gage Paris and his family.

"Why do I have to hide? I want to stand with you. Preferably in front of you," Chase groused. The blue-green color of the ocean in his eyes gleamed wetly. She knew he was still struggling with his emotions. Dani wrapped her arms around his waist and let him hold her for as long as was possible.

She was forcing him to watch from a hidden position on the sidelines and it was pissing him off. She explained that his choices were to agree with her or be forced to behave through mind control. He didn't need to know she was feeling telepathically useless after the effort she had put into controlling his body and mind earlier. He piped down but she knew punishment would follow this day. Dani would gladly repent in any way Chase saw fit as soon as this mess was over.

Abel emerged from the trees and Chase snarled, "Is this your savior? I'm not impressed."

Abel ignored the comment and started walking away. "Are you going to help me or not, Dani?" he grumbled over his shoulder. "I did what your mother asked, against my better judgment. Now it's your turn."

"I'm coming," she called. She kissed Chase quickly before pushing him back into his hiding place and catching up with Abel.

"I'm sorry about this, but it has to look real. I can hear him getting closer. Remember, you're a sleepy prisoner. And remember he doesn't know what happened with your mother. He has no clue you should be dead." He apologized before lifting her over his shoulder. Dani let her arms hang limply to flop around as Abel walked.

She was going to kick Chase in the ass if she survived this. He had left his hiding place and was following their progress through the trees. She wanted to send him a telepathic reprimand but the possibility that the Rogue had a few telepaths who would pick it up forestalled her.

"Abel," Darren's deep voice reached out to them from the woods. Chase's outrage flowed to her on a breeze. Darren stepped into their path holding a weak Brandi to his chest. Abel stopped and lowered Dani to her feet. She leaned against him and hoped she looked as convincing as Brandi. Only Brandi wasn't acting. It seemed like Darren had given her just enough Hypno to put out her flames but not enough to put her down.

———◆———

Abel struggled against the intense need to go to his mate. She rested limply against Darren and the sight was making him a little crazy. He had to stick to the plan in order to keep both Brandi and Dani safe today.

"You claim not to care if she dies, but I know you're lying." Darren stroked Brandi's cheek. A tear slid down her pale face. Abel stiffened. It was clear Darren had told her his lie. He couldn't worry about that now. Tessa would help him clear up all of the misunderstandings. "I don't care about your Master's war. I don't care about the Council or any of the rest of it. You want your freedom? I'll help you get it. Give me my mate. I'll give you yours and together we will work this out."

Darren was so sincere, Abel almost felt bad for him. He still believed he had a chance at a life with Dani. Abel wished there was a way to release him from his self-imposed half bond, but Darren would never go for it. Just like Abel's mother would never destroy her bond to his father. It was part of the madness. They believed it would all work out. The difference between Darren and Abel's mother was that Darren was willing to crush anyone between himself and his mate, where Abel's mother was willing to wait an eternity for her mate in silent misery.

"And how exactly do you propose we go about assuring my freedom and my mother's release?" Abel asked and tightened his arm around Dani's neck. Darren took a step forward.

"I propose we go in together and bring your Master out. We're skilled enough to take him down, and I have enough Hypno left to make it that much easier. We will take him to the Council and exchange him for immunity. We've both made mistakes. With the Rogue in Council hands and your mother free from him, we can all walk away. I'll have the time I need with Danielle and you can take your mate and mother wherever you like." Darren looked hopeful. Again, he was totally delusional if he thought the Council would let him just walk away.

"Abel, it's okay. Go save your mother," Brandi slurred.

She raised her hand to reach for Abel. He had to tighten his grip on Dani to keep himself from grabbing her outstretched hand. "Send Brandi over to me and I will release Dani."

"No. I will walk to you and we will trade," Darren demanded.

"Fine." Abel stood his ground and prayed Chase wouldn't come charging through the trees. This had to be difficult for him to watch, but this had to play itself out. He didn't know what was coming, but he did know Tessa would never have sent her daughter into this if she believed Darren was going to get a chance to take Dani again. Darren came forward with Brandi and waited for Abel to release his hold on Dani's neck. As soon as he did, Darren pushed Brandi at him and jerked Dani to his chest. He backed away quickly but he didn't go far. He just held her.

He tilted her head back to look at her face. "I'm so sorry, baby. I know I went about things the wrong way, but I swear if you give me a chance, I'll make a good life for us." Darren ran a hand through her hair. Dani's eyes drifted shut. Abel hated putting her through this.

Abel checked Brandi over to confirm that there were no real injuries. He was assuring her in quiet undertones that he loved her more than his own life and this would all be over soon. They would go someplace safe and he would spend his life proving his love to her. "I love you, Sparky. I've got you now. It's almost over," he whispered against her ear.

A shrill voice cut into Abel's vows to his mate. His mother stormed toward them and Abel stared in shock at her. She didn't look weak and confused right now. She was a tall woman with long, wavy, sable hair and dark eyes. She was beautiful but her expression held pure menace. From the corner of his eye he saw Darren retreat a little farther into the woods to shield Dani.

"How could you betray us this way? Is this how you repay us for teaching you to be a strong male? By stealing the power we deserve?" his mother screamed and her chest heaved.

"Mother, how did you get free?" Abel walked toward her but stopped when Brandi refused to move with him. He didn't blame her. The woman wasn't making any sense.

"I knew you were up to no good so I followed you. It just doesn't matter how many times you are punished, does it? Why do you insist on disobeying us?" she asked with a growl.

"Us?" He was confused. "You have never punished me, Mom. Let's get out of here and we'll talk about this later." Abel tried to smile. He needed to explain things gently to his delicate mother. It broke his heart to see such a beautiful and once-vibrant female so utterly lost in her own mind. He turned to introduce Brandi. He had to tread lightly if he wanted her to come away with him and his new mate. He would find someone to help her sort out her mental tangle as soon as possible.

"This is my mate, Brandi. You're going to love her, Mom. I want you to come with us. We'll find a safe place and make a real home for the three of us. We need to leave now while the Master is down," Abel pleaded with his mother. She completely ignored the reference to his new mate.

"You knew that bitch was drugged! You knew and you let him feed on her?" she bellowed.

"Mom, please calm down. He can't hurt you while he's unconscious," Abel explained. "He had a lot of innocent people captive who needed to go home. I was coming for you next, as soon as I had my mate safe."

Abel's mother began to laugh. The sheer insanity carried in that incredulous cackle made the hair on the back of his neck stand on end. Movement in the woods got his attention briefly and he knew Chase had changed position to prevent Darren from making a run for it with Dani.

"Oh, my boy, as intelligent as I know you to be, it amazes me that you still don't understand my relationship with your father." She attempted to still her maniacal laughter. Abel was so confused. He'd never seen his mother behave this way. She was a quiet, frail female. "You are just as gullible as the foolish purebloods. They believe they are above the rest of us, especially us poor mixed-breed creatures." She laughed again.

"Mom, you're human, not mixed." Abel felt like he was speaking to an unreasonable child. What the hell was she talking about? She had to be drugged. He needed to get his mother and his mate to safety and get them both medical attention.

"Is that so? Yes, I guess you would believe that. The rest of the world did, even your father. You see, when I met your father he thought I was just another human piece of ass he could screw and move on. When in actuality my father is as much a vampire as yours."

Abel shook his head in confusion. His mother was human. He was part human, so he knew it to be true.

"Yes, love. I am just like you. I suppose that actually makes you more like three-quarters vamp, doesn't it? Well, anyway"—she waved a dismissive hand—"for some reason I didn't inherit any vampire traits except for a touch of mind control. I don't even need to drink blood. My human mother died in childbirth. My father was trying to hide his dirty little secret so she was alone when she went into labor. My father paid a vamp couple who couldn't have kids to raise me. He didn't want me ruining his reputation. But that's a story for another day." She shrugged.

Abel struggle to comprehend what his mother was confessing. "You know none of that matters to me, Mom. We can leave this all behind and be a family. Come with me now." He held out his hand.

"You aren't listening, dear. I'm not leaving and neither are you. You have work to do. This is my show. Your father is a puppet with my hand up his ass. David has been basically asleep for over twenty-five years. He thought he could dismiss me. I believed him when he said he had to end our relationship because of a bonding agreement made by his parents. But he lied. He met that Vaughn bitch and bonded with her in secret. He dumped me and mated with that mousy little psychic. So I used his sad little power against him and ruined his whole world. I tried to bring his mate out in the open so we could steal her precognitive power before she died. David wouldn't give in to me entirely, not as long as his mate held his soul. So, I killed her."

Brandi was backing toward Dani and Darren. She was trying to tug Abel along with her a step at a time. When his mother admitted to the murder of Brandi and Dani's aunt, they both gasped. This seemed to remind her that she wasn't alone with her son. Abel felt suddenly like his head would explode. "You said you were mated and it didn't stick. You told me he turned you away," Abel reminded her. None of this could be true. It just couldn't! His father had done something to her. This wasn't his mother.

"The mating part is true enough and it did fade. I did some research and it seemed on the rare occasion your father's particular talent appeared, the only bond they could maintain was the first. But, I haven't been pining for him all these years. Oh, hell no! I've been off spending his money while he worked on the plans I programmed into his little brain. My telepathic control only works on select individuals. It works like a charm on David and I believe that could be due to our past bond. You, on the other hand, no dice; I had to threaten and beat you into submission."

Abel just couldn't wrap his head around what was happening in front of him. It made absolutely no sense. How could his helpless mother be the cause of so much pain in his life?

"Come with me now, Abel. After you've been punished, I have a job for you," his mother demanded.

Abel's world, his whole life, shattered around him. He loved his mother. He'd sacrificed his life along with the lives of many others, his dignity, and flesh and bone to keep her safe. She was his mother. And she was the cause of a lifetime of pain and misery for him. He stood there feeling lost and unable to absorb the enormity of his mother's deception.

Dani knew it was time to go. She had Brandi back safely. They needed to make it to the Paris family house and away from this crazy bitch before she had a chance to test her mind control on the rest of them. Brandi was still too weak to run on her own, so Dani and Chase would have to help her. Dani had the feeling Abel was going to need a minute to sort things out in his own head.

Dani watched as two black-eyed freaks appeared out of the woods as if they had just been waiting for Abel's mother to give the word. They must have drawn the unlucky mind control cards. They were planning to take Abel with them whether he liked it or not. This was a really bad time for her telepathy to go on the fritz.

Dani sidestepped Darren to grab Brandi's arm. Brandi was not at full power and these guys didn't look the type to give a shit that she was just trying to protect her mate when she'd interfered. When Dani came into view, Abel's mother hissed.

"You! You stupid bitch! Just like that other Vaughn bitch, David just had to have you. The only damn thing I can't control is David's obsession with you. Well, that ends now." She pointed to Dani and bellowed, "Kill her!"

Oh shit! Dani had never seen this woman before but she obviously knew Dani. Abel grabbed Brandi and forced her to the ground so he could cover her body with his own. The sound of objects whizzing through the air made Dani turn to run. Her telepathy and telekinesis were useless at the moment but she could run like hell. Dani heard things flying past her as she weaved in and out of the trees. Something embedded itself deep in her left arm. She screamed and staggered but kept moving. The sound of heavy footsteps made her move faster but she didn't get far before she was tackled to the ground.

Dani landed on her side with a huge weight on top of her. She was waiting for the attack to begin but it didn't come. She opened her eyes and realized Darren was on top of her. His hot blood ran over her but his eyes watched hers. Dani shifted and he slid to his side. She tried to sit up, but he pulled her back down into his arms.

"Not yet. Not safe," he wheezed.

Dani could hear the sounds of fighting nearby. She looked down to find a three-inch-thick tree branch protruding from Darren's chest. He was still focused on her face. Blood was beginning to seep from his mouth. He had taken the strike meant for her. Tears filled her eyes. This was a fatal injury. There was too much blood loss to get him help in time. The branch had ripped through his body. She knew she shouldn't care after everything Darren had done to her. She should be glad, but Dani just wasn't built that way.

"I don't deserve your tears, baby." He brushed his fingers over her cheek and carried the tear to his bloody lips. "Do you think one day you can forgive me? I will rest easier if I know you can at least try." His eyes begged her for absolution.

"I forgive you now, Darren. It's all over now."

She wrapped an arm around his side and stroked his back. Her other hand traced the long scar down the side of his face. The blood flowing out of his chest slowed to a trickle, but he smiled.

"I may not have lived in your arms, Danielle, but at least I'll have the honor of dying in them."

Darren rested his spiked blond head against her shoulder and struggled for a few more painful breaths before he drifted away.

Twenty-four

Missiles were flying through the air and Brandi found herself pressed into the ground under Abel. It was a hell of a time to be useless! At least she was starting to feel less groggy. She had the sudden fear this might be her last chance to speak with him, so Brandi confessed the depth of love in her heart.

"I know this is a really bad time to say it, but, I love you. I love you so much, Abel." Brandi turned her head to press a kiss against his cheek. "We will get through this. Our plan still stands. That is, if you still want to be with me. We will find a little house and make a comfortable life. I won't let them take you away from me."

She hugged him tight. Abel didn't respond. He was watching his mother flee the area while her minions did the dirty work. Out of the corner of her eye Brandi saw movement. Chase came out of the woods behind the killer vamps. Silently he crept up to them, carrying a huge branch. He took aim and swung away at the head of the largest male. The thud of wood meeting bone echoed through the trees and made Brandi a bit queasy.

The sound distracted the second male and Abel leapt at the chance. He was on his feet and delivering a roundhouse kick before Brandi could blink. The extra time it took him to get up gave the bad guy time to gather himself and deflect the kick by grabbing Abel's leg. Abel used the guy as leverage and swung up his other leg to connect with the guy's head before he fell to the ground and rolled back up to his feet. The two males shifted from foot to foot like prizefighters in the ring, trading punches and kicks.

Brandi started crawling away and immediately drew the bad guy's attention. He still had a target to kill and his first priority was to search out the target. Brandi was female and the right size, so he lunged for her. That was the end-all for her mate. No more fighting fair. He leapt on the male and snapped his neck with a sharp twist and a crack. His lifeless body hit the ground and was forgotten. Abel's mother was long gone and both of her henchmen were dead. Chase took off into the trees in the direction Dani and Darren had gone.

Abel strode to Brandi and lifted her to her feet. Without a word, he checked her from head to toe for injuries and then pulled her into his arms and kissed her. Brandi felt every bit of love he had in his heart for her in that kiss and the telepathic connection they shared as mates. That close, she was able to feel his presence within her mind again, and she couldn't wait until their bond grew and they could sense each other's emotional state all the time. Abel was confused and hurt by his mother's confessions, but above all, he had been terrified he would lose Brandi. His family had done her family so much harm. He feared she would hold it against him.

"I love you. We will get through this," she repeated her earlier promise when Abel released her lips.

A noise to the left had Abel on the defensive. Chase and a blood-covered Dani came toward them. Brandi's shock must have shown on her face because Dani raced to reassure her.

"It's not my blood. Well, some of it is, but not too much," Dani explained.

"We will have to come back for Darren's body. He gave his life for my mate. The least I can do is ensure he receives a proper final resting place." Chase ripped a strip from his shirt to fasten tightly around Dani's injured arm.

"Well. Well. It looks like we missed the party, guys."

A voice came from behind Brandi and she started. Abel pushed her behind him and glared at the newcomers. Dani squealed and ran at the male. He caught her midair and smiled widely while he gazed into her eyes.

"Now there's a sight I've missed. How are you, Angel?" Kayden hugged her tight until she hissed at the pain in her injured arm.

"I've had a rough day, if you must know. And as soon as I'm over it, I'll be getting in the line of people waiting to kick your ass. Where the hell have you been?" She kissed his cheek.

"Could you please remove your hand from my mate's ass and speak to her from a respectable distance?" Chase was seething just a bit. No male wanted to see his mate in the arms of another.

"Sorry, man." Kayden placed Dani's feet on the ground and smiled down at her from his impressive height.

"I'm looking forward to that ass whipping. I'll definitely pencil you in. As for where I've been, I have some friends to introduce to all of you."

Kayden nodded and dozens of people appeared from all around them. One really huge guy stepped up next to Kayden and looked curiously at Dani. He wore head-to-toe black and his duster waved a bit in the wind.

"This is Hawk. He's the unofficial father of all these hoodlums." Kayden pointed a thumb at the skyscraper of a male. The male he called Hawk was so tall he even looked down at Kayden. The others laughed at Kayden's paternal description of the big male. The circle tightened around them and Abel pulled Brandi protectively back against his chest.

"You don't need to worry, man. I would never hurt Brandi. She's like a little sister. I used to hide her dolls and pull her pigtails," Kayden said when he noticed Abel's discomfort.

Chase came forward to embrace his oldest friend in a back-thumping man hug. Dani was walking around the circle of strangers and inspecting each person she passed. Brandi could iden-tify two-thirds of them as clearly vampire, and the rest seemed human, but not.

A blonde sidled up next to Kayden and crossed her arms over her chest. She was cute with pale ringlets and strikingly bright blue eyes. Her all-black fatigues fit like a glove on her long, lean body. With a raised brow, the chick glared at Dani. Oh, now that was interesting. It seemed Kayden had a new friend.

"We found a few more friends on the way in. I think these are buddies of yours." Kayden nodded to Abel.

The crowd parted and a small group pushed in. Karrie and Nate stood out in front. Brandi didn't know the rest, but Abel did, and he left her to go shake hands and welcome them. Kayden was explaining that they were ex-Shade who had defected with Nate when the Rogue attacked the Enclave. They'd set up camp nearby to wait for a chance to catch up with Abel. He was the strongest of the group. They were looking for his guidance as to where to go and what to do next. That was when Kayden's new friends had found them.

"They're all like me," Dani interrupted Brandi's thoughts.

The blonde next to Kayden stepped closer to him and sniffed disdainfully. Dani didn't seem to notice the slight, or she didn't care.

"Well, they're like I used to be. They're demi-vamps." She beamed at the crowd.

"They call themselves the Horde. They think it's funny." Kayden frowned. Dani laughed uproariously, hugging her injured arm to her chest.

"The Mongrel Horde. I love it." She smiled. Chase's frown joined Kayden's. The others approved of Dani's reaction and started introducing themselves and asking her questions. No one seemed to notice or care about her blood-covered clothes. Brandi was sure most of the vampire nation would have heard of Danielle Vaughn, the powerful demi-vamp turned vamp.

"You take everything so seriously, Kayden." The blonde stroked his arm but he shook off her hand.

"I once loved a girl like you guys." He snuck a look at Dani. "Believe me, Jamie, she is no mongrel."

Jamie growled under her breath.

"Alright." Chase cut into the crowd and retrieved his mate. He had removed his sweater to give her something to change into and pulled his jacket back over his undershirt. "Now that the introductions have been made, what brings you out tonight?"

"We are here to offer our services," the big man named Hawk answered. "You've got some asses to kick and we're wearing the right size boots. We're here to help with that pest problem over at the Enclave. The Shade and their master have taken over. We'd like to help you get it back."

"I've been training with my new friends for a few weeks," Kayden explained. "It's time they stop hiding in fear from our people. I can't think of a better way to introduce our society to the fact that they exist and that they are strong and worthy of notice than to allow them to help us deal with our little infestation. What do you guys think?" Kayden asked.

"I think there's no time like the present. The Rogue is down and out from his own drug and his troops are without direction." Chase smiled and kissed the top of Dani's head.

"We just need to tuck the girls away someplace safe," Chase added.

Karrie scoffed and both Brandi and Dani howled their outrage. In the end, all three girls went to the Enclave in spite of their mates' protests. Kayden was none too happy about their participation in the strike either, but the dispute ended when Dani said, "Either you take us with you or we'll find our own way in. It's up to you," and she planted her hands on her hips.

———•———

They were going in without the knowledge of the powers that be. They all agreed it was better to ask forgiveness than permission. They had to strike while the Rogue was incapacitated. They were a group of misfits and rebels with a few strong females, a warrior, and a future Councilman mixed in for good measure. As a unit, they moved in through a little-known emergency exit in the gutter system that carried runoff water out of the Enclave. One by one the group dropped into the dark manhole a few blocks from the Enclave. Many of the warriors who were trapped during the invasion had escaped this way. Once inside they fanned out in groups of six with one lead on each team. The element of surprise was on their side. As much as Abel didn't want Brandi to see this side of him, there was no time for mercy. They had to strike down as many Shade as possible on the first wave.

Abel managed to convince Brandi, Dani, and Karrie to hang back in the tunnel until they were needed. If the guys could sweep the grounds without raising alarms, they would. They used the excuse that they could be hurt if they were distracted by their mates. The girls grudgingly gave in.

When the teams advanced, they were each assigned a building of the barracks to clear. They would take out the sleeping Shade to reduce their numbers quietly. Abel's team, which included Chase, Nate, and three of his old Shade chums, cleared their building's floor and found not a soul. Abel couldn't help worrying that when the time came the ex-Shade wouldn't be able to do the job. It was hard to end a life, especially if it was someone you knew.

When they rejoined the other teams, they learned every other building was vacant as well. Abel knew it wouldn't be this easy. It wasn't like the Shade would have abandoned their post because the Master was taking a long nap. A chill crept up his spine and Abel called a retreat. This had to be a trap.

Before they reached the tunnels an alarm sounded and floodlights bathed the night in a yellow glow. The sounds of a far-off battle reached the ears of every male.

Now that they'd lost the cover of darkness, the group moved quickly toward the sound of battle. Abel was relieved beyond belief for the sight that greeted them at the top of the last rise that led to the grounds between the security fences and the Enclave. This was no trap. The warriors were storming the gates and the Horde was there to prevent the enemy from retreating. It was perfect. They would squeeze the Shade between them and meet in the middle. Abel prayed Brandi and the other females would stay put in the tunnel until the fighting was over.

The field of battle was a mass of darkly clothed, black-eyed males with guns, knives, and fangs. The Horde along with Abel, his ex-Shade, Chase, and Kayden entered the field of battle as one. They had an advantage at first because the Shade weren't expecting an attack from behind. The Shade hanging back in the rear were quickly picked off until they were finally noticed. That's when the real fighting began. There was pandemonium as half of the Shade forces turned to meet them while the other half focused on the warriors ahead. The less experienced fighters like Chase and some of the younger Horde members hung back and picked off the approaching enemy with firearms while Abel and the rest pressed forward with blades and fists as well as guns.

The biggest difficulty was trying to be sure you didn't take out one of your own guys. Males fell and were trampled underfoot as the line progressed. The battle was bloody and both sides were suffering major losses. The Horde was making headway and the warriors were in sight when they hit a wall—a telepathic wall. Abel watched as, one by one, his people and the warriors turned on each other. There were telepaths in there sending out illusions and mental deceptions to trick them into fighting each other. The center of the field was Shade territory and Abel had no idea how to break through.

***

Dani's plan was crazy, but all three of them prayed it would work. It took real trust to allow another person any level of mind control. Brandi didn't like it, but she did it. It was harder for Karrie because she was a control freak from top to bottom, no doubt about it. Dani explained that only one telepath could enter a mind at a time and it all made sense. If they let Dani in, the bad guys would be locked out. They could enter no-man's-land in the center of the field and take out the two pricks Dani suspected were running the show.

Abel had told them earlier that David had four high-ranking henchmen, two telekinetics and two telepaths. They had killed the telekinetics earlier. These two had to be the remaining telepaths making a stand for their fallen leader. Brandi feared the Rogue would be waking up very soon and Sheena, Abel's mother, would be in charge again. It was a very pretty name for a female with such a demented mind. Brandi kept waiting for her to suddenly appear and strike them down. She could still hear Sheena's insane cackle floating through the trees.

They needed to take out the Shade ringleaders with their telepathic weapons, and they needed to do it now. She took a deep breath and nodded to Dani when she was ready. Dani entered Brandi's mind gently and sat quietly in the rear. It was kind of like having another presence tucked up next to Abel's. He had been too

busy fighting to think about what she was up to until he felt someone horn in on his territory. He flared to life in her mind and
roared at her.

"Territorial much?" Dani asked.

Karrie was holding her head, so Brandi imagined she was getting a good scolding from Nate, as well. Brandi felt like a third
wheel when Dani directed Abel to pull his guys back and prepare
to take cover.

"Let's move while I'm feeling strong, girls," Dani directed.

Karrie took the lead and kicked a path through the Shade and
the confused warriors and Horde who were fighting each other.
Dani sent out waves of clarity and sight to hopefully pull them from
the cloud of illusion. Many of them began to fall back to either side
of the field. It was working. What they had to do was get through
the battle raging around them alive, and Brandi was never so grateful for her martial arts training. She and Karrie fought through the
battle, slipping around the action when they could, while Dani
concentrated on releasing the minds of the confused warriors from
the grip of the Shade. They were lucky it wasn't mind control being
used on the field, instead of a mass illusion of sorts. There would
have been nothing Dani could do about a mind under the influence
of another telepath.

Once they reached the ringleaders, it would be up to Brandi to
end the fighting. She still wasn't sure how that was going to work
out, but she had to do it. Dani couldn't help because telepaths can't
control each other and the best Karrie could do was kick their asses
until they cried uncle. Dani seemed to know something Brandi
didn't, and she suspected Tessa had shared her vision of the future
battle, because Dani was sure that if she just got Brandi to the
center of the fight, it would end quickly. Considering the amount
of Shade they were up against, Karrie wouldn't get much of a chance
to reach their targets.

They hit resistance in the form of a mountain of Shade surrounding the telepathic terrorists. Karrie never stopped when she reached the blockade. Terrorist number one was a female, and she looked at Brandi and snarled. They were trying to breach her and Karrie's minds unsuccessfully. Karrie battled on while Brandi and Dani held their own back to back. This wasn't going to work. They couldn't breach the line and Brandi didn't know what she would do if they did. All she did know was that the flames she worked so hard to keep banked were building to a critical level.

Karrie screamed and Brandi turned to find a long blade handle sticking out of her shoulder. Karrie's pain shot through Dani via their telepathic link and took Dani to the ground as well. Brandi could feel Dani's presence wavering in her mind. They could not be stuck out on this field and turn against each other. Brandi refused to allow herself to harm the ones she loved, and she couldn't carry both of her friends to safety.

"Dani, tell them to get down now!" Brandi screamed over the cacophony of battle. Dani nodded and her eyes lost focus as she reached for the minds of their males.

Brandi thought about her allies and their strength of character. She focused on the need to protect them all. She concentrated on the darkness she imagined flowing in the veins of their enemies. They had to be stopped and she was the only one who could end this without spilling another drop of honorable blood. Her body burned, her clothes smoked, and her heart ached for what she was about to do. She would be feared and possibly hated after this. Brandi reached out and put a hand on each of her friends, hoping her touch wouldn't burn either of them, before she released the hell storm churning in her belly. A mass of energy crashed out of her, searing the very air and scorching the earth. It was like a superheated tornado that claimed some and skipped over others. Brandi directed her flaming rage to seek out only the darkness and protect the strong of heart. Eyes closed tightly, she held on to her friends for comfort. People would die at her hands today. How would she learn to live with that?

Screams reached her ears very briefly before silence prevailed over the landscape. There were no more sounds of clanging knives or gunfire. The war cries of impassioned males and the screams of fallen combatants came to a halt. Brandi was too afraid to open her eyes. What if she'd killed them all? What if she were the only one left? How would she explain this to the families of so many good males? What if she had killed her mate, her love, her life?

"Brandi?"

She didn't answer. She wanted to believe for just another few seconds that she was not a murderer. If she opened her eyes, she would be faced with the reality of the blood on her hands.

"Sparky? Open your eyes for me, baby." Abel encouraged her to look at her shame. She was terrified that he would fear her now and she didn't want to see that in his eyes.

"Oh, Sparky," he sighed. "You saved so many lives today. You saved your people from each other and destroyed the Shade. You are not a murderer. You are a phoenix rising from the ashes of a battle well fought and won."

Brandi imagined twisted and charred bodies. She expected a scene straight out of hell when she opened her eyes. What she was confronted with was even more horrific. The field was covered inches deep with ash. Mixed in with the gray remains of so many of the Rogue's Shade warriors were the injured and dead warriors, Horde, and other vamps who had been under the influence of the telepaths. Her power had obeyed her command to take only the lives of her enemy. The disbelieving faces of every male she passed would be burned into her memory. Her people would fear and ostracize her for sure now. Abel kissed her forehead and returned her earlier vow to him.

"I love you. We will get through this," he told her.

She nodded, but Brandi didn't believe it. The fight to reclaim the Enclave was over, but the battle of her life was about to begin.

———•———

There were some very tense moments when the captain of the warrior class came to confront his son. From what Abel understood, Kayden had been missing without a trace for weeks. Kayden's biggest concern was how the captain would react to the Horde. They were Kayden's people now, and if they weren't accepted, he would go when they left.

Father and son stood on guard, both with a line of brethren at their backs. Kayden gave not an inch to his father. Gage looked up and down at the ragtag line of demi-vamps Kayden had helped train and reform. Slowly a smile broke over Gage's face and he crossed the imaginary line in the sand to greet his son.

"Welcome home, kid." Gage pounded lovingly on his only child's back, crushing him in a bear hug. "Your mother will be so relieved to see you."

Both lines of fighters took their cues from the Paris men and crossed to greet and congratulate each other on the joint victory. It was a good beginning and more than Abel could have hoped for.

The male Councilmen, with Mason in the lead, retrieved a groggy and confused David Deidrick from the training facility. Given Sheena's confession, it was unclear what should be done with David. His crimes were many and varied, but how much of it was actually his own doing? Sheena was still on the loose, having fled when the fighting started, so there was the possibility of her overcoming him again.

In the end, Abel was left feeling adrift. He had spent his whole life defending a lie. The mother he worshipped had only used him to further her own cause. He'd sat still for beating after beating to protect his mother, when all along she was the one who had ordered the abuse. The animosity Abel felt for his evil, sadistic bastard of a father now had to be shifted to his mother instead.

Sheena had fed him this bullshit fairy tale about how in love his parents were when he was conceived and now he realized that couldn't have been further from the truth. She had manipulated David into her bed after she had killed his one true love and made it look like suicide. It was all just too much, and Abel needed time to soak it all in and deal with the aftermath of his wasted life.

Abel did his part to help restore the Enclave after the battle in spite of his personal turmoil. It took days to put things back to rights, and he worked side by side with the warriors, the Horde, and his fellow ex-Shade to get it done. There was a tentative friendship between the three groups that was strengthening by the day. He used the time he toiled away at backbreaking labor to sort out his thoughts and reexamine his past. He also spent time with Kayden helping train the Horde, and got to know the Deidricks, his father's family. He spent every night with Brandi at the apartment she'd rented so they would have privacy and time to bond, but they didn't really talk. He came home late and weary every night. He would shower and crawl into bed next to his beautiful mate, where he would claim her body, taking her like a madman, making her scream his name over and over until he could no longer move. Once again sweaty and physically and mentally exhausted, Abel would find peaceful oblivion in a dreamless sleep where he didn't have to think about the countless lives he'd taken and destroyed.

Brandi absentmindedly stepped out of the shower in the apartment she'd rented for her and Abel and toweled herself dry. She was lost in her thoughts of Abel and the ocean of space that had opened between them since the battle at the Enclave weeks ago. She'd feared the worst that day but prayed for the best, and it looked like her prayers were going unanswered. Her first concern was for Abel's mental well-being after learning of his mother's lifelong deception. Abel was a strong male who'd never had anyone to lean on or confide his troubles to. So it was understandable that he needed time to adjust to having a mate who wanted to help shoulder the burden. The problem was that Abel wouldn't talk about it at all. If she brought up his mother and father he would get upset and walk away. Not only did he refuse to talk about his feelings, he wouldn't talk to her about anything.

Abel had volunteered to help rebuild the damage done to the Enclave during the invasion. He'd helped dig the graves of the warriors who were killed in the fighting. At the funeral for those warriors, he'd stood in the back of the chapel, refusing to take his place in the pew with her family. She suspected he felt responsible for those deaths by association. After things on the Enclave were righted, he began working with Kayden and his new friend, Hawk, to train his fledgling warriors known as the Horde. The large group of demi-vamps was unorganized and still fearful of being too close to the vampires they'd been hiding from their whole lives, but they were motivated and for the most part eager to be accepted.

So Brandi watched Abel's life become an endless loop of work and training with short breaks for sex and sleep. She believed helping out was his attempt at community service or penance to make amends for the hurt he'd caused over the years. He worked from dawn until dusk at anything and everything that needed to be done at the Enclave or with the Horde.

The relationship between her and Abel had declined to little more than daily bouts of sex—and she called them bouts because there wasn't anything loving about it. He would use her body to further exhaust himself and drop into a near-dead sleep. He was aggressive in his lovemaking, but he always satisfied, leaving her mindless and sweaty before he took his own pleasure. Their mental bond as mates was nearly nonexistent. She was catching echoes of his self-loathing and guilt. It was clear that he was having trouble dealing with the guilt of his past. She wanted to comfort him. She wanted him to know that she would never judge him if he needed to unburden himself and tell her of his crimes, but she couldn't tell him any of that unless she wanted to push him even further away.

There were times she wondered if Abel was regretting his decision to become her mate. He was definitely blocking her mentally and that hurt her more than anything. She tried to convince herself that it was his guilt making him so distant, but what if she was wrong? It was widely known that she had been the vampire to end the fighting at the Enclave. Her pyrokinesis was a dangerous ability that many would fear. What if he was disgusted by her actions? Could she blame him? Not really. She'd murdered hundreds of people on the field of battle. She'd turned them to dust where they stood. Those people had been, if not friends, then colleagues of his. He'd worked and lived with most of them for years. It was possible that Abel wasn't as accepting of her gift after seeing it in action. She just didn't know, but she had to find out soon. She couldn't continue living this way and loving him while he ignored her. Damn it! This should be their honeymoon period. They should be spending time working to strengthen their blood bond, not building walls against each other.

Brandi rummaged through the closet they shared for something to put on while she made dinner. She had a special dinner planned for her mate, and she wanted to look pretty but it was too early to get dressed. It would be a while before Abel got home. When her hand brushed by one of Abel's shirts, she pulled it from the hanger and slipped it on. Feeling silly for needing to do anything to feel closer to the man she loved, she buttoned it up. She'd change it before he got home, but at the moment his much-too-large shirt was a comfort to her.

The kitchen was very small but a bright, cozy place to spend time. Brandi bustled around assembling ingredients from a list in one of her new cookbooks. Cooking was a skill she'd only recently developed. She enjoyed the act of cooking for her man, and she was pretty damn good at it. He hadn't refused to eat anything she'd made yet. Growing up in a mansion with maids and cooks hadn't prepared her for life on her own. Her mother had never cooked, but Brandi would want to spend time in the kitchen with her kids. She could already imagine the children with their father's dark eyes sitting around the table while she served them meals made with love. The thought had her eyes filling with tears. She loved Abel so much. She wanted those babies and she wanted her lover and her friend back. She needed her mate more than he could ever imagine.

Pulling herself together, Brandi began to sauté the vegetables for the meal. Lost in thought and busy with her task, she hadn't noticed that she was no longer alone in the apartment until Abel pressed himself against her back. She drew in a shocked breath before relaxing against his solid chest. He wrapped his arms around her and kissed the top of her head. There was an odd tension radiating from Abel that gave her hope. Maybe he was finally ready to talk. This was what she missed. This closeness to her mate was what she needed. Carefully she tested the connection between them only to find it solidly blocked. Her heart fell. He would let her get close physically but that was it. He wouldn't give her any more than that. Brandi stepped away from him to stir the food in her skillet. She didn't know what to do but she couldn't handle this constant emptiness.

"You're home early. Dinner will be ready in about an hour," she told him flatly. He didn't reply. She wasn't surprised. He just stood behind her as if waiting for her to turn and give him her attention, but she refused. She couldn't look into his eyes and see nothing but lust staring back at her. She needed more than that from her mate. Abel reached around her and flipped the knob on the stove to shut off the flame. "Hey!" Brandi complained, but her cry was cut off as Abel spun her around and cupped her face in his hands, claiming her mouth and demanding her full attention. She was helpless to deny her mate the contact he needed. He invaded her mouth, his tongue delving deep to stroke and taste every corner. Brandi moaned and opened wider, accepting him. She ran her hands up his chest to explore the dips and ridges of his muscles. Abel's hands slid down her neck and over her collarbone to cup her aching breasts. His touch excited her body but her mind instinctually searched for the link to her mate. Being one with him while they made love was an incredible experience she'd only enjoyed that first time, the night they mated, and she desperately needed it now.

"Let me in, baby, please," she whispered against his mouth, but the barrier between them remained in place. Abel opened his eyes and looked down at the shirt she wore. He gripped the shirt in both hands and pulled hard, causing buttons to fly in every direction. Her bare breasts were revealed to his dark gaze, and he bent to suck one tight nipple into his mouth while sliding the shirt down her arms. It pooled on the floor at her feet. Brandi's belly tightened in anticipation when Abel's hand delved into her panties. He made a sound of aggravation. She knew she wasn't wet enough to take him. Abel was a big man. Her mind was busy trying to unravel the puzzle of her mate instead of absorbing the physical pleasure he gave her.

The room spun when Abel lifted her into his arms and turned to bend her over the kitchen table. Wide-eyed she said, "Abel, baby, maybe we should talk." She tried to stand up but he pushed her back with a hand between her shoulder blades. Brandi obeyed. His hands splayed across her ribs and traveled down to her hips. He traced the line of her lace thong and hummed. Then, without warning, the delicate garment was ripped from her body with one strong tug. He used one knee to spread her legs farther apart. Brandi knew her charms were totally on display in this position and she blushed. Lord. They were in the kitchen and she was totally nude!

Abel dropped to his knees behind Brandi and she could feel him looking at her, but he didn't touch her. As embarrassed as she was having Abel back there staring at her girl bits, it excited her at the same time. He rubbed his big hand over the globes of her ass before smacking one cheek and making her yelp, but, again, it was exciting. He was getting her wet without even touching the places she needed him most. She squirmed and panted as the need for stimulation grew in her belly. He smacked her ass again but she didn't have time to register the pain before he spread her wide with his hands and his face was pressed in tightly, his tongue lapping at the wetness he'd caused. She moaned. Oh, it was so good. He nibbled and licked, sucking at her clit, alternating between teasing licks and deep thrusts of his tongue into her channel. Brandi shook and pressed back against him, wanting to come. He purred and gave her what she needed. Abel's fingers delved into clenching heat while he sucked her clit into his mouth and vigorously strummed it with his tongue. Brandi came with a scream, the violent clenching of her body rendering her unable to stand. The world around her faded as her orgasm swallowed her.

Abel moved to his feet and she heard the rustling of fabric as he undid his pants. His hands explored her body as his manhood probed at her entrance. Slowly he pushed into her, parting her with his impressive girth. She moaned and relaxed her muscles to accept his invasion. Abel twisted his hips and rocked until he was fully seated. She panted and gripped the edge of the table. He moved then, pulling out slowly once and gradually sliding back in. The motion caused friction between her clit and the edge of the table. Shit. She wouldn't last long. He already had her body primed for another orgasm. Abel pulled back again, slammed back in, holding her body still for his thrusting. He pounded at her entrance again and again, claiming her in the rough and mindless way she'd come to expect from him. Her clit was ground into the table with every inward stroke and Brandi was screaming his name again in no time. It went on and on. Abel made her come over and over until she lay limply across the table, no longer able to move or even think. His strokes became erratic and he leaned over her, holding on to the table with one hand and her hip with the other. He grunted and strained against her when he finally found his own violent release. Warmth spread through her body but her heart and mind were still sadly empty. There had been no glorious joining of souls to make her feel loved and cherished, only a physical joining of bodies to relieve the tension. Abel's hot breath blew across her cheek. He lifted his weight from her body and kissed the back of her neck before backing away. She couldn't move at all.

"I'm not hungry, Sparky," he told her and left her there on the table. It was the first thing he'd said to her since he entered the kitchen.

Brandi felt the tears welling up and sliding down her cheeks to make little puddles on the table. This was what he needed from her. This was all he needed from her and she couldn't live with it anymore. She peeled her sweat-slicked body from the table and turned to survey the room. Her attempt at a special meal for her mate sat congealing in the pan on the stove. Her panties were shredded on the floor next to the shirt with its missing buttons scattered around the room. The sound of the shower coming on stirred her to action. Walking naked to the bedroom, she pulled down the suitcase from the top of their closet and began to fill it with her things. She loved Abel too much to let things go on this way. If he didn't want to talk, that was fine, but she would not stand idly by and watch him wallow in guilt. If he regretted their mating, she couldn't change that, and letting him use her body while he rejected her heart and soul was destroying her a little more every day. She would give him the space he needed. If he wanted there to be distance between them, she would grant his wish.

———•———

Abel had taken his mate in the kitchen like an animal. There hadn't been any thought behind it at all. He'd gotten home early after his newfound uncle, Mason, pulled him aside to talk about how Abel was dealing with the situation with his mother and father. That was easy. He wasn't dealing with it and he didn't want to deal with it. He just wanted to move on from here. Frustrated with everyone for wanting him to talk about his feelings, Abel headed home. He'd been trained not to have feelings. Now his love for Brandi, his sense of betrayal by his mother, and the concern of the crowd of new family and friends threatened to choke him. He needed time to think without everyone watching and waiting for him to finally crack. When he couldn't even come home without being pestered to "talk things out," Abel did what he'd always done when shit got too heavy. He shut out the world.

Abel didn't notice exactly how large the distance between Brandi and himself had grown until it was nearly too late. He was so caught up in his own misery that he didn't take the time to look at what his struggle to come to terms with his sins was doing to his mate.

When he'd stepped out of the bathroom to find Brandi straddling a suitcase near the door he knew things were far worse than he'd imagined. Her curly hair was in disarray, like she'd been running her hands through it. She was crying, big tears rolling down her delicate face and dropping onto her jeans.

"I can't do this anymore, Abel," she'd said with trembling lips.

Those words echoed around the room now that she was gone. He loved her so much and he didn't want the ghosts of his past to taint their future. What he had actually done was let his own fear that he would never be more than his past drive a wedge between them. Watching her walk out of their home had opened a black hole in his chest. Nothing could exist without his Sparky. His world was sucked into that dark, empty space the moment the door closed behind her.

He'd been unknowingly blocking her out of their mating bond. He hadn't even known it was possible. He'd been doing a better job of shutting out the world than he thought. Shit! He'd honestly believed his humanity was the cause of their weak link. He'd been beating himself up about not being able to give Brandi the kind of bond she deserved but he'd been wrong. As Brandi had paced back and forth explaining her reasons for giving him space, she'd reminded him of the night they'd tied their lives together. That night they had been one, together, complete. That's what she was asking him for now. He had to find a way to give it to her before she would come home to him.

She'd given up searching for the emotional and mental connection she deserved and needed from her mate. He was devastated by her leaving. You don't just walk out on your mate. But he'd quickly realized that was figuratively what he'd done to her. When things got rough, he'd ducked out on their relationship instead of learning to be a real mate and letting her in, letting her help him.

If Sparky could clearly read his emotions, she would know that she was the only thing keeping him sane. Her love, her devotion, and her patience were teaching him how to be a better man. He was healing and finding out what it took to deserve the love of a woman like his precious mate. Abel lay across the bed and watched the room darken as night fell. He was still staring at the ceiling when the dawn came, but he knew without Sparky the sun would never truly shine on him again. It was a new day. It was the first day of forever, and Abel was ready to claim his mate, again. He had a plan but this time he was going to need some help. Okay, a lot of help. He climbed off the bed and dug the phone out of his jeans on the floor. It was a good thing he had a family ready and willing to support him, because it was going to take a small army to pull this off before his mate gave up on him completely.

"Are we having fun yet?"

Sheena smiled down at the little slut who thought she could replace Sheena in David's affections. The girl was a sweaty mess on the floor. She was shaking with the aftereffects of the new drug they had been testing on her. The drug had been in development for longer than the Hypnovam and they were getting close to a stable formula.

This new creation was the polar opposite of the Hypno and it would be a much more effective weapon against the Council. Instead of rendering its victim powerless, the new formula worked with the chemicals in the brain to cause extreme aggression. It had been great fun to watch David's pretty little toy go against all of her own instincts and attack everyone they put in the cell with her. The girl was horrified by her need for blood. Her introduction to the vampire nation had been less than welcoming and Sheena was doing everything possible to promote the girl's self-loathing. She was having fun turning the girl into her own worst nightmare.

Now that David was in the custody of the Council, Sheena needed a new tool of destruction until she was able to find a way to get him back under her control. At this distance, and without the ability to feed him her blood, maintaining control over him was impossible. Sheena chuckled to herself. She'd bet waking up to thoughts of his own after decades of telepathic mind control had knocked David on his ass. She just wished she'd been there to see him try to explain that he didn't know what he was doing. They would never believe him.

"How does it feel to be the monster you fear most?" Sheena laughed and stalked around the girl, being careful not to get too close. When she came down from the drug the girl was always as docile as a kitten, but if you got too close before the drug completely wore off, she was dangerous.

The girl began to cry again. The limp body of a guy they'd picked up off the street lay next to the leggy blonde David had been obsessed with. He actually had tried to bond himself to the bitch! After everything she had done to solidify her position in his life, he was trying to replace her with a twenty-something-year-old kid. Just like every other man, David was ruled by his lust.

"I think we need to ramp up the dosage," Sheena told the doctor, who watched from the doorway.

"She didn't kill him. That means she has some level of control." Sheena nudged the human guy with the toe of her shoe and he moaned. They had brought in dozens of humans but she never killed them. She would come close and pull back before the deed was done. Until the drug was able to render the subject completely mindless with rage and hunger, it wouldn't be ready.

"I don't think that's wise. An overdose would be lethal. She's already suffering side effects from the dose we're administering. We are skirting the edge of addiction with this one." The doctor looked thoughtfully at the girl. Sheena had no doubt the doctor was also ruled by his lust.

Sheena looked on as the doctor approached the whimpering female to check her vitals. He brushed the damp hair from her forehead to check her pupils. Blood dripped from her chin, staining the front of her hospital gown. Her eyes pleaded for help and Sheena watched him struggle against the urge to give in to her need. Before he could back away, she reached out and plowed her fist into his chest. The doctor flew across the room from the force of the blow. His motion was stopped by the cinder block wall. He slid down to the floor and fought to draw a breath. Sheena roared with amusement. The girl murmured apologies and cried harder. Sheena stepped over the doctor's legs on the way out the door, stopping to glare down at him.

"I don't pay you to worry about whether or not they live, Doctor. Just do as I say, or you'll be the next to get locked in with our little monster." She smiled, but there was no mistaking the venom in her words. She would kill him and find another doctor to replace him.

Nothing would stop her from her goals. Not even the conniving males in her life. Like father, like son, both Abel and his father had abandoned her in her time of need for the love of a highborn vampire debutant. She would have her revenge one day very soon, very soon indeed.

The last thing Brandi wanted to do was attend a stranger's bonding ceremony, but Dani and Debbie were dragging her along. It was only going to make her more heartsick and she knew it. She'd left her mate a week ago and hadn't heard from him since. Well, what did she expect? She'd walked out on him. She told herself over and over that she'd done the right thing. Abel had to commit to a real relationship if he wanted to be with her, and he didn't seem ready or willing to do that. Maybe Abel had the same curse as his father and his bond to her had faded? Maybe he just didn't want a murdering pyro for a mate? Maybe she was going to go crazy wondering why he only wanted her body. She loved him so much but she'd become little more than a receptacle for his pleasure. She sniffed and couldn't hold back the tear that slid down her cheek.

They filed out of the limo and the soft, shimmering fabric of the elegant opalescent gown Dani had brought for her felt good against Brandi's skin.

Climbing the stairs to the chapel doors reminded Brandi of Abel again. This was where they'd met, just inside those heavy wooden double doors. The romantic in Brandi wanted to believe that she had been fated to find Abel and fall in love with him.

She wasn't the only person who recognized the significance of Abel's parentage. Both Debbie and Dani had pointed it out to her. Abel was a child of the House of Deidrick. Brandi was a child of the House of Vaughn. Just like her Aunt Leann's prophecy predicted, they had come together to bring peace to their people. Lightning had struck twice and Brandi had followed in Dani's footsteps. They had both fallen hard for Deidrick males.

Debbie rushed ahead to find Mason. Dani held the door for Brandi to enter the foyer. When she stepped inside, Brandi was sure she was seeing things. He was a figment of her heartsick imagination. He had to be.

Dani bumped her shoulder and smiled. "Be glad I'm already mated. I might have fought you for that one." She winked and headed off into the chapel.

Standing in the foyer in the very spot where Brandi had first laid eyes on his handsome face was her mate. Abel looked dashing in a black suit and crisp white shirt. She had never seen him in anything but dark jeans and casual shirts or fatigues. He also looked nervous as hell when he came to take her hand.

"Are you ready, Sparky?" he asked before placing a kiss on both corners of her mouth. She stared up at him, absorbing every inch of his anxious face. She'd missed him so much.

"Ready?" she replied dumbly.

"Yes, are you ready to be my wife? I know we've already done the all-important blood bonding but a wedding ceremony would mean a lot to me. So, are you ready?" he asked again.

"I . . . of course, I would love to marry you." She shook her head to clear the buzz of seeing him again. She did want to marry him but she couldn't carry on with him the way things were. "I want to, but I can't, Abel. Not yet." Her eyes filled with tears. "I need all of you." She choked on the words and Abel dropped to his knees, wrapping his arms around her waist and burying his face in her flat belly. She stroked her fingers through his hair and he looked up at her hopefully. Then she felt it, she felt Abel there buzzing quietly in her mind.

"I love you, Sparky," he told her, and then he flooded her mind with that love. He made her feel all the things that were so very hard for a man like him to say. He was afraid of failing at this new life and letting her down and of never being able to be the kind of mate he felt she deserved. But most of all he was terrified of losing her. "I'm trying, Brandi. I was so wrapped up in my pain and guilt that I didn't see what I was doing to us. I'm sorry, baby." He rose to his feet and took her face in his hands, wiping a tear from her cheek with his thumb. "I'm begging you to give me the chance to be a better man. Please, I can't do this without you."

She kissed him then. She couldn't help falling into those deep, beautiful eyes. The warm glow of his love for her lit up the connection between them. It had been so long since she truly believed he felt the bond the way she felt it. She craved his attention, and ached for his love. Relief washed over her heart like a soothing balm, filling in all of the cracks and holes. Abel was in her arms and he wanted her to be his mate and his wife.

Abel pulled away first. "Is that a yes, Sparky?" He nuzzled her neck and she shivered. "Say *yes*," he pleaded.

"Yes, Abel, I will be your wife," she said and kissed him again, deeply, slowly, and with all of the love she felt in her heart. Abel pulled back again when they both were panting and he grinned widely down at her. He looked so young and full of life when he smiled like that. Brandi hoped to see a lifetime of those happy smiles.

Abel took her hand and led her to the chapel doors. When he knocked, they opened wide to reveal a room full of family and close friends. The entire Horde and many warriors were also in attendance. To her surprise Greyson and Candice were seated together with his arm wrapped around her shoulder. Brandi and Greyson shared a smile. Sometime things worked out just the way they should.

Conspicuous in her absence was Brandi's own mother, but her twin, her little brother, and her father were front and center with the Deidricks.

Abel and Brandi stepped through the chapel doors together, and when they closed behind them, several Wrath guards took up positions. Brandi looked at Abel inquisitively. He leaned over to kiss her nose and whisper in her ear.

"I'm not taking any chances, Sparky. I learn from the mistakes of others."

Brandi laughed out loud. The attendants cheered and clapped when Abel and Brandi walked up the aisle hand in hand to the altar. They applauded again in celebration of their once-forbidden bond when they returned down the aisle as man and wife.

About the Author

Cat Miller was born and raised in Baltimore, Maryland. An avid reader and fan of all genres of romance, from historical to contemporary to paranormal, Cat began writing her first novel on a dare from her eldest daughter. She's never looked back. When Cat is not reading, writing, or indulging her addiction to café mochas, she is a certified medical coder. The mother of two daughters and a stepson, Cat lives in Maryland with her husband and their dog. She loves hearing from fans; please visit her online at www.catmillerbooks.com. *Unforgiven* is the second novel in the Forbidden Bond series, following *Unbound*.